Mischief in the Glen

To Anne

from Ian

with thanks

Mischief in the Glen

Ian McLaren

To order additional copies of this book, contact:
Xlibris Corporation
0-800-644-6988
www.XlibrisPublishing.co.uk
Orders@XlibrisPublishing.co.uk
301649

To Bill Munro. A stalker, a friend, an inspiration.

To my wife Jane for her generous input and tireless support.
Without her this book would never have reached publication.

To my mother who made all things possible.

My apologies to the people of Inverness for some
liberties taken with your local geography.

Chapter 1

The Moray Inn was always busy on a Friday night. Tonight it was heaving: it was ceilidh night.

A young man watched the crowd with interest, honing his policeman's eye. He was DC Jamie Ross, LL.B. He sat back contentedly sipping his pint, beside him was his sister Alison. A cheer from the bar greeted a group of lads that entered, kilts swinging. It was great, Jamie thought, that young folk were now wearing the kilt with pride. Kilts were no longer for older men to dust off for weddings and young men to hire for the occasion. He wished he'd worn his as Ali had suggested, but he'd planned only a couple of pints and an early night—though the arrival of this new bunch of lads had probably changed that. All of them were his mates from the rugby club so a good night was in prospect.

Sitting opposite Jamie was big Hughie MacRae, Jamie's best friend from schooldays and captain of his rugby team. He smiled at Jamie and waved in the direction of the new arrivals. 'They're hooligans: a wild bunch o' buggers. A hope they behave themselves tonight.'

A kilted figure detached from the group and came over. He sat down on a spare seat beside Alison and threw an arm over her shoulder—he'd clearly had a few drams on the way to the pub. He smiled across the table at Hughie. 'Where's Lizzie then? Let you out on your own, has she?' Lizzie was Hughie's wife.

'Havin' a hennie tonight with some of her pals at home,' said Hughie laughing. 'Two of them pregnant and not up for drinkin'.'

The newcomer was Gus MacRae, Hughie's cousin. He nodded at the almost empty glasses in front of the other two. 'You'll be needin' refills.' Not waiting for an answer he headed for the bar where the rest of the lads were shouting their orders.

The Moray Inn was an old coaching house converted many years ago to a hotel. An outhouse became a big bar, fine old stone walls retained. The stables and coach house had also been converted and extended to create a large hall, The Barn, complete with old oak beams and a new sprung floor—and tonight it was hosting the ceilidh.

The bar in the Moray was a cosy friendly place. In the winter the big stone fireplace next to Jamie would have a roaring wood fire. It was a popular meeting place and was Jamie's and Hughie's local. The owner was Malcolm Fraser, a local character and amateur historian. His passion was the '45 Jacobite Rebellion and the Moray was almost a shrine to its memory. The walls of the bar were hung with genuine weapons of the period. Maps, lithographs and contemporary pictures, tartans and other memorabilia were everywhere. Above the huge fireplace was an oil painting of a kilted Highland gentleman, Archibald Fraser of Glen Dorran, chief of a minor sept of the clan and Malcolm's ancestor who had died at Culloden. The locals loved the place and tourists flocked in to admire the exhibits and listen to Malcolm's stories. Malcolm had been a close friend of Jamie's father, a fellow enthusiast, and when Jamie's father had died, most of his collection had been donated to Malcolm for display.

By the time the last pints had gone down it was almost 10 o'clock. The bar was emptying as folk moved through to The Barn for the ceilidh, and Ali was agitating to join them. Hughie wasn't up for it, wanting to get home to Lizzie.

'She'll maybe be ready for a wee dram o' this,' he said, pulling a bottle of Famous Grouse whisky from an inside pocket of his leather bike jacket which was hung over the back of a chair. 'My prize for winnin' the darts tonight,' he laughed. 'Pity you were stuck workin'—this might just have been yours, man. Bit more like the thing, eh? Hardly worth winnin' a box of chocolates, that's why A didnae try too hard last week.'

Hughie and Jamie were members of the Moray darts team. Hughie was the Captain but Jamie was probably, on a good night, the better player and had beaten Hughie in last Friday's singles match, winning a big box of Quality Street. Jamie stuck his empty glass under Hughie's nose. Hughie scowled good-naturedly. 'Well, you did give me some o' yon chocolates last week A suppose.' He opened the bottle and poured Jamie a generous dram. 'Don't suppose Lizzie could manage it all onyway.' Hughie got up, pulled on his bike jacket, and went round to give Ali a big hug.

'But Hughie,' protested Ali, 'it's only just 10 o'clock. Are you sure you're not up for a wee dance?'

Hughie shook his head. 'A told Lizzie A'd no' be late. And Jamie, A'll see you Wednesday night at rugby trainin'—if you're no' out catching criminals, that is.'

Jamie's job as a policeman was accepted by Hughie and his old mates, but Jamie understood that it sometimes set him a bit apart.

In The Barn the ceilidh was just starting to swing. When Jamie and Ali entered, everyone was lining up for a *Strip the Willow* and Gus pulled them into his set. His partner was a rather nervous, very pretty American tourist whom Gus introduced as Mary Jane. She had reason to be nervous—Gus was a wild dancer, the more so with a few drinks in him.

'Reckon she'll be up for learning the best kept secret then?' Jamie whispered to Gus as they lined up. Gus's coarse answer was drowned in the music as the ceilidh band struck up.

The last dance was called at 1.00: a slow waltz. Alison and Jamie had danced every dance and both were ready for bed. Gus and most of the wild bunch had disappeared some time before. One survivor was Andy Craig, a dairy farmer and club prop forward. A big, handsome, but very shy man, he'd managed to be in the same sets as Alison all night, and now finally found the courage to ask her for the last dance. Jamie sat, content to finish his beer as he watched them. They made a nice couple, he thought; it was about time his beautiful sister found herself a good man.

One of the good things about a ceilidh is that you quickly dance off the drink, so Jamie was tired but clear headed as Ali drove them towards home. He couldn't resist teasing his sister about Andy Craig.

'The big lug, he kept standing on my toes,' she retorted.

'Only because you were holding the poor man so close!' laughed Jamie. Alison punched him playfully on the arm.

'Asked you out, has he?'

'As a matter of fact he has—would that be OK by you?'

The tone was sarcastic, but the appeal for his approval was there. Since losing both of their parents in a plane crash five years before, the pair, always close, had grown even closer.

Jamie squeezed her shoulder. 'Andy's one of the best. A gentle giant, a real gentleman. He must really fancy you if he plucked up the courage to ask you for a dance—and to ask you out. Never seen him with a girlfriend. Usually he just has a few beers and goes home to his cows—not that I'm implying anything, you understand. You'll need to be right gentle with him though—I don't think he's very experienced!'

'At least he's not your typical rugby jock,' said Ali indignantly. 'They usually either get too pissed to care, it seems, or can't believe you won't climb into bed with them. "No" is not a word they understand at the end of the night. And anyway, they're usually too drunk to be capable of doing anything.'

'So you'd know about that,' teased Jamie.

Ali thumped his arm again. 'As it happens I do—and I'm not about to elaborate.'

'Well, you better get on with it, little sister. Another few weeks and you're back in Edinburgh.' Ali was about to start her final year at medical school.

'Anyway; you're a fine one to talk. There were at least two nice girls drooling over you tonight.'

Jamie shrugged.

'It's time you finally put that woman behind you.' She was referring to Fiona Lawson, a very long-standing girlfriend and fellow lawyer who'd dumped Jamie when, disillusioned with the legal profession, he'd left law and joined the police—there had been serious talk of marriage.

'I'm sorry Jamie, but if she'd really loved you, you'd still be together. She was a high flier and wanted her handsome high flying trophy on her arm.'

Fiona and Ali had never got on. Ali had always found her to be a snotty bitch and resented the wedge that Fiona seemed to have been deliberately driving between her and Jamie. Jamie slumped in his seat and said nothing—they'd had this conversation before. He knew Ali was right, but the pain of Fiona moving out, and worse still, her taking up with one of his mates almost immediately, still hurt.

His thoughts were drifting towards the work he'd be facing in a few short hours when Ali nodded ahead. 'Something's up.'

A blue flashing light could be seen ahead through the trees. Jamie's immediate thought was that his colleagues had caught up with someone the worse for drink: he hoped it wasn't one of his mates. An ambulance was stopped by the Monnie Bridge, and behind it, a police car. Jamie told Ali to pull in. As they stopped, a body on a stretcher was being loaded into the ambulance. A uniformed policeman came over as Jamie stepped from the car. He was about to ask Jamie to move on when Jamie showed his warrant card and the policeman introduced himself.

The constable shook his head sadly. 'Nasty business. He came off his bike—looks as if he hit the end of the bridge and ended up on a rock in the river. Fair smashed up, he is. Young fellow too—he was pissed, most like.'

Jamie's heart sank as an awful possibility hit him, but he had to ask.

The policeman flipped open his book. 'Name on his licence: Hugh Robert MacRae. Identity confirmed by a friend of his.' The policeman gestured towards a figure sat slumped on the parapet of the bridge: it was Gus.

Gus lifted his head as Jamie and Ali approached him. His face was ghostly white and tear-stained; he was visibly shaking. Ali put her arms round him. His clothes were dripping wet and he was shivering with cold.

'I'm going to get him a blanket from the ambulance,' said Ali hurrying off.

'He's deid, Jamie. Hughie: he's deid.' Gus's voice was a painful whisper. 'A couldna dae onythin'. He wis cold—and all that blood, all that blood.' Gus slid off the parapet, turned and dry heaved into the water. Alison returned with a blanket and draped it over Gus's shoulders, hugging him from behind.

Gus wiped his mouth on his sleeve. 'A saw his bike at the end o' the bridge; just sittin' there, leanin' against the fence. A thought maybe he'd stopped for a piss or somethin'. A stopped and shouted for him—nothin' but the noise o' the burn. A looked ower the bridge an' A saw him, spread-eagled on that big rock there, arms oot like this. A shouted "Are ye a' right man, are ye a' right?" His heid moved up an' doon an' A thought maybe, maybe he's fine, no' hurt too bad. A ran doon tae him, through the water—he wis so cold an' white. He wisnae noddin' at me, Jamie: it wis just his heid in his helmet bobbin' in the water. He wis deid, Jamie—A couldnae dae onythin'. A pulled him off o' the rock ower tae the side—the blood, Jamie—a' that blood.' Gus looked at his hands and rubbed them down the blanket. He turned and leaned back on the parapet. 'He's deid Jamie: Hughie's deid.'

The paramedic came over to check on Gus and Jamie suggested that Gus should go with the ambulance. The paramedic nodded: Gus must go to hospital. 'Aye, he can't go home in this state, but maybe best the police take him. Sharing the back of the ambulance with his dead mate'll no' help him. He's in shock though—I'll give him some sedation.'

Jamie put his arm round Gus's shoulders in silent comfort, he himself struggling with the reality of the situation as Gus was helped into the back of the police car. By the light of some spotlamps, the policemen were measuring the skid marks of the motorbike and taking photographs of the scene. Hughie's bike was strangely undamaged—almost parked—as Gus had observed. There was, however, a long scratch on the right faring, which Jamie showed to the policeman with the camera.

'Aye, it's a scratch right enough,' agreed the policeman as he ran his hands over the fibreglass. 'Think it's fresh? Could have got it anytime.'

Jamie knew that the bike was Hughie's pride and joy, and had someone scratched it everyone would have known about it. He said as much to the policeman who just shrugged. 'Maybe someone in the Moray car park tonight—didn't see it in the dark, and him pissed—he stinks of whisky.'

Jamie bristled at that. The bottle of whisky in Hughie's jacket pocket must have smashed and soaked Hughie's clothes. Hughie had not been pissed—he'd had a few beers, but he was a big lad and could hold his drink. Jamie felt a twinge of guilt though. Had Hughie drunk too much? Should he have tried to stop him using the bike? In his heart though, he knew he couldn't have stopped him. He'd have been told to stop being a copper for the night and to fuck off—he knew Hughie only too well. He also knew that Hughie could handle his bike. He always drove very carefully. As a pillion passenger, Jamie never felt in the least bit nervous when being driven by Hughie—the same couldn't be said for some of his other mates with bikes. Late at night, with a few drinks in him he'd have been taking it easy, well aware of the risks on the small road: only the week before Hughie had hit a roe deer in his car.

Taking his torch from the car, and driven by the strange compulsion which draws friends and relatives to the scene of the death of their loved ones, Jamie climbed over the fence and slid down to the burn, the bank slick and muddy from the traffic of feet and the evening's rain. As he sat on a rock and felt the tears on his cheeks, suppressed grief welled up and he cried quietly to himself. A second figure slid down the bank, and Jamie felt Alison's hands on his shoulders. He rose and took her in his arms and they wept on silently together.

One of the policemen called, saying the ambulance was leaving. Jamie and Alison were heading back when Jamie noticed a partially smoked cigarette in the rocks on the river bank. The wetness of the stones had extinguished it, but the cigarette itself was dry. He called to ask if anyone had been smoking a cigarette: no-one had. He carefully picked up the cigarette and wrapped it in a clean tissue from a pack in his pocket. Jamie showed it to his two uniformed colleagues, but neither showed any interest; even when he pointed out that it was a very unusual brand.

The policeman shrugged. 'Quite a few cars come down this road, flicked out of a window maybe, or someone walking a dog—lots of explanations. I bet you'd find loads of fag-ends if you looked.'

'But the cigarette's dry,' protested Jamie. 'When did it stop raining tonight?'

The policeman told him it had rained until about 10.00.

When Jamie pointed to the position of the skid mark and the relatively undamaged bike, his colleagues became irritated.

'Look,' said one, 'I think it's bloody obvious. He'd had a night's drinking and probably swerved to avoid something—a deer or fox maybe, and came a cropper. We see the likes all the time. Unfortunately this one ended up dead. Another one for the drink-driving statistics.'

Jamie was getting angry at the callous and dismissive attitude of his colleagues, but appreciated that they were not Hughie's mates. To them this was just another accident: just another body. Perhaps longer in the job he'd become like them . . . he hoped not.

He felt Alison take his arm. 'My God—Lizzie, what about Lizzie, his wife—has she been told yet?'

The policemen shook their heads. 'A woman PC is on her way here—she's got that job.'

'No she hasn't,' said Ali. 'Lizzie's a friend of ours—we'll do it.'

The policemen agreed, saying that would be fine. Gus's car was a problem. It couldn't be left where it was. Jamie offered to drive it to Gus's house which was only a few miles further on. The alternative was the pound, and Gus would have enough to face the following morning without the hassle of finding his car. A transporter was on the way to collect the bike.

Gus appeared to be asleep in the back of the patrol car: the sedative was clearly working, and Jamie envied him the release.

Jamie rubbed his face. 'My God, Ali. Lizzie—how do we tell her? What do we say?'

Ali looked at his tortured expression. 'I don't think we'll have to say anything, Jamie—she'll know the moment she sees us; and from the looks on our faces.'

Chapter 2

Like most people, Detective Superintendent Jock Anderson was no great lover of Monday mornings. The knowledge that a new load of trouble probably lay in store at the office always somehow managed to take the edge off the weekend.

Jock chewed the stem of his unlit pipe as he flipped through the reports from the previous two days and noted with some pleasure that nothing untoward had happened: nothing likely to intrude on the afternoon's golf with the Chief Constable when he'd fill him in on the relative non-events of the weekend.

Before him on his desk, however, was a small pile of blue folders: four to be exact. Each file related to a burglary, none of which, until this morning, had been his concern. The burglaries had been committed in various parts of the area, well spread geographically, miles apart and had been investigated by the police in whose backyards they'd occurred. A quick reading suggested they were all the work of one villain, or, most likely, a bunch of villains; each job was almost a carbon copy of the others. Clearly these were not casual affairs, no opportunist break-ins for odds and ends to pay for some drug habit. Big remote houses, all high value stuff taken—much too organized to be locals. Some smarter lads from the smoke: most likely a gang up from the south, which would make catching them that bit more difficult.

What intrigued Jock was the nature of the stuff being taken. Not the usual petty crime stuff. No TVs, computers or electrical goods; no watches or jewellery, no missing cash or credit cards. They were dealing with unusual, more discriminating villains here. Antiques: nothing very big. No Queen Anne tables or Regency wardrobes. All small, easily carried items: but very expensive small items. Persian rugs: he whistled as he read their value. He marvelled that folk would ever pay thousands of pounds for a wee rug.

As he ran his eyes down the list he was amazed at the wealth of treasure concealed in these houses—though clearly not concealed well enough. Paintings were popular: a Landseer and several old Scottish masters. There were even a couple of Picassos taken, along with many first edition books and several Ming Chinese vases. Whoever was involved knew their business. The houses had been targeted—quick in and quick out, no mess.

What was obvious to Jock was equally obvious to the Chief Constable who'd pulled the reports together and dumped them in Jock's lap. The biggest pain for police, however, was that people with lots of cash who live in big houses and are robbed, tend to be influential and make lots of noise in embarrassing places. The fact that one victim was an MP, and another a prominent industrialist from England was grist to the mill.

The press, as yet, had failed to get a good smell of it, but that couldn't last. The headlines would come along soon enough, followed by the inevitable police-baiting. He could imagine the headlines: *Another £100,000 Inverness-shire robbery—police confounded.*

Willie Ferguson, the Chief Constable, was already under heavy pressure. Now it would be Jock's turn to take some of the heat. While it seemed that considerable efforts had been applied to the investigation, there were as yet no clues: no leads to follow.

Jock looked at his watch. Only about five minutes to "Morning Service", as the troops referred to his regular Monday morning meetings with his team. He called for his cup of tea and lit up his pipe as he waited for his lads, and lass, to arrive.

First in was his new right-hand man, DI Bob McLean. Jock's DCI, had taken early retirement some months before and both Bob and Jock were anticipating Bob's promotion. They made an odd pair. Jock was a big man, fifty-two years old, over six foot and built like the rugby player he used to be. His rugged "farmer's face" was full of character. He was handsome in an ugly kind of way. His nose had been rearranged several times during his long rugby career but this somehow added to the lived-in appearance of his face.

In contrast, his number two was short and slim, thirty-two years old but as bald as his boss was hairy. In his wire-rimmed glasses he looked more like an accountant than a policeman. He was as sharp as a razor. A university man: a law graduate.

Bob McLean was waving another blue folder. 'Sorry Boss, we've got another—a good one: it's that wee gobshite, Councillor Archibald MacPhee. He's been away for a few days—a nice welcome home for the little shit.'

Jock groaned. Councillor MacPhee was a member of the Police Relations Committee and a constant thorn in Jock's flesh. MacPhee regarded it as his mission to single-handedly improve policing in the Highlands.

'Ah well,' said Jock with a grimace. 'So we'll no doubt be getting a visit from him this morning. It'll be a rare Monday morning that he doesn't appear bitching about something or other. Got any details?'

'Nothing much yet. I'll be sending DC Ross and DC Annie Miller up to see him after your Morning Service. Seems to be the same MO. Maybe get some leads on this one, but I'm not holding my breath. These lads are slick operators. We've been spared the wrath of the press until now, but the good councillor can be guaranteed to change all of that—loves his wee bit of publicity, does our Archie.'

Jock nodded to DS Alan Clark, Jock's choice for promotion to DI, and DC Murdo Morrison as they took their usual seats at the back. DC Annie Miller, DC Ross and DS Dave McKay trooped in and found themselves some space in the small office. Jock fired up his pipe, waved away a cloud of smoke and eyed his officers through the fug. He wished them all a good morning and proceeded to review the activities of the previous week. A few minor items, crimes—or perhaps more accurately misdemeanours, remained for further action, but largely the books looked good. Congratulations and praise were awarded where appropriate. Criticism, where necessary, he preferred to make in private.

'Something here for you to get your teeth into,' said Jock, picking up the now thickened pile of blue files. 'We're being made fools of here. Five cases now, the latest being our friend Councillor MacPhee.' Jock heard a muted 'Oh my God' and smiled in its direction. 'Indeed you may groan, DC Miller.' Jock outlined the cases then picked up the files.

'First one Fort William a month ago. A week later Fort Augustus. Five days after that they were busy in Dingwall and last week in Nairn—and this weekend the good councillor on our patch in Inverness.

'On the face of it the local boys have done a good job. Reports are comprehensive: if nothing much in them of any help. They've all missed something, they must have: and it's our job to find out what. Copies of the files have been prepared for all of you. Familiarize yourselves. DC Miller and DC Ross will be off to speak to Mr MacPhee. I want a very thorough job please you pair; we need something to go on. Hopefully you'll come up with something—and we can't have our good councillor complaining we're neglecting his case. The whole team will be on it. We're going to town on this with a full scene-of-crime investigation. DI McLean will allocate jobs for each of the rest of you. An interview with all victims. I want some good news by the end of the day.

'Use your brains. It's possible these robberies may be being done to order. We need to know where stolen items were acquired and when; with luck we may find a common denominator.'

They all trooped out except for DS Clark. 'Quick word, sir?'

'Sure Alan, got some gem you want to impart?'

'Sadly, no sir. Been talking to young DC Ross. His best mate died on Friday night: came off his motorbike. The traffic boys seem happy to file it away as a simple accident, but Jamie's not at all happy about that.' The sergeant gave Jock the gist of Jamie's story and sat back, a little embarrassed. 'Probably nothing to it of course, him being right upset about his friend's death—emotionally involved and all that. I told him that I'd have a word with you. He's a good lad—got the makings of a really good copper. I just don't want to dampen his enthusiasm.'

Jock eyed Alan and chewed on his pipe. He thought back to his own days when he was fresh on the job. On one of the first cases he'd been involved in he'd picked up on a strange inconsistency. When he dared to voice his concern to his own Detective Superintendent he'd been sent off with a flea in his ear. It turned out he wasn't so daft after all. The case was finally cleared up, but if they'd listened to him in the first place they'd have saved everyone a lot of work.

Jock nodded. 'Send him in. I'll have a word with the lad.'

Jamie arrived a few minutes later, nervously took a seat and adopted as confident a demeanour as he could muster.

'OK lad, let's have it. I've had a distilled account from DS Clark. Give me the full version.'

Jock puffed away quietly, not interrupting as Jamie spoke. He couldn't but be impressed by his confident presentation, delivered clearly and articulately—like a lawyer, in fact. Jock decided that all that education maybe wasn't a complete waste of time after all.

'Can you really be sure that the faring wasn't scraped before he left the pub, sometime earlier in the day maybe?'

Jamie shrugged. 'No sir, not a hundred per cent, but I know Hughie. He loved that bike sir. I'm sure he'd have said something about it to someone. His wife knew nothing of it either. I'm sure he'd have said.'

'You mean you've interrogated his poor missis? Can't believe she'd have been in much of a state to talk about scratched motorbikes.'

'Not interrogated exactly sir; just kind of slipped it in in passing—I am a policeman, sir.'

Jock eyed him through the smoke. 'Aye, lad, you are that. But maybe best not to be mentioning your doubts to her or to anyone else for now—only makes things worse. An unfortunate accident's bad enough for her to deal with. That someone's maybe responsible for killing him is something else—she doesn't need any added pain.'

Jock took out his tobacco and began filling his pipe again. 'So what are you suggesting? Hit and run? You don't think the scrape could have been the result of hitting a sheep or a deer? And how does this cigarette end fit into things? OK, a strange foreign brand. But you told me yourself the pub was full of tourists—must be lots of exotic smokes round. Flicked out the car window perhaps?'

'But sir, the cigarette was dry. It could only have been there about three hours or so, and I think it was too far away from the road to have been just flicked out a window. The faring was scratched. If he'd hit a sheep or a deer it would maybe be damaged: dented maybe—or cracked, but not scratched.'

'So where does that get us? OK, then. Circularize all the local repair shops. Let's see if any car's acquired any suspicious knocks. But if it was a tourist they could be long gone by now, and I don't really think we can justify a nationwide search for damaged hire cars on this one. Check with local repair shops and car hires.'

Jock leaned forward and adopted what he hoped was his avuncular voice. 'Look Jamie, I understand that it's really horrible about your friend, but I think I have to agree with the traffic boys. This was a tragic accident; but I'm happy to keep an open mind. Off you go. We've got a lot of other stuff on our plates right now, but let me know if you come up with anything. Councillor MacPhee will be expecting you . . . I want your mind on the job, and mind to bite your tongue—our Archie's not an easy man to deal with.'

When Jamie had left, Jock leaned back in his chair, buzzed the canteen for a fresh cup of tea and dialled the Chief Constable. He and Jock were friends from police college days: an invaluable relationship, especially during trying times.

'Morning, Willie. I think we'd best put off our golf this afternoon, I'm getting a wee bit busy—aye, the burglaries. No, I've not spoken to the good councillor yet. In a bit of a state, is he? Poor man. I'll no doubt have the pleasure later this morning. If he got wind of us playing golf in the middle of this national emergency there'd be all hell to pay—and the crime correspondent of the *Courier*'s finally got a decent crime to write about and will be chewing my arse for a statement. Been calls from the *Press and Journal* this morning, so I expect a visit from that reporter of theirs. Trouble is, there's not much I'm prepared to tell them. What we know is we're dealing with professionals. Same slick MO, targets are all remote houses. Somehow they knew the premises would be empty. My guess is that they knew what was inside. All victims insured—quite well insured—and all through the same company. We've got the local agency in Inverness. It could be—just could be an inside job. A nice list of addresses and insured valuables passed on by some clerk? Could be—we're working on that one. I know the manager down there. He runs a tight ship, and I can't think he'd employ a bad one. DS Clark will be having a word with him this morning.

'But Sunday for golf as usual? Meg's having a day with daughter Jo and wee Gordie. She can't get enough of her grandson so I've got the whole day off.'

DC Ross and DC Miller were having a less than pleasant time at the home of Councillor MacPhee. MacPhee, a scrawny little weasel of a man, notoriously irascible even on a good day, was giving the two officers the full vent of his spleen. He was not in the least mollified by the conscientious efforts of the scene-of-crime officers as they dusted for prints and popped various items into plastic bags for further investigation. As a "very important member of the community, whose home had been horribly violated", he expected results immediately. As he raged at the policemen his wife sobbed quietly into a wet handkerchief as she sat in the corner of a sofa. Jamie was thankful for the diplomatic ability of Annie Miller who finally calmed things down and got everyone sitting round the kitchen table with a cup of tea.

Between them, the MacPhees managed to put together a list of stolen items: not impressive in length, but very impressive in value.

'So you're a stamp collector. Your collection is really worth that much?'

'Indeed,' said a very pompous Councillor MacPhee. 'And I'm not a "stamp collector": I'm a philatelist. Treasurer of the Highland Philatelic Society, in fact.'

Jamie hoped his expression registered that he was suitably impressed.

'Are all these items covered by insurance, sir?'

'Indeed they are, young man.' He thrust the policy at Jamie who glanced through it.

'But each and every one is irreplaceable, quite irreplaceable. My stamp collection is the result of three lifetimes' work: my grandfather, my father and myself. Irreplaceable.' Only one missing item had been acquired recently:

a Persian carpet for which MacPhee had paid fifteen hundred pounds, and Jamie was shown the receipt from a shop in Edinburgh.

The mention of Mrs MacPhee's large collection of Dalton figurines reduced her once again to tears. 'We should have had a better security system, Archie, didn't I tell you? We should have got that nice man to install one for us. "State-of-the-art" he said it was. He wasn't asking much, but you said "no" and it would only have cost about five hundred pounds—and now look what's happened.'

As part of his police training Jamie had learned a lot about, and had taken a keen interest in security systems. A state-of—the—art system for only five hundred pounds struck him as odd.

'When was this, Mrs MacPhee? Was it recently?'

'Oh yes, just a few weeks ago. Such nice boys. Came to the door—so polite. They were quite right, Archie. People in our position in such a nice house with such valuable things should be properly protected. But you said "no".' A further bout of sobbing ensued, terminated again by the caring, diplomatic DC Miller.

'So they came into the house?' persisted Jamie.

'Oh yes, such nice lads. I gave them a cup of tea while they showed me their brochure and they told me what they could do for us, Archie. They had one of these laptop things, showed me their website: pictures of all the jobs they'd done. I showed them round the house. They did all sorts of measurements and gave me a quotation. It was only five hundred pounds, Archie. Only five hundred—and you said "no"! They said what nice things we had. You'd have liked them, Archie. One of them showed such an interest in your stamp collection, said he collected stamps too.'

'So you pointed out all the things that you thought were of value then?' asked DC Miller.

'I didn't have to for most things. They were experts; they pointed out things. And they were so careful. They had special gloves they wore when they handled our nice things.' The officer who was dusting for fingerprints overheard. He smiled at Annie and shook his head.

Mrs MacPhee continued. 'That awful nice wee painting: the one from your grandmother that was at the top of the stairs. They said that was worth at least five thousand pounds. Oh Archie, if only you'd listened to me. Everything's lost. All gone! We'll never see our lovely things again.' Jamie felt genuinely sorry for Mrs MacPhee, and even felt a twinge of sympathy for the obnoxious, though thoroughly chastened, Mr MacPhee.

'In case you decided on a system, did they leave you any details of how to contact them? Their brochure—or a card maybe?' asked Jamie.

Mrs MacPhee looked blank for a moment. 'A brochure, aye: I have it somewhere.' Mrs MacPhee got up and raked through some stuff in a sideboard drawer, produced a brochure and a business card and handed them to Jamie.

'Did they ever contact you again?'

'Oh yes, I got a call during that week, the Thursday I think it was. They wanted to come round and talk to my husband like I wanted them to. They wanted to know when we'd both be in. But Archie and I are both very busy people,' she said, her Morningside accent resuming as she pulled herself together.

'Most days I'm out. I'm involved in a lot of charity work, and I do enjoy a bit of golf with my friends some afternoons. Our evenings can be busy too. Archie has a very important position in the community. We have lots of functions and he has very important meetings to attend.

'Such a nice young man. We had a bit of a laugh on the phone. He said it might be easier for me to tell him when we wouldn't be in. He suggested Saturday morning. They work every day, he said, to fit in with their clients. Such a nice boy. I told him that was no good either as we were to be away on holiday for ten days. He said he'd call again when we got back.'

'Would you mind if I borrowed these?' asked Jamie, picking up the card and brochure. 'You could say security systems are my special interest area.

Could be these lads have something to offer.' Mrs MacPhee nodded as she sipped the last of her tea.

Jamie fingered the card as Annie drove them back to the station. 'Ex-Cell Security Systems,' he read. 'An Edinburgh address—and a mobile number: presumably for the Mr Charles McKenzie whose name's on the card.'

'You thinking what I'm thinking, Jamie?'

Jamie nodded. 'Let's get back to the station and do some checking out.'

DI McLean looked up from his desk as DC Ross and DC Miller came into his office. He was amused by the smug grins on their faces and hoped it portended good news. He opened his hands questioningly. 'Well, what have you got?—Spill it.'

Jamie gave an account of their visit to the MacPhees, at the end of which he laid the business card and brochure in front of his boss.

'Nice card: looks very professional,' muttered DI McLean.

'Yes sir, but nothing that couldn't be run up on a computer with a wee bit of effort and knowledge. Turns out that the company is genuine enough. Head office of Ex-Cell is on an industrial site in Craigmillar. I've had a long chat with the owner, his name's Duncan Lewis. They have no employee named Charles McKenzie. They have got plans to open up in this area in the future but none of their teams are currently up here. At the moment they don't go further north than Perth.

'Lewis is seriously not happy about their good name being involved in this. I told him it needn't appear if they cooperated fully with us. Ex-cell has only got four employees: all with the company since they set up and they're all accounted for. I asked him to supply photos and backgrounds of the employees anyway.

'He's right keen to help, sir. I can't help feeling, though, that there must be some connection to the company. Just in case there is, I told him to say nothing about this to his people. If there is any connection word could soon get back to our villains. I tried the cell phone on the card: it's a pay-as-you-go number—it's switched off.'

DI McLean grinned at the pair of them. 'Well done; I think you've got something here. You know what to do, don't you?'

'Yes sir,' said Annie. 'Get back out to Mrs MacPhee for descriptions—and anything else we can coax out of her.'

As they closed the door of his office DI McLean, a man not noted for displays of emotion, jumped out of his chair and danced a little jig.

Jock Anderson was equally heartened by the news. He called Jamie into his office and was shown the card and brochure. He looked up and smiled at Jamie. 'Well lad, I think this just may prove to be the breakthrough we've been hoping for. Well done.' Jamie's smile broadened at the praise. 'Pass on the news about the con men to the teams doing the interviews with the other four victims. Hopefully we're onto something.'

Jamie told Jock that MacPhee was insured by an Edinburgh company, and DS Clark had reported that the manager of the most popular local insurance agency was adamant that any leak from his office was out of the question. His staff of five had been with him for years, and all of them were beyond reproach: it seemed that any connection with an insurance company could be ruled out.

Unfortunately the great euphoria was short lived, but they were on the right lines. All the burglary victims had been visited by the spurious salesmen in the previous few weeks. In every case they'd soft-soaped the wife who was proud and happy to show them round and to point out her valuable possessions. However, other than that one was tall and slim and the other medium height and stocky, there was no consistency when it came to descriptions of either of the men. All reported two very smartly dressed, nice polite young men whose accents were not local—Edinburgh maybe—but there the agreement stopped. They were described as variously dark haired, blond, hair cut short or long, bespectacled, moustached. There were no prints—each customer had been very impressed when the nice lads insisted on wearing gloves when handling items.

They had something, but not a lot, to go on. A couple of very clever lads simply—but effectively—disguised, it seemed, in each case. The question was: to put out the word now warning the public to beware, in which case there was no chance of catching the thieves who would pack up operations and run with their loot to try it on somewhere else—or to say nothing, and somehow use the information they had to lay a trap. With the current insured value of the stolen goods at now well over a million pounds, and with a very agitated bunch of important folk wanting their valuables back, it was not an easy decision: but one that would wait. What couldn't wait was a statement of *some* sort to the press.

It was the duty of the police to warn owners of the kinds of items being stolen to be extra vigilant, and the local press would be happy to oblige. The irony of this, of course, being that the thieves could have a field day—who wouldn't be tempted to buy a cheap alarm system when there's a bunch of clever burglars on the loose?

Jock sighed as he slipped on his jacket and prepared to face the reporters.

During the week Jock's team worked on the cases. From information received from the local insurance companies they'd compiled a list of likely candidates. Hours were spent on the telephone contacting likely target households and giving discreet warnings. Four of those contacted, all of whom lived within a few miles of Inverness, had been visited by Ex-Cell, one during the current week. They'd all been visited by the police and statements taken—with the usual ambiguous descriptions obtained. None of the four were reckoned to have enough antiques to interest the pair, so hopes were not high that a trap could be baited yet. The good news was that the men were still at it, and in the immediate area.

Saturday evening at home; and Jock sat pondering, puffing on his pipe and sipping a favourite malt. It was a beautiful evening as he sat on the terrace of his house watching the last of the sun illuminate Ben Wyvis. A black head rested itself on his thigh: it was Nick, his Labrador, and Jock played with the dog's ears as he sipped his whisky.

The house sat high above Inverness and had a panoramic view east to the sea and north over the Moray Firth to the Black Isle and the mountains of Easter Ross. It was the old family home and had been the farmhouse for the large hill farm which had been worked by three generations of his family. While Jock loved the farm and farming, he'd recognized that there would be no long-term future for himself and his brother on the farm. He'd joined the police, and Iain, his younger brother by a year, had gone to university and got a degree in agricultural engineering. Iain had worked with his father and tried to make a go of the place, but as a hill farm with very little good arable land it was a hard grind. When their father died and was laid alongside their mother, Jock and Iain came to a very amicable agreement: Jock got the old house and about a quarter of the land, Iain got the remaining land and what cash his dad had left to build a new bungalow on the place. It was an arrangement that well suited Margo, Iain's wife, who was happy to swap the big draughty old farmhouse for a cosy new bungalow.

Much of the top hill land was let off for grazing, but they kept the best for a few sheep: prime blackface, from which they produced top-level breeders: they'd won first prize at last year's Black Isle Show. Iain's pride and joy, though, was his small herd of Highland cattle. He'd capitalized on the increasing popularity of the beasts and he'd now exported champions all over the world: but that was a hobby. Iain's wife, Margo, a solid farmer's daughter, did most of the day-to-day work round the place. Iain's day job was his agricultural engineering business in town. The children, both girls, had flown the nest. Neither had any interest in farming and both were working in Edinburgh.

When he had time, Jock loved to help out on the farm. He felt it kept him in touch with reality—with what was important. His wife Meg loved the old farmhouse. A bit of money well spent got rid of its cold draughty aspect. With soaring Highland property prices it was not a bad investment either.

Jock's only current regret was that he saw little of his two sons. Both had had itchy feet and had set off to explore the world in their university gap years and neither had returned permanently. One, Angus, had met and married a farmer's daughter in New Zealand. He was raising thousands of sheep, and producing Jock's and Meg's grandchildren: a boy and a girl so far. He and Meg had yet to see the younger one. There had been some talk of his son bringing his family to Scotland again, but Angus, however, wanted his parents to come to New Zealand.

Jock's elder son, Fergus, was the serious athlete of the family. He'd narrowly missed a cap for Scotland at rugby, having broken a finger in a warm up match. He was playing professional Aussie rules football in Australia, was still single and making the most of it by all accounts.

Jock's daughter Jo lived locally. A single mother, she owned an upmarket boutique in town. Gordie, Jo's son, was four years old, and was Jock's first grandchild—Jock and Meg just wished that they saw more of them.

Meg, Jock's wife, was a slim, very attractive forty-nine-year-old and was Head Teacher of the local primary school. She disturbed his reverie as she sat down beside him with a glass of wine. 'What time will we be expecting Willie then? Will I put on the tatties?'

Jock looked at his watch. 'About 8.00: it's almost that now. Aye, stick them on, he'll be here—he's never late.' As he spoke, Nick gave a welcoming bark and ran to the back door, tail frantically wagging. Jock took Meg's hand. 'He's here love, and he'll be ready for a wee dram.'

Willie Ferguson, the Chief Constable, was joining them for dinner, a regular occurrence when Willie's wife was off visiting her mother in Glasgow.

As Jock's confidante and sounding board, Meg had no problems with the men talking shop throughout the meal. There had been many a time when her perceptive views, opinions and suggestions had been invaluable. As Willie once said, "Meg, you really know how to cut through the crap and get to the heart of things." Tonight she just listened with interest as they discussed the problem currently uppermost in their minds: the spate of burglaries.

'We've got to let it roll, Willie. Blow the whistle now and we'll no' see them for dust. Poor wee MacPhee's stamp collection lost forever: who'd have believed it, a few wee coloured bits of paper worth that much.'

'Aye, almost half a million quid,' said Willie shaking his head.

'More, Willie. Broken up and spread round?—probably much more. These guys have hit a winning formula. If they run from here, they'll set up somewhere else. They've got to be stopped now. Trouble is, we've got next to bugger all to go on yet.'

'Actually,' said Meg, 'you've got a wee bit to go on. Unless there are teams of lads out conning the locals, which is unlikely, you've got two lads, at least one of whom is good at disguises and make up. An effective disguise must be expertly applied: you can't just stick a moustache or beard on and expect it to look convincing. Someone, maybe one of your burglars, knows what he's doing—works in the theatre maybe? Maybe a girlfriend with them? You'll have to ask the witnesses, but I suspect you'll find one of the lads did the talking on the antiques, the other about the alarm systems. You've got a clever pair of youngsters here, Jock. One's an expert on antiques, the other knows his stuff about alarm systems, and someone knows about disguises.'

Meg smiled at the men. 'It's not much, but it's something.'

Willie rubbed his chin thoughtfully. 'What do you think Jock? Need another word with a few witnesses?'

Jock smiled and nodded.

'OK Jock, we'll keep quiet about their MO for now, but you'd better get them soon. I'm the one getting jumped on—and that wee MacPhee's got big boots. Him on that Police Relations Committee—he's got influential contacts. Wrap it up quick, man.'

As Meg cleared up, the two men wandered out to the terrace, each with a healthy dram in his hand, Jock on his pipe and Willie with a Havana. Nick went for a sniff round the garden, having given up hope of any scraps. The two men sat in silence for a while, taking in the evening. Willie, a keen birder, sat up as a barn owl called from close by.

Jock smiled. 'Aye, she's nesting in the corner of the hay shed again this year.'

Both Jock and his brother Iain were enthusiastic naturalists and conservationists. Between them they'd made quite a few changes to the place to encourage wildlife. They'd planted lots of new hedges and native deciduous trees, and had implemented a list of other measures recommended by Scottish Natural Heritage. The farm was fully organic, of course—not that that affected the price of a Highland cow, but Jock reckoned the farm's chickens and eggs tasted better.

'Bad business the other night eh Jock? Young Hughie MacRae,' said Willie, breaking the silence.

Jock recalled his conversation with Jamie Ross. 'Dangerous bloody things, these big bikes,' he muttered. Surprised at the mention of the accident, Jock asked Willie if he'd known the lad.

'A bit, aye—knew his dad very well, and you knew him too. Kicked your head in a few times. You played in the scrum against him often enough.'

Jock sat up. 'You mean Sandy MacRae? Sunk a few pints with him too—aye, he was a grand lad. Oh God, I didn't make the connection. Didn't he kill himself on a bike too?'

'Yes and no. He was minding his own business—a drunk tourist hit him.'

Jock frowned as he laid down his whisky. 'So you've read the report on Hughie's accident then?'

'Aye, a bad business.'

'History repeating itself?' Jock was interested in his friend's reaction to the police report which he'd not yet seen. He suspected that young Jamie's account was likely to be the more accurate.

Willie shook his head. 'Not according to the traffic boys. He was over the limit, but only just. That makes him a drunk driver in their books. He was a big lad, could handle his beer. That lad was brought up on a bike, could handle anything. Used to do the Scottish Six Day Trials: wild stuff that. Amazing what these lads can do on those cross bikes. The skid marks suggested he wasn't going fast—and it would take more than a sheep or deer to get that lad off. Bad business—strange business.'

Jock thought back over his conversation with Jamie, but decided not to mention Jamie's misgivings. He'd let the matter rest for now.

Chapter 3

The CID was buzzing when Jock walked in on Monday morning. DI McLean was in Jock's office before he could even sit down and order his tea. 'Family in Aviemore we have on our danger list and have notified. Mr and Mrs eh . . .' He consulted a paper in his hand, 'Mr and Mrs Smyth-Willerby. The husband's abroad on business, but we just took a call from his missis. Seems our friends are busy down there. She's made an appointment for 2.00 this afternoon.'

'Same company?' asked Jock. 'When you warned them you didn't mention Ex-Cell, did you? Kept it general, told them a bunch of cowboys were round ripping off good people with bum alarm systems?'

DI McLean nodded. 'No, she gave us the name. I'm getting the team organized now.' He rubbed his hands. 'Nice start to the week. I'm going myself, taking DC Morrison and DS Clark.'

Jock tried to shake off the feeling that this all seemed to be a bit too easy as he ordered his morning tea and fired up his pipe. Maybe he was just a touch envious that his Number One was having all the fun: a nice drive down the A9 and some action, while he was stuck in the office with a pile of paperwork.

One bit of paperwork on his desk this morning did, however, interest him. The information from Ex-Cell had come through; e-mailed, he noted, and all nicely set together in a folder by DC Jamie Ross. Jamie had been about to head off with DC Miller when he got the summons from Jock.

Jock tapped the Ex-Cell file with the stem of his pipe. 'These burglaries. I think there could be a connection somewhere to Ex-Cell.' Jamie was treated to a blast of pipe smoke. 'What's your thinking?'

Gathering his thoughts, Jamie leafed through his own copy of the file. 'I've been thinking about this. Certainly no direct connection, sir. I'm really impressed by their operation. I had a long chat with the owner. He's not much older than me—a real livewire. Started on a shoestring, and they're still hanging on to the shoestring. If their product's as good as he says, they should be onto a winner. They've even got their own research and development department; all their stuff is designed and built in-house. Seems like a fantastic and very cheap system. There's minimal installation involved. We should be encouraging these guys—could make police life a lot easier. If the news got out that their name's connected to the burglaries it would ruin them.'

Jamie laid the folder on the desk and looked at his boss. 'But I think there could be a connection sir. At least one of our pair knows the electronics and the alarm business very well. He can very easily disable existing old systems. He impresses and scares his victims by disarming any system they might have in seconds. My guess is he's got an unwitting contact in Ex-Cell—we just need to find the connection.'

Jock nodded. 'OK lad. Get down to Edinburgh and check it out, but tread carefully. You'll need a cover story for the staff.'

'Already done sir. It's agreed with the owner: industrial espionage. I'm investigating Chinese infiltration of the market, that sort of thing.'

'So you think you're one jump ahead of me then?' said Jock smiling. 'I spoke to the boss, he's expecting you. You'll not be wrapping this up in a day. Quick as you can though, and no five star hotels, mind.'

DI McLean and his team were in place in good time. A very nervous Mrs Smyth-Willerby served them tea and biscuits as Bob gave her instructions. She was such a bundle of nerves he doubted if she was capable of acting at all naturally. If the villains were as smart as he thought they were, they would smell a rat and run. Leaving DC Morrison hidden outside to lock the gate once they were in would take care of that eventuality. Once inside, he and DS Clark would quietly confront them.

Satisfied with his arrangements, they settled down to wait and had some more tea—Mrs Smyth-Willerby had a large gin and tonic to settle her nerves.

At 1.45 they got the signal from DC Morrison: a van had come through the gates and he was in the process of locking them behind it. By then Mrs Smyth-Willerby had had a few more nerve-settling gins. DI McLean suspected that she was no stranger to gin for breakfast and hoped for the best.

DI McLean and DS Clark took up their positions as their hostess made her way unsteadily to answer the knock on the back door. From his place in the kitchen DI McLean could see her as she opened the door, heard her mutter something unintelligible and watched in horror as she fell backwards into the passageway. Oh my God, he thought, I set that poor woman up to be attacked—there'll be hell to pay for this. He ran from the kitchen, leapt over the body of Mrs Smyth-Willerby and threw himself at the figure in the doorway. He was shouting 'Police!' as he did so, but as the young man on the doorstep was too busy trying instinctively to defend himself, the call went unheard. DS Clark heard the shout from his position in the lounge and ran out to investigate.

DI McLean had taken a knock on the head from a swung laptop and was sitting stunned on the ground. On seeing DS Clark, the man laid down the valuable computer and readied himself for the new attacker. Sergeant Clark decided there was something not quite right here. The young man in the smart suit was alone. Where was the accomplice? He wasn't behaving like a criminal caught in the act: he was acting like a frightened, innocent man defending himself.

Clark pulled out his warrant card, waved it and said, 'Police. You're under arrest.' The man in the suit looked stupefied, then terrified as DC Morrison arrived and grabbed him from behind, put him in an arm lock and forced him over the bonnet of his car.

'What the fuck are you mad bastards doing? Let me go—you're breaking my fucking arm!'

DC Morrison relaxed his hold as Clark approached with handcuffs.

'Resisting arrest is a serious offence,' warned DC Morrison. 'Just take it easy.'

Submitting to the cuffing, the man then turned to face his assailants. 'Would you mind telling me what the fuck's going on? What are you arresting me for?'

DI McLean had by now got to his feet and was dusting himself off. Clearly he was still a bit stunned and not fully back in the game, so DC Morrison took the initiative. 'Would you mind telling me what you're doing here, sir, and can we please see some identification?'

'I'm here to sell a fucking alarm system. I assume to that women lying in the hallway!' The man indicated with his head. All thoughts of Mrs Smyth-Willerby had been forgotten in the skirmish. Morrison looked in horror at the supine figure and hurried to her side.

She opened her eyes and smiled at him as he tried to take her pulse. 'Give me a hand up, will you love—I need a drink.' Morrison got her to her feet, helped her into the lounge and deposited her on the settee.

Back in the driveway, DS Clark was examining the contents of the wallet extracted from the young man's pocket. He was reading a business card for Ex-Cell and compared the name with that on a driving licence. 'Says here Neil Murray. You work for Ex-Cell?'

'I am Neil Murray, and yes, I work for Ex-Cell,' said the man indignantly. 'Will you please take these fucking cuffs off? They're hurting. Please get these fucking things off me!'

Clark called the number on the business card, had a short conversation, then stepped behind the man and unlocked the cuffs. 'I'm sorry sir, but it seems there's been some sort of mistake. We were expecting . . . eh, someone else.'

Mrs Smyth-Willerby called from inside. 'Anyone like a cup of tea?'

DS Clark smiled sheepishly at his erstwhile villain. 'Cup of tea, Mr Murray?'

Among DI McLean's other excellent qualities was a fine sense of humour. He was also a gifted raconteur—an invaluable aid when it came to presenting his report.

It turned out that Mr Smyth-Willerby, alarmed by the news of the burglaries and by the fact that his many valuables lay unprotected, decided to install an alarm system. He had, however, omitted to tell his wife. The sales department of Ex-Cell, having been kept in the dark about activities up north, could not but respond positively to the request. Although currently they were only operating as far north as Perth, business was business and Aviemore was only a shortish hop further up the A9—Mr Murray had been despatched.

What could have been a messy PR incident blew over. Neil Murray, fortunately, also had a fine sense of humour. His brother being a policeman in Perth helped matters—he was well aware that a policeman's lot was not always a happy one.

As for Mrs Smyth-Willerby, she thought that the whole thing was a great hoot and was clearly soft on Neil Murray. Ex-Cell would get their contract, so everyone was happy. Except, of course, Jock Anderson. But he too had a sense of humour. What wasn't funny, though, was that they were back to square one on the case.

For DC Jamie Ross, his trip to Edinburgh was like coming home. He'd had four good years at university there and he hoped he might have time to visit some old stomping grounds and look up a friend or two.

He found the premises of Ex-Cell without trouble on a new industrial estate. The owner, Duncan Lewis, greeted him warmly, firmly closed the office door and sat him down after ordering some coffee and leaving instructions that he was not to be disturbed. Files on the employees were on the table and they spent half an hour reviewing them. They were comprehensive enough, but gave little in the way of personal details. Lewis was uncomfortable with the hush-hush nature of the investigation. He valued his team highly and felt he knew each member very well. What's more, he trusted his staff and didn't like deceiving them. But he had agreed that there was no choice. After lunch would be soon enough to start the interviews so Lewis and Jamie retired to a nearby pub for a pie and a pint.

Duncan Lewis turned over his office for the interviews, there being no other space available in the small unit. Only two of the team were available. The two salesmen were out on the job but they would be back in the office first thing next morning.

The sales and marketing department was Mrs Alice Rogers, a very attractive, dynamic twenty-five year old graduate in business studies. Somewhat bemused by the whole thing, she answered Jamie's questions with total candour and humour. Her husband was an accountant, and they had no remotely questionable friends or contacts. She pretended to ponder the question about any Chinamen acting suspiciously. Her answer was a laugh and a shake of the head.

The Research and Development department was from a different mould: it consisted of Frank MacTavish. Frank MacTavish was a nerd—a classic textbook nerd. Twenty-eight years old, skinny, scruffy, with unkempt long hair and a pair of John Lennons on his long, thin nose. He was a Glaswegian with an accent even Jamie occasionally struggled to cope with. Interviewing him was like pulling teeth—he clearly was not of this planet. He was single, lived alone and had no friends that he could name or think of other than his associates at the computer club: his only social outlet it seemed. He certainly looked and acted shifty, but Jamie was not convinced. He felt that poor Frank was just a congenitally shifty looking character.

Reviewing what little he had with Duncan Lewis, Duncan noted one inaccuracy. MacTavish didn't live alone. To share costs he had a flatmate, or certainly used to have. He was only fairly recently heard to complain about the antisocial behaviour of the man he shared with. Duncan gathered that this related to the playing of music very late in the evening and his activities with his girlfriend, which apparently disturbed Frank throughout the night.

Tackled on this apparent discrepancy, Frank assured Jamie that he now did indeed live alone, he had moved into a one—bedroom flat, leaving his noisy friend behind. Despite the social friction, it turned out that he was still a friend. Both were computer and electronic freaks. They'd met at the computer club and the mutual need for cheap accommodation had brought them together. He admitted that he had talked a lot about his work with his flatmate. As his only interest—and a mutual interest—it was difficult not to. His flatmate, he said, was very enthusiastic about Ex-Cell, and was keen to help promote it and help his friend. He had said that if Frank could provide him with a bunch of brochures, he was sure he could interest a few folk. As far as he knew, his friend was still in the old apartment—he was quite happy that Frank had vacated as he had another friend who wanted to move in. Frank provided his old address and gave Jamie the name of his old flatmate, John MacDonald, and that of John's new flatmate who, he thought, was an Ian Forbes.

Yes, there were photos of the two. Frank liked digital photography and they were on his computer at home. He was sent off to his flat and within half an hour some very useful pictures were being downloaded on the office computer. Jamie immediately forwarded the photos to Inverness, then picked up the phone and called his boss.

Jock was clearly very happy with Jamie's results and told him so. 'Get yourself back up here laddie; forget the salesmen you've missed: they've got bugger all to do with this. And no, don't you be worrying about checking out MacDonald's flat, that's a job for the locals. I don't believe for a minute there's anyone there anyway—they're having too good a time here in Inverness.'

Jamie phoned up and cancelled the meeting he'd planned with two of his Edinburgh friends. As he was about to leave Duncan Lewis's office, there were sounds of voices and laughter from the hallway. The sales rep had returned from his trip to Aviemore and was recounting his story. On being introduced to Jamie his reaction was understandable.

'Bloody hell—not another fucking bobby!'

Chapter 4

Jock took a couple of lazy practice swings as he waited for his two playing partners. A 9 o'clock tee-off meant just that. Miss it, and the next in line was in there like a shot, and that would be it. Chief Constable or not, if he didn't show soon it would be home to the Sunday papers. It was three minutes to the hour and the foursome to follow were already inching forwards when Willie Ferguson, and the third in their party, Colonel Dougie Sanderson, hurried onto the tee.

Willie pulled a driver from his bag and extracted a ball from his pocket. 'Sorry we're a wee bit late—I had to collect Dougie, his car's in the garage.'

The Colonel was a good friend of both men and a regular playing partner. Older than both, in his late sixties, he was a smallish, wiry man, every inch a soldier. His white military moustache was permanently stained by the small smelly cheroots he habitually smoked. Scots to the core, his accent, however, was straight out of Sandhurst.

The good weather was persisting. An occasional gust of east wind sent a few drives into the rough—and some miss hits sent a few more. All three were very steady golfers of comparable ability. They played for the fun of it and didn't take it too seriously, which was why they hadn't played in any club competition for years, so their official handicaps were somewhat historical. Dougie never went anywhere without a well charged hip flask from which the winner of each hole was obliged to take a generous sip of good malt—they all considered this handicap enough. The loser of course had to buy the drinks on the 19th.

Jock chipped in his last shot from a bunker for a round of 84. The other pair putted out at 86 and 87. Willie was buying—again.

'Damned fine chip, Jock. You're a lucky bugger—ball was going like the clappers. If the pin hadn't been in we'd still have been looking for the ball,' joked Dougie.

'It's your own fault Dougie,' said Jock laughing. 'The last swig you forced on me at the 17th just steadied my nerves nicely. Bar-time—I could kill a beer.'

The bar was comfortably busy when they walked in. Some quick words and nods were exchanged with fellow regulars as they passed through to find a spare table. Jock and Dougie sank gratefully into the comfy chairs while Willie headed to the bar to order. Dougie was in the process of lighting a cheroot when he suddenly stiffened. Jock followed his gaze. A pair had just entered: a small overweight man in checked golf trousers leading the way. Behind him, clearly his companion, walked a tall, athletically built, strikingly handsome blonde man, casually dressed, but not for golf. The pair stopped, leaned on the bar, and the smaller of the two ordered drinks.

Lifting his beer, the tall man turned. Casting his eye round the room, he found Dougie staring at him. Jock had never seen that look on Dougie's face before. But what was it? Surprise? Anger? Contempt? There was something else, a flash of emotion Jock couldn't identify. The tall stranger lazily raised his glass in greeting and turned to his companion.

'Friend of yours, Dougie? Impressive looking character.'

Dougie completed the lighting of his cheroot, took a heavy draw and lowered his head. 'That, my friend, is the Honourable Richard Ogilvie, the Eighth Duke of Dunmorey.'

'Well, he certainly looks the part. I gather from your reaction not a pal of yours.'

'Long story, Jock. His father was my best friend. How he spawned the Honourable Richard I'll never understand.'

Jock fiddled with his pipe. 'He's keeping strange company. His mate's Owen Evans, the slimiest lawyer this side of the border.'

Dougie looked towards the bar. 'Welsh, is he? Suppose he must be with a name like that.'

Jock nodded.

Dougie looked at him. 'How come a Welshman's practicing law in Inverness?'

'Aye, Dougie, how indeed. He came to Scotland during the oil boom; a lawyer with some company in Aberdeen. Met and married a woman from Inverness and ended up in practice here. She divorced him pretty sharpish if I remember rightly. He's remarried to a local girl, good bit younger than him—so he stayed on, unfortunately.'

'Well, what a coincidence, Douglas, imagine meeting you here.' Jock looked up in surprise, Dougie in irritation at the figure towering over them.

'Mind if I take a seat?' Less imposing but nonetheless impressive when seated, the newcomer extended his hand to Jock while fixing him with penetrating blue eyes. 'Ogilvie, Richard Ogilvie.'

Jock returned the handshake and introduced himself. Ogilvie also shook hands with a reluctant Dougie.

'Surprised to see you here,' said Dougie coldly. 'Fancying a spot of golf?'

'No, afraid not Douglas. Not much time for golf these days—much too busy. No, I've been at the estate for a few days, bit of business to attend to. Off back to London this afternoon. Hope to get a bit of stalking in soon though. Fancy a day on the hill, Douglas? Few years since you've bagged a stag, eh? Nice to see you again Douglas, and to meet you, Mr Anderson, but you must excuse me—business to attend to. Gather they do a nice spot of lunch here, eh? Perhaps we could have a drink together after lunch? Sorry, but I must go.'

Jock watched the retreating figure and turned to his friend who was clearly none too happy. A whirlwind had come and gone and they sat silent in its aftermath.

'Where are these bloody drinks?' muttered Dougie. 'Hope he's got me a large one; I damn well need it.'

Willie, who'd been chatting to a group of friends at the bar, had missed the whole episode. He apologised for the delay as he set the drinks on the table. Dougie picked up his double whisky and downed it in one.

Willie looked at him in surprise. 'You OK man, you look a bit pale?'

'Can you get me another of those please, Willie? I need it.'

His second glass he drank more slowly while Jock described what had happened. Dougie refused to be drawn on the matter of the Honourable Richard Ogilvie and by the end of lunch he was back to his old self and was even laughing about the incident.

Chapter 5

When the call came in, it was almost as a relief. There had been no reported burglaries for almost two weeks, and Jock was becoming concerned that the birds had flown: that he'd lost them.

'This one's a bit different though sir,' said DI McLean. 'We've got a body.'

'What do you mean you've got a body?' said Jock rising to his feet, his smoking pipe forgotten on his desk.

'A dead man at the scene.'

Jock grabbed his jacket and his pipe. 'Come on—fill me in on the way.'

Jock hadn't recognized the address, but he knew the house very well: it was the home of his friend Dougie Sanderson. Any doubts or desperate hopes were shattered as he looked down at the body. Dougie Sanderson was lying on his back down the length of a short flight of patio steps. His feet rested on the second step, his head on the edge of the bottom. There was a large pool of black congealed blood on the pathway below; a trickle had run into a rose-bed. On Dougie's hands were green rubber gardening gloves and a trowel was still held loosely in his right hand.

Despite himself, Jock felt his eyes moistening and he tried discreetly to wipe away a tear. He blew his nose, and then walked across to Doctor Paterson who had examined the body. Round them, cameras flashed as the scene-of-crime team continued their work professionally and dispassionately. Not for the first time in his career, Jock was finding it difficult to remain professional and detached when faced with the body of a close friend.

Dr Alex Paterson rubbed his hand over his face and cleared his throat. 'He was my friend too, Jock. Many's a time we've sat together at yon table with a few beers admiring his garden and watching the birds. Was a great gardener: loved his roses and his birds.' The doctor cleared his throat again, found a tissue in a jacket pocket and blew his nose.

'You'll be wanting to know the time of death,' he said, anticipating Jock's question.

Jock turned to him and nodded.

'As near as I can guess at the moment, an educated guess, mind, is that he's been dead about . . .' He thought for a few moments. 'More than twelve hours for sure. It was cold last night, which affects things.'

'Sometime late yesterday evening then?'

'No, earlier. He's got lots of fly eggs in his eyes and mouth. No flies round at night. No flies about just now, too cold yet.'

'So what are you saying? Maybe yesterday afternoon while it was still warm?'

'Aye, that's about right. Late afternoon or early evening I'd say. Maybe manage to narrow it down a bit for you later. Need to get him down to the morgue now for a proper examination and post mortem. I'll try and have some answers for you as quick as I can.'

Jock was joined by DI McLean. 'Accident maybe?' said the DI, indicating a fallen rake lying by the top step. Beyond it were some pots beside an open bag of potting soil. A bunch of dried-out seedlings destined for planting were scattered around.

'Could be.' agreed Jock, sighing. 'Working on his planting, stands up, legs tangled in the rake when he stepped back? Could be. I hope it was, Bob, I hope it was. But this will be a crime scene until we prove otherwise.'

Jock had pulled himself together and was now all business.

'Who found the body then?'

'I did sir.' It was Jamie Ross. 'We were nearest when the call came through about the burglary. That's all we thought it was sir—another burglary. Reported at . . .' He consulted his notebook. 'At 9.42am by Mrs Jean MacInnes. She's his . . .' He looked towards the body being loaded onto a stretcher . . . 'Was his house-lady. Says she always comes in every morning about that time. She says the back door was unlocked, didn't need to use her key. She soon realized that there had been a burglary. There was no sign of Colonel Sanderson, so she dialled 999. I took a wee look round the outside of the house. That's when I found him, sir.'

Jock cleared his throat. 'Mrs MacInnes, I'll need a word with her.'

The constable indicated the house. 'Inside sir: in the kitchen with Annie—DC Miller.'

Mrs Jean MacInnes was a slimly built, middle-aged lady, early sixties Jock guessed, grey haired and bespectacled.

'You feel up to answering a few questions, Mrs MacInnes?' asked Jock.

'A am that. Bittie shook up, but that nice cup o' tea's helped. Thanks dearie,' she said, touching Annie Miller's arm.

'Can you just tell me everything that happened after you got here this morning? Take your time,' said Jock as he sat down opposite her. 'Can I have a cup of that nice tea please, Annie?'

Mrs MacInnes took a packet of cigarettes from her bag and lit one, took a couple of puffs and stubbed it out. 'A got here aboot half past nine. A wee bittie later than A normally come in. Had tae tak my sister doon tae the doctor's—trouble wi' her bowels again. A keep tellin' her tae eat mair fibres but she'll no' listen tae me. All Bran an' prunes every mornin' keeps ye regular; tak a tip frae me, Mr Anderson.'

Jock smiled and thanked her for her advice.

'A parked ma wee car in ma usual place. The Colonel's Land Rover wisnae there, a thought he must hae gone oot.'

'You saw nothing out of the ordinary then?'

A shake of the head. 'The back door wis open—no' standin' open mind, just no' locked.'

'Was that unusual?'

A head shake again. 'If he's in it wid be open. If he's gone oot for just a wee while; gone for a wee walk lookin' for birds, or maybe popped doon tae the shop, he usually leaves it open. If it's locked A've got ma ain key. A cam intae the kitchen; A ey wash up his breakfast stuff first. He's a gid cook but no' sae very gid at tidyin' up after hissel' whiles.'

'You'll not have done any dishes this morning then?' commented Jock, looking towards the sink.

'No, none tae wash this morning, all tidy. Just a mug an' a glass. A washed them.'

'He never did his own washing up then?'

'Oh aye, but no' when he kent A'd be comin' in.'

'So if he'd cooked anything last night the dishes would be left?'

'Aye, that's right. A just cleared up here a bittie an' went through tae the lounge. The place looked empty—just kind o'empty. A' his lovely Persian carpets—no' there. The big wall—a' his lovely bird pictures gone. A' the walls empty, just a few family photies still there. Yon big display cabinet, doors wide open. A shouted oot for the Colonel, he's often busy in his office, but he wisnae in there, A looked in to see. So A called the police, A dialled 999 like ye're meant tae dae. Never done that afore.'

Jock asked her when she last saw the Colonel.

'Friday mornin'. A only work fir twa oors in the mornin's. Dinnae cam in weekends. Hardly enough work fir me tae dae. The Colonel is, wis, a very tidy man. Wis in the army ye ken. They learn tae be right tidy in the army.

He wis workin' in the garden wi' his roses when A left. Loved his garden; he grew lovely roses.'

'On your way here, in your car, did you see anyone, see any cars coming or going?'

Mrs MacInnes thought for a moment. 'A waved at old Mrs Harris: hers is the wee cottage at the bottom o' the drive. She wis in her garden. Nae cars though.'

'If you're feeling up to it can we take a wee walk round the house, maybe you can give us an idea what's missing?' said Jock getting up from the table. 'We'll start through here.' Mrs MacInnes followed Jock into the Colonel's office, and she looked round. The walls of the office were well covered with photos, a record of Dougie's life.

'There wis a few nice bird pictures over there, see them empty spaces? They really wis his favourites. Birds, lovely they were, a' mair than five hundred years old he telt me.' An in-tray full of papers lay on the desk, and Jock flipped through them idly. There was the usual collection of bills and domestic papers, but in the midst, the familiar red brochure for Ex-Cell. On a tour of the house they found many more spaces on the walls, and many display cabinets stood open, their shelves cleared. Mrs MacInnes couldn't be very specific about what was mising, and Jock hoped, with a bit of luck, that the insurance company would have a list and descriptions of valuable items.

He called over DI McLean. 'We'll leave the forensic lads to get on with it. I want all the houses between here and the main road visited. We need to know what the neighbours saw yesterday afternoon or evening. We'll pay a visit to old Mrs Harris. A last wee word with Mrs MacInnes first.'

Jock found her back in the kitchen. 'This brochure: have you seen it before?'

Mrs MacInnes took the Ex-Cell booklet and flipped through it, shaking her head.

'Did the Colonel have any visitors that you saw over the last few weeks? Anyone that looked like a salesman maybe?'

The shaking of the head again. 'A wis only here fir twa hours o' a morning; bit o' cleaning, an' his laundry, no' much tae dae, an' no' at the weekends either. He didnae hae that many visitors A dinnae think. Sometimes A'd hae tae clear up a puckle glasses an' wash up mair than one plate, but no' often.'

'Did you get on well with the Colonel?'

'Och aye, he wis a lovely man; we had many a gid laugh.'

'Ever share confidences? I mean, did you have real talks with him?'

'No. He was a right private man, even mair so after his wife died. Kind o' drew intae his shell so tae speak. A cam tae work here when she got sick, she couldnae manage. She wanted me tae stay on after she died tae tak care o' hissel'. She wis a gid one. A real lady—cancer it wis. He never really got ower it ye ken, it hit him hard, it did. He kept hissel' busy but A often felt his heart wisnae in it if you follow me: a sadness aboot him. Been mair doon than usual recently, thought maybe tae dae with the anniversary comin' up. She died five years ago cam first o' September.'

'Many phone calls?' Jock felt he was fishing in empty waters but pressed on.

'Aye, A suppose he did. He had lots o' friends, ye see.'

'Any calls that you'd remember? Ever overhear anything interesting?'

Mrs MacInnes smiled. 'There wis some woman a while back kept callin' him up—frae Edinburgh A think. He never said onything, but he seemed tae manage a few visits tae Edinburgh—business trips he called them. That wis ages ago, nothing cam of it. Pit a gid grin on his face for a wee while it did.'

'Any calls that didn't make him happy?'

Mrs MacInnes thought for a few moments. 'There wis one A mind well. Must hae been aboot a month ago. It wis on his mobile. He answered it in here but went ootside tae talk. Someone got him right angry; shouting on the phone he wis—no' like him at all. Couldnae mak onythin' oot though. He cam back in lookin' right upset. Poured hissel' a big dram—a never saw him dae that in the mornin' afore.'

Jock took a quick last look round before he left and found DC Ross in the office. 'No computer sir. Top-of-the-range colour printer, but no computer. They must have taken that too.'

'Check with Mrs MacInnes, will you. She didn't mention a computer was missing.'

Jamie did as instructed. It turned out that the Colonel had got rid of his old desktop and replaced it with a new laptop only the previous week. She said he didn't always have the laptop on his desk; it was often in the lounge or the bedroom. The laptop computer couldn't be found anywhere in the house. Neither was there any trace of Dougie's mobile phone.

The talk with old Mrs Harris at the end of the drive wasn't a total waste of time. Being a bit hard of hearing, sensible conversation was difficult. She was, however, still very sharp, and like many old people, took a lot of interest in what was going on round her.

'Aye,' said Mrs Harris. 'Yesterday afternoon, A saw the Colonel in a car going up. It was a big red car, he was wi' another man. He gave me a wee wave. He was a right nice man the Colonel, he never forgot me at Christmas.' Mrs Harris dabbed some tears from her eyes and blew her nose. 'It was just after lunch. A was in the front garden. A wee whiley later the red car cam back doon again. A thought maybe A heard a car go up later in the afternoon, maybe two cars, or maybe it was the same one coming back doon again. It wisnae the Colonel's car: A ken his noisy old Land Rover.' It was, she said, before she turned the TV on, so must have been before 5.00. She couldn't hear anything outside with the TV on. She had neither heard nor seen anything early that morning, except for Mrs MacInnes who passed in her car when she was in the garden. Before that she'd been in the kitchen with Radio 4 making scones, and the kitchen was at the back of the house away from the road.

Jock and DI McLean sat in a pub with a beer, reviewing what they had, which didn't seem much. No other neighbours had reported seeing any vehicles on the Sunday afternoon or evening. The preliminary post mortem report was due early that afternoon: the Doc had promised to get right on it. Jock just finished his pint and was contemplating another when his phone rang.

'Alex, what have you got?' Jock listened for a few minutes, grunted his thanks to the doctor and returned the phone to his pocket. 'Get me a dram will you Bob: a large one.'

Bob McLean returned from the bar and handed his boss a whisky. Jock looked shaken. He downed his drink and looked at his DI.

'Alex stressed that this was just a preliminary report; a kind of quick look-see I suppose. Not sure I want to hear any more. Dougie had a large bruise on the centre of his chest. Back of his head smashed in, consistent with it hitting the step. The Doc thinks he was punched pretty hard on the chest and went backwards down the stairs. The punch probably stunned him—the head wound killed him; but not instantly. His heart was going long enough to create the big bruise and the puddle of blood.'

'So we've got a murder on our hands. Shit, we badly need a fucking break on this one,' said DI McLean as he thumped his empty glass on the table. 'How can we keep this quiet? The press will be all over us. We're starting to look as stupid as they'll say we are.'

Jock shook his head. 'You're not thinking, Bob. Dougie's death will be reported as an accident. The murder bit we can keep quiet till it suits us. But you're right, we do need a break—fucking or otherwise.' Jock took his mobile from his pocket. 'I have to speak to the Chief Constable.' Jock called Willie Ferguson and broke the news to his friend. 'This is also a professional call, Willie. You dropped Dougie off at his house after the golf, didn't you? Then it seems you were the last person to see him alive. I'll be in your office in twenty minutes.'

It was a pale-faced Chief Constable facing Jock over his desk. 'I can't believe it Jock, just can't believe it. Not often murder strikes so close to home.' He rubbed his hands over his face.

Jock cleared his throat. 'We all left the golf club at about 2.00. You gave Dougie a lift home; must have got there about 2.15 or so. You'd tell me if you saw anything unusual. Did you just drop him off and go?'

Willie stood up, took a bottle and two glasses from a cabinet and poured them both a whisky. 'No, we went inside. He offered me a dram. He had one, but I had a coffee. I wasn't there long, maybe half an hour. I was ready for a kip. When I left him he was in good form, said he'd have a wee kip after he checked his e-mails. We took a quick walk round his garden—he wanted to show me his roses, then I left.'

Jock finished his whisky and stood up. 'We'll be keeping the details of Dougie's death quiet, Willie. As far as anyone else is concerned, it was a tragic accident. I just hope to hell if the bastards think they've got away with it they'll hang around until we can grab them.'

Jock was reluctant to risk doing anything that would scare off his suspects. There was no doubt in his mind that MacDonald and Forbes were the men he was looking for. As an electronics and computer wizzo, MacDonald fitted the bill perfectly. Forbes, they had learned from investigations made by Jock's Edinburgh colleagues, was a former assistant in the top Edinburgh auction house—he was an expert on antiques. That the men would eventually be apprehended there was no doubt. Jock had photos of the two which he could give to the press, but the men could then go to ground and the stolen antiques would be lost. Wee MacPhee's stamp collection and all the other valuable knick-knacks aside, this was personal. Jock was going to find the Colonel's killers and get his stuff back—he owed it to Dougie.

Chapter 6

Some might say that it was good police work that finally got them their men, but it's unlikely that Jock Anderson would claim as much. His intelligent use of the media certainly was, however, effective.

Mrs Catherine Symmons was a formidable widow of some sixty-five years. She lived alone in an old manor house on the Black Isle surrounded by her cats—numbering about fifty—an elderly Great Dane and four terriers of indeterminate breed. As a semi-retired specialist in animal behaviour, her passion in life was animals—all animals. Her particular passion was, however, for cats.

The manor house had once dominated a very large estate. Most of the land was now gone, but there remained several farm holdings: houses, barns and steadings which had, over the years, been converted for holiday rentals. Why anyone wanted to holiday on the Black Isle was a continual source of amazement to Mrs Symmons. That tourists were prepared to pay such outrageous rents for the privilege delighted her, this being her principal source of income. Being the height of the holiday season, all her properties were rented, and she discreetly visited all four of them as part of her daily routine, either on foot, or, as today, on her mountain bike. She rarely needed to intrude on the privacy of her guests and only did so in extreme circumstances—such as incorrect disposal of litter. Pedalling past one of the bigger properties she was annoyed to find large pieces of polystyrene foam blowing round the old farmyard.

She dismounted and prepared to confront the tenants but found them absent. She noticed that the barn door, which normally stood open to facilitate the movement of the many birds that nested there, was closed. Not only closed, but locked by a hasp and staple affixed, apparently, by her current tenants. She was preparing to cycle on, determined to return later to confront the offenders, when she heard the plaintive cry of a kitten trapped, she presumed, within the barn—this could not be tolerated.

An old store shed still contained some rusting tools, amongst them a crowbar with which she made short work of the lock and the door swung open. Astounded, Mrs Symmons gazed upon an Aladdin's cave of treasure whilst the liberated kitten fussed round her ankles. With the cat securely stuffed inside her back-pack she hurried home, found the current copy of her local paper featuring the news of the burglaries and the police appeal for help, and called the contact number provided. Jock Anderson was speaking to Mrs Symmons within minutes, and was with her within half an hour.

The hoard in the barn was as she had described: dozens of items carefully wrapped in cardboard and polystyrene, and many many others awaiting attention. Amongst these, Jock recognized some of the valuable bird pictures from Dougie Sanderson's house. Jock's radio crackled a warning that a truck had pulled off the main road and was approaching the farm. Jock prayed that these were his boys—long stakeouts were tedious. He instructed Bob McLean to park their car out of sight while he remained inside the barn, closed the door and waited.

The truck pulled into the yard. Jock heard it manoeuvre and, through the crack between the doors, saw it reverse towards him. Two figures jumped from the truck and headed to the door. Remembering the broken body of his friend, Jock felt a moment of uneasiness. He'd allowed himself to be trapped in the barn and was about to encounter two potentially violent and fit young men. His experience had taught him that the mildest of men can become the most violent when cornered and desperate—these men were about to be trapped.

Jock took a deep breath and waited.

The men outside were alarmed at finding their lock broken and quickly threw open the barn doors. Facing them was the imposing figure of Jock Anderson. 'Misters MacDonald and Forbes, I presume?' said Jock—he did enjoy a bit of theatre. Behind the men appeared a smiling DI McLean, a police car drove into the yard blocking any exit and four uniformed constables jumped out. Whatever inclinations the men may have had, to fight or to run, evaporated. Both clearly realised that their position was hopeless. They were read their rights as the cuffs were clapped on.

Jock addressed his captives. 'Me and you, lads, are going to have a wee chat.'

Back at the station, Jock identified John MacDonald as the leader of the two, and he was his. DI McLean prepared to interview Forbes, MacDonald's partner.

From an adjacent room, Jock watched MacDonald for a few minutes through a one-way window. The lad was clearly distressed: his hands were shaking as he tried to drink his tea. Jock suspected that this was MacDonald's first offence. There was no record of previous convictions for either of the two men. MacDonald was terrified and confused—in the perfect state to be interviewed.

Jock and DS Clark went into the interview room and took chairs facing MacDonald, The sergeant switched on the tape recorder and formally commenced the interview. MacDonald asked for a cigarette. Jock nodded and DS Clark gave him one from his pack.

Jock laid his pipe on the table. 'Why did you do it, lad?'

MacDonald accepted a light for his cigarette, blew out some smoke and shrugged. 'Seemed like a great idea. What could go wrong? I knew about alarms, my mate knew his antiques. Aye, seemed like an easy way to get us started, sir. We needed some money. It was just going to be the one time—enough money to get us set up in our own businesses.'

Jock tapped his pipe on the table. 'The old man. Why did you have to thump him?'

MacDonald looked up, his cigarette half way to his mouth. 'Old man? What old man? What are you on about?'

Jock looked at him coldly. 'Last Sunday. Your last burglary. You robbed the house on Northmuir drive.'

'Aye sir, we did.'

Jock nodded and continued. 'In the course of the robbery you encountered an elderly man, the owner of the property: Colonel Douglas Sanderson. One of you hit him. He fell backwards down some steps and smashed his head. One of you killed him, and you are both facing a charge of murder.'

MacDonald's face paled as he stared at Jock and DS Clark in shocked disbelief. 'Murder? Get off, Superintendent. We nicked a load of antiques from the house you're talking about; and a few other places—hands up, it was us. But murder? We didn't see any old man—we didn't kill anyone.' He asked for another cigarette and his hands shook as he lit it. He realized he was in trouble, very serious trouble. The police knew he'd been there, he'd admitted to being there.

'There was no one in the house sir. We'd done our usual thing—couple of phone calls to the house, no reply, a quick last call just before we went in to be sure. The door was unlocked—there was nobody in. We grabbed the things we wanted and got out of there quick. There was no-one there sir; we saw nobody alive or dead—honest.'

Jock leaned forward in his chair. 'What time were you there?'

'About 5 o'clock; maybe a bit before.'

Jock slowly shook his head. 'Not looking good son, not good at all. Colonel Sanderson was killed between 4.00pm and 7.00pm. I think you'd better get yourself a lawyer.'

Jock felt an almost overwhelming urge to grab MacDonald and beat the truth out of him. He was tortured by the image of his friend callously left for dead on the steps of his house. Jock knew he was too emotionally involved with the case. The Chief Constable had wanted to relieve him but had relented to his continued involvement.

In the next room DI McLean was having no better luck. Forbes was not bearing up well, and though he readily admitted to the burglaries he was tearfully proclaiming his innocence of any involvement in the murder.

'Maybe Johnny hit him, I don't know. Maybe when I was loading the van and never said anything to me. Maybe that's it, aye, maybe he thumped him, but not me sir—I never saw anyone, honest I didn't.'

Hours of questioning wore down both police and murder suspects. Jock had a clear picture about the burglaries but no confession to the killing. It was midnight, Jock and DI McLean were comparing notes in Jock's office, and Jock refilled his and McLean's glass from his emergency bottle of malt. Both of the accused had been appointed lawyers. In the light of the evidence both lawyers had advised their clients that when the case went to court they would both risk a conviction for murder. The police were willing to accept that there was no intent to kill. With a confession, a lesser charge of manslaughter could probably be considered—but neither MacDonald nor Forbes was prepared to compromise. They were adamant that they were innocent.

Bob McLean sat back wearily. 'Well, are we going to formally charge them?'

Jock sipped his whisky before answering. 'Would seem pretty obvious it was them. But I'm just not sure Bob. They're very frightened young lads.

This is their first venture into crime. They're not streetwise criminals, and there's no history of violence. Got a fright when they saw Dougie? Panicked and punched him? Maybe. But the body language is all wrong, Bob; their denials are so emphatic—they sound so sincere. If I was them, and I'd done it, I'd be grabbing at a chance to get off with manslaughter. I just don't know. Let's sleep on it.'

But sleep wouldn't come easily for Jock. He was too tired, too wired to sleep. Meg prescribed a large hot toddy and they lay in bed talking through the case.

'MacDonald, he's the really bright one, Meg. He's the leader. He's mad about computers and micro-electronics. Had started a course at college but dropped out, got bored—he said knew more than the teachers. He could still get a very good job and was no layabout, but he wanted money to fund his own business and develop his ideas.'

'Forbes, the auctioneer's assistant. Another bright boy. Knows all about antiques and fine art. He's big into amateur dramatics, loves dressing up—he's the make-up artist.'

'They met one night at a party, hit it off and over a few pints came up with the idea. Their big plan was to get some money together for MacDonald to start his electronics business, and to get a few antiques together for Forbes who wanted to open an antique shop. If they sold off all the traceable stuff they'd stolen they'd get a nice pile of cash: enough for a bit of the good life and to get their businesses started. Forbes would fill his shop with legitimate things along with the untraceable stolen items. Forbes knew he could move the traceables through the many less than scrupulous customers of the auctions.'

'We were right lucky, got them just in time Meg. Caught them as they were planning to load everything up. They were heading off down south tonight—to London. We'd probably have picked them up easy enough in

Edinburgh as the Edinburgh lads are watching their flat. But London? We'd have been lucky to have got any of the stuff back. As we knew their names and had photographs of the pair they'd have been caught soon enough, but probably not before the goodies had gone. MacPhee's stamp collection: they'd planned to sell that first as they'd already set up a buyer for it. We've got the names of their customers for the stuff down south which might interest our friends in the Met. They'd even rented a place in Edinburgh to stash the untraceable things and Forbes had put down a deposit on a wee shop. Plans o' mice and men, eh?' mumbled Jock as he drifted off.

The news of the recovery of the stolen goods and the arrest of the burglars was headline news in the morning paper. Councillor MacPhee, greatly relieved that his stuff had been recovered intact, was all over Jock like a rash and had said very laudatory things to the reporters about their wonderful police force. MacPhee's grinning face was on the front page and Bob McLean smiled as Jock swore and deposited the paper in the recycle bin. 'How long will his good-will last do you think Bob?'

Bob looked at his watch. 'Probably about another ten minutes. He's coming in expecting to collect his stuff and I'll be having to tell him it's being held as evidence—but I suppose MacPhee being nice to us for twenty-four hours is a bit of a record eh?'

Jock sighed as he got up from behind his desk. 'Let's see how Jamie and Annie are getting on.'

Jamie Ross and Annie Miller had been given the job of cataloguing the stolen items and, as well as they could, allocate them to their various owners. Jock was told that there was a problem with Dougie's missing laptop computer and his mobile: they had not turned up. There were no computers or mobile phones amongst the retrieved stolen items.

Jock and Bob then re-interviewed the burglars, but MacDonald and Forbes were adamant about not touching a computer—about not even seeing a computer or cell phone. They pointed out that there were laptops in the other properties; and other valuables like digital cameras that they hadn't touched. They didn't want those sorts of things. New to the game, they had no fence on whom to offload them.

'Believe them?' asked DI McLean.

Jock nodded. 'I do, actually. And I'm starting to maybe believe them about Dougie.'

DI McLean ran his hand over his head. 'Me too. In this job you get to recognize when someone's not being straight. But if they didn't take them, who did? And why?'

Jock suddenly recalled something from his talk with the Chief Constable on the day after the killing. He picked up the phone. 'Willie, you mind when I spoke to you on the Monday after Dougie died and you said he was going to check his e-mails? Did you see his computer?'

Willie seemed surprised at the question. 'Aye, I saw it. He wanted me to see it: he'd just got it, a neat little laptop. Real chuffed with it, he was. Said he'd downloaded everything from his old desktop and got rid of that. When I left, he had it there on the coffee table trying to get on line.'

Jock explained the significance of the laptop.

'So it was there when I left, but wasn't when your friends pitched up—or so they say. So where the hell is it? If they didn't take it—then who did?'

'Exactly, Willie—who did?'

Chapter 7

The funeral of Colonel Douglas Sanderson VC was a big affair. With the arrest of the two burglars the fact that Dougie had been murdered had been made public and there was the predictable media interest. That Dougie was a holder of a Victoria Cross added extra spice to the stories. Groups of reporters and cameramen were hovering, presumably in the hope of some interesting copy from the dignitaries present.

Dougie had had many friends and was a well-loved and respected member of the community and beyond. Mourners had come from all parts of the country to pay their respects, and many senior soldiers in uniform stood out in the crowd. Most members of the golf club were there along with many dozens of others. Jock Anderson and Willie Ferguson watched in silence from the edge of the large group of mourners. They could barely hear the words of the minister as the body of their friend was lowered into the ground to lie beside his wife and two sons. Both of his sons had met violent deaths. The elder, Captain Alan Sanderson in the Falklands war, and his brother Major Donald Sanderson, ten years later in the first Gulf War.

A bugler from Dougie's old regiment stepped forward and played the *Last Post*; a lone piper struck up a lament, and it was over.

As the crowd slowly began to disperse, a figure joined the watching pair: it was Alistair Chambers, Dougie's lawyer, and a friend of both Jock and Willie. 'A good turnout, eh Jock—he'd have been right pleased. But surprised though, he was a right modest kind of a man. He had no idea he was so loved and respected. You lads'll be needing to come round to see me. You're named both as unofficial executors and beneficiaries of his Will.'

Jock and Willie looked surprised. 'But surely we can't be both executers *and* beneficiaries,' said Willie.

'Aye, that's right—as I said, it's unofficial. Ye've got no legal responsibilities. Aye, he's done you both just fine. But you'll have to do a bit o' work for it as executors: official or no'. Tomorrow about 10 o'clock suit you? It's getting right cold; I'll no' be standin' round—tomorrow then.'

The men smiled as they watched the plump, dapper figure hurry towards his car. 'They're all the same these lawyers: all business,' said Jock shaking his head. 'Come on then, let's go and do this.' In his hand was a wreath Meg had made with roses from Dougie's garden. They walked to the graveside and Jock laid the wreath beside the many others. He wasn't a religious man but he said a silent prayer for his friend.

When he lifted his head he saw a group of men lingering on the other side of the grave. One he thought he recognized as the Honourable Richard Ogilvie, Dougie's acquaintance from the golf club. The man caught his eye, smiled and turned to speak to his companion. Jock couldn't hear what was said, but the accent, unlike that of the Honourable Richard, was pure Scottish. The hair was different: the same blonde colour but in a short military cut. There were the same blue eyes, but the figure was slightly smaller and trimmer perhaps. Thoroughly intrigued, Jock walked round and introduced himself.

The young man laughed as Jock explained his dilemma. 'You're not the first to make that mistake. I'm Robbie, and Richard is my elder brother. Yes, I'm told that we do bear a striking physical resemblance.'

'Fortunately that's where the resemblance stops,' said the man at his side.

'Sorry, forgive my manners,' said Ogilvie. 'Allow me to introduce Duncan Munro, and his son Calum.' Jock shook hands with the men, both dressed in matching tweed plus-fours and deerstalker hats.

Duncan Munro smiled at Jock. 'Actually, man—we've met before.'

Jock looked again at the bearded tweed-clad figure. He had a good memory for faces but was momentarily flummoxed.

'Try takin' off aboot thirty years, an' the beard,' suggested the man.

'My God,' exclaimed Jock—'it's wee Dunkie!' He grabbed the man's hand again and held it warmly. 'I've not seen you since we were kids.'

'Aye, that's right. When we were eighteen. You went off tae the police an' me tae the army.'

The pair had been great mates at school and stars together in the school pipe band. They stood grinning at each other, warm memories flooding back.

Jock laughed. 'We've picked a right place for a reunion.' He took a card from his pocket and handed it to Dunkie.

In turn Dunkie wrote his number on a bit of paper. 'Stalkers dinnae run tae business cards.'

'I'll call you at the weekend, Dunkie. We've got a bit of catching up to do. Wee Dunkie—A canny believe it.'

Robbie Ogilvie was grinning at him and Jock gave him his attention. 'Aye, my encounter with your brother was brief, but I can agree with Dunkie here that you would seem to be from a different mould. I take it you were a friend of the Colonel?'

Ogilvie's face saddened. 'More than a friend. He was a second father to me.'

'A right fine gentleman he was,' said Dunkie Munro. 'Bad business. We're right glad ye caught the killers, Jock. That's no way fir a man like the Colonel tae die. Terrible business.'

A cold wind had blown up and it was starting to rain.

'Time to be off I think,' said Jock pulling up his coat collar. 'Been good to meet you, Mr Ogilvie.' Jock clasped Dunkie's shoulder. 'And you too, man. And you, Calum.' He excused himself and returned to join Willie who was chatting to some friends from the golf club. As the rain became heavier they all hurried to their cars.

Back in the privacy of his office, Jock read yet again the whole file on Colonel Sanderson's murder. It was now fairly thick. Jock considered that every aspect had been covered: no stone left unturned. A thorough search through Dougie's home had produced very little in the way of relevant letters or other documents. It had to be assumed that if there was any correspondence relevant to the case it was on the missing computer. His uneasiness about the guilt of MacDonald and Forbes had led to a thorough investigation into the life of his friend, social and professional.

Jock knew Dougie from the golf club. They had initially met there and had bonded further by a keen interest in nature, particularly in ornithology. Dougie had often talked to him about Dunmorey, and Jock knew that Dougie was involved in a conservation project with the old Duke of Dunmorey. Dougie had encouraged Jock to visit the place on several occasions but it had never happened. Socially, beyond the golf club, the lives of the two men had rarely intertwined. He was amazed and impressed by what he learned of Dougie's many interests and involvements. He'd known nothing about Dougie's VC, a further illustration of the modesty of the man. He appeared to be widely admired and respected, without an enemy in the world.

The identity of the caller who had caused Dougie so much distress still niggled. What who had provoked Dougie to behave in a manner so out of character? He recalled the subsequent interview he'd had with Mrs MacInnes, the house-cleaner.

'A canny see how I can help ye onymair, Superintendent,' she'd said. 'Aye, it wis aboot a couple o' months or so afore the Colonel died. A mind now, it wis aboot the time ma sister wis up seein' me frae Glasgow, an' she wis up fir the first twa weeks o' May.'

'There was nothing you can think of that was bothering the Colonel at that time? You said he'd been a bit down for a while.'

'Aye, doon an' a wee bittie grumpy. But he wis a right gentleman—he'd ey apologise fir bein' grumpy. No' that it bothered me, mind.'

'But he never said what he was grumpy about?'

'Aye, sometimes he would, like when his roses got attacked by greenfly or somethin'. An' the computer. Got right upset aboot the computer he did. The old one that is. It kept goin' wrong an' he kept pittin' it in tae get fixed—spent a lot o' money on it, he did. Got right angry wi' the shop. Aggie, that's ma sister frae Glasgow, her man Harry kens aboot computers. He's a programmer or somethin'. He took me tae work one mornin' when ma car wis in the garage. Harry an' the Colonel got talkin' aboot computers an' Harry had a wee look tae see if he could find the problem. A think he telt him it wis a "heardware problem", whatever that is, and telt him tae tak it back tae the shop.'

'So this was about the time the Colonel had that phone call you told me about?'

'Aye, right enough, it wid be,' agreed Mrs MacInnes

A check with the shop confirmed that they had had some less than friendly communications with the Colonel about his computer round the time in question, but no-one recalled, or would admit to having one as acrimonious as that overheard by Mrs MacInnes.

Nothing. A dead end. Jock closed the file and drummed his fingers on the cover. Closed for now but this one would not be filed under cases solved. He'd had no choice but to charge MacDonald and Forbes with Dougie's killing. But his last conversation with MacDonald had guaranteed that the case would not be firmly closed.

'We didn't do it, Mr Anderson,' MacDonald had said. 'What's more, I don't believe that you think we did it. We're not going to admit to something we've not done and we're relying on you. You'll come up with the evidence to clear us.'

Chapter 8

As the last soil was being added to the grave of Dougie Sanderson, Richard Ogilvie, Eighth Duke of Dunmorey, was reclining comfortably in his seat in the first class lounge of a BA 747. Any thoughts, had he ever entertained any on the death of his father's old friend, were far from his mind.

Opposite Ogilvie to his right sat the bespectacled figure of David Rubens, a thin, birdlike figure, every inch the brilliant Jewish lawyer. To the right of Rubens, endeavouring to look more relaxed than he felt, was Arthur Cavendish, Ogilvie's accountant and financial adviser. A tall, urbane, handsome man in his early forties, he was the best in the business. Both men felt uncomfortable under Ogilvie's cold stare. Ogilvie enjoyed intimidating people, believing that fear produced the best results. Perhaps he was right. He demanded—and got—the best from these two men.

He snapped his fingers imperiously at a passing attendant and demanded a double malt whisky: Glenfiddich—no ice or water. The hostess was clearly taken aback by such rudeness and her friendly façade slipped momentarily. Cavendish and Rubens, embarrassed by their boss's behaviour, each asked politely for orange juice. Ogilvie continued his silent scrutiny of his two employees as he awaited the return of the hostess. She received nothing in the way of a thank you as she placed his whisky in front of him on the table. Her offer to provide anything else he may require was gruffly dismissed.

'Well gentlemen, we've got several hours until we hit Miami. Let's make use of them, shall we? I want a review of everything you've got. You first, David.'

For the next three hours both men were grilled mercilessly. Numerous incisive questions sent them searching through a small pile of documents or clicking frantically on their laptops.

Finally, apparently satisfied, Ogilvie sat back and smiled at his men. 'It certainly looks good: all bases covered, so let's have a drink—proper ones for you two this time.' In fact, both men would have preferred orange juice. Neither were big drinkers and both disliked whisky which was ordered on their behalf. Ogilvie, who was aware of every aspect of the lives of the men, knew this. Ever the sadist, he would relish their distaste as they sipped their drinks. In excellent spirits he actually managed a smile and a thank you for the hostess who served them—perhaps because this one was blonde and very pretty.

With some hours of the flight remaining, he returned to his seat in the first class cabin to grab a bit of sleep. As it was, his mind was too preoccupied with what lay ahead and he contented himself with a private review of the deal to which he was about to sign.

His bank had been approached by a group in Florida to invest in an expansion programme for an already large condominium, golf and marina complex on the Gulf Coast. Paradise Glades was already a multi-million dollar business and they were looking to double the size of their present operation to include a second championship golf course, more hotels; hundreds of villas and condos, a state-of-the-art hospital, a shopping centre and a greatly enlarged marina. The prime target of the new development were the retirees: the golden oldies from the rich, cold north seeking to buy their place in the sun. The buyers would want for nothing—as long as they could afford to pay for it. On paper, the investment was very attractive. The track record of the existing project was impressive and the projected profits for the new operation were irresistible. There lay the source of part of Ogilvie's unease. The deal on offer—their share in the venture and the likely return—was almost too good to be true. In his experience something too good to be true was usually exactly that. He was also uneasy about the other investors involved. Not the investors themselves: they were solid and there had been numerous discussions with them. It was the fact that they were all foreign. There were only three backers: his own bank, a Saudi prince with whom he'd had successful dealings in the past, and a sheikh from Dubai. Both Arabs were completely happy and had already passed over ten percent of their promised investment.

But why were no American investors involved? Ogilvie felt that for the deal on offer, the locals would have been queuing up to get in on the act. On that question he had been assured, that indeed, there was no shortage of willing American partners, but there was also a political dimension. The new governor of the state of Florida wanted to attract foreign capital. It was one of his election pledges. "Foreign money—local jobs." A reasonable explanation, but he still felt a twinge of unease. Perhaps, he argued with himself, this was nothing more than a reaction to his first dealings in The States when he had been young and inexperienced and had tried swimming with the sharks. He'd lost the bank five million pounds on a bogus property deal and had no desire to repeat his mistake. This time he was risking twenty million. Reluctantly he decided to swallow his misgivings for the present—along with another large whisky, whence he dropped off for a couple of hours sleep.

It was morning in Miami when they touched down. Ogilvie was a seasoned traveller and minimized the pain by travelling first class. He did, however, hate flying with the sun, when his body clock seriously demanded one thing and his eyes another. He always found the conflict worse when heading west. Also, he was not relishing another American experience.

He considered America a vulgar, cultural desert, the Americans loud and uncouth, their effusive, overt friendliness extending only as far as his wallet. He recalled a friend telling him that an American's smile was as warm as a whore's embrace and as sincere as an Arab's handshake. Whilst he was afraid England was losing some of its national identity, unlike America at least it had one—and hundreds of years of culture, history and tradition to fall back on. America he saw as a bunch of largely autonomous states populated by bewilderingly disparate inhabitants. They had no real history, and the only recognizable national identity they could grasp at was a pretty flag and a three octave anthem very difficult to sing—and their only cultural icons were hamburgers and Coca Cola. Of most concern was that the only glue that held the whole lot together was money. The American dream had bred a culture of greed. When their economy slipped down the tubes, as it surely would as their empire declined, and when the *nouveau riche* bully was on its way out, then two hundred odd million people would be left tearing at the carcass—and then at each other.

He didn't like America, and he had agreed to come to the country only on the condition that his passage through immigration be smoothed. His passport showed many stamps for Arab countries, and on a previous visit the anal immigration officer had decided that he must therefore have terrorist sympathies. Ogilvie was detained for an hour of interrogation, and was almost denied entry—not because of the stamps but for threatening to punch the obnoxious inquisitor. He was saved by the intervention of a superior officer who was clearly impressed—as Americans generally are—by his English title.

In this thoroughly negative frame of mind he stepped into the arrivals hall where, to his huge relief, he was met by a friendly uniform who led the party painlessly through immigration. Sadly, the friendly uniform was also the first to insist that they "have a nice day y'all."

Unfortunately for the travellers their final destination that day was on Florida's west coast, which necessitated another plane trip. The expected two-hour lay-over became five due to some mechanical fault with their plane. It was a tired group sadly lacking in good humour that eventually arrived at Tampa.

The representative assigned to meet the party had no trouble in identifying his charges. Amongst the throng of other passengers in their light, colourful summer clothes, the three Englishmen in dark business suits stood out like creatures from another planet. Of the three, only Ogilvie retained a dignified indifferent demeanour. With or without distinctive clothing Ogilvie was a man who stood out in any crowd. Even he, however, was somewhat nonplussed by their welcome. A large, grossly overweight figure in a garishly floral shirt suddenly materialized before him proffering a meaty hand.

'Al Scheiffer; welcome to Tampa, my Lord.' Ogilvie smiled to himself as the man actually gave a small bow. Ogilvie returned the wet, meaty, bone-crushing handshake and introduced his two colleagues.

Most of their dealings had been with Scheiffer. He was a Senior Vice President and the Financial Controller of Paradise Glades, and Ogilvie was initially pleased that a senior figure had been sent to receive him. After a few minutes with Scheiffer he wasn't so sure. For the next five minutes they were subjected to effusive Scheiffer verbiage, most of it relating to the wonders of America and the delights of Paradise Glades, until finally the carousel disgorged their luggage. It was by now late afternoon but the heat hit them like a wall as they exited the terminal.

'Bit warm for y'all, uh?' laughed Scheiffer as he wiped his brow. 'The goddam humidity. You get used to it man. Hope you've brought something lighter?' He indicated their suits. 'No sweat man, Lord, soon get y'all fixed up.' Ogilvie couldn't quite see himself in Scheiffer's floral garb, but he had come prepared.

A white stretch Mercedes pulled up at the kerb and they gratefully climbed into its air-conditioned interior. Paradise Glades, they knew, was about fifty miles south of Tampa and Ogilvie had resigned himself to a journey of an hour or so. An hour of Scheiffer would be more difficult to take. It was with huge relief, therefore, when the plush saloon, after only a short drive, pulled into the private airfield adjoining the main terminal and pulled up beside a gleaming helicopter. Red carpet treatment indeed—very welcome, but unnecessarily extravagant. Ogilvie was a man who counted the pennies.

Scheiffer continued his monologue as the helicopter headed south along the coast, his prattling increasing as they approached Paradise Glades. Ogilvie could not but be impressed as the helicopter circled the resort. Below him was a beautifully landscaped development which Ogilvie would have been happy to appreciate in silence, but Scheiffer was in his element. Every feature was identified: the hundreds of villas, the Paradise Marina full of colourful yachts; the golf course beautifully crafted round a small inlet. At the mouth of the inlet, set at the end of a short peninsula was a green that looked an impossibly small target. The tee was on the opposite shore and as they watched, a golfer dropped his shot in the water ten yards short.

'The dreaded 13th, man,' said Scheiffer. 'Th'all call it "Murphy's Grave". Arnold Palmer designed the course. For inauguration w'all had a charity celebrity Pro-Am tournament. Eddie Murphy, poor sucker, dropped three balls in the water—three balls man—three goddam balls, way overshot into the bunker with his fourth. Poor sucker ended up over the green into that rough by the shore. Poor bastard putted out for thirteen—thirteen on the 13th. Poor sucker's partner was Arnold Palmer. The lucky sucker got a hole in one! Can y'all believe that! Yeah man; all good fun man, an' w'all had a real good laugh. Yeah man, even got on CNN—great publicity man, yeh great publicity. Yeah, Murphy's Grave! Th'all love it and th'all hate it man—scares the goddam shit out of them. Don't play myself. Heard you're a real mean golfer Lord. Yuh aimin' to fit in a round or two?'

Ogilvie watched as the golfer landed his second ball on the green. 'I'd not intended to, but it does look a beautiful course—we'll see.'

'Yeah, the new one's gonna be even more beautiful man. See over there— they've started clearing ground, gonna be a real beauty man, a real beauty.'

The hundreds of villas, each with its own sparkling blue pool, had been moulded into the gently rolling landscape. It was impressive and Ogilvie complimented his host.

'Yuh ain't seen nuthin' yet man, my Lord. Phase Two will be even nicer. Th'all wanna a piece o' the place man; eighty per cent sold off plan. Goddam unbelievable. The suckers are queuein' up man, queuein' up A tell ya. Goddamit we can't build enough for them goddam Yankees. Them suckers, they got the money man, they got the money A'm tellin' yuh.' Ogilvie knew the figures and was impressed, very impressed indeed, but wished he could silence Scheiffer.

'Started expandin' the offices too, man,' continued Scheiffer, pointing ahead. Workers could be seen busy on the half completed roof of a large annex. 'All offices bein' refurbished man. W'all moved to the conference centre for a couple a' weeks—y'all be meetin' the rest o' the boys there tomorrow. Guess y'all must be tired.' Scheiffer tapped the pilot on the shoulder and pointed down. The pilot nodded and dropped the machine towards a large building on the shore north of Paradise Glades.

'Glades Regency, Lord: five star—reckon ya'll be comfortable here, Lord. Got yuh the penthouse suite, Lord: it's nice—real nice.'

The penthouse suite was indeed "real nice" with a spectacular view over the sea and the Paradise Marina. Ogilvie would have loved to be sitting on the balcony with a large scotch, relaxing and watching the sun go down over the gulf, but Scheiffer: his shadow—without being invited—had poured himself a beer and had settled himself comfortably in a large armchair.

'We reckoned seein' y'all would be mighty tired, we didn't arrange nuthin' for ya'll this evenin'.'

Ogilvie agreed that he was indeed a little fatigued and thanked him for his consideration.

'Eight o'clock OK for ya'll tomorrow mornin'? Great. A'll meet y'all in reception and A'll take y'all to meet the boys. Y'all need anythin' see ya'll give me a call,' he said handing over a business card. He drank his beer in one swallow then struggled out of his armchair.

'One little thing for yuh if you'd like, Lord. Thought yuh'd maybe like a massage. Nothin' like a massage after a long trip, eh man, Lord? Nothin' like a *special* massage from Susie to really loosen ya'll up.' He gave Ogilvie a meaningful wink of a podgy eye. This type of hospitality was not new to Ogilvie and he nodded to Scheiffer—he even managed a smile.

'Nine o'clock for Susie suit yuh then?' Ogilvie checked his watch. He nodded to Scheiffer as he led him down the hallway.

'Nine's fine.' With a sigh of relief he closed the door.

Fortunately the sun was still an inch from the horizon as he picked up his whisky and settled down to enjoy what promised to be a spectacular sunset. After the second whisky he was beginning to think that America wasn't such a bad place after all—except, of course, for Scheiffer.

By 9 o' clock Ogilvie felt fully restored. After a long hot shower and a fifteen-minute power sleep followed by a light meal from room service, he was eagerly anticipating the arrival of his "masseuse". He was relaxing with a fine malt on the balcony enjoying the cool evening breeze when there was a discreet knock on his door. Ogilvie glanced at his watch. 9.00 on the dot—he appreciated punctuality.

The girl he admitted didn't walk in: she floated. She was, by any standards, beautiful. Not a drop of makeup, tanned, long blonde hair, a slight, lithe athletic figure in loose fitting white pants and a very skimpy top which exposed her naked abdomen. There was a small diamond stud in her navel, but other than a gold watch, that was her only jewellery. Ogilvie was taken aback. All the previous "hospitality packages" he'd sampled had been beautiful, but all had been wrapped in sexy outfits and their profession, though not glaringly obvious, could be guessed at. The girl laid down her bag and turned to face him. She looked so natural and he found it an amazing turn-on. She accepted a drink: a glass of chilled white wine. He topped up his whisky and they moved out to the balcony where they leaned on the rail and watched the moonlight on the ocean. It was a beautiful night, silent but for the sound of waves on the beach and some distant music from the marina.

Conversation came easily with this girl Susie. She was obviously well educated and seemed genuinely interested in His Lordship. Perhaps she was simply obeying the first rule for a good hostess: let the man talk about himself. After a second wine she laid down her glass and floated back into the lounge.

'Massage time: and you're overdressed for it—not much fun in slacks and shirt.'

Ogilvie went to the bedroom, threw off his clothes and returned to the lounge with a towel round his waist. Susie was preparing her bottles of oils beside a massage table which had been set up in anticipation of Ogilvie's acceptance of Scheiffer's offer. Susie watched appreciatively as he walked over and joined her.

She ran her hands professionally over his muscular chest and arms. 'Mmm. Nice, very nice—you have excellent musculture, Mr Lord; you're in good shape. But you're still over—dressed.' She undid the towel from his waist and dropped it on the floor. 'Yes, very very nice, Mr Lord Stallion. On the table, face down.' She dimmed the lights and slipped a CD into the player and the room filled with soft soothing music. As the pleasant smoke from a joss stick completed the scene change, Ogilvie closed his eyes and patiently awaited Susie's ministrations.

He had never before experienced such an exquisite massage. Susie was a professional. Such was his state of pure physical relaxation that he was almost forgetting that the provider was a stunningly beautiful girl hired for his pleasure. A pat on his naked backside broke his reverie.

'OK Mr Lord—flip side.' Ogilvie turned over as ordered. He was fully aroused and he groaned as Susie stroked him gently. 'You *are* a big boy, Mr Lord: a very big boy—but not too big for Susie.' She rubbed some warm oil on her hands and gently anointed the length of him. Ogilvie had never before achieved such an intense arousal as she worked him gently with both hands. Their eyes met and she gave him a devilish smile as she lowered her head and took him in her mouth. Susie's timing was perfect and she finally, many minutes later, brought him to the most intense orgasm he had ever experienced.

'So how was it, Mr Lord?' she asked playfully as she gently stroked him.

'Wonderful. Bloody incredible—and just fine for starters.'

Susie looked at him in surprise. 'Starters? No, Mr Lord, that's it. I do massages, hand jobs and blow jobs—that's it. Didn't Scheiffer tell you?'

Ogilvie felt his anger rising. 'You teasing little bitch! No, he did not tell me.' He saw the slight fear in her eyes as he climbed off the table. Had she disguised her fear, calmly collected her stuff and left, perhaps she might have escaped—but for Ogilvie, fear in a woman was a deadly, irresistible turn-on.

He was already once again fully aroused. Susie made to move away, but he grabbed her and spun her round. She was a small girl and no match for his strength as he forced her face down over the back of a couch. While one hand held her wrist behind her back the other pulled down her pants and ripped off her brief thong. Ignoring her sobbing protests and weak struggling, he forced her legs apart.

'Let's see if this isn't too big for Susie.' He forced her face into the cushion and muffled her cries as he forced himself roughly into her. Having come once he was in no hurry to come again. He could now stay hard for hours and he fully intended to enjoy himself. Susie's breasts were magnificent and with his free right hand he fondled them cruelly.

'Now let's try some of that nice oil of yours, shall we?' He reached behind him and picked a bottle from the dresser, unscrewed the top with his teeth and poured half the contents between the tanned cheeks of her buttocks. Susie writhed frantically as he lubricated her anus and inserted a finger.

'Please,' she begged, 'please, not like this, please, not in the ass. I'll behave, I'll let you fuck me any way you like but not like this—please; please not in the ass.'

Ogilvie relaxed his grip on her wrist and pulled her upright. She didn't resist. She knew she was in an impossible situation. As a masseuse well known for her special services, she could hardly scream rape. If the cops got involved they'd most likely fuck her themselves—as had happened to a friend of hers. She knew karate and could hurt the bastard, but crushing a Lord's balls would finish her with Paradise Glades and they'd probably hound her out of town.

Susie turned to face him, rubbing her bruised left wrist. 'Well, you bastard,' she said wiping tears from her eyes, 'get on with it, but please don't hurt me.'

Ogilvie gave her a cruel smile. 'That's more like it—spread your legs, you little whore.'

Susie's ordeal lasted until midnight, when Ogilvie finally spent himself inside her, pushed her aside and fell asleep. He had left the worst until last, when, too exhausted to resist, she had been brutally sodomized. She could barely walk to the bathroom where she sobbed as she examined herself in the mirror. A bruise was already forming on her swollen cheek and an eye would be black by the morning. A split lip had stopped bleeding but the pain of that was minor by comparison to her other injuries. Her body was a mass of developing bruises and she flinched as she explored the teeth marks on her badly bruised breasts and inner thighs. Her body was a sea of pain inside and out and she groped in her bag for aspirins as she collected her clothes and dressed.

'You bastard. You fucking English Lord Bastard. I'll get you for this—I'll fucking get you.' She smiled painfully as she began plotting her revenge.

Chapter 9

Ogilvie, smartly but casually dressed in slacks and a polo shirt, strode into the restaurant shortly after 7.00. He was in high spirits, invigorated by the night's activities. Rubens and Cavendish had already finished breakfast and were chatting over a coffee.

'A very good morning, gentlemen—sleep well? No jet-lag?'

It was a rhetorical question and both men knew it. Ogilvie didn't give a damn if they'd had a good night, but Cavendish answered anyway on behalf of both men. 'Very well sir, and yourself?'

Ogilvie beamed at him which was answer enough.

He appraised the men over the top of the menu he was examining. 'Undertaker's convention I've not been invited to?'

Both men looked suitably puzzled. 'Sorry sir?' queried Cavendish.

'Look at the pair of you, for God's sake!' Both men were in dark suits, stiff white shirts and sober ties. 'You're in Florida, not the bloody City of London. The Americans think we're a bunch of stuffed shirts as it is—no need to dress the part. At least get rid of the jackets and ties. You were told to bring some light stuff with you.'

Once again Cavendish replied. 'Yes sir, but we thought that would be for social wear, not . . .'

Ogilvie cut him off brusquely. 'I don't care what you thought. Go and get into something more appropriate—don't make us a laughing stock. Eight o'clock in reception. See you then.' He turned his attention to the menu and ordered a full English breakfast.

It was 8.15 before Scheiffer waddled into the hotel: he was already sweating profusely. Fat people in general disgusted Ogilvie. He also disliked gays, small men, ugly people, coloured people, most foreigners and Jews. Rubens he regarded merely as a useful tool and tolerated him as such. Scheiffer he found particularly offensive.

'Thought A'd give ya'll a bit longer to finish your breakfasts,' said Scheiffer jovially. Ogilvie bit back a comment, nodded coolly and led his men out of the door to a waiting limousine. Scheiffer seemed oblivious to Ogilvie's displeasure and his own bad manners and recommenced his inane prattling. He informed them that they'd be meeting with "the boys" at 10.00. He was now going to drive them round the resort.

'Looks even finer on the ground, man. Y'all really gonna love this place, Lord—ain't called Paradise for nuthin'.'

The trip should have given opportunity to ask questions, but Cavendish made the innocent mistake of asking the very English question about the weather in this part of the world and was rewarded by a month-by-month climatology report—questions best avoided.

First stop was the golf club. Ogilvie liked his golf club to look, and feel, like a golf club. The Paradise Glades Club wasn't just plush: it was opulent, the foyer reminiscent of a five star hotel reception. The place was already busy—to escape the heat of the day an early-morning tee-off was essential.

They were introduced to the club's pro, a Scottish former professional golfer who'd been moderately successful on the circuit, and Ogilvie vaguely recognized his name. A very handsome, quietly spoken man in his early thirties, he told Ogilvie wryly that he'd been hired as much for his looks and accent as his golfing skills. He provided a bit of the exotic, and was in more demand from rich bored retiree's young wives for off the green activities. His presence was a relief to Ogilvie. He hoped he would have the opportunity to gain some insight into the workings of Paradise Glades from this civilized insider; perhaps during a round of golf. He was about to suggest a meeting when the Club Captain bullied his way into the company. He was an effusive ex-marine General who threw his arm round Ogilvie's shoulder and welcomed him to the "good old U.S. of A." The General then treated them to a grand tour of the facility, an unlit half-smoked cigar clamped in his mouth.

The club was undeniably impressive, but vulgar in its ostentation. The General's irritatingly loud parade-ground oratory continued over a coffee on the shaded outside patio overlooking the 18th green, where he relit his well chewed cigar, cussing the "goddam politicians" for banning smoking indoors. Ogilvie declined the offer of a Havana as he flipped through the resort's glossy magazine he'd found on the coffee table. Unimpressed by photos of the many grinning celebrities who seemed to grace the resort, there was one item in particular that did, however, catch his attention. He excused himself for a few minutes while he consulted his palm top notebook, rejoining the party as they were leaving to continue the tour of the resort.

Ogilvie had had more than enough. Pleading a slight headache he asked that they cut short the tour and head for the conference centre. He managed to dodge a bear-hug from the General who settled for a crushing handshake while promising Ogilvie a round of golf with himself and a couple of "good old boys". Ogilvie thought not.

Although they were some thirty minutes early, Scheiffer's "boys" were already in their seats in a small conference room drinking coffee, and their effusively warm welcome was returned with polite smiles and formal handshakes.

The owner and CEO of Paradise Glades was Luigi Capello, a small swarthy man with thinning dark hair. From their research they knew he was in his late sixties. He did, however, seem older and frailer than the man depicted on the company website. He explained that he'd been ill: a heart attack followed by triple by-pass surgery. Ogilvie expressed polite concern; sorry that he hadn't been informed. He was in fact furious with Cavendish as it was his job to know all that was to be known about their future partner.

Capello smiled. 'Not many folks did know. Kept real quiet. Sick CEO's not good for investor confidence.' Ogilvie was assured that Capello was now "as right as rain, he'd played nine holes yesterday." He apologised that, as he was still under strict doctor's orders to take things easy, he wouldn't be taking much part in any meetings.

'You're in safe hands with the boys here: they do most of the work anyway.' He indicated Scheiffer and two other men who had been introduced as Karl Muller, Paradise Glades' lawyer and Mike Sabelli, the company accountant. Faces were put to names—they'd been dealing with these men for some months.

'Just give me a shout when you need a signature,' called Capello jovially as he left the room.

Ogilvie looked round the table. 'Well, gentlemen, for the moment I think I'm also surplus to requirements. I'll leave you all to get down to the fine details. My headache's getting worse.'

Ogilvie didn't like the looks of either Sabelli or Muller. Sabelli had the greasy Italian look and would cast well in a Mafia movie. Muller was strictly Aryan: blond with cold blue eyes. Ogilvie reckoned the melting pot could do with a good stirring—he was dealing with full-blooded Krauts and Spiks.

Ogilvie had a headache, but not the kind you could fix with an asprin. Back in his hotel room he sat on the bed and re-examined the Paradise Glades magazine. In the pocket of his suit he found and examined the business card Scheiffer had given him the previous day. Although still only mid-morning he downed a large whisky, then picked up the phone and dialled a number. A cheerful girl answered and transferred him to the office of Mr Luigi Capello.

Two hours later, Ogilvie rejoined the meeting, assured everyone that his headache had cleared, took a seat and demanded a progress report. All seemed to be going smoothly, a few minor legal points to be clarified, but all were confident that documents would be available for final signatures by late the next morning. He was assured that his presence was not required. Ogilvie nodded and seemed satisfied. They were planning to break for lunch shortly and would he be joining them? Ogilvie declined and told his men that he wanted them back at the hotel, apologizing that something had come in from London requiring their attention.

He laid a large manila envelope on the table.

'I've been having some further thoughts, gentlemen.' Ogilvie tapped the envelope. 'I've drafted out some additional proposals for your consideration: everything's in here.' He slid the envelope across the table to Scheiffer. 'We'll meet again back here after lunch, say 2 o'clock?'

On their arrival back at the hotel, Ogilvie, Rubens and Cavendish gathered in Ogilvie's suite. Rubens and Cavendish were ready for their lunch but curious to learn about the new developments. "Something from London" could mean just about anything and they were puzzled about the contents of the large manila envelope Ogilvie had given to Scheiffer.

Cavendish asked if there was a problem in London.

Ogilvie shook his head. 'No problem, gentlemen—that was just a polite excuse to escape. I've told Capello that I'm prepared to increase our investment by ten million, to thirty million pounds but in return I want an investment from them of five million in my Scottish project.' If the two men were surprised by their boss's last minute moving of goal posts, they had sense enough not to show it. Rubens muttered that it might take a bit of time to prepare the new contracts.

'You really think they'll go for it, sir?' interrupted Cavendish.

Ogilvie turned to him with a rare smile. 'They'll go for it all right. You'll remember they originally wanted us in for twenty-five million? Not a bad deal for them: a great deal, in fact. They'll now get what they said they needed. They probably won't be too enthusiastic to part with five million, but they'll go for it. With a bit of persuasion perhaps, and probably some arm-twisting, but they'll see that the deal's in their best interest.'

'But they have no details of your Scottish project sir,' continued Cavendish.

Ogilvie give him the familiar cold look. He tapped his laptop. 'I downloaded everything. All they need's in that envelope. They'll be poring over the stuff as we speak—a nice aperitif for their lunch. Not that burgers and French fries deserve an aperitif. Talking about lunch, let's continue in the restaurant shall we?'

Ogilvie was quite correct. The Americans welcomed enthusiastically his offer of extra investment, but were singularly unenthusiastic about any reciprocal deal. Even after a very professional presentation of Ogilvie's Scottish project by Cavendish they remained intransigent. After two hours of fruitless negotiations, Ogilvie finally stood up, collected his papers, thanked the Americans for their time and told them that he regretted that he and his bank would no longer be interested in any investment in Paradise Glades. The Americans were momentarily stunned by this development. Scheiffer's fat, florid features dropped and paled as he stammered in disbelief. He looked frantically at his colleagues.

'Perhaps you'd like a few moments to discuss the matter between yourselves?' suggested Ogilvie as he and his men headed for the door. 'We'll just go and have a coffee while we await your decision.'

Seated in the cafeteria, Ogilvie grinned at his two puzzled employees.

'Bit of brinkmanship, sir?' asked Cavendish. 'I hope they come round, the board won't be too happy to lose this one.' He idly stirred his coffee. 'And as your financial adviser, I think . . .'

Ogilvie silenced him with a look. 'They'll be out crawling all over us in a few minutes.'

They'd barely finished their coffee when Scheiffer, beaming all over his face, joined them. He explained that they'd had to make some phone calls. Mr Capello, had been contacted again and had now agreed to sanction the deal. 'It's going to be just fine, no problems guys.' Scheiffer mopped his brow. Dark sweat patches under his arms stained his shirt almost to his ample waist. 'We need your bucks, and you need ours—good business for us, good business for y'all.'

Ogilvie nodded and forced a smile. 'I want everything tied up by lunchtime tomorrow—and I plan an early lunch.'

The subsequent afternoon meeting concluded on an up-beat note, the only negative being an insistence from their hosts that the Englishmen join them for a meal and entertainment that evening. There was no enthusiasm from the group, but good manners, unfortunately, demanded their acceptance.

The evening proved to be surprisingly pleasant. A plush limousine had collected the three men and delivered them to Club Florida, a refreshingly unpretentious, but clearly up-market restaurant. It had been agreed that there would be no reference to business during the evening. The food was excellent, and Ogilvie, seated comfortably far from Scheiffer, enjoyed the company of Luigi Capello who regaled him with entertaining stories and scathing insights into American politics. Ogilvie's colleagues, seated either side of Scheiffer, seemed less enamoured and politely declined an invitation to join the party when the suggestion was made to move on to a local casino club. Ogilvie was no gambler and had contempt for those addicted. For him, roulette, or any game involving pure chance held no attraction. He was, however, an excellent card player and enjoyed a profitable hour of poker, winning five hundred dollars. Ogilvie was appalled by the amounts of money staked by his fellow players. Ogilvie gambled in tens of dollars, others at the table in hundreds or even thousands. Scheiffer, he was pleased to observe, lost heavily. Capello seemed content to observe and Muller and Sabelli lost modest amounts.

From the poker table they adjourned to the bar where Ogilvie was impressed by the range of excellent malts available but was disgusted to watch as Scheiffer and Muller drowned the most expensive malt whisky in Diet Coke. Capello had a soft drink, then apologised that he was off home to bed.

Ogilvie was also about to leave but changed his mind when a beautiful girl appeared at his side. She took his arm and purred that her name was Lucy. While fully aware of his own sex appeal and attractiveness to women, he had no doubt that here was the latest special hospitality laid on by his hosts, a suspicion confirmed by a drunken nod and wink from Scheiffer. Scheiffer, Muller and Sabelli had also acquired stunningly attractive escorts. Ogilvie was horrified to watch as Scheiffer drunkenly pawed the petite Latino girl seated beside him. She was somehow managing to laugh and pretend that she was enjoying his company and the experience—Ogilvie hoped she would be getting very well paid.

Ogilvie's companion was a tall full-bodied statuesque blonde and he wondered if his hosts had researched his taste in women or were they—and he—simply lucky? Whilst a slim redhead or busty brunette wouldn't have been a disaster, he knew what he preferred.

Lucy had not been hired for her conversational abilities, but Ogilvie found himself fully enjoying her company. He felt relaxed and found the girl genuinely amusing. She was good fun and when they had finished yet another round of drinks and she suggested they all move through to "The Club", he was happy to follow on. From the presence of muscular bouncers by the discreet door towards the rear of the casino, Ogilvie guessed he was entering an exclusive inner sanctum. He was struck first by the smoky atmosphere— clearly the place excluded itself from the draconian American anti-smoking regulations. This was a meeting place for the rich and influential. Ogilvie didn't particularly like nightclubs, and as they entered, a crooner murdering a Sinatra song didn't encourage him. A compere in tight black pants and a white sequined jacket then proceeded to tell a series of very bad jokes which the audience found hilarious. Ogilvie eyed the beautiful girl by his side. She smiled at him and squeezed his thigh—bed would be much more fun.

The next act was a striptease. The girl on stage was extremely beautiful, and the act very erotic. It was close to midnight and Ogilvie was now ready to slip off with Lucy. He whispered in her ear it was time to go but she indicated the stage and said that maybe they should wait a few more minutes. The naked girl was still on stage, legs apart and arms akimbo. From the darkness behind appeared a muscular and rampant young man. Standing behind the girl he cupped a breast in each hand, then ran his right hand down between her legs. She spread her legs wider to accommodate. He then bent the girl forward and entered her from behind. On a couch which had rolled silently onto the stage, the couple proceeded to have sex in every imaginable position—a few new to the highly experienced Ogilvie. Lucy nibbled Ogilvie's ear and whispered throatily—'now we can go.'

Lucy proved to be much more amenable than Susie from the previous night. But unfortunately for Lucy, even though no coercion was required, brutal dominance and infliction of pain was integral to Ogilvie's full sexual satisfaction. Lucy fared better than Susie, however. Whether from the whisky consumed or tiredness affecting his libido, Ogilvie contented himself with a brief session and—mercifully for Lucy—rolled off and fell asleep.

Chapter 10

At 9 o'clock the following morning, the Americans and the English were facing each other over a table in Paradise Glades' conference centre. Cavendish and Rubens had been up until the small hours completing the contracts for signature. Everything had been scrutinized by Ogilvie over breakfast when he'd declared himself satisfied with their efforts.

The contract referring to the Americans' private investment with Ogilvie was now being studied by Muller and Sabelli, while Cavendish and Rubens read through the final draft of the bank's contract with Paradise Glades. To the relief of all concerned, by 11.30 both sides declared themselves satisfied that all was in order, and Ogilvie and Capello added their signatures. It had been agreed that on signature both parties would authorize immediate transfer of funds by telephone. Ogilvie made his call while Scheiffer made his on behalf of Paradise Glades.

The sense of relief in the American camp was almost palpable. With ill concealed delight Scheiffer pulled a bottle of champagne from an ice bucket and popped the cork, declaring that this was a great day and they must all have a drink in celebration. Ogilvie smiled and agreed that for him the outcome was most satisfactory, but asked that they call for more glasses; and perhaps another bottle as he was expecting guests.

Scheiffer, engaged in filling glasses, looked at him in puzzlement. 'More guests? Sure man; let's have us a real party.' Swallowing a glass of champagne he moved to the telephone. 'I'll git y'all food—y'all like that commie caviar stuff? Nuthin' but the best for y'all. We's all gonna celebrate! Lemmy tell ya'll, this is a real big day for us, ya'll don't know just how big.'

Ogilvie smiled at him. 'You're wrong, Mr Scheiffer, I know exactly how big you think it is, but first, let me introduce my guest of honour.' On cue the door to the room opened to admit an elderly, small, slim, distinguished-looking figure. There was a crash behind Ogilvie as Scheiffer dropped his champagne glass. The other Americans were frozen where they stood. Ogilvie, thoroughly enjoying the moment and determined to savour it fully, eyed them each coldly in turn.

'Gentlemen, I would like to introduce you to Mr Luigi Capello, CEO of Paradise Glades.' There was a moment of stunned silence before Muller exploded from the group, swung an easily dodged punch at Ogilvie and made a run for the door only to find it blocked by a uniformed policeman, pistol drawn. He stopped in his tracks and turned his hate-filled face to Ogilvie. Ogilvie smiled, picked up a glass of champagne and raised it to Muller in a toast.

He turned contemptuously from the furious figure of Muller and contemplated the other Americans. Sabelli was slumped in a chair trying to light a cigarette with shaking hands.

The Capello impersonator, ashen faced, was looking appealingly at Ogilvie. 'They paid me to do it sir, I'm just an actor. I needed the money; they made me do it.' He sank sobbing into a chair.

Scheiffer, his puffy face contorted in fury, glared at Ogilvie. 'How did you know, you English mother—fucker? How the fuck did you know? The whole goddam thing was fucking perfect.'

Ogilvie took a step towards him. 'Mr. Scheiffer, a few words of advice for you and your associates: if you choose to sup with the devil, be sure to use a long spoon—a fucking long spoon.' Ogilvie nodded to the armed policeman who holstered his gun and left the room, closing the door behind him.

'Gentlemen, I told you I was expecting a few more guests. Just who, and how many, will depend on yourselves. Would you mind, please, resuming your seats?' With some hesitation they complied. Ogilvie took a seat facing Scheiffer and a smiling Luigi Capello viewed the proceedings from the head of the table.

'About just how we blew your little scheme we will leave you gentlemen to agonize over. I suggest however, that for the moment you concentrate your minds on your immediate situation. But firstly, would you mind please giving me your names? I do like to know to whom I'm talking.' He played with a cigarette as Cavendish noted each name in turn.

'Gentlemen, I do congratulate you on a very clever—I'd even say almost brilliant fraud which all but succeeded. My Arab colleagues have yet to be advised that they've been fleeced so cleverly. My friend here, Mr Capello, assures me that should it be required, a trip to the Middle East for all of you could easily be arranged. Rendition, I believe—legal or illegal—is something of the norm in this country. My Arab friends would, I'm sure, be very keen to have words with you, and as your government knows, these people have perfected the art of interrogation. An alternative, of course, is to cast you into your own American legal system. Less physically painful perhaps, but Mr Capello assures me that your period of incarceration would be lengthy and very unpleasant.'

Ogilvie focused a cold-eyed glare on Scheiffer. 'Everyone hates traitors, Mr Scheiffer, least of all your boss here.' He indicated Capello who nodded grimly. 'In your role as Financial Controller you had access to everything. It's small wonder you managed to fool the best in the business—my people were assessing genuine Paradise Glades' documentation.' Ogilvie managed a cold smile for Cavendish and Rubens.

Ogilvie lit a cigarette as he turned to "Muller' and "Sabelli". 'And you pair,' he glanced at Cavendish's notes, 'Mr Nieuman and Mr Romano. I understand that the real Misters Sabelli and Muller would relish some time alone with you two—armed with baseball bats.'

The deflated bogus accountant and lawyer slumped dejectedly in their seats.

'I do offer you grudging praise for your professional abilities. You fooled everyone: myself included. And as for you, "Mr Capello", aka Mr Sabatini—a fine actor. You mastered the role perfectly—you fooled me completely.

'Now, I've offered you two choices, gentlemen, neither of which I imagine you will find particularly appealing. As the latter would involve unfavourable publicity for Paradise Glades, Mr Capello is in favour of losing you all in Dubai or Saudi Arabia.' Sabatini, the actor, recommenced his sobbing. Ogilvie shrugged. 'For me it's a matter of complete indifference, though I tend to agree with Mr Capello. Court cases can be long and tedious affairs and I have no desire to be forced back here to testify.'

Ogilvie once again turned his attention to Scheiffer. 'Mr Capello tells me that you have been Financial Controller for the company since its inception—that you've done an excellent job and have been extremely well rewarded.'

Scheiffer dropped his head and stared at his hands.

'He also tells me that you have the imagination of a slug—which brings me to yet another option for you to consider.

'None of this was your idea, Scheiffer. I want to know who was pulling your strings: who set this up; who's been paying the bills? Tell me all you know and I walk away—no Arabs, no Sheriff. You're all fools—you're as much victims as I'd have been—you've been suckered. I could almost feel sorry for you. Someone's currently sitting on several million dollars kindly donated by a pair of Arabs.

'How much have you been given? How much were you promised? Two million? Three million?—enough to pull you in and to provide you with a new life in anonymity somewhere? That's not how it works, gentlemen. You've got yourself involved with some very unpleasant people—you'd have been hung out to dry, first in line when the shit finally hit the fan.'

Scheiffer hid his face in his trembling hands.

'Well,' said Ogilvie, 'what's it to be? Will I invite some more guests? The Sheriff and the DA I'm sure would love to share some of your . . .' Ogilvie picked up the bottle. 'Californian champagne. Once again I'm going to give you gentlemen some time to come to your senses. The armed guard will be outside the locked door, so please doesn't be tempted to do anything stupid. Mr Cavendish, will you please relieve these gentlemen of their mobile phones and remove the office handsets. We'll be in Mr Capello's office. When you feel ready to talk, just knock on the door and the policeman will call us.'

Unbeknown to the imprisoned men, the room had been bugged prior to the morning's meeting and in Capello's office Ogilvie, Cavendish, Rubens and Capello sipped their coffees as they listened to a heated discussion.

That Scheiffer was the principal player and the others merely well paid pawns was confirmed. When it was apparent that things were getting a little rough: when Nieuman seemed to be beating up Scheiffer, Cavendish wanted to intervene but he was firmly overruled. A blubbering Scheiffer could be heard pleading to the others that he knew very little about who was behind the scheme. He'd been blackmailed—he was a paedophile—they had photos. They had put the screws on him—he hadn't wanted to do it. He'd had most of his information and instructions by e-mail. All the money he'd received to pay them and to cover expenses had come to him in cash delivered by courier. The bank, whose details he'd been given for deposits, had been set up in the name of Paradise Glades and was in the Caymans. He'd been given a coded message for the bank to expedite the five million transfer to Ogilvie.

It was as Ogilvie had expected. He felt no sympathy for Scheiffer. He needed a name. Alarm bells would soon be ringing. No money had, of course, been transferred from London, so questions would soon be asked.

Ogilvie toyed with Scheiffer's mobile. He scrolled through Scheiffer's list of contacts and the call register. He knew Scheiffer must have a phone contact for the puppeteer. It may prove to be as anonymous as a numbered bank account in the Caymans, but it would be a start. If his controller got very anxious, as he would when no transfer appeared and Scheiffer dropped off the radar, he would certainly try to contact him—he'd have to phone. Ogilvie spent some minutes dialling numbers, then slipped the phone into his pocket.

Meanwhile, over in the conference centre the puppets were getting desperate and more violent. They believed that their fate depended on Scheiffer providing some concrete information and he clearly had little to offer. It was time to intervene—a dead Scheiffer was of no use to Ogilvie. Ogilvie had a few private words with Capello, then led his men from the office.

The short journey back to the hotel was completed in silence. Cavendish and Rubens had screwed up. Ogilvie was intolerant of failure, of any weakness, and they were both resigned to the inevitable—they'd almost certainly be out of a job in a few minutes. Their apprehension and fear, however, were almost overridden by curiosity as to how Ogilvie had worked out that they were being scammed.

Ogilvie ushered them into the hotel bar and they sat in a quiet corner. He ordered his usual large malt but allowed the pair to choose their own drinks. They both ordered small beers.

Ogilvie looked over the table. 'A question, gentlemen.'

Both men sat to attention.

'Why is American beer like screwing in a canoe?'

The men looked at each other and then in puzzlement at Ogilvie.

'I asked: why is American beer like screwing in a canoe?'

Rubens, a man with zero sense of humour, studied his glass in the hope of finding an answer that would please his boss.

Cavendish, a closet comedian, realized that Ogilvie was actually telling a joke—a previously unheard of event.

'I don't know sir. Why is American beer like screwing in a canoe?' He gave his reply in what he hoped was in an appropriately light-hearted tone.

Ogilvie downed his whisky and laid his glass on the table.

'Because both are fucking close to water.'

The built up tension in Cavendish snapped as he laughed until his tears ran. He didn't give a damn any more, and as a collector of jokes he thought it was the funniest he'd heard in a long while. Rubens didn't get it and Cavendish had to explain.

'For God's sake, you two—relax a bit—join me in a decent drink. How about a Jack Daniels? It's a crap American so-called whisky, but sweet and smooth. For me it's a bit like cough mixture, but the Americans seem to like it—you might enjoy it.' Of course they agreed and Ogilvie made the order which included another large malt for himself.

Cavendish was familiar with, and did indeed enjoy Jack Daniels and, after his second, plucked up the courage to open conversation. 'Sir, I know we screwed up. We can only apologize for that. Had you not been here Ogilvies would be down for twenty million. But how did you twig? Those bastards hooked us and reeled us in like willing bloody fish—what tipped you off?'

Ogilvie sipped his third malt and smiled at him, stood up and walked through to the hotel reception and returned with a brochure for Paradise Glades in his hand.

He looked at the two men facing him. 'We all screwed up. They did a wonderfully professional job on us, even down to the poor pathetic look-alike for Capello. As you know, even though I had some doubts about the deal, I swallowed the same bait. Mind you, had we gone down for twenty million I'd be feeling somewhat less philosophical—my balls would be in a vice and you two would have been history.'

He slid the brochure across the table. Cavendish read it through once, puffed in frustration and started again. 'Nice brochure. Just manages to convince me again what a great deal we had on offer. Sorry sir, you've got me.'

Rubens took the brochure but had no more success.

Ogilvie pulled Scheiffer's business card from his wallet and passed it to Cavendish with the brochure. 'Try again. A clue: ignore the blurb and the pretty pictures—don't be fooled again by window dressing. Look at the small print—last page.'

'Bloody hell!' swore Cavendish after a further few minutes' scrutiny. 'The clever bastards.'

Cavendish passed the brochure and card to Rubens. He took longer, but finally for him too the penny dropped.

'Yes gentlemen, very, very simple. In a magazine at the golf club I spotted that the e-mail address and telephone numbers we'd been using were not those of Paradise Glades. Doesn't look much, but there's a world of difference between paradiseglades and paradise_glades. And there's only one digit difference in the phone number. It's this I noticed first. As you know, I never forget a telephone number. While you pair were in the meeting with your oppos, I called the real Capello. The rest you know or should have worked out. The reverse scam was a bit of fun—some punishment and some reward for the inconvenience. I've had a text message from London—the five million from our mystery benefactor has arrived.'

'But who's behind it, sir?' chipped in Rubens who was both enjoying, and feeling the benefit of his Jack Daniels. 'The Mafia? Organized crime? Not a good idea to tangle with those people sir.'

Ogilvie laughed. 'My first thoughts also, but Don Luigi Capello assures me I should look elsewhere.' He pulled Scheiffer's phone from his pocket and slid it over to Cavendish. 'Have a look, what do you think?' He ordered another round while Cavendish scrolled through the many numbers.

Ogilvie toyed with his whisky. 'He must have a contact number, but I doubt if any of these numbers will ring on our Mr Big's desk or mobile. He's too clever for that. And no number will be traceable.'

'Germany, Switzerland and France,' said Cavendish. 'There are nine, no, ten received calls from those countries, all different: they look like mobile numbers.'

Ogilvie nodded. 'I've already tried them: they're all dead. No German, Swiss or French number among his contacts.

'Mr Capello is very displeased about this whole business and is very eager to help. He'll be having a nice little chat with our Mr Scheiffer and if there's anything to learn I'm sure he'll convince Scheiffer that it's in his best interest to tell all. He's also got his computer people going through all of Scheiffer's files and papers. In the meantime, we can only wait. I have my suspicions who might be behind it. There are not many non-American big boys fishing in these waters—the locals don't appreciate the competition. But someone somewhere will be wondering why thirty million pounds has not arrived in their account.' He picked up Scheiffer's phone. 'Scheiffer should be getting a phone call very soon.' Ogilvie grinned. 'I've got five million of someone's money. Whoever that someone is, will perhaps, be very interested in talking to me.'

Ogilvie was in his room freshening up for dinner when his phone went: it was Capello with a progress report. Scheiffer had been "persuaded" to come up with a telephone number: a German mobile number. He said he'd been told to use it only in emergency. He'd only had cause to call the number once, when Ogilvie had demanded the five million investment and he'd called from a public landline. He claimed not to know the identity of his contact, only that he was foreign: perfect English but a foreign accent. There had been extensive communications by e-mail from a Swiss address.

Capello said he would e-mail everything he had. He thought they'd got all they were likely to get out of Scheiffer, but they'd squeeze him a bit more in the morning.

Ogilvie thanked Capello, switched on his laptop and was wondering how he could best make use of the new information when Scheiffer's phone rang. Ogilvie took a deep breath and pressed receive: it was Scheiffer's wife. She was wondering if he'd be home for dinner. In his best American accent Ogilvie told her that Scheiffer was very tied up at the moment and wouldn't be home for a long while. It was a half-truth. Scheiffer was certainly very tied up somewhere, but he wouldn't be the one to tell her that her husband wouldn't be coming home—ever.

Ogilvie opened his e-mails and downloaded the information from Capello. The whole scam was laid out step by step. Scheiffer had followed clearly laid out instructions. There had been very regular communications. All very interesting, but it didn't get him much nearer to Mr Big. Ogilvie had an e-mail address and a telephone number, not much use unless he could somehow use them to lure his man in—and he wasn't optimistic. He logged off and went down to dinner.

Cavendish and Rubens were both relieved that Ogilvie was still in an up-beat mood when he joined them at their table. There were no more jokes, but conversation flowed fairly freely, lubricated perhaps by a very enjoyable Californian wine. Ogilvie told them about the latest developments and, unusually, sought their advice and suggestions. Just as they were finishing their main course, Scheiffer's mobile phone rang yet again. Ogilvie quickly flipped it open. 'German number,' said Ogilvie as he pressed receive.

'Yeh, A'm Scheiffer, who's callin'? Gotta real bad line man, whadja say? Gotta real bad line—sorry man, can't hear yuh. Try hangin' up and callin' again. A'm in a bad area for reception. If ya'll can hear me, gimme an hour and call again—Sorry man—can't hear nuthin.'

Ogilvie switched off and slowly laid down the phone.

'Fucking Scheiffer: he's still trying to screw us. It was our man. I was trying to play for time. He kept hissing "codeword", said nothing else. I've switched off the phone. It might give us a bit more breathing space.' On his own phone Ogilvie quickly called Capello and told him what happened. He listened for a few moments, then finished the call. Cavendish and Rubens were looking questioningly at him. 'He said he'd have another word with Scheiffer and get back to us as soon as he can.'

What Don Luigi Capello had actually said was—"The stupid mother-fucker; guess we'll be seeing how he likes the fucking blow-torch."

It took less than fifteen minutes for Capello to call back. The code word was "hardball". Ogilvie switched on Scheiffer's phone and the three men stared at it, willing it to ring again. Ogilvie's coffee had gone cold. He ordered another with a brandy and cursed the no smoking regulations—he needed a cigarette. He pulled a pack from his pocket and was reaching for the phone to take outside with him when it rang.

'Sorry sir—that you called earlier? Sorry yeh, yeh, hardball, hardball—sorry sir, bad reception earlier—couldn't hear nuthin'. Yeh, it's all just fine, no problems, was gonna e-mail you in the mornin'. Whatja mean money's not come through? Heard him make the transfer. A was in the room. A'll see him, yeh, we're all out kinda celebratin'. Sure A'll tell him, must be some mix-up with the bank—he'll sort it out. Yeah man, OK, right, right.' Ogilvie laid the phone down and picked up his cigarettes.

'You think you fooled him?' asked Cavendish.

Ogilvie slowly shook his head. 'A man of very few words—but enough. I'd recognize that bastard's voice anywhere.' He was pulling a cigarette from the pack as he headed for the door.

There was nothing further to keep them in Florida, and Cavendish managed to get them booked back to London the following day. Capello arrived as they were finishing breakfast. He and Ogilvie had a brief meeting before Capello saw them all off to the airport in a limousine. He insisted that he take care of the hotel bill, and Ogilvie didn't argue. As they were leaving, Cavendish asked Capello what would happen to Scheiffer and his accomplices. Ogilvie barked that it was not their concern. The old Ogilvie was back—end of conversation.

That morning as he was relieving himself, Ogilvie had felt a slight tickling. As the day wore on, the urethral discomfort steadily increased. By the time he landed in London, he felt he was passing barbed wire; he had a copious yellow, bloody discharge and painful sores were erupting on the head of his penis—Susie had got her revenge.

It had been simple enough to prepare. A friend of Susie's had contracted a particularly unpleasant and, to date, intractable venereal infection. Susie had guessed that special hospitality would be arranged for Ogilvie for the following night. A quick swap of girls was arranged and the irresistible "Lucy" was in place. "Lucy" needed the money and quite enjoyed it "a bit rough". A very happy arrangement—except of course for the Honourable Richard Ogilvie.

Chapter 11

Myrtle, the old hill pony, stood quietly as Calum Munro heaved the heavy deer saddle onto her back and began to fasten up the girths. This was her fifteenth season and she was well used to the procedure. Calum clapped her neck, rubbed her muzzle affectionately and slipped her a few polo mints which she loved. She'd been bought when he was ten years old. She had been a frisky little thing when he'd adopted her and learned to ride, and he still loved the old girl. Saddling up Myrtle wasn't really Calum's job: the pony man should do it, but if not done correctly, the girth straps would rub and Myrtle would end up with painful girth galls. The pony man looked on smiling: he was Lachie Donaldson, the ghillie. Lachie had done the job every year since he was sixteen and knew perfectly well how to put the saddle on, but he was happy to humour Calum.

It was now a perfect morning on the Dunmorey Estate. The heavy rain which had looked set to ruin the day had stopped, and there was now a clear blue sky with high scattered clouds blown by a fresh north wind.

'Great day fir stalkin' now,' said Lachie. 'Thank God the rain's stopped, we got soaked to the arse yesterday.' He looked at his watch. 'We're right late in gettin' started. We'll need tae be findin' somethin' close tae home today—nae time tae get oot the heid o' the glen. You stalker again today then?'

Calum nodded. 'Aye, Dad's no' feelin' too good.' Calum's title was Assistant Stalker. His father Duncan, wee Dunkie, was Head Stalker to the Dunmorey Estate.

Calum stroked Myrtle's muzzle. 'I hope Lordie behaves himself today.' He was referring to the Honourable Richard Ogilvie who wasn't really a lord but a duke. He liked to be addressed as "Your Lordship" nonetheless. His Lordship had been none too happy the day before, when his antics on the hill had cost them a good stag. The stalk had involved a long crawl through a very wet bog in the rain—or should have involved a long crawl. Calum crawled, but Lordie, not relishing a swim through the mud decided that walking bent over was good enough. The stag, of course spotted him and was off. Calum was accused and abused. Lachie also somehow drew his own share of the blame for the failed stalk and both lads were treated to one of His Lordship's famous tantrums.

'A dinna ken why we put up with it.'

'Aye Lachie, the man's an arsehole,' muttered Calum as he tightened a girth.

'Someone should tell him the age of feudalism's long gone. The bastard treats you guys like a bunch of bloody serfs—he thinks you're a load of peasants for him to kick round.' Both men turned: it was Colin Buchanan, a vet student and an old friend of the Munro family. Colin always tried to manage a few days on the hill before the start of university in Edinburgh.

'Fuck him,' said Calum as he fed Myrtle another Polo.

'At attention, here he comes,' hissed Lachie.

His Lordship emerged from the Lodge and was walking purposefully towards them. 'Morning lads, lovely day now, eh?'

'Fuck him,' said Calum under his breath as His Lordship walked past and entered the gunroom.

For Ogilvie, the previous day hadn't been a complete disaster. Cold and wet, heading down the glen at the end of the day and in sight of the

Lodge and home, they'd spied a magnificent stag. The light had been poor, but through their telescopes they had made out that the beast was a huge royal, his twelve points beautifully balanced: a perfect trophy head and one of the biggest stags Calum had ever seen. His Lordship's black mood had evaporated. He'd been beside himself with excitement, and was determined that he'd get the stag the following day.

Dunkie appeared in the gunroom doorway and waved Calum over. Both men disappeared inside where Ogilvie waited impatiently.

'Ye realize, m'Lord, that the beast is unlikely tae be onywhere near where ye last saw him.' said Dunkie. 'The rain's stopped, and the wind's changed since yesterday, so he'll likely be headed higher up, and with that north wind he could hae moved ower the top or maybe up intae Corrie Bhraken.'

'Or almost anywhere,' added Calum.

His Lordship turned and looked sharply at him. 'This is my last day. I've not shot, or even had a decent chance at a good stag all week.' He cast an accusatory look at Calum. 'That head's going with me to London tomorrow!'

Dunkie cleared his throat. 'Well, m'Lord, if he's there we'll get him. If ye gae up the path tae the corner, tae the first spy point, ye'll get a look up intae the corrie. If he's there ye'll never get tae him, forget it, he'll see ye a mile off. Normally fir a beast in there, ye'd loop roond an' come intae the top o' the corrie, but no' wi' this wind. He could be on the flats below the corrie, but if he's no' ye'll likely find other beasts there. Tae spy in there ye'd need tae gae up the burn frae the spy point. Calum kens fine, we've taken a few beasts oot o' there.'

Calum pocketed some bullets, picked up the rifle, slid it into its carrying pouch and slipped it onto his shoulder. 'We'll get him if he's there, m'Lord.'

'Hopefully you'll do better than yesterday,' said His Lordship as he headed out the door. Calum waved two fingers at his back and followed.

The first spy point that Duncan had referred to was no more than half a mile or so from the Lodge, and the stalking party generally stopped there and spied the glen ahead. Calum and His Lordship were spying up into Corrie Bhracken, and Colin sat beside them and spied up the glen as Lachie arrived leading the pony, sat on the bank and busied himself with his mobile phone. Colin made out a small group of stags on the slopes of Ben Carrick, too far away to be of interest. Mindful that the day was short, he began to search closer to home.

On the hillside almost opposite their position was a small group of deer feeding high up on the slope. A movement above them caught his eye. Emerging from a dip in the ground was their stag. There was no mistaking him: there couldn't be two stags like that on Dunmorey. He quietly poked Calum with his stick and pointed. Calum turned and aimed his glass where directed. A huge grin broke his face. The stag was heading up the slope, but with this wind he'd go over the top into Strathgellie, the neighbouring estate.

'The bastard'll no' be taken that heid tae London tomorrow, A'm thinking,' whispered Calum to Colin.

Calum called to the Duke. 'Excuse me, m'Lord, but maybe ye should have a wee spy this side—he's up there.'

A stalk has to be well planned: wind direction assessed, the ground studied and the best route decided on, how to get within shooting distance: no more than a hundred and fifty yards from the stag without being seen either by the stag—or by any other deer. It's a skill, it's an art, and Calum was very good at it. In the unlikely event that the stag decided to stay where it was, or at least stayed on Dunmorey, Calum was considering his options as Colin continued his spying of the far side.

Calum heard him curse. 'On the skyline—right above the beast.' They could be seen with the naked eye. Two figures were crossing the skyline. Calum smiled at Colin—it was a stalking party from the neighbouring estate.

The march, the dividing line between the properties, once a fence, but now a line of rusting poles, ran about fifty yards below the ridge. Still below the march was their stag, and he was heading up towards it and the other stalking party. Three telescopes watched the two men drop below the skyline and head north below the ridge towards the rim of Corrie Mhor which opened onto the Strathgellie side of the crest. They watched the party freeze, then drop to the ground. They'd seen the stag, or more likely his antlers as they broke their skyline. The stag was now over the march and could be no more than a hundred yards from the party, and was still heading slowly towards them.

It was almost voyeurism as they watched the stalker slowly remove the rifle from its cover, slip bullets into the magazine and carefully pass the gun to his companion lying beside him. The rifle went to his shoulder; he aimed, and for long minutes the stag continued up the hill towards the waiting gun.

Suddenly, from behind Calum and Colin came a terrible wail of anguish. His Lordship had leapt onto a large boulder above the path and was shouting at the top of his voice whilst waving his arms and jumping up and down. Calum and Colin watched his antics in astonishment. Much of His Lordship's tantrum was unintelligible, but the sentiments being expressed were clear enough. Then he screamed at Calum. 'Get the rifle out, fire it—make some fucking noise—scare that fucki . . . !'

Lordie's shout was cut off in mid-curse, his knees buckled and he fell backwards off the boulder into the heather as a distant gunshot echoed weakly in the glen.

'Fuck me, he's had a heart attack,' shouted Colin as he jumped up and ran to His Lordship who was lying on his back with his arms spread. His mouth was open, still shouting its final curse and his glazed blue eyes gazed sightlessly at the sky.

Colin knelt beside the body searching for a pulse. 'Shit, he's dead!' He shook his head. 'Stone fucking dead.' Then he stared in horror at the spreading patch of red on His Lordship's chest and looked up at the shocked faces of Lachie and Calum.

'That phone of yours, Lachie: are you getting a signal here?'

'Aye, just aboot—no' very strong mind. Who are ye wantin' tae call?'

Colin looked back at the bloody corpse. 'I think 999 would be a good start, don't you?'

Chapter 12

Any incident involving firearms automatically becomes the business of CID—a dead duke becomes a priority. Jock Anderson and DI McLean were in a car and heading for Dunmorey within minutes of the report coming in.

As they drove, Jock told DI McLean about his meeting at the golf club with Richard Ogilvie, the Eighth Duke of Dunmorey, and the chance encounter at Dougie Sanderson's funeral with the Duke's brother Robbie and Jock's old school friend, Dunkie Munro. It was the first time Jock had been through the gates of the estate and he was impressed. The tree-lined drive took them through acres of fine farmland; fields were lined with mature oak, beech and huge ash: these trees he could identify, many other species he couldn't—some previous duke clearly had had a taste for exotics. Many of the fields held grazing cattle and sheep, and a fine herd of Highland cattle caught Jock's interest. The well-kept tar road led them up through old mixed woodland then alongside a long lochan alive with birds and Jock had to resist the temptation to stop.

At the head of the lochan stood Dunmorey Lodge, the seat of the Dukedom of Dunmorey. It was a magnificent two-storey ivy-clad house with arched mullioned windows. Surrounded on three sides by mature trees and with the backdrop of the mountains, the effect was breathtaking.

Bob McLean was shaking his head. 'Bloody hell sir. What a place. How the other half live, eh?'

Someone they took to be an estate worker directed them to the back of the Lodge, where sat another fine old two-storey building. Most of the ground floor appeared to be old stables and a coach house, and as they pulled up, a smiling Dunkie Munro emerged from a doorway and strolled over.

'Glad ye've cam yersel', Jock. We've got a wee bit o' an incident here.' Dunkie explained that he'd just got back from the site of the Duke's death, and as instructed, nothing had been touched. The lads were still waiting up the glen with the body.

'A'll tak the pair o' ye up there on the quad. Just room fir one on the back though. DI McLean'll no' mind sittin' on the trailer—it's no' very far.' As they headed up the track, Jock could see that indeed they didn't have far to go. In the distance, no more than half a mile away, he could see a horse grazing at the side of the path. Beside it, three figures were sitting. As they got nearer, Jock could see that they were contentedly eating their lunch.

Colin Buchanan, the most articulate of the three, gave his account, with the occasional—mostly irrelevant and irreverent interjections—from his companions. As he talked, Jock and DI McLean took in the scene: the source of the shot high on the opposite slope; the body on the ground.

Jock shook his head sadly. 'Certainly looks like a tragic accident.'

'There's nothing bloody tragic aboot it,' retorted Calum, swallowing the last of his tea. 'Good bloody riddance. Almost restores ma faith in God. A've bin prayin' fir one o' ye're "tragic accidents" fir years.' Jock wondered if he'd ever hear a good word spoken about the late Duke.

'What now Jock?' Dunkie had seen a flashing blue light by the distant Lodge.

Jock turned and looked down the glen. 'Doctor Paterson will want to take a look, but he shouldn't be too long.' Jock stepped up on the boulder Ogilvie had been standing on when he was shot. 'He was right unlucky right enough,' he muttered. Jock knew that in order to discourage hill walkers during the stalking season a lot was made of the risk of getting shot. The chances of that were infinitesimal—it was all a ploy to keep walkers off the hills and the deer undisturbed. But it seemed that the virtually impossible had happened.

Jock turned and looked down at Colin. 'Is this how he was standing when the bullet hit him?'

Colin smiled and shook his head. 'If you jump down sir, I'll try and show you.' Colin took his place on the boulder and re-enacted Lordie's last moments, much to the amusement of Lachie and Calum. Both agreed Colin's demonstration was spot on. Calum thought that Lordie had maybe been waving his arms more, but all agreed that His Lordship was definitely facing the opposite hill—and the other shooting party when he was hit.

Jock scratched his head. The significance of his Lordship's position seemed of little relevance, but Jock liked to have all the facts. 'Aye, right unlucky, right unlucky,' repeated Jock.

Dunkie looked down the glen and then back at the body in the heather. 'We'll no' be gettin' yon ambulance up here. We'll need tae be gettin' the body doon, A suppose.'

Calum grinned. 'Well, Myrtle old girl, ye're goin' tae enjoy this. A'm certainly goin' tae enjoy tyin' the bastard on—or maybe we could just pull him like we drag a stag off the hill eh.' Jock pretended to ignore the continued irreverence, but noticed that the others were smiling broadly at the joke. DI McLean looked bemused.

'Yes,' confirmed Jock, 'the horse will have to carry him, but not until the doctor has seen it all as it is now. It shouldn't be long before he's here, so hold off touching the body for a while yet. And we'll be needing statements from everyone. There will be a constable back at the Lodge, but would you mind restraining yourselves when he takes your statements. I gather there's not much love lost between yourselves and your late employer. Bottle it. I just want the facts—and only the facts on paper. Please keep any crap to yourselves.'

Jock turned to DI McLean. 'We'd best be getting up to Strathgellie, they'll know nothing about this. Someone's in for a bit of a shock.'

Strathgellie Lodge proved to be a much smaller version of Dunmorey. The estate had fallen out of noble hands long ago, and was currently owned by a German industrialist. The old Lodge, had suffered cruelly as a result, and the lovely sandstone building now demonstrated the execrable taste of the new owner: an obscene glass and steel structure had been affixed to one end of the house, and a red brick extension to the other. To add insult to injury, a large German flag fluttered from a pole on a turret.

There was a group of men at the rear of the building where they had just got out of a Land Rover. Two men, whom Jock guessed to be ghillies, headed into an old stable block. A slim, middle-aged man in plus-fours and deerstalker approached the two detectives and some steps behind him was a short, strutting figure dressed more for the Tyrol than the Scottish Highlands. Uninvited visitors were never welcome on the estate, the more so during the stalking season, and it had been with some difficulty that Jock had managed to talk his way through the locked gates at the entrance. The men's demeanour was not friendly, but a flash of Jock's warrant card forestalled any unpleasantness.

'I'll be needing to have a word with you gentlemen, if I may? Is there somewhere we can talk?' As they were led into Strathgellie Lodge the Tyrolean had already begun to complain about the intrusion in a grating, arrogant German accent which was as nails down Jock Anderson's blackboard. Jock thought that the little man, in his wire-rimmed glasses and small moustache bore an uncanny resemblance to Heinrich Himmler.

Seated in the lounge, both the policemen were offered a whisky which they declined. A large glass was poured for the Tyrolean and introductions were made. Jock learned he was talking to Mr John MacDougal, the Head Stalker to the estate, and one Klaus Steiner: the owner. Mr Steiner provided them with the unsolicited information that he was a very important leading figure in German industry who strongly resented this current inconvenience. When Jock explained the nature of his visit, the German's bluster was replaced by grovelling sycophancy, encouraged perhaps by DI McLean's toying with a pair of handcuffs—the man was clearly terrified of being arrested. Jock told him it was unlikely that he would be charged with murder. Manslaughter was a possibility, and this carried a lesser sentence of no more than five years or so. John MacDougal got into the act by promising to take care of the estate in Herr Steiner's absence and assured him that Scottish jails were quite nice.

Announcing that he was leaving DI McLean to guard Herr Steiner, and instructing that the handcuffs be used if required, Jock left the room with John MacDougal.

'Little Kraut shit,' muttered MacDougal as they sat at the large table in the kitchen. 'What a fuckin' day. He missed the best stag A've ever seen on them hills. He could hae clubbed the beast wi' the rifle we were so fuckin' close—an' shoots a fuckin' duke instead.' He burst into an infectious uncontrolled laughter, Jock couldn't restrain himself and joined in.

'What'll happen now then?' Asked MacDougal after the two men had recovered.

Jock shrugged. 'Formal inquest, verdict of accidental death most likely.'

'A'll keep the little shit wound up fir a while yet, though,' grinned MacDougal.

'Aye, and you can have some more fun later if you like. Couple of my lads will be up shortly for formal statements. But I need you to tell me what happened up there.'

John MacDougal got up and took a bottle of whisky from a cupboard. He waved the bottle at Jock who nodded. MacDougal filled two glasses, handed one to Jock and resumed his seat at the table.

'We were needin' tae hae a look intae Corrie Mhor. We'd spied some beasts in there an' wanted tae get ontae them so we had tae cam roond frae the Dunmorey side—well above the march, mind ye. We were goin' along just below the ridge an' A looked roond tae check that the wee man wis still wi' me. He's no' very fit an' keeps fallin' ahent. Right lucky that A did. A saw the tips o' a beast's horns doon beneath us an' we baith got doon quick. A managed tae get the rifle tae the wee man. We'd got bugger all cover: bald as ma arse up there an' A wis sure the beast wid hae tae see us, but he just kept comin'. There wisnae much wind, hardly onythin', just a wee bit o' a breeze frae the north, so the beast widnae be gettin' oor wind.

'A've never seen a beast like him for years, Mr Anderson. Huge bugger— an' the horns on him: a beautiful big royal. The wee man wis aboot wettin' hissel' he wis so excited—he's ey bin ontae me aboot wantin' a big royal. The beast wis in nae hurry, just wanderin' up, comin' heid on. He wis right on us. No' a bad shot tae tak an' he should hae managed it fine. He's a right wee shite o' a man but he's a bloody gid shot. The beast spooked a wee bit, pit his heid up an' turned just as he fired. Maybe it heard somethin', or caught a sniff o' us or they lads in Dunmorey. A've nae idea—he missed him onyway. Nae chance fir another shot, he wis off like a bat oot o' hell. The wee man wisnae right pleased A can tell ye. He had tears in his een, but maybe that wis just frae the wind.'

Jock sat forward in his chair. 'Mr MacDougal, at any time did you see the other party in Dunmorey?'

'No, A wisnae lookin'.'

'And the wee man: Herr Steiner?'

'Him? Nah, he's as blind as a bat at the best o' times.'

'If you had looked, could you have seen them?'

'Withoot ma glass, A doot it.'

Herr Steiner was still blubbering when Jock returned to the lounge, but DI McLean had managed to extract his account of events.

'Shooting people's a very serious offence in this country, Herr Steiner,' said Jock grimly. 'But if this is the first person you've killed in Scotland, the courts may take a more lenient view.' He nodded to DI McLean that they were off and left the room—enough was enough.

When they got back to the station, DS Clark was waiting. 'Just had a call from London sir: about the dead Duke. News of dead nobility travels right fast, eh?'

'Seems so, but how in the hell did they find out?'

DS MacKay looked up from his desk. 'I think I know, sir. That Owen Evans was in here this morning visiting one of his clients: that Johnny Lennox.'

'Drunk last night, beat up his girlfriend again?'

'Aye, sir.'

Jock shook his head. 'Bloody Evans will get him off with a wee wrist-slapping again.'

'Anyway sir,' continued MacKay. 'Evans saw that there was a bit of a flap on and asked what was up. PC MacAlister, that new young probationer was on the desk and the silly bugger told him about the dead Duke. I heard him from the back office. I hauled him in and gave him a right bollocking sir—he'll no' be opening his big mouth again in a hurry.'

Jock frowned. 'Can't be helped. Evans just loves to stir shit. So what was London on about?'

'It was a real snotty bastard on the phone sir—why do these people have to be so deliberately unpleasant?'

Jock looked at him. 'They live in a different world down there man: a cruel, back-stabbing jungle of a place. They all hate each other—and everyone else. You ever been to London?'

DS Clark shook his head.

'You've not missed bugger all, but you'd need to go there to even begin to understand.'

'Is that it?' said DS Clark. 'Anyway, they're sending two men and their own medical examiner up Monday morning, first flight. They'll be landing at 9.00. We've to collect them and arrange suitable accommodation. I was instructed to advise our doctor that the body must not be interfered with. Dr Paterson wasn't well pleased. Said it's his body in his morgue and they can go and stuff themselves.'

Jock grinned. 'Sounds like Alex. Who are "they" anyway?'

'Home Office.'

Jock groaned. 'So we'll be having big boots all over us on Monday then.'

'Aye,' said DI McLean. 'The Duke of Dunmorey is—was establishment. These bastards look after their own.'

Jock sighed. 'Ah well then; we'll not be rolling out the red carpet, but let's at least be polite, eh?'

Chapter 13

Early Monday morning, Jock paid a visit to Dr Paterson at the morgue. It was almost 7.30, but the doctor was already working on a post mortem. He always liked to make an early start—Dr Paterson "liked to get at them when they're still warm". Jock declined the invitation to join him and had a coffee while he waited.

Dr Paterson came into his office looking grim-faced. 'Another drug overdose, Jock. There's some right nasty stuff around just now. A young lad: just a teenager. That's the third one in as many months.'

'Aye Doc, we're on to it, but we're not making much headway. Nobody will talk to us. We've lifted a load of small dealers but the stuff's still coming in. It's like holding back the tide.'

'Anyway Jock, what brings you here so early on a Monday morning? Don't tell me—the Duke?'

Jock nodded. 'Aye Alex, the Duke.'

Dr Paterson looked at him over the top of his reading glasses. 'Something bothering you about the case?'

Jock shook his head. 'No. Just that I've got statements about what happened, I've been out to Dunmorey but I've not seen a report on the body. I'd just like to pull everything together, that's all. I assume you got the order to leave the body undisturbed?'

Dr Paterson smiled and gave Jock a wink. 'Aye A did, but unfortunately a wee bit too late, you understand. You want to have a look?' Jock nodded, and Dr Paterson made a call to the morgue to get Ogilvie out of his cold drawer. Jock followed the doctor into the morgue where there were several tables occupied. An assistant was busy suturing the post mortem wound on the body of a young man on the central table. Dr Paterson indicated the body. 'Bloody drugs—just a young kid.'

On a trolley at the far end of the room was a figure covered by a sheet which the doctor pulled back to reveal the naked body of Richard Ogilvie. In the centre of the dead man's chest was a small, somewhat irregular hole about an inch to the left of his right nipple. The doctor called over two assistants who turned the body over to show the exit wound: a larger, messier hole.

Jock hated the morgue, the omnipresent stink of death with the background smell of chemicals always made him feel slightly nauseous. He felt an uncomfortable movement in his stomach, said he'd seen enough and headed for the exit.

Back in his office the doctor sat at his desk and took a folder from a drawer. 'As you saw, I haven't opened him up, but here's what I've got for you.' He pulled some photographs from the folder and passed them to Jock, who flipped through the photos, picked up the folder and read through the doctor's report: lots of medical jargon describing what he'd seen on the body and was obvious on the photographs.

'Any idea about the bullet?'

'Difficult. It's not a very nice clean entry wound. Looks like the bullet hit his sunglasses in his top pocket which made things a wee bit untidy.' Jock held up photos of Ogilvie's left and right buttocks which showed several areas of bruising and looked to the doctor for an explanation.

'Injection sites. The poor bastard had had quite a few painful injections which were, I'd say, to treat this.' Dr Paterson showed Jock a blown-up photo.

'Is that the end of his dick?'

The doctor smiled, nodded and pointed out some healing sores. 'The Duke's been a naughty boy; been dipping it somewhere a bit dirty. He was being treated for a nasty dose of the clap.'

The three suits from London: a Commander Clive Millington, a medical examiner and a DCI Bernard Pendleton, had been collected from the airport. The Commander and the DCI were seated in Jock's office by 9.45—the medical examiner had been delivered straight to the morgue.

Millington, a pompous little middle aged man very rudely dispensed with any pleasantries, curtly dismissed the offer of coffee, and immediately demanded a report on the incident. He showed some surprise when a neatly prepared and well presented document was handed over.

'I think you'll find this preliminary report to be comprehensive, gentlemen. I'll leave you to digest it at your leisure,' said Jock rising from his chair. 'I have some much more important business to attend to.' Nonplussed, Millington changed his tone, and politely requested that Jock be good enough to brief them on the contents of the report. Jock resumed his seat and ordered coffee, once more offering his guests the same as a deliberate afterthought. To their obvious horror he proceeded to fill, and then light his pipe. The room quickly filled with more smoke than usual.

Millington coughed theatrically and glared at Jock through the pall of smoke. 'The Scottish Government,'—he spat the words with a contemptuous smirk on his face—'is, I understand, about to ban smoking in public places: which, I believe, will include the workplace.'

Jock smiled, waved his pipe and shrugged. 'Aye, the buggers are right concerned about our health. Bloody nanny state—it'll be the whisky next.'

'We, ourselves and our medical examiner, will of course require to visit the scene of the incident,' said Millington an hour or so later.

Jock laid down his pipe. 'Certainly, gentlemen—a vehicle and a driver are at your disposal.' He had given the driving job to DC Ross with instructions to keep his lugs flapping. When they'd left, Jock called Dunkie Munro and told him to prepare for their arrival, adding: 'Dunkie, that fine wee quad bike of yours: keep it out of sight, will you—let the bastards walk. Pissing with rain, is it?—even better.'

Jamie Ross arrived back in the early afternoon and reported to Jock. He'd returned three wet and very disgruntled suits to their hotel, and they'd informed Jamie that they would contact DS Anderson later in the afternoon.

'Something to look forward to,' muttered Jock.

Jamie reported that little had been said in the car on the way to Dunmorey, the men seemed content to pass the time dissecting Jock's report. It had been raining steadily when they arrived at the Lodge. Dunkie had found the three of them an old combat jacket each and some leaky wellies. The jackets kept nothing out, and all three were soaked to the skin by the time they arrived at the scene of the incident. Jamie and Calum in their all-weather gear enjoyed a nice walk. The rain had stopped and the mist had lifted long enough for the men to make out the top of the hill where the shot had come from. From their conversation Jamie gathered that they were quite happy that the death had indeed been an accident. There had been more conversation on the way back, little to do with the case: mostly derogatory comments about the depressing countryside, the terrible weather and the awful people.

Jamie smiled at Jock. 'I don't think they're enjoying their wee trip to Scotland, sir.'

Commander Millington called shortly after and told Jock that they were returning to London the following morning, though this evening would have been more convenient. Jock had to agree that it was unfortunate that there were currently only two return flights daily from Inverness to London and that it was sad indeed they'd missed the afternoon flight. Millington's rider: that two flights a day was probably adequate for demand, and that he couldn't understand why anyone would wish to visit this place by choice infuriated Jock, but he refused to rise to the bait. The good news was that they felt no need to interview anyone in connection with the incident and that they intended to take up no more of Mr Anderson's valuable time. Their medical examiner, on the basis of his preliminary examination, was satisfied that the post mortem features observed were consistent with the account of the accident provided. Arrangements were being made to return the body to London. Millington told Jock to refrain from making a statement to the press; that he himself would call a press conference on his return to London.

'Snotty bastard,' growled Jock as he put down the phone. He called Bob McLean to his office. 'Get onto the big Scottish papers, Bob. *Press and Journal* first. That bastard Millington's planning to drop this nice Scottish story into the laps of the English papers. Bugger that, Bob. Prepare a statement and get it off quick as you can.

'Try and get hold of some photos of the dead Duke—not the Duke dead, though; that would be a bit too gory. Maybe Robbie, his brother, could oblige.' Bob McLean smiled as Jock stomped out of his office, still muttering angrily to himself.

Chapter 14

Monday evening was practice time for the Dunmorey Ceilidh Band. When Jamie had returned to the area, he'd blown the dust off his fiddle, banjo and other instruments and was determined that his mates would do the same with theirs. With himself on the tenor banjo and guitar, Calum Munro on the small pipes and whistle, and Lachie Donaldson on the accordion and melodian, they were already making a good sound. Ali, Jamie's sister, had a great singing voice for traditional music and was hot stuff on the bodhran: she could really make the little drum talk. Colin Buchanan, who played guitar and five-string banjo, was also part of the band. Unfortunately he and Ali would be heading back to university shortly—but they'd be periodic members. The pair hoped they'd somehow manage to get home to Inverness most weekends. They all missed big Hughie MacRae. Hughie on bass had made all the difference. But he was missed for more than his musical contribution—the hole in all their lives couldn't simply be filled by another musician.

They met at Calum's place. He had a cottage on the Dunmorey estate with an unused barn behind, and there they could make as much noise as they liked and disturb no-one. The rest of the band was already there when Ali and Jamie arrived. Lachie and Calum were sitting together on a hay bale, each with a can of beer in his hand, and Calum was laughing at something running on Lachie's phone video camera.

'Sick pair of buggers,' said Colin when Jamie asked what the fun was about.

'Lachie caught Lordie getting shot on video. I couldn't stand the man, but I still think this is a bit sick.'

'The dumb pair of bastards.' Jamie laid down his banjo case and went over to the pair.

Lachie waved his camera. 'Have a look at this, Jamie. A'm thinkin' aboot puttin' this on the net, what dae ye think, man? Or maybe A could mak mysel' a wee bit o' money, eh? How much wid A get fir this frae Sky News dae ye think? It's been on the TV an' it's a' ower the papers—must be worth somethin' eh?' He held up the camera and gave it to Jamie. Lachie had spent a week's wages on the mobile phone: it was top of the range and the camera's photo quality and sound were excellent. It was all there: from the screaming tantrum to Colin kneeling beside the body by the rock.

Jamie shook his head. 'You'll be doing nothing of the kind. Whatever you thought about that man, this is sick. I'd have thought you'd have more sense.' He turned to Calum shaking his head in disgust. 'What's more to the point, what both you idiots seem to be oblivious to, is the fact that this is material evidence. A man was killed, there will be an enquiry; so what you have here is an invaluable record of exactly what happened, can you not see that? And you want to put it on the fucking internet or have it on the TV to entertain a few more million sickoes. I'm telling you, you'd have been in real trouble if you had.'

Jamie ran the video again. 'I just can't believe you guys could be so daft. Keep your big mouths shut about this. It'll be just like the thing for reporters to be chasing you lot for your stories.' Jamie waved the phone. 'Mention this and you'll be in trouble.' Jamie took out his own phone. 'Transmit that lot to me. My machine's crap but good enough—something to show my boss anyway.'

Ali tapped Jamie on the shoulder. 'Mr Policeman, if you don't confiscate that evidence now, your arse'll be in the fire tomorrow. You think DS Anderson will be impressed when you tell him you didn't want to upset your mate by arresting his phone? Think Jamie. What if Lachie gets pissed tonight—a good possibility—and his camera ends up down the toilet?'

They all gaped at Ali. Jamie closed Lachie's phone and slipped it into his pocket. 'Sorry Lachie.'

Lachie shrugged. 'You're right, Jamie, I'm sorry. Get it back as quick as you can, will you? Just hope Megan doesn't send any dirty messages for your boss to read. She can be a wee bit, eh . . . what's the word?'

'Explicit?' offered Colin.

Lachie smiled. 'Aye, that's it: explicit—she's a right dirty wee thing. Oh my God, Jamie—the pictures!' Lachie blushed scarlet. 'He'll no' be lookin' at my other pictures, will he Jamie?'

'I hope he will—and posts them on the internet.'

They all turned at the sound of Colin plunking the opening notes of "Duelling Banjos". 'Now are we going to play some music or what?'

Jamie was undeniably pleased with himself. He knew he had something of great interest, if not a great deal of importance. He was bursting to show the film to his boss and was hovering in the corridor first thing the following morning, and trying not to look predatory when Jock arrived.

'Morning sir, I've something here I think you might find interesting when you have a minute.'

'Important, is it? More important than a Morning Service? I've called one for this morning.'

'Wouldn't say that, sir—but very interesting certainly.'

Jock was acquiring a respect for the young policeman and knew that he wouldn't be pestering him with trivia. 'You best come in then,' he said, opening his office door.

Jock was flabbergasted. He tried to conceal it but failed. The film was good, and useful, but what interested Jock most was the soundtrack: much of His Lordship's tantrum was in German.

'You speak German, lad?'

'Aye sir, enough to get by. I can pick up most of it.'

'Well? I'm waiting.'

'Mostly swearing, sir. He's right upset about someone called Steiner coming onto his land and shooting his deer, and a bit about what he's going to do to Steiner. He says, eh . . . sorry sir—that he'll really fuck him over this time. That's the gist of it sir.'

Jock re-ran the video. 'I think your mate Lachie will have to manage without his phone for a few days.'

'Actually sir, you don't need the phone.' Jamie handed Jock a CD. 'It's on here, I downloaded it all. You'll find it's much clearer on the computer screen.'

'Well done, lad—very well done.' He handed the phone to Jamie and waved the CD. 'This is much more important than Morning Service—in fact, I'm going to cancel it.' Jock slipped the disc into his computer and made a copy which he gave back to Jamie.

'I want a full and accurate transcript. If you can't do it, find someone who can—and quickly. Jot down what you can make out for me now.' Jock passed a pad and pen to Jamie and re-ran the recording. After Jamie had left, Jock watched and listened to the recording several times, and then summoned DI McLean who sat in stunned silence as he watched the replay and read Jamie's rough translation. Together they reviewed the statements previously taken from Herr Steiner and MacDougal. They'd tallied in the most part, though Steiner's account seemed to overstate the distance of the target and the degree of difficulty of the shot which both the policemen had attributed to damaged ego.

'I think, Bob, that we should get our wee German mannie in for another wee chat.'

John MacDougal answered the phone when Jock called to Strathgellie: he wanted to see him and Herr Steiner in his office first thing in the afternoon.

'Yer man'll be no' right happy aboot that, Mr Anderson. He's bin ontae his lawyer so he's no' so scared aboot the jail noo. A'm thinkin' he'll maybe no' cam withoot his lawyer.'

'He can bring his lawyer,'

'But it's an Edinburgh lawyer.'

Jock sighed in exasperation. 'If you're not both here at 2 o'clock—with or without a lawyer—your wee German mannie better start getting worried about the jail again.'

DI McLean reminded Jock that he had a press conference in ten minutes. Jock looked at him and swore under his breath. The death of the Duke, under such strange circumstances, had attracted a lot of press interest and representatives of all the major newspapers were gathered downstairs. Thanks to Jock, all the Scottish papers had got the jump on those south of the border.

'The TV boys are here too,' said a grinning Bob McLean. 'They're still setting up so I think we've time for a cup of coffee.' DI McLean's smile dropped when Jock told him he'd be facing the cameras with him.

Jock and DI McLean took their seats on the small podium set up at the end of the cleared cafeteria and Jock addressed the gathering of newsmen. There was little that Jock could, or would, add to the statement previously issued by DI McLean, so he merely reiterated the statement with some embellishment. No names, other than that of the late Duke had been given and the assembled reporters were, of course, hungry for such details. Steiner had been identified as the owner of the Strathgellie estate, and Jock confirmed that indeed Herr Steiner was the man who had accidently caused the death of the Duke. Some photographs of Ogilvie had been found at the Lodge. They showed Ogilvie posing appropriately, rifle in hand, beside various dead stags on Dunmorey, and these photos were issued to the reporters. The press was very keen to have some photographs of Herr Steiner: these, unfortunately Jock could not provide, but he thought he could remedy that.

Jock stressed that there were no suspicious circumstances and that the Duke had died as the result of a multi-million-to-one accident. He then referred them to the statement already issued by Commander Millington in London. As Jock was leaving the podium he whispered to DI McLean to discreetly drop the word that Steiner was due to visit the station that afternoon. Jock smiled as he wondered if the press would pick up on the man's uncanny resemblance to Heinrich Himmler.

On his way back to his office, Jock met Jamie who handed him a neatly prepared copy of the translation of Ogilvie's tantrum. Jamie told Jock he'd had his old German teacher listen to the recording and fill in the gaps he'd missed.

Jock read through the revised version. 'You did well lad; you got the meat of it—just missed a few good swear words by the looks of it.'

Jamie smiled. 'Aye sir, Mr Tulloch, my German teacher said he'd not heard language like that since he worked on the docks in Hamburg when he was a student.'

MacDougal and Steiner, accompanied by a lawyer, arrived at the station at 1.55 to be met by an army of reporters. An infuriated Steiner fought his way into the building without comment to the press, leaving his lawyer to face the cameras. Finally, both Herr Steiner and the lawyer were lead to an interview room.

Jock and Bob McLean had watched the episode from Jock's office window with some amusement, and John MacDougal was still laughing when he was shown into Jock's office.

'Thank you very much for coming in, Mr MacDougal. I've a few more questions for you if you don't mind: some that you, as an experienced stalker, can best answer.'

Jock took out a large scale map of Dunmorey and asked MacDougal to draw the route they had taken, and to mark—as precisely as he could—the spot from which the shot had been fired, and the position of the stag.

MacDougal put on his reading glasses and studied the map for a few moments. After some thought he confidently traced their path. 'It's no' right easy tae be awful precise, but A think we were lyin' aboot here when he fired,' said MacDougal as he drew a cross. 'An' the stag when he fired: aboot here.' MacDougal added another cross.

Jock indicated a cross he himself had drawn on the map. 'That's where the Duke was standing.' Jock laid a ruler on the map—the three crosses were more or less in line.

'What was the distance between your man and the Duke, do you think?'

'Nae mair than three quarters o' a mile A'd say. The glen's quite narrow there.'

Jock took the ruler. 'You're not far off. According to this,' he said, waving the ruler, 'it's about a thousand yards. You told me already that you didn't see the other party.'

'That's right. A broon pony, an' men dressed fir the hill wid be right difficult tae pick oot at that distance, especially if they're no' movin'.'

'And if the pony had been white?'

'Still no' easy,' insisted MacDougal

'But not a problem with a telescope?'

'Naw, nae problem wi' a glass.'

'Herr Steiner has a good rifle, does he?'

'Aye, the best: a Manlicher, wid hae tae be the best. Nothin' but the best fir the Führer—that's whit we a' call him.'

'And his telescopic sight: good is it?'

'Good? Best that money can buy.'

Jock chewed for a moment on his empty pipe. 'So through his rifle scope it would have been possible to see the other party?'

MacDougal nodded. 'Aye, nae bother.'

'Mr MacDougal,' said Jock leaning forward, 'would you, in your professional opinion, think that with a good rifle and scope it would be possible to hit a target at a thousand yards?'

'Ye're no' suggestin' . . . ?'

'I'm not suggesting anything, Mr MacDougal, I'm just asking for your professional opinion.'

'Aye, it wid be. Bloody difficult shot, though. It's a long way, an' doonhill—a right difficult shot tae gauge. At that distance ye'd no' be shootin' directly at the target. The bullet would be droppin', so ye'd hae tae mak allowances fir that. No' easy, but we used tae target practice snipin' at that distance in the army.'

'A last question, Mr MacDougal. Approximately how long did Mr Steiner have the rifle before he fired the shot? How long was he peering through that expensive telescopic sight?'

The stalker scratched his head for a few moments. 'A few minutes. Aye, it wid be a gid few minutes. The beast wis in nae hurry. A'd say maybe four or five. Felt like forever lyin' there holdin' ma breath. Aye, the beast wis in nae hurry.'

His wait for an hour or so in the interview room had done nothing to improve Herr Steiner's humour and he was protesting loudly when he and his lawyer were finally invited into Jock's office. He curtly refused the offer of coffee, but his lawyer gratefully accepted as he introduced himself to Jock. He had driven up from Edinburgh that morning and was Mr Justin Cooper, of Marston, Boyd and Cooper: a very reputable law firm.

Jock and DI McLean took their seats and Jock turned to the German. 'Herr Steiner, were you familiar with the deceased: Richard Ogilvie, the Duke of Dunmorey?'

'He was my neighbour, I was familiar with the name, yes.'

'That is not what I asked, Herr Steiner. Were you familiar with the man—did you know him?'

'No I did not.'

'Are you quite sure that you did not know him and had never met him?' persisted Jock.

'I believe my client has answered the question, Super—intendent,' interposed the lawyer.

Jock rotated the screen of his computer. 'I would like you gentlemen to watch a short piece of video, then I will ask the question again.' He handed a paper to Cooper. 'This is a transcript—you may find it useful.'

Both men were shocked by the video, and Cooper was stunned by the transcript. 'If you'll please excuse us, I would like to confer with my client.' Both men rose and left the room.

'Well, Bob, that's got the wee man squirming a bit—be right interesting to see what story he'll concoct with his lawyer.'

DI McLean looked at his boss. 'Are you really considering the possibility that Steiner deliberately shot Ogilvie?'

Jock shrugged. 'Could be. He's lying there waiting for a stag, sees the other party and recognizes Ogilvie through his telescopic sight. A good chance to even an old score, maybe? MacDougal says the man's an excellent shot. So how did he miss that stag? Still an awful lot of questions Bob—and I want answers.'

Steiner and the lawyer returned to Jock's office half an hour or so later. Steiner sat in sulking silence, the lawyer did the talking. Cooper said that as the result of some ambiguity in the questioning, his client, not being a native English speaker, had been confused. The lawyer assured DS Anderson that his client had had no intention of misleading the police. His client insisted that he'd had only one brief meeting with the Duke, which was about two years previously, and that all subsequent communications had been by either e-mail or telephone. Herr Steiner and Mr Ogilvie had had some business dealings in the past which had not been concluded to his client's advantage. His client was not, however, prepared to discuss with DS Anderson any details of his business involvement with Ogilvie.

Jock had no option but to dismiss the pair. He was tempted to demand Steiner's passport but accepted the lawyer's surety that his client would remain in Scotland pending further investigations.

Later that evening Jock was back in his office. Nick, who had insisted on coming along for the ride, took his usual place under the desk as Jock sat down. Jo, his daughter, and Gordie, his grandson, were at the house. He loved them dearly but twittering women and a noisy, boisterous four-year-old were not conducive to a clear thought process—he had a lot to think about.

From his desk drawer he pulled out Dr Paterson's report on the dead Ogilvie, quickly read through it and flipped through the photographs. Something wasn't right. He laid out the large-scale map of Dunmorey on which was marked the site of the Duke's death and the source of the shot as marked by MacDougal. From the contours he got an approximation of the relative altitudes of the two and the horizontal distance between. With a bit of arithmetic and some graph paper he produced something he hoped was to scale. For an hour or so he worked away, before finally deciding that fiddling round with sums and rulers wasn't his line—he wanted something else. A trip back home was called for—he needed something from Jo.

'A mannequin, Dad? You want to borrow a mannequin?' Jo shook her head in disbelief.

'Aye Jo—a male one. Just for a day or so.'

'I'm not even going to ask what you want it for—you'll not tell me anyway. So when do you need it?'

Jock looked at his watch. 'You'd not planned to go to the shop this evening?'

'No, I had not,' retorted Jo indignantly. 'It's after 8 o'clock at night for goodness sake—the shop's closed. Some people actually take time off from work, you know Dad.'

Jock sighed. 'Then I suppose it'll have to be tomorrow morning.'

'Tell you what, Dad. I'm sure whatever awful things you're planning to do with my poor mannequin must be frantically urgent, but they'll just have to wait. How about you having a bit of quality time with your grandson? She picked up young Gordie and put him in Jock's arms. 'Gordie; your grandpa wants to play football.'

Chapter 15

'Well, there's a hell of a lot here, but nothing much,' muttered DI McLean as he laid a manila file on Jock's desk and sat down. Jock pulled the file towards him and read the title: Klaus Adolf Steiner. Jock opened the folder and flipped through. 'There's a lot in here; how about giving me a short version?'

Bob McLean smiled and reclaimed the folder. 'He maintains he's a leading German industrialist. He may be a leader of something but not of any industry you'll find on a stock exchange. He's a real shadowy figure. Rumoured to be involved in everything from gun-running to illegal gambling, people trafficking, drugs and money laundering with lots and lots in between. His name comes up everywhere: Interpol, FBI, CIA. I spoke to one of my contacts in London. Scotland Yard would love to nail him but the clever little bastard never leaves his prints on anything. There are lots of layers between him and anything dirty. He works out of Switzerland mostly, where sensibly he keeps his nose nice and clean. Anything goes in that place as long as it involves big money. And it is *big* money we're talking about here sir: big, big money. You'll love his background. Son of a leading Nazi who made his fortune in munitions during the war, all tucked away nicely in Swiss accounts. He capitalized on the post-war regeneration and the accounts got fatter. The father died a few years ago and young Klaus took over and diversified, so to speak.'

'I thought he was my kind of man when I first saw him,' said Jock grimly. 'Any connection with Ogilvie?'

DI McLean shook his head. 'We're still compiling on Ogilvie. On the face of it, Ogilvie's a highly respected and influential merchant banker, but it seems some of his affairs are about as shady as Steiner's. They make a right pair, sir: fine pillars of society with their feet in the dung heap, I'd say. Would be nice to pin a murder on Steiner, sir—it would make a lot of folk right happy.'

'Aye, Bob but that'll not be so easy. Come on, let's get our wellies and take a wee walk in the country to stretch our legs. Got your camera?' DI McLean fished in his pocket and nodded.

Wee Dunkie was at Dunmorey Lodge when they pulled up. For the trip up the glen he had had provided a second quad bike so DI McLean could travel in more comfort—that he had to drive the bike himself occasioned a few moments of nervousness on his part.

Jock had the mannequin delivered earlier. It was already up the glen at the death scene, and the finishing touches were just being added to Jock's creation as the party arrived. Jo's mannequin stood on the rock occupied by the Duke in his last moments. The figure was clad in an old combat jacket and trousers, and Lachie was examining his handiwork.

'That it?' asked Jock. 'You sure that's as His Lordship was standing when he was shot?'

Lachie looked at Colin Buchanan and both men nodded. 'We think so,' said Colin. 'It's as we remember.'

Jock took some photos from his pocket: stills from Lachie's video. He nodded and grunted. 'Looks about right. We ready then?'

'Almost,' said Lachie. He jumped up beside the dummy and stuck an old deerstalker on its head.

Jock smiled. 'Aye, Lachie, that's much better.' He turned and focused his binoculars on a group of figures high on the hill on the opposite side of the glen. Jamie Ross, Calum Munro and stalker, John MacDougal were easily identifiable—a significant point noted by Jock. Jamie was watching Jock's group through his binoculars. Jock raised his arm in greeting and Jamie returned the wave. Jock called Jamie on his mobile. 'You all ready up there?'

'Aye, sir. John MacDougal's sure we're in exactly the right spot—we've even found the ejected cartridge. John says the wind's pretty much as it was on the day, and same visibility.'

'OK, when you're ready then. We'll get out of the way.'

Jock pulled the group back a safe distance and turned to Dunkie. 'Think he'll hit him?'

Dunkie shrugged. 'He's a bloody gid shot.' He gave a painful cough and rubbed his chest. 'A'd rather it wis me wi' the rifle, but A'm no' up fir the hike up the hill. There'll be a gid drop on the bullet at that distance, an' ye need experience tae gauge that. A did some wee sums based on the loadin' o' the bullet an' the type. If he does as he's telt he should hit him nae bother. There's no' much wind tae worry aboot.'

Jock grunted and turned the glasses back to the opposite hill. Calum, with Steiner's rifle, had taken up his position on the ground. Jock lowered the binoculars and looked at the mannequin—he found he was holding his breath. He saw the dummy give a slight shudder then they clearly heard the crack of the shot. Jock waved a signal to the hill and headed back over to the dummy. Lachie lifted it off the rock and Jock stripped off the combat jacket. He fingered a small hole in the centre of the chest then turned the mannequin over—in the lower back was an exit hole.

Jock flicked on his mobile. 'DC Ross. Congratulate Calum, he was spot on. You lads hang on up there for a bit.'

Jock turned back to the dummy. In addition to the bullet holes there were two additional, much larger. Jock had drilled holes representing the entry and exit wounds on Ogilvie's body.

He pulled off the tape which was masking his additions. 'OK lads, set him up again.'

Happy with the positioning, he called for a two-metre length of rigid two-centimetre plastic pipe which he slid through the holes he'd drilled. From behind the dummy he spied through the pipe and gave a satisfied grunt.

The far side of the glen, about half a mile south and almost directly above the Lodge was clad with a Scots pine plantation, the edge marked by a deer fence. For a few moments Jock spied through the pipe. He called up Jamie Ross, directing him and his party to cross to the fence line and follow it down until told to stop. The field of vision through his two-centimetre pipe, even at over half a mile, was very limited. He could, however, make out the fence and finally the figure of Jamie Ross. Calling the party to stop, he instructed Jamie to flag his position by the fence then join him in the glen.

He turned to DI McLean. 'Well, what do you think?'

Bob McLean smiled and nodded his head. 'I'm very impressed sir—simple, but hopefully effective. I'm sure the computer boys could have done a simulation for you, and you'd not have had to leave the office.'

Jock laughed. 'Aye Bob, but how long would it have taken, and where's the fun in that? I've enjoyed my wee bit of fresh air and exercise. First thing tomorrow we'll get some lads up there for a fingertip search.' Jock picked up his binoculars and watched as Jamie Ross tied what looked like a scarf on the wire of the deer fence.

'Up there, or thereabouts, is where I think the fatal shot came from. Aye man, I think we're a wee bit further forward.'

Colin and Lachie were standing by the big rock grinning; between them stood the dummy. DI McLean, who'd been making a photographic record, smiled, lifted his camera and took a photo. 'I'll send you a copy. Thanks to all of you. You've been assisting in a serious police investigation. Keep your mouths shut, no blabbing to your pals. Not a word to anyone—especially not the press. Everything to do with this case is highly confidential—you understand?' All the lads nodded. 'OK, then—pick up your friend and back to the Lodge.'

'Hey Jock,' called Dunkie, who was sitting on a bank with his telescope in hand. 'Can A drag ye away frae yer police business tae introduce ye tae some friends o' mine?' Puzzled, Jock joined him on the bank. Dunkie lay back and pointed up. Circling above, at no more than five hundred feet, was a golden eagle. 'An' there, an' there,' said Dunkie, pointing again. 'Mum an' dad an' this year's bairn. There were twa youngsters in the nest this year, but only one's made it.'

Jock was smiling as he followed the birds with his binoculars.

'Mair interestin' than deid dukes, eh Jock?'

'You said there were two in the nest; you mean you saw the nest? Counted them?'

Dunkie nodded. 'Mum an' dad are old friends, been aroond fir years. They nest the same place every year.' Dunkie pointed up the glen. 'See the crags on the face o' yon hill: Ben Darrach? That's where the nest is. Wi' a bit o' climbin' and scramblin' ye can get a gid look ontae the nest, an' far enough away no' tae bother the birds. A'll get Calum tae tak ye up next spring if ye're interested—ye'll manage it fine.'

Jock beamed at him. 'Ye're right Dunkie. As you said: much mair interestin' than deid dukes.'

Back at the Lodge, Jock was about to get into his car when he was approached by Colin Buchanan. 'I gather from that wee bit of fun up the glen just now that you're not too happy about the, eh . . . perceived circumstances of Lordie's death.'

'Aye, lad, but you'll be keeping that to yourself I hope.'

Colin smiled and nodded. 'Can I show you something sir?'

Colin led Jock over to the larder, a small building set back among the trees. 'This is where we skin and hang up the beasts,' he informed Jock as they went inside. Two skinned stags were hanging on hooks.

'Have a look, sir,' said Colin, indicating the carcasses.

Curious as to what this was all about, Jock poked the first suspended animal. 'Nice bit of meat. What am I meant to be looking at?'

Colin pointed to a small hole in the side of the animal's chest.

'Bullet hole,' said Jock.

Colin nodded and rotated the stag to show the opposite side and looked at Jock, smiling. 'Anything missing, sir?'

Jock looked blankly at the carcass until the penny dropped. 'There's no exit wound.'

Colin nodded. 'There rarely is. We're shooting beasts at no more than a hundred and fifty yards, usually less—maybe nearer a hundred: a wee bit more sometimes if Calum or Dunkie trust that the gent's a good shot. Dunkie and Calum never let Lordie take anything over about a hundred yards though—pissed off Lordie, that did.' Colin turned and picked up a jam jar from a shelf, rattled it and spilled a few of the contents into his hand. He selected what looked like a flattened piece of lead and handed it to Jock.

'This is a bullet: these are all bullets I've collected.' He shook the jar. 'When the bullet hits the stag it mushrooms: flattens out. We usually find it in the chest or inside the skin on the opposite side. Goes right through sometimes, right enough—if the beast's taken close enough or if it's not stopped by a rib. 'When we loaded Lordie's body there was blood on his back which I thought a bit odd. And your wee experiment needed an exit hole.' Colin shrugged. 'Seemed a bit strange to me that a bullet fired from the top of that hill would pass right through. That's all sir. Just a thought—it's maybe nothing.'

Jock smiled at Colin. 'No lad, you're right I think. It's not nothing. I'm going to have a word with Dunkie.'

Jock found Dunkie in the gunroom where he was oiling a rifle. When he told him about his conversation with Colin, Dunkie swore to himself. 'He's right, Jock, he's quite right. Why the hell did A no' pick up on it?'

Dunkie opened a drawer in the gun cabinet, took out a box of bullets and emptied a few on the baize-topped gun table. He picked one up and showed it to Jock. 'These are what we use. 0.243, copper-jacketed lead. When it hits, it's like a dum-dum. Ye saw the wee mushrooms Colin showed ye. Maks a bit o' a mess inside—kills the beast even if ye're a wee bit off target. One o' these widnae gae right through at the distance we're talkin' aboot.'

Dunkie lined up six bullets on the table. 'Best bullets on the market, but they're mass-produced, an' each has got its ane wee personality, so tae speak. Wee differences in loadin', an' wee irregularities on the surface.' He picked up some bullets. 'They look the same but they're no'. Fired under a controlled situation they six bullets here wid mak a group aboot maybe the size o' a wee tin lid: maybe twa or three inches at a hundred an' fifty, two hundred yards—which is just fine fir takin' beasts. Aerodynamically they're no' designed tae gae a long way either.' Dunkie shook his head. 'Why did it no' click aboot the exit hole? Bloody stupid.'

'So someone planning to deliberately kill the Duke wouldn't be using a bullet like this, then?'

Dunkie shook his head. 'No way—an certainly no' at the distances we're talkin' aboot. There's lots o' different kinds o' bullets, Jock. Ye select the kind ye want fir the purpose. Tae pot onybuddy at a distance ye'd want a bloody gid rifle: a sniper's gun ideally—they're designed fir the job—an' wi' a bloody gid scope an' a high powered hard-nosed bullet. A mind in the army the snipers wid load their ain bullets an' polish them up. They needed tae ken that the bullet wid gae where they wanted it—nae point in clippin' a lad's lug or gaein' him a bit o' a haircut when ye want the bloody thing between his een. Calum did a bloody gid job hittin' that dummy o' yours. Yon wisnae an easy shot. A'm thinkin he was maybe a wee bittie lucky—but dinnae be sayin' that tae Calum. Yer man that shot Lordie widnae be wantin' tae be takin' a chance on hittin' his man—he'd no' be countin' on a wee bit o' luck.'

Chapter 16

J
ock and DI McLean stopped off for a beer in the Moray on their way
back to Inverness. Jock sat back puffing on his pipe, his beer untouched
on the table.

'A lot of food for thought, Bob,' he said blowing out a cloud of smoke.
'We've confirmed that a decent shot could hit Ogilvie, but it seemed pretty
obvious to me from the wounds on Ogilvie's body that the bullet hadn't
come from the top of that hill. That exit hole was all wrong. There's no way
a bullet hitting square on the chest could have come out near enough his
left armpit—no way. I think we've maybe confirmed something today with
my wee experiment.'

'Aye sir, but that means another shooter firing at the same time as
Steiner. Starting to get a wee bit far-fetched, is it not? Dr Paterson said the
bullet hit the Duke's sunglasses. No chance that that could have deflected
the bullet?'

Jock shook his head. 'I asked about that. No, a wee bit of plastic wouldn't
do it.'

'Colin Buchanan said your man was bouncing about a bit on that rock.
We could see that on the video. You don't think that maybe on a bit of a
bounce he could have caught the bullet a bit differently?'

Jock shrugged. 'Aye, could be right enough, could be. But we've got
another wee complication.' He told Bob about his conversation with Colin

Buchanan and Dunkie. 'Anyway, with a bit of luck your modern technology will give us some answers.'

Back at the office, there was an e-mail waiting for Jock: it was the results of the analysis of the video he'd sent to the lab. The results were unambiguous. All extraneous sounds had been filtered out and the lab had produced a trace showing a flat line with two distinct peaks, the first slightly wider and lower than the second: two distinct sharp sounds from two different sources. What had been recorded were two gunshots, from different rifles fired three quarters of a second apart. A series of still photographs confirmed that Ogilvie had been standing square onto the party on the opposite hillside at the moment the shot hit him. Jock laid down the report and called for Bob McLean.

'Bugger me, you were right sir,' said DI McLean as he read through the report. 'So it certainly wasn't an accident. A calculated, cold-blooded murder. But not by our wee German friend, unfortunately. That would have been nice. Damn sight easier too, sir. Now we've got a bit of a job on. You going to advise our London friends about this development?'

Jock looked at him as if he was daft. 'No bloody way. You want those big boots back here, and a load more of them clomping all over us? They had their sniff at it and blew it. No, Bob, this is our body, our case.' He smiled at DI McLean. 'We'll just solve it and then rub their smug noses in it. That'll be much more fun. But we better try and find ourselves a suspect. Any ideas?'

DI McLean shook his head sadly. 'From what little we've learned about our late friend, he seems to be the sort who'd have a queue of folk happy to see the end of him.'

'Got that search on Ogilvie done yet?'

'Just about. I'll get you what we've got.'

'First thing tomorrow, Bob, I want you down there. Take a team to Dunmorey. We'll need to thoroughly check out the Lodge. Hopefully

Lordie's personal stuff's still there and hasn't been rummled around too much. And I want you to take some of the lads up the hill. The shot must have come from the edge of the trees, and I need to know exactly where. I want a really thorough search of the area. We've got bugger all to go on, so let's pray for a wee clue or two.'

Jock opened his large-scale map of Dunmorey on the desk. He pointed with the stem of his pipe. 'There's the Lodge. See this wee road here? It runs from the Lodge and up the hill through the woods. And see here, from my wee experiment I think the shot came from round about there.'

Bob bent over the map. 'And the wee road's about fifty yards from the edge of the wood—quite handy, eh?

'Aye Bob. Now let's see what you've got on Ogilvie.'

The weather the next day was cloudy and windy but dry as the team began their search. It had been some days since the shooting and expectations of finding anything of significance were not high. Someone sitting in the woods would be unlikely to leave much long lasting evidence of their presence. Fortunately, protected by the tall canopy of the pines, a path through the carpet of needles was apparent. Clearly someone had made the passage from the road to the edge of the wood more than once. Unfortunately no identifiable footprints are made on a carpet of pine needles. The small forestry road, though not busy, was well enough travelled by estate workers to have obliterated any signs of a vehicle which may have been involved. DI McLean's team returned with little to show for their efforts. Jamie Ross did feel, however, that he'd found the exact spot from which the shot had been fired.

He spread out some photos on Jock's desk. 'See here, sir; the moss has been scraped off the bark of a pine tree, and off the top of this wee branch. The tree's right on the edge of the wood. I think that's where he . . .'

'Or she.'

'Right sir, he or she rested the rifle. Just the right height for somebody to sit and fire.'

A search of the Lodge had been barely more productive. Ogilvie's personal effects were still there, and his mobile phone and laptop were taken for examination but nothing else offered any promise.

Jock re-read the report on Ogilvie compiled by DI McLean. It was interesting but not particularly helpful in identifying any likely suspect. On the face of it, Richard Ogilvie was a respectable businessman. On the death of his father he had taken over the directorship of the family business: Ogilvies, a small, very respectable, very exclusive merchant bank in the City of London—patronized, apparently, by the very rich. He had been very much part of the establishment with friends and contacts in the highest of places. There was nothing finite about the shady aspects of his dealings. Nothing was ever pinned on him, but a very strong suspicion—more than that, an unproven certainty remained. From his contacts in Scotland Yard, DI McLean had got more interesting, but still useless, information, really little more than gossip. Ogilvie was considered a nasty piece of work. They'd love to nail him for something, but couldn't.

Jock closed the file in exasperation. He needed to get a proper handle on the man. He'd got nothing from down south so he'd try closer to home. He picked up the phone and called Dunkie Munro. Dunkie offered to come to Inverness, then suggested that as the whole story might take a while, Jock and his wife could maybe come over at the weekend and have a decent talk with a few drams. They could stay over Saturday night and there would be a nice haunch of venison for Sunday lunch.

Meg was excited at the prospect of the visit to Dunmorey. Jock had described the place as best as he could, and had given her a fascinating picture of wee Dunkie. Meg was intrigued. But it was more than that. Meg and Jock were not really very active socially. Their weekly bridge with the Chief Constable and his wife, the occasional golf club do, or the odd professional function was about the limit of Jock's and Meg's social life. Occasionally, if there was a good play or concert at Eden Court Theatre, they would enjoy a night out together. Meg had her own circle of friends and was involved with the local Hospice, which took her out in the evenings more often than she would perhaps have wished. Jock had his golf and his birdwatching. He reckoned he saw enough folk during the day at work, and the last thing he needed was to go out and see more folk at night. Meg had accepted that Jock was very selectively sociable. Given the right environment and gathering, he could be the life and soul—and that usually meant socializing with old friends. He could be dragged out, and he often was—Meg didn't always take no for an answer. Once out, he usually enjoyed himself. Occasionally however, he'd get his dram and retire to a quiet corner somewhere with his pipe. So for her and Jock to be visiting an old friend from Jock's past—and staying overnight with him and his wife on Dunmorey was really something special.

It was late afternoon on Saturday before Jock returned home from his golf and Meg was agitating to leave for Dunmorey. He quickly showered and changed and joined her and Nick in the car—then returned to the kitchen to collect the bottles of wine and whisky he'd forgotten. The last of the sun was forcing its way through some threatening storm clouds and there were already big spots of rain on the windscreen as they drove through the gates of Dunmorey. The deteriorating weather didn't detract from the impressive beauty of the estate and Meg complimented Jock on the description he'd given her. There was, however, no wildlife in evidence and, apart from a few sheep, no livestock either. The weather forecast for Sunday was good, and Jock reassured Meg that a tour of the estate had been promised. Meg was desperate to see the Lodge, and Jock smiled at her eagerness as he let Nick out of the car. He took Meg's hand as they hurried through the rain up the path to Dunkie's back door, where they were met by Morag who took their wet coats and ushered them into the warm kitchen. Jock retrieved his coat and returned to the car to collect the wine and whisky he'd left on the back seat.

Nick had an exciting first meeting with Gyp, Dunkie's young black Labrador bitch. He and Gyp, and Meg and Morag hit it off from the start. The fact that the wives were almost the same age and came from the same small town in Easter Ross helped. They quickly discovered that they had many old friends in common. Morag had cooked up a stew of Dunmorey lamb, after which the men excused themselves and retired to the living room.

Chapter 17

Dunkie's living room was a homely place uncluttered with unnecessary furniture. A sofa and two comfy-looking big armchairs faced a blazing log fire, on either side of which were well stocked floor-to-ceiling bookshelves. A standard lamp behind Dunkie's chair by the fire provided a warm glow to the small room. It was a very cold, wet night and the strong wind drove the heavy rain against the lounge window. Dunkie closed the curtains on the storm.

At the opposite end of the room was a rustic old dresser where Dunkie stood pouring their first drams of the evening. Beside him, Jock stood examining the many framed photographs arranged on the wall above. Arrayed there was the record of the lives of Dunkie and his family. Many showed Dunkie in uniform and one in particular caught Jock's attention: a much younger Dunkie posed between two officers.

'Aye, that's me.' Dunkie handed Jock a large glass of whisky. 'Company Sergeant Major—Pipe Major—Duncan Munro. Ye'll maybe recognize him: the one on the left?'

Jock took out his glasses, put them on, and studied the photo. 'Dougie Sanderson?'

'Aye, that's him: Major Douglas Sanderson. You'll no' be knowin' him on the right though—that's his best mate Major Donald Ogilvie, the late lamented Lordie's faither. Aye, the three o' us went through a lot thegither—

wi' quite a few wee nicks tae show fir it A can tell ye. Aye, A could be tellin' ye a few stories.'

'There'll be a story to go with this one,' said Jock, pointing to a grinning young soldier holding up a medal.

Dunkie shrugged. 'Me with ma Military Medal presented by Her Majesty the Queen. A gid story right enough, but A dinnae like talkin' aboot it, Jock. Aye, some gid men died that day; them mair deservin' o' a medal than me. Morag wants the picture there, says it makes her feel proud.'

'And this one here?' Jock indicated a happy family group. Between a younger Dunkie and his wife stood three children: a tousle-haired lad of about eight or nine years old, an older boy of ten or eleven, and between them a pretty blonde girl who looked a bit older. 'One of these lads must be Calum, and the lassie must be your daughter Cathy. And the other wee laddie?'

Dunkie nodded. 'Aye, as I telt ye; there's a lot A'll be wantin' tae tell ye tonight. Just ye sit yersel' doon an' get some o' that Glen Grant intae ye.' As they settled down by the fire they could hear a clatter of dishes and the distant chatter and laughter from the kitchen.

Dunkie smiled at Jock. 'We'll no' be needin' tae worry aboot them eh?' He settled into his armchair. 'It's no' easy tae ken where tae start, Jock. It's the late Lordie ye want tae learn aboot. Stuff ye'll maybe no' find in *Who's Who* or *Debrett's*? Maybe some modern kind o' stuff, then we can gae back a bit?'

Jock nodded. 'Anything that's not relevant I'm sure will be entertaining.'

Dunkie lay back in the chair and took a good sip of his whisky. 'Ye'll no' be knowin' that this wis tae be oor last season. Lordie had grand plans fir the estate that didnae include us. A dinnae just mean us, me an' the wife an' family. All o' us were tae be laid off. The Farm Manager: that's Donnie Cameron, Cathy's husband; the foresters, ghillies, farm workers—the lot o' us tae be kicked off—awbuddy. Farm shut doon, the cattle: all the beasts sold—a kind o' mini Highland Clearance tae mak way fir a new kind o' prosperity.'

'He was selling the place then?'

'Worse than that, Jock—a championship golf course; the Lodge tae be a five star hotel. The place wis tae be raped—the end o' an era. So ye'll maybe understand why naebuddy here wis too upset aboot Lordie's sudden demise. I ken it wis right disrespectful, but we a' got thegither up at the Lodge an' drunk a toast tae whoever killed the black-hearted bastard. Quite a few big toasts—we drank a' his bloody whisky. We never had as much as a cup o' tea frae him when he wis alive so we thought maybe the tight bastard owed us a few drams. Didnae steal it, mind. Robbie, that's Robert his brother—ye've met him—telt us just tae help oorsels. He wisnae there though, at least no' in body—he wis on duty at Fort George. Aye, ye met Robbie at the funeral: he's a right fine lad. We a' felt that a tight noose had been taken off o' oor necks, Jock. It wis a grand night.'

Jock was clearly stunned at what he'd heard and couldn't conceal the fact.

Dunkie looked at him smiling. 'Aye, Mr Policeman. Mair than a few folk are glad that he's deid. There's lots o' folk wi' a bit o' a motive. Real Agatha Christie stuff eh? How are yer little grey cells, Mr Poirot?'

Jock leaned back in his chair and blew out air. 'I think you'd better fill my glass up, Dunkie—and bring over the bottle.' Dunkie smiled as he got up, topped up both glasses and laid the bottle of whisky beside Jock.

'He wis a right clever man, Jock. He must hae been plannin' it fir years. His faither kent fine he wis up tae somethin' but A'm sure he never suspected onything like this. Primogenitor, they a' still stick tae it nae matter what kind o' shit the son may be. A few gid second an' third sons hae walked away wi' bugger all ower the years. Army or the church—tak yer choice.

'The first Duke, General Arbuthnot Ogilvie, a lowland Scot, wis granted the estate by the Duke of Cumberland fir his sterlin' butchery after the '45.

Ye can see his portrait in the Lodge. The estate's been in the family ever since. The ancestors were a right mixed bunch. Some dissolute bastards managed tae lose a gid chunk o' the land, but somehow the estate managed tae hold thegither. The auld Duke wis desperate that nothin' wid change. He loved this place, an' he devoted hissel' tae creatin' whit it is now. He really built the place up. I'll tak ye roond tomorrow an' ye'll get some idea. Fantastic man: a character an' a real gentleman. An' that bastard Richard just couldnae wait fir him tae die.'

Dunkie caught Jock's sharp look.

'Naw, nothing suspicious there—well, maybe no' directly. He wisnae a well man. Prostate cancer an' a bad heart. The cancer wis eatin' intae him an' his heart wis buggered. He wis set fir a triple by-pass when he had the heart attack that killed him.'

'So Robert would have inherited nothing from his father?'

Dunkie shrugged. 'Bit o' money maybe, ye'd hae tae ask him yersel'. He's never mentioned it. As A said, army or the church, an' he's right happy in the army.' Dunkie leaned over, threw more logs on the fire then sat back with a sigh.

'One thing did upset him though. His mother: fine lady, a beautiful woman. She wanted Robert—Robbie we ey call him—tae hae her English estate. She'd a big place doon in Devon. Richard an' her didnae get on, she saw right through the bastard, but she loved Robbie though. She wis much younger than the Duke. For years he'd been married tae the regiment. They didnae meet until the auld Duke, Richard's grandfaither, died an' he had tae tak ower the family business. He wis the Colonel o' the regiment then, aboot forty A think. They own a merchant bank in the City o' London. He didnae want tae leave the army and tak it on, but family duty won—they're great on family duty, them aristocrats. Onyway, he met up wi' Lady Elizabeth, twenty years younger she wis. Devoted couple they wis. Inseparable. Just aboot killed him when she had her accident. It gaed him his first heart attack. He never really got ower it, an' he went a couple o' months efter. A ridin' accident. She loved her horses and huntin'. A dinnae ken the details, but her horse fell an' crushed her. A lovely woman. Many a cup o' tea she's had in yon kitchen.' Dunkie nodded his head in the direction of the door. 'Aye, a lovely lady; real doon tae earth, no' one o' yer snotty types.'

Dunkie sat back and gazed into the fire. For the first time Jock noticed how thin and drawn his friend's face, lit by the flickering fire, had become. He allowed the silence to continue for a few moments.

'You said Robert was upset by something?'

'The death o' his mother knocked him fir a six, Jock. He kent his faither didnae hae long tae live, an' he'd aboot cam tae terms wi' that—well, just aboot. But his mother? They were right close. Devastated he wis. Devastated. A mind at the funeral, that evil bastard brother o' his smirkin' at Robbie's grief—a just wanted tae thump the bastard in his smug grinnin' face.'

Dunkie paused in thought for a few moments. 'Robbie: he's like a son tae me. He never got on wi' his brother. Chalk and cheese, Cain and Abel. A year younger, Richard treated him like shite. He wis a bully tae a' the kids but worse tae Robbie. When they were younger they used tae spend maist o' their school holidays here. Robbie loved the place. He wis well intae nature an' wildlife. He loved the animals. Richard just wanted tae tak oot a gun an' shoot everythin'. They used tae cam up here thegither until the accident.'

Dunkie gazed into the fire, his mind wandering. He wasn't drunk, but with the help of the whisky he was slipping back through the years. Jock refilled his pipe, content to wait for him to continue.

'They used tae cam up fir their holidays in the summer. There were other kids roond the estate an' they'd a' get thegither. Richard, he ey insisted on being called Richard; never Rickie or Dick. He was the eldest, an' the biggest and strongest. A right bully he wis. A think maybe he'd just had a year at Eton, he must hae been aboot eleven or twelve. A remember thinkin' that he'd be a right Flashman by the end o' his time there. A little shit he wis, but he wis clever enough tae be really sweet an' polite tae adults. Maist folk were taken in but we werenae. Like Flashman he wis a coward. Never did onythin' dangerous hissel', but he'd goad the other kids intae daein' right dangerous things—but never him. The wee shit wid just laugh at them if they refused, or hurt themsel's when they did. A got a' this frae Calum years later, A never kent the half o' it at the time. What parents ever do Jock?

'Ye were lookin' at that photo earlier. The other wee laddie in the picture is Davie. He wis ma eldest boy, a year older than Calum. They a' used tae play thegither. Calum, Davie, Robbie and Richard an' a few o' the sons o' some o' the estate workers. It a' seemed innocent enough tae us parents. This wis a paradise fir kids, Jock. They'd build their tree hooses an' swings an' played their cowboys and Indians, an' they fished an' swam an' sailed boats on the lochan. Where the River Monnie comes oot o' the lochan, no' far frae here, there's a big deep pool wi' a waterfall. We call it the troot pool: it's a grand place fir the troot. An' it's a grand place fir swimmin' in the summer.

'A big larch tree had fallen ower the pool, right across it but aboot forty or fifty feet above. There were only three kids there that day: Richard, wee Davie an' the farm manager's son, Willie Stevenson. The story we got wis that Davie had jumped off the fallen tree intae the pool. Richard cam runnin' tae the hoose here an' telt us that there had been an accident an' that they couldnae find Davie. We found him—at the bottom o' the troot pool.'

Jock watched his old friend relive the agony of that day. No word or gesture seemed appropriate.

Dunkie gazed into the fire, ran his hand over his face and continued. 'An awful accident. Thae things happen. How many crazy things did we dae when we were kids, Jock, an' got off wi' them? This time it wis ma lad Davie. He didnae get off wi' it. Just aboot destroyed his mother and me. Can ye imagine livin' wi' the loss o' yer kid, Jock? Yer eldest son? It's wi' ye every day o' yer life. The wife still cries at night whiles. She still celebrates his birthday, tortures hersel' every year. She still cannae let go."

Dunkie leant forward and tapped out his pipe in the fire.

'A'm goin' tae tell ye somethin' that must never leave this room.'

Jock smiled and nodded.

'Willie Stevenson: the other lad there that day. The poor kid became a basket case after the accident. Nightmares, bed-wettin', depressed—totally withdrawn. Awbuddy pit it doon tae grief at losin' his friend—the trauma o' the experience. He wis sent tae a' kinds o' therapists tae try an' help. Maybe it wis time, maybe it wis drugs an' a clever doctor in Edinburgh, but aboot a year after the accident his faither cam tae me and telt me what had happened that day: his lad wis finally able tae talk aboot it. He'd watched as Richard an' Davie had walked oot ower the troot pool on the fallen tree. Richard had goaded Davie tae jump intae the pool frae the tree. I telt ye it wis maybe fifty feet up. Davie didnae want tae dae it an' wis tryin' tae get back tae the bank. Richard pushed him, Jock. He pushed him off that tree an' Davie fell intae the pool. Willie saw it a'. He saw Davie hit the water, gae doon an' no' cam up again. He tried tae run away but Richard caught him an' pit the fear o' death intae him. We dinnae ken whit wis said but it really fucked him up, Jock, an' he wis terrified tae tell onybuddy what had happened. The family left no' long after. They emigrated tae Australia, A think.

'A never telt the wife, Jock. She couldnae hae handled it. She'd hae killed that little bastard. Nae gid wid hae cam o' it. It's bin ma awful secret a' thae years. A've often wondered why A kept it tae mysel': it wis an awfy burden tae carry. He wis deid, Jock, an' nothing could hae brought him back. A think maybe it wisnae just fir Morag. It was fir Richard's faither. A worshipped that man. How could he hae coped wi' the fact that his son wis a killer?'

Jock sat in stunned silence, his pipe cold and empty in his hand, whisky forgotten, the only sound the crackling logs on the fire and Dunkie's gaze was locked into the flames. A burst of laughter from the kitchen pulled him back.

'That wis the last time we saw Richard here fir years. Robbie cam every year fir the summer, an' some other holidays, tae. Lived here wi' us as part o' the family. Sometimes he'd gae doon tae his mum's place in Devon, he loved it there too, but he'd never gae ony place his brother wis. Refused tae gae tae Eton. Upset his dad a bit, broke the tradition it did. Credit tae the Colonel, he didnae try tae force him. Robbie wanted tae stay in Scotland an' went tae Gordonstoun: he loved it there. It wis right handy. When he wis young A used tae pop ower there an' pick him up fir long weekends. Whenever he could get away A'd collect him an' bring him hame. He used tae share a room wi' Calum which wis fine, but then the Colonel built a wee extension fir us wi' a room fir Robbie. When he got a bittie older he'd hitch-hike tae Inverness, or the village if he wis lucky, an' A'd pick him up. Aye, he wis a second son right enough. When he got his drivin' licence then it wis nae bother. Except that he started bringin' girlfriends wi' him. Didnae bother me, right nice girls they were but Morag was a wee bittie funny till she got used tae it. A' this cohabitin' didnae gae doon well. She's a wee bittie auld fashioned ye ken. Widnae let Calum dae it mind, but it wis different wi' Robbie. Aye, she got used tae it. Robbie ey asked if he could bring them an' she couldnae say no. She got used tae it—there wis nae bother.

'Richard never cam here again until he wis a teenager. Arrogant little shit, liked tae lord it ower awbuddy. He cam fir the stags—he just loved killin' things an' got right upset if he didnae gae off wi' a nice heid.' Dunkie refilled his glass and topped up Jock's.

'So the two boys hated each other?'

Dunkie shook his head. 'No, Robbie didnae hate Richard. At least if he did he never showed a sign o' it. No, I ken Robbie too well. He didnae like him, an' he avoided him. Chalk and cheese, oil and water.'

'You mean no sibling rivalry? There must have been something?'

'Nah, tae hae rivalry ye need competition fir somethin'. Robbie wisnae interested. His mum adored him, an' his faither an' him were right close.

He kent tae keep his distance frae Richard. Robbie's got it all: handsome, charismatic, an athlete an artist; and a bloody good musician. No' that Richard didnae hae talents mind. He wis a great athlete: got a blue fir cricket an' rowin' at Oxford and a scratch golfer. That made his faither right proud. Had nae interest in art or music though. Robbie's no' stupid, but it wis Richard got the biggest share o' the brains. Brilliant he wis, or so awbuddy said. Robbie didnae want tae be a duke. He had his own life an' wis happy.'

'But you said something really upset him?' Dunkie drained his glass and nodded. 'Aye, really upset him.'

Dunkie explained that Robbie's mum didn't approve of all this primogenitor stuff. Ogilvies, yes, she believed it should go to Richard. He, for all his faults, was brilliant and loved banking, London, and all the city stuff. But she felt the Dunmorey estate should go to Robbie. The Colonel was adamant. It was the seat of the Dukedom and must pass to the elder son and heir to the title. Besides, he knew that the estate was not viable as an entity. It more or less broke even under his efficient management, but city money was needed to sustain it. The bank and the estate were inseparable. But Robbie's mother had her own money and her estate in Devon, and that was all to go to Robbie.

'And Robbie was happy with that?'

Dunkie laughed. 'Happy? He wis bloody delighted. The news o' it pulled him oot o' the bit o' a depression he wis in after his mother got killed. He loves Dunmorey but he wis content tae accept the inevitable.'

Jock looked at Dunkie, prompting him to continue, but Dunkie was in no hurry. He leisurely topped up both glasses, loaded his pipe, fired it up, sat back and looked at Jock.

'Ye asked if the twa boys hated each other. A telt ye aboot Robbie, he hates naebuddy—it's no' in him. But Richard hated Robbie. Makes little sense, but he did. Maybe the man wis just so full o' poison he hated awbuddy. A psychiatrist's dream, A reckon. He resented Robbie: his talents, the obvious love o' his parents, his personality. He didnae want Robbie tae hae onything so it stuck in his craw when his mother's will left the lot tae Robbie.'

'OK, don't tell me, Richard contested his mother's will?'

Dunkie nodded. 'Clever Mr Policeman. Got his smart lawyers in London ontae it. Richard won again. Robbie learned a couple o' weeks ago that the will's been overturned. He disnae hae the money tae fight back. He's bin well and truly shafted. Richard wis set tae get the lot.'

Jock's head was spinning, and not from the whisky. 'Bloody hell, Dunkie, you've just set up Robbie with the perfect motive.'

Dunkie smiled. 'A've no' finished yet Jock. A'm no' telling ye onything ye widnae hae dug up yersel'. A ken yer reputation. Just savin' ye a bit o' time.'

Dunkie took a sip of his whisky and relit his pipe. 'We were talking aboot Richard. He used tae pester Cathy. Ye've seen her picture on the dresser: she's a lovely looking girl. He seemed tae think it wis his lordly right tae screw the peasants. Cathy hated him, an' she wis ey on edge when he wis up here.'

'He had the sense to back off then?'

Dunkie gave him a look that sent a shiver down Jock's spine. There was more—and worse, to come.

'Aboot eight years ago; aye, Cathy wid hae been aboot eighteen. He wis up here wi' twa o' his pals: a right pair o' aristocratic tossers they wis, baith oot o' the same mould as Richard. Supposed tae be here fir the stalkin'. One o' them couldnae walk the length o' hissel' an' just sat in the Lodge an' drank whisky a' day. But the other made it up the hill. Yon wis a hell o' a day. Moaned the whole time until we finally got ontae a stag. Big beast it wis. Sitting target, but he faffed aboot an' the beast saw us an' took off. That should hae bin that, but no, he wisnae goin' tae lose that beast. He took a shot at it as it wis runnin' off—the daftest thing onybuddy could ever dae. Smashed a foreleg. Took us six hours, an' the length o' the bloody estate tae finally get on him and finish him off. No' Mr Hoity-Toity Lordie's pal o' course, he headed off hame in the huff right after he wounded the beast—wi' a right flea in his ear A can tell ye. A wisnae tae moderate in ma language ye understand.

'That wis on the Thursday. On the Friday they took off in the Colonel's Range Rover. The Colonel wisnae here, ye understand, but he ey kept the car here. Dinnae ken where they went but they were pissed drunk when they got back an' had took oot the side o' the car somewhere on their travels. A right mess they made o' it. The old Colonel loved that car: it wisnae new, maybe five years old, but immaculate. Richard wis right keen that his faither widnae ken aboot it. A'd hae been right happy if he had, but tae avoid upsettin' the Colonel, A sent Richard doon tae see a young lad in the village who'd just set up a body repair shop. Hughie MacRae, a real artist he wis. Poor Hughie, cam off his bike and killed hissel' no' long ago. Anyway, Hughie made a beautiful job o' it. Gid as new. Spare parts on thae cars cost a fortune, especially new body panels. Beatin' oot wis nae gid fir Richard, a' had tae be replaced. Hughie had tae buy the lot in on his credit. Wis quite a few thousand pounds just fir parts. Richard threw him a cheque fir five hundred, said it wis a crap job, an' that was a' it wis worth. He just laughed at Hughie—an' the cheque bounced. Just aboot broke him, him just startin' oot, workin' on a bank loan as it wis. Fortunately his bank extended credit. Unfortunately the Colonel wis oot o' the country at the time an' his office widnae let me hae ony contact details fir him. It wis a month or so efter, when he cam up here afore A could tell him whit had happened. He wis right upset. Paid Hughie what he wis owed, wi' a generous bit extra. He wis sittin' where you're sittin' noo when A telt him. He wis right shook up. Didnae say much, just that that boy was becomin' a constant source o' pain an' disappointment, so God knows whit else he'd been up tae. The Colonel never said. He just finished his dram an' went off—he widnae even stay fir his dinner. Right upset he wis.'

Jock relit his pipe and passed his pouch to Dunkie. Both men sat in companionable silence sucking on their pipes. Jock was eager to pull

Dunkie back to the subject of his daughter Cathy. He could see that Dunkie was getting tired and Jock was afraid that tonight would be a one-off. An atmosphere like this was unlikely ever to be recreated.

'You were talking about Cathy. There's something you want to talk more about?'

Dunkie looked sadly at Jock. 'Ye're a policeman Jock. An old friend, but a policeman. A maybe shouldnae be talkin' tae ye like this.'

Jock nodded. 'Aye, Dunkie, maybe you're right, but I need all the help I can get on this one.' Dunkie got to his feet and walked to the dresser and picked up the old family photo. He wiped the glass with his sleeve as he made his way back to his chair. He studied the picture for a few moments, lost in thought.

'This is the only photo we've got o' us a' thegither Jock: the only one.'

Jock was sure he'd lost him, when Dunkie suddenly stood up. 'I think some coffee would dae us gid. A've got a bit tae gae yet.' He patted Jock on the shoulder as he headed for the kitchen. As he re-entered the lounge he turned and called to his wife. 'Proper coffee mind, none o' yon instant rubbish—an' strong.'

Dunkie sat down and relit his pipe. 'That same weekend, when he messed up the car, Richard wanted his mates tae hae a slap-up meal. Fresh shot venison an' a' the trimmin's. Nothin' unusual in that, an' he was even very polite when he asked the wife if she'd mind preparin' it. Morag did maist o' the cookin' fir the guests at the Lodge; got well paid fir it mind, so she wis happy enough tae agree tae dae it. But she'd hurt her ankle an' wisnae very mobile, so Cathy offered tae help. Morag wis back aboot 10.00, an' we went straight tae bed. Cathy had stayed on tae finish clearin' up an' tae gae them their coffee. She didnae cam doon tae breakfast the next mornin'. It wis Sunday so we thought nuthin' aboot it. Morag took her up some tea, said she was havin' "wimmen's trouble" an' took her up some Asprins. A had tae tak Richard and his pals tae the airport, an' Cathy wis still in bed when A got back, but Morag didnae seem bothered. She didnae look too good on the Monday but went off tae school as usual. But when she couldnae get oot o' bed on Tuesday we called the doctor: old Dr Cameron, oor doctor—he'd delivered Cathy.'

There was a knock on the door and Morag came in with a large jug of steaming coffee and a plate of her homemade shortbread. The men thanked her as she poured cups for them and, realizing that conversation was not wanted, she discreetly left.

'As A wis sayin: Dr Cameron. A real good doctor o' the auld-school. If it had been one o' his assistants, one o' thae youngsters, God knows whit wid hae happened.'

Dunkie sat back and sipped appreciatively at his coffee. 'Naebuddy kens ony o' this Jock, ootside the family that is. An' you a policeman.' He took a deep breath and continued. 'The doctor wis wi' her fir ages. Me an' Morag were sittin' oot there in the kitchen when he cam doon lookin' right upset—he wis real angry. We thought at first Cathy had upset him, but it wisnae that. He didnae ken whit tae say an' we just looked at him, appealing like. I got up an' poured him a dram; he ey had wee dram when he visited. He threw it doon in one an' cam oot wae it. You're a policeman Jock, have ye no' guessed?'

'Aye Dunkie. She'd been raped.'

'No' just raped, Jock. Raped an' buggered—bruised an' teeth marks a' ower. They'd really messed her up. Cathy said she remembered nothin' aboot it. Said she remembered one o' the men comin' intae the kitchen an' gaein' her a glass o' wine. She remembers wakin' up lyin' on a couch in the big lounge in the Lodge. Her body telt her something awful had happened but she'd nae recollection. Somehow she made it hame tae bed. Poor kid didnae want tae say onything tae us, didnae want tae mak ony trouble. Dr Cameron was spittin' mad, wis goin' tae call the police. He's meant tae report that sort o' thing but we talked him oot o' it. Cathy widnae press charges onyway. He understood oor loyalty tae the Colonel—he wis an old pal o' the Colonel hissel'. It wisnae right that thae lads got off wi' gang rapin' Cathy but nae gid would hae cam o' makin' a scandal o' it.'

Jock reached over and took Dunkie's wrist. 'It should have been reported, man! You let them get away with it. How many other girls have they done that to? Did you consider that?'

'Aye Jock, we did—but we read the papers. We see whit happens when the press get hold o' stories like that. This widnae hae been a juicy bit o' local *Aberdeen Press and Journal* scandal; this would hae bin national tabloid, *News o' the World* scandal. Ye ken how the victim gets dragged through the dirt. Three fine upstandin' members o' the nobility an' a wee country servin'-girl. She'd hae bin made tae look like dirt. They'd hae destroyed her. No, Jock, we did the right thing.'

Jock shook his head. 'Is there anything you wouldn't have done to protect the old Duke?' Dunkie looked at him, smiled and shook his head.

'And the Duke, did you tell him about it?'

'No' at the time. We even managed tae keep it frae Donnie Cameron fir a long while. Donnie wis Cathy's boyfriend, her husband now. He widnae hae bothered wi' ony policeman; he'd hae been doon tae London wi' a gun—A'm nae kiddin' ye. No Jock, it stayed in the family. Even Robbie wis never telt aboot it.

'An A kept it frae the Colonel until a couple o' years ago—it wis efter Cathy an' Donnie got married. The Colonel kent she wanted lots o' kids an' wondered why nane were comin' along. She'd bin telt that because o' the damage inside it would be unlikely she'd hae ony kids. We were a' right upset when it looked as if the doctors were right. Onyway, one night the Colonel an' me were in here havin' a few drams an' A cam oot wi' it. He broke doon Jock. A'm tellin ye, he sat in your chair blubbin' like a bairn. If he didnae ken it before, he kent it then—he'd conceived a monster. He loved Cathy an' he's bin payin' for top specialists, a' this IVF stuff. Cathy an' Donnie are on their third try—it's a hell o' a business.'

Jock sat back in his chair and rubbed his face with his hands. Dunkie gave him one of his tired smiles and chucked another log on the fire.

'For God's sake, Dunkie, I came here tonight without a single suspect in this case and you've presented me with—how many? Robbie, a sharp-shooting soldier. Donnie Cameron: I assume he's handy with a gun?'

Dunkie nodded.

'Your daughter, can she shoot?'

'Aye, a real Annie Oakley.'

'Even your own wife, for God's sake. Four perfectly good candidates.'

'Five,' said Dunkie, grinning. 'Dinnae forget me. A should be number one on the list. A've hated the bastard an' had a good reason fir longer than onyone. Gettin' kicked off the estate an' the rape o' Dunmorey wis the final straw.'

'Dunkie—are you confessing to the murder of Richard Ogilvie?'

'Well now, Jock, that will depend very much on who ye may set yer sights on. Ye've had a few confidences tonight—just another wee one fir ye.' Dunkie lay back in his armchair and sighed.

'A'm dyin' Jock. Maybe a year or so: bittie more if A'm lucky—lung cancer.' Jock felt as if he'd been slapped and his shock was obvious.

'A thought that wid mak ye sit up. As A said, it's in confidence. Naebuddy kens. Just me—an' now you.'

'Morag?'

Dunkie shook his head. 'No' yet. Only found oot masel' last month. Routine medical fir insurance picked it up. Been a bit below par fir a few months; been a bit breathless fir a while wi' a wee bit o' pain here, side o' ma' chest, an' a bit o' a cough. Had chronic bronchitis fir ages because o' this.' He waved his pipe at Jock. 'Never really thought there wis much wrong.'

'Oh my God, Dunkie, I'm sorry. Bloody hell, man—what about treatment?'

'Fir lung cancer? Forget it Jock. They put folk through hell. Surgery, radiotherapy, chemo, an' a' that fir what? For fuck-all. Awbuddy dies—A've seen enough o' them. Nah, A'll just go quietly wi' some dignity.

'So ye see Jock—suspect number one. Motive, means, an' fuck-all tae lose. Ye want tae arrest me noo?'

Chapter 18

Jock and Meg were first up on Sunday and took Nick and Gyp for an early morning walk. It was a glorious, calm, clear morning; the woodlands with their hint of reds and yellows were fresh from the night's rain, and a low-lying mist was still hanging in places.

'No wonder they all love this place, Jock. It's a wee bit of heaven.' Jock hugged Meg, and she tucked her arm in his as they took a path along the bank of the River Monnie. Jock needed to talk through the events of the previous evening and his wife was the perfect sounding board and confidante. He needed to get his thoughts in order. He talked as they wandered; Meg listened but offered little comment. Jock stopped suddenly and Meg felt him stiffen. Any words would have been drowned by the roar of the Monnie as it waterfalled into a large deep pool. Jock drew Meg further down the path until the roar of the water was pleasantly muted and together they sat on a fallen log overlooking the pool.

'The troot pool.'

Meg looked questioningly at him—he'd skipped that part of the story.

'Aye, the troot pool. You can see a few big ones from up here.'

'If it was a wee bit warmer Jock, I'd be in for a swim. It's not too cold for them though.' Nick and Gyp were both straight into the water after a stick thrown by Jock.

'Aye, Meg, used to be a right popular swimming place. Aye, used to be.' He told her the story and put his arm round her as she quietly sobbed.

'The bastard, Jock. What a hateful person. And it's your job to find out who killed him. My God Jock, what if it was Dunkie, or Cathy—or even Morag?'

Jock shrugged and lowered his head. 'Aye Meg, bit too close to home this one. It's getting a wee bit difficult for me to retain my policeman's cold objectivity.' He looked at his watch. 'Come on love, we said we'd be back for breakfast.'

Sunday breakfast was a late affair in the Munro household, a special family occasion and all attended if they could. When Jock and Meg got back, the whole family was there. Morag and Cathy were setting up the outside table while the men: Dunkie, Calum and Donnie Cameron stood chatting in the warm sunshine. All conversation stopped for a few moments as the newcomers joined the company. Jock, Dunkie's old friend, but sadly also Jock the policeman, had arrived. The women laid out a slap-up meal, a full "English" breakfast, made a bit more Scottish with lots of fried black pudding, fried oatcakes and dumpling. It was a very relaxed affair. If there were any guilty consciences in the group, anyone nervous about Jock's presence, it certainly didn't show, and there was no talk about Lordie to dampen the atmosphere. It was a very happy family gathering and Jock felt privileged to be included. Looking round, he couldn't imagine a cold-blooded murderer amongst them. He'd been a policeman too long to be easily fooled by outward appearances, but he tucked such thoughts behind him as he buttered another slice of Morag's homemade bread.

Jock was sitting beside Donnie Cameron who proudly told him about the farm. Jock was especially interested in the Highland cattle and complimented him on the large bull he'd seen in the roadside field.

Donnie beamed at him. 'Aye, that would be old Arthur: Benlochy Arthur, Pride o' Dunmorey, to give him his posh name. Champion three years running at the Highland Show. He's thrown some lovely calves. The old Colonel loved his beasts, but Arthur was his favourite, though.'

Jock felt Dunkie tap him on the shoulder.

'Is yersel' an' Meg up fir a wee tour o' the establishment?'

'Me too!' called Morag. 'A'm leavin' this mess fir you lot tae clear up.' Calum gave a good-natured moan of complaint and started gathering the dishes.

'Ye'll be travellin' in style,' said Dunkie as they walked to the front of the house. 'Compliments o' Robbie, jump in folks.' Dunkie climbed into the driving seat of a Range Rover parked by a mud-splattered Land Rover. 'This is a wee bittie mair comfy than that auld thing,' he said, indicating the Land Rover.

With the two men in the front, the two women chatting away in the back and two excited dogs running along behind them, Dunkie drove the half mile or so to the Lodge. The dogs would be allowed to run round at the Lodge, but on the reserve they would be confined to the Range Rover—busy dogs and nature reserves don't mix.

Jock had seen the Lodge many times before but was still blown away by the tasteful grandeur of the place. In all weathers the Lodge would be impressive; but that morning, bathed in bright sunlight, set in a park of mature woodland by the shore of the lochan, the view of Dunmorey Lodge was breathtaking.

Dunkie was smiling. 'Quite a place eh? Granite, Jock. Built by the first Duke. Took ower four years tae build. The granite wis carted—an' A mean carted—horse an' carted a' the way frae Aberdeen. They didnae rush things in them days. Built tae last, no' like yer modern rubbish.'

Meg shook her head in amazement. 'How many rooms?'

Morag thought for a few moments. 'Bedrooms ye mean? Twenty; no' countin' the servant's quarters. A' thegither A've nae idea—ye can hae a wee count yersel' when A tak ye roond!

'Back in them days they needed lots o' space. Folk just didnae pop up fir the weekend. Guests had tae cam up frae the South, frae London even. A hell o' a journey. A'm telt maist cam by boat tae Inverness, but even that wis a bit o' an adventure. When they got here they stayed fir the season. The place wis often full up. They had some right wild times it seems. There's a couple o' old diaries in the Lodge ye can hae a look at. One o' them, written by a Lady Camilla Somethin' Or Other wisnae meant tae be read by onybuddy else—real intimate stuff ye could say. No' whit A'd call lady-like behaviour. They Victorians were only stuffy on the ootside. Yon Camilla was a right rompy wee thing. It's a' written doon in graphic detail: the orgies, the wife swappin', how big Lord So An' So wis, how useless the Duke O' Wherever was. It's a' there in immaculate, but tiny handwritin'.' Morag smiled at Meg. 'A'm guessin' by the look on yer face yer keen tae hae a wee peek at it, eh?'

Meg stared in awe at the face of the Lodge. 'The windows, Jock. Just look at those windows.' Meg walked over and ran her hand over the heavily-leaded frames. 'The stained glass: it's magnificent—Jo will have to come and see this.'

'Aye, ye must bring yer daughter roond soon; A'm dyin' tae meet her. Ye've no' seen nothin' yet though, come on inside.'

An hour later, sitting in the big kitchen with a cup of tea, Meg was still trying to contain herself. 'You remember that country house we went to a couple of summers ago, Jock? Hopetown was it; that big place near Edinburgh? That place was grand right enough—fair crammed full of all those antiques, but I could never imagine livin' in a place like that. But here in the Lodge—lots of antique stuff right enough, but nice tasteful antiques that suit the place, nothing posh and showy. It feels so homely, it's so comfy looking. The pine floors and wood panelling, and all those Persian carpets; those huge fireplaces—and the four-poster beds! I'd live here in a minute. But I didn't like all those animal heads on the walls though: I'd get rid of them. Aye, it's a place to die for.'

Meg threw an embarrassed hand to her mouth when she realized what she'd said. 'I'm sorry, Dunkie, Morag, I didn't mean to . . .'

Morag patted her arm and laughed. 'Aye Meg, but ye're right though.' Morag excused herself and left the kitchen returning a few minutes later carrying two books. One was a leather-bound diary which she handed to Meg. 'Have a read, A'm sure Robbie'll no' mind ye borrowin' it, An' Lady Camilla's long past carin'. A've no' read it a' masel' yet. The writing's right neat but too small tae pick up easy; strained ma eyes it did. A often wonder aboot it. It wis hidden. Robbie asked us tae hae a bit o' a clean oot after Richard got killed. It wis in that room ye loved, the one wi' the big four-poster lookin' oot ower the lochan. A found it when A pulled oot a drawer and turned it ower tae get a' the dust o' years oot. The bottom fell oot—an' the diary. It had been hidden under a false bottom. A often wonder aboot Lady Camilla, why did she leave it there? Maybe she just forgot a' aboot it when she left, easy done A suppose. Like Dunkie forgettin' his passport when we wis gaein' tae Spain. Silly bugger. Calum had tae drive like hell tae Inverness wi' it. Just got the flight.

'An' this other one. Right interestin'. A found it wi' some auld books in another bedroom.'

Meg flipped through the second book which was larger, also leather-bound. It was a journal, clearly written by a man. No name, only his initials imprinted on the leather cover. Meg was intrigued, and Morag told her she was welcome to borrow both books. Meg was very interested in history, in anything historical. The Victorian period she had always found to be fascinating, so she was excited at the prospect of an intimate insight to the life of early Victorian gentry.

Even to drive round the estate, with lots of stopping to take in the views, took almost two hours. Where the road out of the glen started to drop into the strath, Dunkie had pulled over and stopped. Beneath them the wide strath stretched from the Cromarty Firth in the east and towards Glen Affric in the west.

'How much of it is Dunmorey?' Meg asked.

Dunkie pointed out the boundaries and Jock whistled. 'A fair whack o' land right enough Dunkie—it would make a right nice golf course.'

Dunkie threw him a dark look. 'A'm taken ye doon now tae the old Duke's pride and joy—tae his nature reserve. Ye can see some o' it frae here. See that big lochan an' all them big trees? That's it, or a wee part o' it. A see ye've got yer binoculars wi' ye Jock. Ye'll be wettin' yersel' in a wee minute. Ye fancy seein' a few ospreys?'

Jock put the glasses to his eyes. 'You're winding me up, ye wee bugger.'

'Wid A dae that tae you Jock? Come on then, jump in.' As they drove, Dunkie described the old Duke's and Colonel Sanderson's vision for the reserve. He explained that the whole estate was really a nature reserve, that the farm had been run organically for years, and farmed, as far as practicable using traditional practices to encourage as much wildlife as possible.

'"Maximum diversity", the Duke called it.' They've done a right gid job. Ye'll see mair birdies an' beasties here than onywhere else in Scotland. Ye'll like the otters, Jock. Maybe none aroond today but we've got lots o' them. But you're a birdman A'm thinkin'—got lots o' ducks fir ye.'

When they tried to take a walk along the side of the lochan, Meg was reminded of something her old mother used to say to her. "If you want a good walk, never go with a photographer or a birdwatcher." They only made a few hundred yards as Jock was locked to his binoculars every few paces and was all for just sitting and watching. The world stood still for him as he watched a pair of ospreys swoop and pluck fish from the water.

Jock was entranced. 'Ye were no' kiddin' me, Dunkie, ye lovely wee man, ye were no' kiddin' me.'

At the head of the lochan, set back among the trees on a grassy hill with a commanding view over the whole, was a small white croft house: a picture postcard of a place.

Dunkie pointed up the hill. 'Colonel Sanderson's hoose. Well no' his exactly, but near enough. The Colonel, the Duke that is, had some deal wi' Dougie aboot it. Dougie did the whole place up. Made a real nice job o' it. Used tae come here a lot fir his birds. He had a right lot tae dae wi' the reserve. Hissel' an' the Duke, they worked thegither on it. Right close that pair were. Ye'll be wantin' a wee look at the place?'

The party followed Dunkie up the hill; the short climb exhausted Dunkie, and he was breathing heavily as he took a seat on an old wooden bench by the cottage door. He leaned back against the wall of the old building. 'This'll be older than the Lodge—had a wee bit o' renovation since, mind ye. It would hae had a turf roof at one time. Aye, built tae last. Ye'll see the thickness o' the walls: must be three feet.' Dunkie stood up, took some keys from his pocket and opened the small wooden door of the croft house. 'Don't suppose Dougie'll be mindin' eh?' Jock had to duck through the entrance, and inside he felt his that head almost brushed the low ceiling.

Dougie had indeed done a fine job on the renovation. To one end was a small bedroom with an en suite toilet and shower, and the remaining space was a lounge and small galley kitchen. Comfy armchairs were set round a big fireplace and colourful rugs covered the old flagged floor. In front of one small window was a big worktable on which a large map was laid out. Dunkie leant over the map and his finger traced a red encircling line. He smiled at Jock. 'That's the reserve.' He pointed out the main features. 'Lots o' new developments planned. See here an' here, mair native woodlands were tae be planted, an' this stream here wis tae be dammed tae mak another wee lochan—that whole area there wis tae be a wetland. An' that was just fir this year.'

Dunkie bent to look out of the small window.

'The 16th tee.' Jock looked at him. 'Aye, the 16th tee, just ootside the door there. An' ye see doon there on the other side o' the burn goin' intae the lochan? There's yer 16th green. The lochan would be a nice big wet bunker, eh Jock? You're a golfer—a tricky wee par three? Aye, it wis a' planned oot. We found a' the maps o' the course up at the Lodge. Ye can hae a look at them later.'

'Aye, Dunkie. Under different circumstances I could get quite excited about a golf course here. Your Lordie had vision, whatever else he had or hadn't got. This place would put Gleneagles in the shade if it was developed.'

Dunkie smiled at him. 'Wid be nothin' left o' the place as we know it, though. An' an awfy lot o' birdies an' beasties widnae be right happy either.'

After a quick trip round the home farm and a closer look at the Highland cattle, they headed back home. The rest of the family had gone, the women headed for the kitchen to prepare the promised haunch of venison, and Jock and Dunkie resumed their chairs in the lounge with cups of tea.

Dunkie was relaxed and seemed happy to talk, but Jock felt that he'd exhausted the subject of the death of Richard Ogilvie for the moment. Dunkie drained his tea, got up and poured them each a dram.

Jock took a sip of whisky. 'I only learned about Dougie's VC after he died.'

Dunkie sipped his drink and smiled. 'Aye, he never talked aboot it. Winnin' medals usually involves killin' folk, Jock. You dinnae think aboot it at the time—ye cannae—it's them or us. It's afterwards it haunts ye whiles. The look on the terrified faces when ye pull that trigger or put the knife in.' Dunkie was lost in thought for a few moments. 'A'm thinkin' ye want me tae tell ye aboot the Colonel's VC?'

Jock smiled and nodded. 'So you know all the gory details then?'

'Aye Jock, A do. A wis there. It's a' in the citation, but that's no' the half o' it. But a cannae tell ye aboot just one medal. Baith wis got in the same action, ma MM and his VC.'

Dunkie refilled their glasses, lit up his pipe, and lay back with a sigh. 'We were oot in Oman. Ye ken where that is?'

Jock nodded. 'Bottom end of the Persian Gulf.'

'Clever man. A didnae ken where it wis when we went there. There's ey been a British presence oot there. It's a civilized kind o' Arab country—well, kind o' civilized. There is, or at least thee wis, British officers in the Omani army. Ex-British army officers. We train the locals, hiv done fir years—an' still dae as far as A ken. Every noo an' again oor lads gae oot there tae dae a bit o' desert trainin' an' tae help oot the locals if there's a bit o' bother. There's ey bother oot there. The tribes are ey fechtin' amongst theresels or havin' a wee go at the government. When we wis there, there wis talk aboot a load o' foreign Arabs comin' intae the country frae the Yemen, that's right next tae Oman. They wis supposed tae hae been trained by the Russians. The Egyptians were right busy creatin' hell in the Yemen at that time an' were sendin' loads o' murderin' bastards intae Oman tae stir up trouble. They said they'd cam up frae Yemen, but they werenae a' Yemenis. There wis a load o' Afghans among them. They were right wild, cruel bastards. Great fighters though—the Afghans that is. The Arabs are right brave when there's a hundred o' them an' a handful o' us, but they're a bunch o' old wimmen when it cams doon tae it. Onyway, nane o' they bastards cared a damn aboot politics. It's a' just a bit o' fun tae them. Chuck them an AK47 and the chance o' a bit o' rape an' pillage an' they're up for it. Nothin's changed wi' thae bastards—they're still at it.

'Onyway, a few of us went oot fir a wee recce: a wee look roond. We wanted tae speak tae a friendly local sheikh tae find oot what he kent. We were only four Land Rovers, twelve men. We didnae expect ony trouble. Oor area wis in the north an' had been quiet fir months. The Colonel o' the regiment wis wi' us, he wanted tae tak a wee jaunt. He wisnae one o' thae desk Colonels, he ey liked tae be oot an' aboot. There wis four o' us in oor Land Rover. Him an' me, an Intelligence Officer who spoke the lingo, an' Dougie. He wis Captain Sanderson then. We wis in the first Land Rover, A wis drivin'. The village we were goin' tae was on a kind o' plateau. Tae get tae it, we had tae gae up a wadi: a dry riverbed, an' it cam oot on the plateau. It wis easy enough goin' fir the Land Rovers. There wis quite a gid track—bugger all water ever seemed tae gae doon the wadi.

'We wis almost at the top when the bastards hit us. A mortar landed right ahent oor Land Rover. We wis a' hit by shrapnel. A took a couple o' bits in ma back an' shoulder, an' Dougie caught it in his left arm an' neck. Ye mind seein' that big scar on the side o' his neck?'

Jock nodded.

'Well ye widnae hae wanted tae see it when it happened—A thought his heid wis fit tae fa' off. The Colonel wis in a bad way—an' the Intelligence Officer. He lost his arm in the end. The Colonel wis still conscious but in a lot o' pain. We wis trying tae get awbuddy oot o' the vehicle an' intae some sort o' cover; but there wis bugger all cover in the wadi, when a second mortar bomb hit the Land Rover ahent—right in the middle. Three o' the lads had already got oot but one in the back who manned the machine gun wis still there trying tae unhitch it. There wisnae much left o' him. Charley Brooks wis his name. Fine lad, had a wife an' twa kiddies.

'They were ready fir us. They'd obviously sighted in on the wadi—nae bloody rangin' shots. They bastards were trained: they kent whit they were daein'. The lads frae the third Rover got oot an' clambered up the side o' the wadi—it wis quite steep wher they wis. As soon as they stuck their heids up they started tae get it frae a machine gun. One o' the lads got hit on the side o' the heid. It wisnae fatal but he wis oot o' action. We managed tae get the Colonel an' the Intelligence Officer oot o' the Rover an' Dougie an' me got oorsels up the side o' the wadi an' had a peek ower. The village wis aboot fifty yards away. There wis a mud wall aboot four feet high roond the place an' the bastards were ahent that, shootin' through gaps in the wall. We couldnae tell how many there wis, but frae the amount o' firin' there wis quite a few. There wis one heavy machine gun an' a light machine gun blastin' awa at us an' more AK47's than we could easy count—an' that bloody mortar kept lobbin' bombs at us. The Colonel an' the other officer managed tae crawl up beside us. A found them a rifle each but neither wis in a fit state tae use a gun.

'They had us cold, Jock. We couldnae move. We had wounded so we couldnae just run away doon the wadi, and they kept lobbin' in the mortar bombs. We were stuck. We couldnae get up oot o' the wadi an' there wis nae cover onywhere. It wis a matter o' time. If the mortar didnae get us, they'd move in an' tak us when it got dark.

'The last Rover wis aboot fifty yards back. We ey kept a goqd spacin' in case o' this sort o' thing. We couldnae communicate wi' they lads though. Sergeant Willie Moore: Mad Willie we called him wis wi' that Rover. A real little terrier he wis—he loved a good scrap. Onyway he decided he had tae dae somethin', so he backs up the Rover, drove it straight up the side o' the wadi ontae the flat an' drove like hell straight at the bastards. There wis a machine gun mounted on the back, and the gunner, Jimmy MacAlistair wis gein' them hell. The Arabs were ahent that wall A telt ye aboot, so A dinnae think he hit bugger all—but he was tryin' tae get them tae keep their heid doon. Stevie Baxter wis in the front wi' Willie Moore an' he wis blastin' away wi' a Tommy gun. They were maist o' the way tae the wall when they ran intae a RPG: that's a rocket-propelled grenade. The Rover went up in the air an' the lads were thrown oot. They werenae deid, nane o' them then, but we could see they wis wounded an' they were tryin' tae crawl ahent the Rover fir some cover—an' a machine gun wis layin' intae them. The Arabs threw a smoke grenade but it wisnae right effective, an' we could see a few o' them runnin' through the smoke towards the Rover. A fired at them and one o' them went doon.

'We kent what they wanted Jock. They wanted prisoners: live prisoners. They liked tae hae fun wi' white prisoners, Jock. A canny describe what they did tae them. A saw the results once.'

Dunkie poured himself another dram and was silent for a few moments. 'Aye Jock, ye wouldnae believe that one human bein' could dae that tae another.

'We could hear the wounded lads shoutin' an' screamin' as the bastards started tae drag them back tae the wall, but we couldnae shoot fir fear o' hittin' oor ain lads.

'Efter that it wis like somethin' oot o' one o' they Hollywood war movies ye see on the TV. Dougie was sare wounded mind an' still bleedin' frae the wound on his neck. The dressin' A'd pit on him wisnae daein' much. He didnae hae full use o' his left arm either. Anyway, Dougie filled his pockets wi' hand grenades; stuck a fresh magazine intae his Tommy gun, shouted for us tae cover him best we could, climbed oot o' the wadi an' ran straight at the bastards, jinkin' tae try an' pit them off their aim. A dinnae ken what got intae me, but A wisnae aboot tae let Dougie gae off on his ain, so A got up an' took efter him. How we made it a' the way tae the wall, A dinnae ken. We baith took a few bullets through oor jackets an' shorts but nuthin' hit us. Dougie flung a few grenades, an' he wis ower the wall afore me an' took oot a few o' them: four A think, twa wi' the heavy machine gun an' twa others. Arabs think they're right brave when they ootnumber ye an' are safe ahent a mud wall, but when the others saw me an' Dougie were ower the wall they started runnin'. Twa o' them were aimin' their guns at oor wounded lads, an' A'm sure they wis gonnae kill them but me an' Dougie dropped them afore they could fire.

'We heard a truck revvin' up in the village. They'd reloaded yon RPG a telt ye aboot, an' it wis lyin' there aside a deid Arab. Dougie grabbed it an' ran intae the village an' A took off wi' him. There wis a pick-up in the wee square in the middle o' the village. There wis four o' the bastards in the back o' it an' it wis just drivin' off, an' twa o' them wis sprayin' bullets at us when we ran intae the square. Cool as ye like, wi' bullets flyin' at him, Dougie tried tae aim the RPG, but his left arm wis buggered. A propped the end on ma shoulder an' he aimed an' fired it. It hit the back o' the cab o' the pickup—got a' o' the bastards: four in the back o' the truck an' three in the front. There wisnae much left o' them A can tell ye—the RPG had set off a load o' ammo on the truck.

'That wis aboot it—or we thought it wis. The Arabs were a' deid, an' we were kind o' draggin' oorsels back tae the others when we found the villagers. They'd been butchered, Jock—all o' them. The women raped then butchered; an'little kiddies wi' their throats cut aside their deid mothers. Aboot a dozen men an' young boys had been lined up against a wall an' machine-gunned. The heid man: the Sheikh, the friendly Sheikh had been nailed tae a door an' cut tae pieces. They'd cut him open an' his guts were on the ground. A couple o' women were raped and deid on the ground in front o' him: they were his wife an' daughter. It looked as if he'd been made tae watch afore they started on him. A whole village slaughtered just because they wis friendly tae the British an' the Government.'

Dunkie looked at Jock. 'Can ye understand noo why we dinnae like tae talk aboot it?'

Jock drained his glass of whisky and nodded.

'A've seen worse, Jock. They Africans in the Congo were worse. Fuckin' animals, they were. It's no' the kind o' thing ye ever get used tae, Jock.

'Onyway, we got one Land Rover serviceable more or less, but nae radio: no' that the damn things ever worked onyway.

'Awbuddy wis wounded, some worse than others. We'd planned tae be oot owernight, tae stay at the village. The Sheikh wis a lovely old guy; he ey killed a couple o' sheep for us an' put on a gid feed. So naebuddy wid be missin' us until late the next day. Ma back an' shoulders were in a bit o' a mess—there were lots o' bits o' shrapnel in me. Hurt like hell it did but A'd no' lost much blood. A wis the fittest o' the lot o' us an' A wis the only one half fit tae drive—the only one wi' twa functional arms an' legs. Another lad, Andy MacIntyre, he cam wi' me. He had a bad leg wound but could still handle a gun if we hit onymair trouble. Afore we went, awbuddy wis got up intae the village an' made as comfy as possible. We'd a lot o' morphine so it wisnae too bad fir the sare wounded. It wis a four-hour drive back tae the base, a shite o' a bumpy drive at the best o' times, Jock. Onyway, we made it. We had one helicopter, but they decided no' tae send it afore the mornin'. It wis dark, ye see by the time we got tae the base.

'We lost twa men killed. Mad Willie Moore took one in the chest an' died just after we rescued him, an' Charlie Brooks who got a direct hit frae the mortar. The Intelligence Officer lost an arm, but awbuddy else wis back at it in a month or so.

'They dinnae usually give oot medals, specially the big ones for scraps in them wee wars—especially wee wars we're no' really meant tae be in. They hand them oot maistly fir propaganda purposes in the big wars. It makes the folk at home right happy tae hae a few heroes. But ony o' they heroes'll tell ye there were braver men than them got nae recognition. We got ours because we saved the Colonel's and the Intelligence Officer's skins—an' A mean that literally, Jock. If they bastards had got us alive—an' they could have—they love tae flay ye alive. Aye an' other things an' all. They just love tae hae fun cuttin' up white men.

'Ye like Kipling, Jock?'

Jock nodded.

'Top shelf there: a' Kipling. Canny mind what the poem's called; it'll cam tae me.' Dunkie took a sip of his whisky and stared into the fire. 'A'm ey minded o' it.

'"When ye're wounded an' left on the Afghan plains, an' the women come oot tae cut up whit remains, ye roll on yer rifle an' blow oot yer brains, an' ye gae tae yer Gawd like a soldier."'

'That wis us Jock. We'd hae fought the buggers off tae the second last bullet.

'The Colonel widnae tak no fir an answer. He pushed like hell an' we got oor medals. That's it, Jock. As A telt ye, oor citations dinnae quite describe what really happened.' Dunkie got up and quietly left the room, leaving Jock in numbed silence.

Being honest with himself, Jock had to admit that he was uncomfortable with what had to be his next step first thing the following morning: to begin investigating these people, his friends, as possible murder suspects. Dunkie came back in with a full bottle of whisky, poured two more drams and sat back down in his chair. Jock looked across at his old friend. He was lying back with his eyes closed. The trip round the estate and the reliving of the horror of Oman had taken it out of him.

Jock wondered if he was he looking at the tired, drawn old face of a calculating killer? He knew that there were few limits to a man's capability in defence of his family. He suspected that Dunkie had often put his life on the line in defence of his Colonel, the Duke, when in uniform. He'd admitted the previous evening that there were no limits to his loyalty to the Duke. Did the son, Robbie and the estate inspire the same loyalty? Jock somehow felt that they did. Killing had been Dunkie's trade for years. Would the shooting of the despised Richard disturb the conscience of a dying man? Sadly, Jock felt that he knew the answer.

Chapter 19

The Monday Morning Service was concluded, and DI Bob McLean was charged with obtaining statements from the list of suspects conveniently supplied by Dunkie Munro. With other pressing matters dealt with, Jock was preparing to enjoy a quiet coffee and a pipe when his phone rang: it was his daughter. Jock had a moment of panic when the switchboard informed him. She never called him at the office, so it was with some apprehension that he took the call—he wished he'd dodged it.

'My mannequin, Dad. Where is it? I need it today. Can you please have it dropped round at the shop? Dad, Dad—are you still there? Damn, have we been cut off?'

Jock was sitting in stunned silence. The last he'd seen of the dummy was in Dunmorey—full of holes and well spattered with mud, being carried down the glen as a sort of trophy by a proud Calum Munro. His heart sank.

'No, no, I'm here, love. I was just in the middle of something important. You were asking about your dummy.'

'Mannequin, Dad. A dummy's something a tailor sticks pins in, or a father who doesn't return something to a busy angry daughter as he promised. I am sorry to bother you at the office, but I need him. I need him this morning. You'd better not have damaged him, Dad—you've not, have you?'

'No, of course not, Jo, but I'm in a meeting right now—I'll get back to you.'

'I don't need you to get back to me Dad; please have him dropped round as soon as possible, got to go.'

Jock slowly replaced the phone and swore quietly to himself. How to screw up an otherwise quite pleasant Monday morning. How was he going to get out of this one? He lifted the phone again and asked DC Ross to come to his office urgently.

An apprehensive Jamie Ross arrived a few minutes later.

'You wanted to see me sir?'

'Aye lad, that mannequin. The one we used as target practice. Any idea what happened to it?'

'Oh aye, the dummy from the glen.'

'Mannequin lad: mannequin. A dummy's someone who pisses off his boss.'

'Yes sir, sorry sir. The mannequin's downstairs, parked in the coffee room. You need it sir?'

Jock felt a slight relief—at least it wasn't lost. Maybe best to say it's lost, or stolen maybe. He couldn't return it as it was.

Jock sighed. 'Aye lad, bring it up, will you.' Jock sipped in distaste at his cold coffee. His pipe tasted bitter.

Jamie was back before Jock had a chance to formulate a convincing story for Jo. He stood the mannequin, now dressed in an old shirt, by Jock's desk. 'I covered him up a wee bit sir—he was putting the girls off their work.'

Jock smiled despite himself as he got up from his chair. 'OK, let's have a look.' He pulled the shirt off the dummy and stared in disbelief—there wasn't a mark on him, front or back.

'Amazing what a bit of filler and a re-spray can do, sir. Friend of mine with a car body shop fixed him up.'

Jock gave an embarrassed cough and sat down. 'Thanks lad; thanks very much. You know the boutique on the walking precinct?'

'Aye sir, your daughter's shop.'

Jock nodded. 'Could you please cover up our friend here and deliver him to my daughter. She seems to be in a hurry to get him back.' Jamie picked up the dummy and was heading for the door when Jock called after him.

'DC Ross. Her name's Jo—and I don't think she's in a very good mood.'

Jamie had learned very early on in the job that there's no sense in moaning about an assignment—whatever it is. If your boss tells you to do something, you do it to the best of your ability even if you know—and he knows, that it's bollocks. But delivery boy for a mannequin on a very busy Monday morning he felt was pushing it a bit. Before leaving with a team to Dunmorey, DI McLean had left him with a load of paperwork—and a deadline. This was the last thing he needed. What was so urgent about a bloody dummy?

As usual there was no parking to be had in the town centre, so he was forced to park in the Rose Street multi-storey parking. Half covered with a shirt, a naked dummy is difficult to carry discreetly through the middle of Inverness, so he was not in the best of moods when he finally got to the boutique. And when a snotty little shop girl called over her shoulder that a deliveryman had arrived with a mannequin, he thought his fuse would finally blow.

Jamie considered himself to be a fairly intelligent person. Nothing much ever seriously fazed him, and he felt he was always pretty much in control— until Jo Anderson entered his life. He'd read about it in books, he'd seen it on TV and in the cinema—the macho reduced to jelly by a woman. He'd even seen it in real life; a friend of his reduced to a virtual zombie. He never believed it could happen, and had never wanted it to happen to him.

Jo wasn't beautiful in any classical sense. Not a tanned blue-eyed slinky blonde; not voluptuous, not even tall and leggy which he usually liked. But when the woman who emerged from the back of the shop smiled and held out her hand and introduced herself, he felt the ground move under his feet and his power of speech removed.

Jo smiled and held his gaze as he struggled to compose himself. When she looked at her watch and asked casually if he'd got time for a coffee, he could only nod and grin inanely.

'It's Jamie, isn't it? Dad called and said you were coming.'

'Look after the shop, Tracy. Jamie and I are going next door for a coffee. Call if you need me.'

Seated opposite in the coffee shop, they looked at each other and broke into spontaneous laughter. They each knew that something had happened to both of them. Neither knew how or what—just that it had.

Finally, Jo dabbed her eyes and grinned at Jamie. 'Thanks for delivering my dummy,' which threw them both into another paroxysm. The other customers eyed them curiously but they didn't care. There was little interest in the coffee, but both concentrated on stirring their frothy cappuccinos for a few moments in silence.

Finally Jamie found his voice. 'I can't stay long—I have to get back to the office.'

'And I've got a new window to set up, that's why I needed the mannequin back.'

'Tonight—are you busy tonight?' asked Jamie; then he cursed under his breath.

'Problem? Got something more important arranged?'

'Jo—right now nothing seems more important than seeing you again. Just that tonight we've got a band practice.'

'Band? You play in a band?'

Jamie shrugged. 'Not a band really—not yet anyway. Just a few of us get together and play for fun—though we do have ambitions.'

'What do you play? I'd guess you're lead, maybe rhythm. I can't see you on bass—and certainly not on drums.'

'No, none of that. Not a poxy pop band. Tenor banjo; few other instruments too, but I prefer banjo. "The Dunmorey Ceilidh Band": that's us, for want of a better name at the moment.'

Jo spontaneously grabbed his hand. 'I don't suppose you could use a fiddler, could you?' Before he could respond she pulled her hand away and sat back, her face serious, almost sad.

'I've got a kid, Jamie. Gordie: he's four years old.'

Jamie looked at her, puzzled and concerned by her sudden mood change. 'So? Bring him along if you can't get a babysitter. Bring him along anyway if he enjoys good music.'

Jo looked at him. 'You mean it really doesn't bother you that I've got a kid—that I've got baggage?'

'Bloody hell, Jo—why the hell should it?'

Jock looked at Bob McLean over his beer and took a bite of his cheese sandwich. 'Well, what have you got? Found us a murderer?'

Bob smiled grimly. 'Take your pick, sir. Could be any or all of them. Motive and means, and not an alibi among them. None of them made any secret of their hatred for Ogilvie. Somebody did that family a big favour. I think all of them would be happy enough to take credit for it. No confessions though, I'm afraid.'

'Your gut feeling?'

DI McLean toyed with his sandwich then flipped open his notebook. 'I'd discount Duncan Munro. He saw the shooting party off that morning and freely admits that he took off in his Land Rover, his own gun with him. Why tell me that? There were no witnesses.'

'Unless, of course, he wants to set himself up?'

Bob McLean shrugged. 'Could be. Said he was after a big dog fox he'd spotted sniffing round down by the river. Says he got back to the Lodge just before Lachie arrived in great excitement with the news.

'I timed a drive up through the woods to the place the shot came from. He had ample time to get up there and make the shot sir—more than enough time. But you're right. I get the feeling he's a bit too keen. He wants us to consider him a suspect.'

Jock nodded. 'I'd wondered if he knows more than he's letting on, but I don't think he does. I agree with you, he'd nothing to do with the shooting, but he's maybe not too sure if one of the family—or Robbie Ogilvie, did have. I made the mistake of involving him in the initial investigations so he knows enough to make a very convincing confession if it came to it—as it would if he thinks we're about to nail any of his folk.'

DI McLean continued. 'The daughter, Cathy. Lovely girl, but just mentioning Ogilvie's name's like taking the top off a volcano. She hated that man with a passion. Self-confessed hot shot with a rifle, she showed me some of her medals and trophies. She keeps her rifle locked up at home. I think she'd be perfectly able to kill him, but I don't think she did.

'Donnie Cameron, her husband. A quiet, controlled man, admitted he would have easily killed Ogilvie when he learned what Ogilvie had done to Cathy. Again no alibi.

'Least likely is Morag Munro. She's a cool customer though. Not much she'd not do in defence of her man or her brood. She says she's fired a rifle often enough, but I doubt if she's got the necessary skill.'

DI McLean sat back with his beer. 'Where next, sir?'

Jock looked at his watch. 'We're interviewing Robert Ogilvie this afternoon. He's coming in from Fort George. There's a man with a serious motive. Opportunity? Wee bit more planning required, but why not? He's a soldier and an officer. That sort of planning's kid's stuff to him. As murderers are usually found close to home, he has to be our number one suspect.'

The interview with Robert Ogilvie was held informally in Jock's office. Coffee was offered and accepted. Jock was struck again by Robbie's resemblance to his brother: the same rugged good looks, blond hair and striking blue eyes. He seemed totally relaxed and forthcoming, freely admitting even the most potentially incriminating facts.

When asked if he was pleased that his brother was dead he shook his head. 'We didn't get on, Superintendent. Never did, even as kids. He was a very strange man, a very unpleasant man in so many respects, driven by something we can't comprehend. But he was my brother, my only family. No, I didn't wish him dead, though I'd be a liar if I didn't admit that his death is very advantageous to me. I was happy to accept my lot as the second born—that's just the way it was.' He shrugged. 'About him manipulating my mother's will? Typical Richard. Was I angry about it? Yes I was. Upset and very, very angry. Prepared to kill to get back what was rightly mine and an awful lot more besides? Definitely not.'

Jock looked steadily at him. 'Were you to receive nothing from your father's estate?'

Robert gave Jock one of his disarming smiles. 'My father was a wonderful man, Mr Anderson. But for him tradition was all important. I know he felt uncomfortable about Richard being sole inheritor. We talked a lot about it—he wasn't entirely blinkered to Richard's faults. My life was to be the army, and I'd no complaints. Did my father leave me anything? I was to get his guns: some rifles and a nice pair of Purdy shotguns. He was going to leave me his London house, but Richard somehow talked him out of that. My father wasn't a well man by the end, and I suspect a bit of intimidation there. He did leave me some shares in the bank, worth about three hundred thousand pounds. I think he didn't want me to be homeless. I could get a nice wee place with that, but I wouldn't be retiring on it. He had known of course that I was supposed to inherit my mother's estate.'

Jock sat back, picked up his pipe and looked at DI McLean who turned to Robert Ogilvie. 'Can you account for your movements on the day of your brother's death?'

'You mean his murder?'

Jock had asked Dunkie and his family to keep the true nature of Ogilvie's death confidential. That Robert was privy, no doubt informed by Dunkie, didn't surprise him.

'Indeed, but can I please ask you keep that fact to yourself for now?'

Robert nodded. 'I was on duty that weekend, from Friday evening to Monday morning.'

'Does that mean that you were confined to Fort George? You didn't leave the base?'

'That's correct, Superintendent.'

'You realize that we will be seeking confirmation of that?'

'Of course sir.'

'Do you own a sports rifle?'

Robert nodded. 'I own several sir.'

'And where are they now?' asked DI McLean.

'On the base, safely locked up in the armoury.'

'You normally keep them there?'

Robert shook his head. 'They're normally kept at the Lodge, but I brought them back here before my brother's arrival at Dunmorey.'

Jock looked at him questioningly.

'I told you my father left me his guns: they were his, the ones my father left me. I'm afraid I didn't trust Richard not to take them. He even resented the fact that the guns were not left to him, especially the Purdys.'

'Nice chap, your brother,' grunted Jock.

Robert shrugged and smiled. 'Have we about finished Mr Anderson? I've got things to do in town.'

Jock had one last question. 'Would you have access to a specialist weapon: a sniper's rifle?'

Robbie smiled. 'Of course, Superintendent—and I'm a trained sniper.'

Jock got up from his chair, thanked Robbie for coming in and showed him to the door.

'Very plausible young man,' said Bob McLean as Jock resumed his seat.

Jock puffed pensively on his pipe. 'Indeed Bob. If Dunkie's to be believed, there's not a flaw in his makeup. I have to admit I like him. I'll take a wee trip to Fort George tomorrow—why do I think his alibi will stand up?'

Jock looked at his watch. 'We're not doing too well, Bob.

'DS MacKay back from Dunmorey yet?' DI McLean had left the sergeant to interview all of the Dunmorey estate employees. 'If he's here, let's have a word.'

DS MacKay had returned and was in the process of writing up his notes when he was summoned to Jock's office. He said that he had interviewed everyone available that morning and had come up with something of interest—Archie Grant the forester and Willie Chisholm the cattleman had each reported seeing a small green car on the estate in the week before the shooting.

DS MacKay spread out his map of the estate on Jock's desk. 'On the Wednesday morning, about 8 o'clock, Grant passed a small green car parked here. Grant was in his Land Rover, and took no particular interest.' DS McKay indicated a spot on the forestry road only yards from the presumed shooting site. 'And coming up this road here about 8.30 on Friday morning. Willie Chisholm was bringing in some cattle for blood-testing and saw it. Again, took no special interest. It seems that area's quite popular with birdwatchers, and the management's tolerant of such visitors in that end of the estate apparently.'

The road DS McKay was indicating looped up through the forest and joined the road leading to the shooting site.

Jock tapped his teeth with his pipe. 'The forester, was he was on his own?'

DS McKay nodded. 'Aye sir.'

'And the cattleman? Difficult to handle a bunch of beasts on your own.'

The sergeant looked embarrassed. 'He didn't say sir.'

Jock threw up his arms in exasperation. 'And you didn't ask? I hope you're not going to tell me you don't have contact details for these men.'

MacKay flipped through his notebook, wrote down some telephone numbers on a pad and handed it to Jock who reached for the telephone.

Willie Chisholm confirmed what he'd told DS MacKay. He was on his own when he saw the car but was joined shortly after by his son Sandy. He put Sandy on the line. He was unable to add anything, but suggested that maybe Hamish Robertson the vet who was to test the cattle may have seen something. Jock called the clinic where Hamish Robertson worked, but he was in the middle of a consultation. Jock gave his mobile number and left a message for Hamish to contact him as soon as he was free.

Jock stood and put on his jacket. 'I think that's it for today. OK, a wee bit of progress maybe, but how many small green cars do you reckon there are in the country?'

Chapter 20

J**ock** got an extra-big big hug when he arrived home, and he wondered why Meg was in such an exceptionally good mood. She sat Jock down in his chair by the fire, poured him a whisky and opened a bottle of red wine for herself. Jock smiled at her in some bemusement. She obviously was bursting to come out with something and he was content to wait.

'We've getting Gordie tonight.'

Jock smiled. Babysitting his grandson was a rare enough event and a pleasure for them both. 'Great, you're obviously right happy about that.' He knew his wife too well. There was more—she was winding him up.

'For the whole night, Jock—for the whole night, not just for the evening.'

Jock laid down his whisky and his half filled pipe. This had never happened before. The wide smile on Meg's face slipped when Jock's mobile rang. She sighed and rose to top up her wine, Jock grunted an apology and pulled the phone from his pocket: it was Hamish Robertson returning Jock's call. Jock explained the reason for his call and listened with interest to what Hamish had to tell him. Jock finally closed his phone and sat back. Meg knew that her news would have to wait a bit longer.

'Interesting, Meg. Maybe nothing, but interesting.' He told her about the sighting of the small green car by the estate workers. Hamish had told him that he'd seen a small green car coming down the road past the steading where he'd been working; he thought round 9.30. He'd caught a glimpse of the driver but couldn't give a description. Beyond the colour he could add nothing more about the car.

'I've asked him to sleep on it and to come in and see me tomorrow.' Jock shrugged. 'It's probably nothing Meg, but we desperately need something.'

'But Jock, this was the Friday morning. Ogilvie was shot on Saturday morning, wasn't he?'

'Aye, Meg, maybe nothing in it.' He took her hand. 'Now, you were talking about wee Gordie.'

Meg squeezed his hand in hers. 'Aye Jock, he's here for the night—staying with gran and grampa.'

'So what's Jo up to?'

'I don't know, but she was fair bubblin' when she phoned me up and asked us to babysit. She sounded just like our old daughter—like an excited wee teenager. Jock; I think she's got a date.' Jock recalled the silly grin on Jamie Ross's face when he'd seen him later that morning. He nodded to himself and smiled.

Jo had been a worry for them for several years. A high flier at university, she'd started a PhD in Aberdeen but suddenly dropped out and came back home three months pregnant. Always an independent, very self-sufficient girl, she had, however, accepted the help and support of her parents and set about rebuilding her life as a single mother in Inverness. To the frustration of Meg and Jock, she refused to talk about what had happened in Aberdeen. It was a chapter in her life she kept firmly closed and it was only through a friend of Jo's from university that they learned anything at all, and even she was vague on facts. It seemed that after a party and a night's drinking Jo had ended up in bed with a member of staff: one of the professors. Jo's friend suspected it was her PhD supervisor.

Her friend had assured them that Jo was in no way promiscuous, but she'd just been dumped by her long-term boyfriend, so was maybe on the rebound. Her friend said it was a one-off, couldn't even be called an affair. She was just unlucky and Gordie was the result. The friend was sure though, that Jo had kept the news of her pregnancy to herself—she never told anyone at university and certainly not the professor who was a family man. She just quietly dropped out and slipped off home. Jo had come home a different person. The happy, carefree fun-loving daughter had gone. With the help of some money left to her by her aunt, she bought herself a flat and set up a boutique in town. Why a boutique, Meg and Jock could never understand. They thought that a first-class degree in computer science and business studies could have been put to better use. As a family, they remained very close, but they could detect very little fun in their daughter's life. She rarely laughed, and she certainly showed no interest in men: to the contrary, she regarded men with an unhealthy contempt.

As a policeman, Jock liked to deal in certainties. Idle gossip irritated him, but Jamie Ross's meeting with Jo and her current behaviour seemed too juicy a coincidence for him not to share it with Meg. He told her about Jamie and the dummy, shamefully admitting his thoughtless abuse of Jo's property. The gentle wrist slap from Meg he knew was nothing compared to what he'd have got from Jo.

Meg sat back and beamed at him. 'Yes, of course. That must be it, Jock—has to be. How many times has she ever left Gordie with us in four years? Five, six times maybe, and just for a few hours even then. Women's instinct, Jock—she's got a date with that lad.'

Meg looked seriously at Jock. 'I hope he doesn't mess her around, Jock. She's had a big wall up for years. I just hope he doesn't break it down only to bury her in the rubble. Tell me about this lad . . . this Jamie—I want to know everything. I'm guessin' from that silly grin on your face that you approve—convince her mother.'

Meg was wound up like a spring by the time Jo arrived to drop off Gordie. Jock had always considered his daughter to be beautiful: she was, but this evening he was astounded by Jo's appearance and demeanour. She wasn't dressed to kill. With no make-up beyond a touch of eye shadow; in tight jeans, knee-length boots and a tweed bomber jacket; tonight she looked stunning. Her eyes sparkled as she hugged her mum and dad—eyes that hadn't sparkled for years. Jock felt a lump in his throat as he watched her. He picked up Gordie who threw his arms round his neck, then turned to wave to his mum. Jo kissed him and assured him he'd see her in the morning. She kissed Jock, gave her mum another big hug and took off. Jock and Meg had agreed that there would be no inquisition—they knew that this wasn't the time.

Chapter 21

Jock was off to the office before Jo arrived to pick up Gordie in the morning. He hoped there would be a mother and daughter episode, and that there would be some news for him when he got back home. He was every bit as excited about the development as Meg, just more composed.

In the police station car park was a mud-spattered estate car, beside it a young man was changing out of a pair of wellies. Jock recognized Hamish Robertson the vet. Jock was a client of Hamish's and they'd met recently when he'd vaccinated Nick. Hamish apologised for his early arrival. He'd been out at a calving and had an hour before morning clinic, was that OK? Jock ordered coffee for them both on the way to his office. They met DI McLean in the corridor and Jock asked him to join them.

Hamish told Jock that he'd been thinking a lot about their conversation of the previous evening but didn't think he could add much, if anything.

Jock smiled at him. 'We'll see, lad, we'll see—you just might be surprised. Just sit back, relax, close your eyes and put yourself back there that Friday morning.'

Hamish laughed. 'You planning to hypnotize me, sir?'

Jock shook his head and smiled. 'Not necessary. Just relax—try and relive that morning. Start by describing where you were, your surroundings—describe what you were doing.'

Hamish nodded, grinned and closed his eyes.

He'd been to Dunmorey to blood-test the Highland cattle and had left the steading to collect blood-sampling tubes from the car. The road was on the other side of a dry stone wall, and he had heard the car approaching.

Jock stopped him. 'You heard the car. Could you tell if it was petrol or diesel?'

Hamish smiled. 'Diesel, I think.'

'Right, was it going fast or slow?'

'He was travelling sir. I wondered what the rush was down that bumpy wee road.'

'You saw the car. Exactly what did you see? How much of it could you see?'

'I turned round when I heard it. I could only see the top half, from the windows up. The sun was on the windscreen so I couldn't see the driver, just a shape.'

'Right-hand drive?' Hamish nodded.

'You said it was green. Light green or dark green; olive, lime?'

'Olive.'

'Shiny or dowdy, dirty—new car or old?'

'Shiny and clean, certainly not old.'

'How long did you see it for?'

Hamish thought for a moment. 'Five or six seconds.'

'You saw the driver as he passed? Window open or closed?'

'Open.'

'The driver. Male or female, white or coloured? Tall or short, old or young? Any beard or moustache. What was he wearing? Hat or no hat; jacket or overcoat? Wearing glasses?'

Hamish, eyes still closed, frowned as he concentrated.

'Male, medium height I'd say. Well built: not fat, not old, maybe early thirties. White, tanned, long nose. I only saw his profile. No hat, full head of black hair: not long, not cropped. Clean shaven, dark glasses. He was smoking a cigarette, and he was wearing a camouflaged combat jacket.'

'Which hand was the cigarette in?'

'Right hand.'

'Any rings?'

'Can't say.'

'The car drove past you. You saw the front—did you see the back?'

Hamish nodded.

'Good. Was it a saloon, estate, hatchback?'

'Hatchback, red and green sticker on the back window. Bottom, in the middle.'

'The sticker, can you describe it?'

'Not big. A strip, rectangular, maybe thirty centimetres by three or four; red border, green with white lettering I think.'

Jock clapped him on the shoulder. 'Very good, very very good.'

Hamish opened his eyes. 'You're good, Superintendent—I thought I'd hardly seen anything.'

'And I'm useless at calving cows. Thanks for your help Hamish. I can't tell you how valuable your information could be, but you'd better run; it's almost 9 o'clock.' He handed Hamish a card. 'If you think of anything else, please call me.'

When he'd left, Jock turned to DI McLean who'd been taking notes. 'Smart young lad. I doubt if we'll get as much from the cattleman or the forester, but have a go, Bob. Not much of a description, but a potentially valuable load of information. But where the hell does it get us?'

Jock looked at his watch. 'Got to go, I'm seeing Captain Robbie Ogilvie's Colonel in three-quarters an hour out at Fort George.'

Fort George, built after the 1745 Jacobite Rebellion to keep the King's peace in the Highlands, was still a major military base. The senior officer,

Colonel David McNair was an affable, middle-aged man who was highly intrigued by Jock's interest in Captain Ogilvie.

Jock was tempted to give him the "routine enquiries" line but had decided that in this case a little more openness was justified.

The Colonel shook his head firmly. 'I've known that lad since he joined the regiment as a fresh second lieutenant. A first class officer; a very brave soldier and a gentleman. Rule him out, Mr Anderson. He'll be the Colonel of the regiment one day—will probably make General. He's just like his father: now *there* was a man, and Robert is out of the same mould.'

The Colonel called in Captain Stewart, the adjutant, who confirmed that Robert had been on duty over the weekend in question and was therefore confined to the Fort. Leaving was a serious breach of discipline unimaginable for Captain Ogilvie.

Jock asked about Ogilvie's car, he had one presumably? The Colonel didn't know, but Captain Stewart informed him that Ogilvie had a small Toyota hatchback: the colour was green, olive green.

In the Fort George car park, Jock counted four small green hatchbacks. Jo drove a small green hatchback—would that make her a suspect?

It was no more than Jock had expected to learn. But Robert Ogilvie, despite all that he'd learned about the impeccable character of the man, had to be the prime suspect. Of all the suspects, he had the most powerful motive. Robert Ogilvie was no fool. The murder had been well planned and executed. Whoever killed Richard Ogilvie would have arranged an alibi with equal efficiency.

Returning to his car, Jock couldn't resist a call to his wife.

Meg was so happy he'd called—she was bursting to speak to him. For the first time in years, she and Jo had actually sat and talked properly as mother and daughter. Jo was desperate to tell her all about Jamie. It hadn't been a conventional romantic evening, her with her fiddle at a band practice, but

Jo had been bubbling with happiness—she'd had an evening in reality more romantic than any candlelit dinner.

'She's in love, Jock. I remember well enough how I was when I first met you. I know the signs—it's so obvious.'

On returning to the station Jock bumped into Jamie Ross, and he couldn't resist teasing him. 'Good band practice last night, DC Ross?' He smiled at Jamie's embarrassment. 'Just try and keep your mind on the job, lad.'

Jock sat puffing quietly on his pipe in his office. Having left instructions not to be disturbed, he opened the file on the Richard Ogilvie investigation and read it through again. Jock had heard somewhere that some folk can do a jigsaw puzzle without the help of a picture—the Queen apparently being one of them. Right now he felt that he was trying to do the same thing—with lots of pieces missing. He felt the answer had to lie with the victim, a man about whose current activties Jock had unearthed little. With a sigh he closed the file. He'd have to go to London. He checked his watch. A meeting with his team was scheduled and he headed for the incident room. The Chief Constable, just back from a short holiday, wanted an update and would be attending. Jock hefted the file in his hands. It was getting impressively thicker, certainly, but that alone wouldn't impress the boss.

Jock arrived first and was able to spend a few moments alone in the incident room. On a large chipboard on one wall was arrayed the story of the investigation. There were photos of the dead Duke, many photos of the dummy displaying the evidence supporting Jock's theory and photos of the suspects with bullet-point notes by each. On an adjacent wall were two new additions: a map, the one from Dougie Sanderson's Dunmorey croft house showing the nature reserve, was pinned alongside another found among the Duke's effects. It showed the planned Dunmorey Golf Development.

The door opened and Jamie Ross came in, the first of the team to arrive. Jock called him over and indicated the maps. It was Jamie's first view of the new exhibits.

'Your part of the country. What do you think? The golf course would have changed things a bit, eh?'

Jamie nodded. 'For sure, sir.' He touched a spot on the edge of the second map. 'That's my wee place; just far enough away not to be too directly affected.' He smiled at Jock. 'Would be worth a bit more though.'

Jamie compared the two maps. 'Your man certainly managed to buy up a lot of land for his big idea, sir. He must have got his hands on these farms. This one was old Will McIver's—used to milk a hundred cows. No money in milk now. And this one, Archie Masterson's. Great soil, he grew lovely potatoes. I heard that they'd sold up. Nobody knew who they'd sold to—I hope they got a good price.'

DI McLean came in and Jock made a move to join him.

Jamie touched his arm.

'Sorry sir, but there's something not right here.' Jock turned back.

'See this bit here, sir?' Jamie traced round an area, a finger of land in the middle of the proposed golf course. 'That, sir, is Hughie MacRae's farm. Hughie MacRae, you remember, my friend? He was killed when he came off his bike. No way would he ever have sold the farm—and he'd never have sold to Ogilvie at any price—he hated the man. They had a run-in a while back, something to do with him not paying Hughie for fixing up his car.'

The men looked at each other. 'Come up to my office after the meeting.'

The Chief Constable sat at the back of the room while Jock reviewed the whole case. The exercise was partly for the Chief's benefit, but there was new information for the team's files and they listened as they were told about the sighting of the small green car and about Hamish Robertson's description of it and its occupant. The forester and the cattleman could confirm only that the car they'd seen was a green hatchback. Copies of the report were handed out.

'We've still got nothing more on our suspects.' He waved another report and outlined what little they had got from the interviews.

'You'll all probably agree that the prime suspect has to be Robert Ogilvie. He maintains that he was confined to Fort George on the weekend in question. I've interviewed his Commanding Officer—his alibi checks out.'

Jock looked round. 'Any questions? Any comments? Suggestions? We've got bugger all. Any constructive input appreciated.'

'I saw him, sir.' All heads turned to look at Jamie Ross.

'Robbie Ogilvie, sir, on the Saturday morning in Inverness.'

There was a loud mutter of conversation round the room, Jock called for silence and indicated that Jamie should continue.

'It was just after 10 o'clock, I was listening to the news on the radio. There was a bit of a hold up at the Longman roundabout. I was heading into town, he was heading out.'

'You had a good look at him?'

Jamie nodded. 'Yes sir, I did. All the cars were stopped, and his window was open.'

Jock tapped Robert Ogilvie's photo on the chipboard. 'You're sure it was him, not another good looking blonde man? You're sure it was Saturday 25th?'

Jamie nodded his head. 'I know Robert Ogilvie quite well, sir; played rugby against him a few times—we've had a few beers together. And I'm sure it was the morning the Duke died that I saw him.'

The Chief Constable had stood up, and everyone looked expectantly at Jock who turned to DI McLean. 'Pull him in, Bob. And his mate, Captain Stewart.'

After a few minutes conversation with the Chief Constable, Jock took Jamie to his office.

'As I recall, Hugh MacRae was a good friend of yours.'

Jamie took a deep breath. 'We grew up together. My best friend sir—my best friend.'

'You said he'd never sell his farm. You're sure about that?'

Jamie nodded. 'It'd been in his family for generations. He loved the place. Didn't do much farming; he was too busy with his garage. Just a few sheep and a couple of suckler cows: meat for the pot mainly. He kept us all in meat. What land he didn't need he rented to his neighbour, Will McIver.'

'Was he ever approached to sell? By anyone?'

Jamie thought for a moment. 'I remember Hughie telling me a while back that he was approached by some smoothie from Edinburgh. Said he was an estate agent wanting to buy a suitable farm for a client down south. He was offering a good price if I remember right—way above the going rate. Hughie told him he wouldn't sell for any price, the farm wasn't on the market and that was that. I think the agent phoned him later with an improved offer. Hughie was intrigued—quite chuffed that he was sitting on so much money, but no way was he selling.'

'And his wife? Do you know if she's been approached since Hughie's death?'

Jamie nodded slowly. 'She's sold the farm. It was Hughie's place and Lizzie loved it too, but she's not a farmer; she doesn't need the hassle. And too many memories there maybe. She's got her eye on a nice wee house in the village, a better place for her and the wee one. She doesn't want to be stuck out on the farm on her own.'

Jock nodded in understanding. He had a file open in front of him and was flipping through it. 'You didn't believe your friend's death was a simple accident, did you?'

'I still don't, sir.'

'You found a cigarette that night near where he died, didn't you? Remind me why you considered it of significance.'

'Well sir, it was fresh and dry. It had been raining heavily all evening. According to the policeman the rain didn't stop until about 10.00. I remember it wasn't raining when Hughie left the pub—that was just after 10.00. And there were no smokers at the scene of the accident. It wasn't a common brand either, sir. There was a broad gold ring below the filter. I don't remember the make, but it was written on the cigarette below the band. It was, I remember, an American name—not Virginia, but something like that.'

Jock consulted the file in front of him. 'Was it by any chance Vermont?'

Jamie looked at him and nodded. 'Yes sir—that was it.'

Jock turned the file so Jamie could read it. 'Bottom of the page. Last paragraph.'

Jamie read out loud. 'Two packs, one opened, brand Vermont.' Jock watched as Jamie's face drained of colour.

'That, as you've guessed, DC Ross, is part of the medical report on Richard Ogilvie. Dr Paterson found those cigarettes in the jacket pocket of the dead Duke.'

'I can't believe it sir. Ogilvie wanted that land—Hughie was in his way, so he just killed him. He killed Hughie for a fucking golf course. Sorry, sir. But what kind of man could do that? We shouldn't be trying to find that bastard's killer to prosecute him; we should be finding him to give him a medal. I'm sorry, sir.' Jamie rubbed his face with his hands and shook his head. 'Maybe I'm a bit too close to this case.'

Jock smiled at him. 'Would I be right in assuming that you've still got that cigarette-end safely stored somewhere?'

'It was evidence sir. It's in a plastic bag at home in the fridge.'

'Very good. Dr Paterson will know what to do with it.'

Jock looked gravely at Jamie. 'This is totally circumstantial. Bloody obvious to both of us what seems to have happened, but of bugger-all use as evidence. The Duke's dead so we've no murderer to convict anyway—but it would be nice for our own satisfaction to nail him properly.

'I'm leaving this to you. Get onto Dunmorey. See what you can find out about Richard Ogilvie's movements on the night Hughie died—if, in fact, he was even up here at the time.'

Jamie forced a smile, then his face crumpled. 'I've just dropped Robbie Ogilvie right in it. Why didn't I keep my mouth shut?'

'Because, DC Ross, you are, whether you like it or not, a policeman.'

An hour later, an apprehensive Robert Ogilvie, still in army fatigues, was facing Jock and DI McLean. He had been cautioned but declined to have a solicitor present. DI McLean switched on the tape recorder and formally noted the start of the interview.

Jock consulted a file in front of him and addressed the man seated opposite. 'Captain Ogilvie. On Monday, the 3rd of September, in an informal interview conducted by myself and DI McLean, you were asked about your movements on the weekend of the 25th of August of this year. You informed us that you were on duty and, as such, confined to Fort George. Do you wish to confirm that statement?'

Robbie Ogilvie slumped slightly in his chair. 'I think, Superintendent, I would like to change my mind and consult with my solicitor.'

Waiting nervously in an adjacent interview room was Captain Stewart. He fidgeted with a packet of cigarettes as Jock and DI McLean took their seats. 'May I smoke?'

Jock nodded. 'Captain Stewart, I must inform you that obstructing the course of justice is a very serious offence. When I spoke to you at Fort George, I asked if you could confirm that Captain Ogilvie was on the base for the entire weekend of the 25th of August of this year.'

Captain Stewart shifted uncomfortably in his seat.

'I am asking you again.'

The officer looked at both men facing him. 'The regiment was just back from a tour of duty. Most of the men were on leave, only a handful still on base. Robbie—Captain Ogilvie—asked me to cover for him for the Friday night. I had a flight south on Saturday afternoon. He promised me he'd be back by 11.00 Saturday morning, so I agreed. I could see no harm in it. It's in breach of the rules but we do that sort of thing when we're on down time. There's no harm in it—the Colonel generally turns a blind eye.'

'Did he know about this particular breach?'

Captain Stewart shook his head. 'The Colonel was off base that weekend visiting his wife in Edinburgh.'

'When did Captain Ogilvie leave the base?' asked DI McLean.

The Captain shrugged. 'I have no idea. I last saw him at about 7.00 that Friday evening. I had duties to attend to.'

DI McLean continued. 'Can you describe his demeanour when you last saw him?'

Captain Stewart looked puzzled. 'His demeanour?'

'Did he look and act perfectly normally?' Persisted DI McLean. 'Happy? Sad? Preoccupied, perhaps?'

Captain Stewart stubbed out his cigarette. 'Actually, Inspector, he seemed very happy.'

'Did he tell you why he wanted you to cover for him?'

'No, and I didn't ask.'

'And when you last saw him, how was he dressed?'

'He'd just had a shower. He was dressing. Casual smart mufti, slacks and a shirt.'

'Captain Stewart, do you consider yourself to be a close friend of Captain Ogilvie?'

'A friend? Yes, I suppose so. I only joined the regiment fairly recently. Close friend, no, but I hope to be one day—he's a remarkable man.'

'So you wouldn't know anything about any social activities the Captain may have been involved in?'

'No. I know he is local to the area. I assumed he'd have social contacts outside the base.'

'He returned to base as promised by 11.00 on the Saturday morning?'

'Yes, he phoned up to my room. It was about 10.45, I think. I was packing my bag.'

'And how did he sound? Upbeat? Happy? Up or down?'

'He sounded a bit tense—tired maybe.'

'Did you see him before you left?'

'Very briefly. I had to give him some keys. To save you asking, Inspector, he looked and acted his normal self.'

Bob McLean sat back, and Jock picked up his pipe and started to fill it. 'Thank you very much, Captain Stewart. I must ask you to be available for further questions.'

Captain Stewart looked at Jock. 'Superintendent, I don't know what this is all about, but of course I'll be available—and I'm sorry if I was less than honest with you yesterday, but in front of the Colonel, it was a bit . . . eh . . . difficult. You must understand.'

Jock nodded. 'Did Captain Ogilvie ask you to lie for him in the event of any questions about his movements?'

Captain Stewart shook his head emphatically. 'Absolutely not, sir.'

'Finally, Captain. If an officer on duty wanted to leave his post for a few hours, and return to the Fort undetected, would it be possible?'

'It's very possible sir. The Fort's not a prison.'

Robert Ogilvie was seated with a solicitor when they returned to the interview room. The solicitor told Jock that he, Robert, was not prepared to answer any questions at the moment. To his surprise, Jock told him that they could leave but to present themselves the following morning and gave them a time.

When they'd left, Jock turned and looked at DI McLean.

'Let's go and chew over this in the pub, Bob. It's nearly lunchtime.'

When Bob McLean returned from the bar with two pints, Jock was smiling as he closed his mobile. 'Just been talking to Meg. I've got a love-sick daughter.' He took a sip of his beer and told DI McLean about Jo and Jamie Ross.

'You couldn't wish for a better son-in-law, sir.'

Jock grunted and sucked down half his beer.

'Whatever Robert Ogilvie was up to, I don't think it was shooting his brother Bob.'

'Protecting someone?' suggested DI McLean.

Jock shrugged. 'Or protecting his own reputation, but I can't see him off visiting some brothel or other, not him. The man seems almost too bloody sweet to be wholesome. Mr Bloody Perfect. No Bob, if he'd been planning to knock off his brother he'd have made sure his arse was better covered. He'd made no attempt to create a decent alibi. When he left the Fort that evening, he had no notion that he may have to account for his movements—but our man better have some answers for us tomorrow.'

Jo's car was at his house when he got home that evening. After a fierce struggle between Nick and Gordie for his attention, he finally made it to the kitchen. Meg and Jo had their heads together at the table as he made a noisy entrance and Jo jumped up and hugged him. The change in his daughter was amazing. It was wonderful to feel like her father again and not some old fart to be merely tolerated.

Meg was beaming. 'Gordie's with us again tonight, Jock,'

Jock put his arms round Jo and hugged her. 'He's a good man, Jo. But don't I remember you giving your poor mother hell about her being married to a policeman? I seem to remember you saying you'd rather marry a dustman, or was it a lavatory cleaner: was one or the other.'

Jo laughed and sat back down beside her mother. 'Who said anything about marriage, Dad?'

Jock shrugged and smiled at his two women. 'That's another problem with policemen—they've got big feet. I'm going to catch the news.'

Their landline rang as he sat down in front of the TV, and Meg came into the lounge with the handset. 'For you, Jock—it's a young lady. She says it's important.' Jock made a face, turned down the volume on the TV and took the phone.

'Superintendent. My name's Carol Evans. I'm sorry to bother you at home; and in the evening, but I have to speak to you. Jo gave me your number.'

'That's OK. How can I help you?'

'I don't have much time—he'll be back any minute.'

'He? Who's he?'

'My husband—Owen Evans. It's about Robbie Ogilvie. I need to meet with you, Mr Anderson.'

'Can you not come into the station in the morning?'

'No, no. He'd—my husband—he'd find out. Could we maybe meet somewhere in town for coffee tomorrow morning? Maxine's in Academy Street, about 11.00?'

Jock agreed, but only if she'd give him some idea about what this was all about.

'I told you, Mr Anderson. Robbie Ogilvie—he was with me that night. Got to go, he's coming back.'

Jock laid down the phone and heaved a sigh.

'Jo, you got a minute?'

Jo sat on the arm of his chair as Jock told her about the call.

'She's a friend of yours then?'

Jo nodded. 'I suppose you could say that. I see her quite often at the gym. We usually go for a coffee afterwards, but I don't really know her very well. Lovely looking girl, and really nice. You maybe knew her dad: Ronnie Henderson. He played rugby for Scotland, she told me. He'd have been about your age.'

Jock's mind flipped back almost thirty years, to that hellish day. Ronnie Henderson. So full of fun and life—and the fittest of them all. Jock could remember it so vividly. Himself running with the ball and passing it to Ronnie, the ball bouncing off Ronnie's chest as he fell to the ground—the shock, the attempts to resuscitate him; his lovely young wife there with her little daughter to watch the final—her terrible grief. Ronnie had died from a cerebral aneurism.

Jock pulled himself back. 'Aye love, I knew her dad very well.'

'Well, Carol's married to that pig of a man: Owen Evans. He gives her a hard time. She called me this afternoon, sounded very agitated. She wanted to speak to you, wouldn't tell me why. I gave her your number—I hope that was OK, Dad?'

Jock squeezed her hand. 'It's OK, love, just fine. So you don't really know much about her—no woman-to-woman, heart-to-heart stuff?'

Jo shook her head. 'I think she wants to talk but is scared to—I think she's got a lot bottled-up. She had a bruise on her face once; had tried to cover it with makeup. I asked her about it and she just burst into tears. She didn't say, but I'm sure that bastard had beaten her up.'

Jock gave Jo another hug. 'Thanks love, go and help your mum.'

Owen Evans. Slimy character, a slimy lawyer; defender of the indefensible. There was mutual contempt between him and the police. Supposedly a fine pillar of the local community: a town councillor, but also a "finger-in-every-rotten-pie" man. Jock shook his head wearily and wondered how any sensible girl could get involved with a man like Evans. He was, however, more interested in her involvement with Robert Ogilvie.

Chapter 22

Nine o'clock the following morning, and Jock and DI McLean were facing Robbie Ogilvie and his solicitor, Mr Alan MacLeod, in an interview room. As is so often the case in a small community where everyone seems to know everyone, MacLeod, a highly respected local lawyer, was a fellow golfer and good friend of Jock's. Robbie looked tired and strained as he sipped a coffee.

Jock spoke to the solicitor. 'I am sure that your client is fully aware of the serious nature of the charge he is facing if he fails to give a verifiable account of his movements on the morning of the 25th of August of this year.'

The MacLeod cleared his throat in some embarrassment. 'My client is, I'm afraid, unable to provide the necessary information.'

'Unwilling, unable, or not prepared? I assume he has a full recollection of the morning in question?'

The solicitor glanced at Robbie. 'Superintendent, there are extenuating circumstances, circumstances totally unrelated to the murder of Richard Ogilvie which preclude any statement from my client.'

'In other words, he was up to something he can't, or won't tell us about?' The solicitor smiled and shrugged.

Jock looked at Robbie. 'I had an interesting phone call yesterday evening—from a young woman named Carol Evans. Does the name mean anything to you?'

Robbie's body language provided the answer.

'I'm having a meeting with the young lady later this morning. I got the impression from our brief conversation that she is very concerned for your welfare.'

Robbie leaned over and whispered to his solicitor.

'My client wishes to defer any statement until after your conversation with Mrs Evans.'

Jock was getting up to leave when Robbie found his voice.

'Superintendent—can I ask you please to be discreet?'

Jock held up his hand. 'I think I've got the picture, lad. We have here a very . . . eh, delicate situation.'

Robbie nodded. 'Very delicate, sir—and potentially very dangerous. Please be careful.'

By 10.45, Jock was seated at the back of Maxine's wine bar sipping an espresso. He'd acquired a taste for espresso when on holiday in Portugal some years before, and somehow now Nescafé didn't hit the spot. He felt distinctly out of place. Maxine's was one of those new trendy places which ordinarily Jock would never think to patronize. He wasn't big on wine: thought the stuff was a waste of perfectly good grape juice. And the only beer on offer was expensive bottled lager—exotic stuff, not even proper beer. Jock was not impressed. Most of the tables were occupied by smartly dressed young people; several of them were tapping away on laptops or talking on their mobile phones. Jock wondered why they were not at work.

He had only a vague description of Carol Evans, and he amused himself by assessing each young woman who entered the café. There was, however, no mistaking the lithe beauty in blue Lycra pants that entered on the dot of 11.00. She'd clearly come straight from the gym; a Nike kit bag was slung over one shoulder. She turned a few heads as she headed straight for Jock's table, sat down and looked furtively round her.

'Best not to act so nervously,' said Jock smiling at her—'attracts less attention.'

She gave him a warm, but nervous smile. 'I'm Carol Evans.'

Jock smiled at the girl. 'I guessed that.'

'It's too crowded in here this morning. Too many people know me and my husband—could we maybe go somewhere a wee bit less public to talk? Maybe take a drive somewhere?'

Jock nodded. 'Where do you want to go?'

'You go out first. I've a red Volvo. I'm parked at the top of Castle Street. See you up there, then you follow me.'

Jock paid for his coffee and left as instructed, amused by all the cloak and dagger behaviour.

Twenty minutes later, parked in a quiet spot by the side of the River Ness, Carol joined Jock in his car and finally seemed to relax. She pulled a packet of cigarettes from her kit bag, lit up, inhaled and sighed in satisfaction.

She waved the cigarette at Jock. 'I even have to have one of these in secret. Smoking's not allowed—the bastard.'

Jock was content to let her come out with it in her own time.

She stubbed out her half-smoked cigarette. 'I don't have very long, Mr Anderson. He comes home for lunch. He insists on a cooked lunch: an elaborate cooked lunch. So I've got to get back to the kitchen where I belong. God help me if it's not on the table at 1.00 on the dot.'

She took a deep breath and exhaled slowly. 'Robbie Ogilvie and me. It's a long story, but to cut it short, we've been seeing each other for about two years. We met at some function my husband insisted I go to with him. You see, I'm nothing more than a pretty ornament to him. A glamorous trophy on his arm to boost his respectability and his fucking ego—sorry about the language Superintendent. A possession, like his flash car and gold Rolex. And, like his Rolex, I get locked back in my metaphorical drawer when he gets home, only to be taken out again when needed.

'Then I met Robbie. God knows how we managed to get it together, Mr Anderson; but we did—love conquering all, I suppose.

'My husband's an insanely jealous man. He doesn't love me; I doubt if he even likes me. He's got other women. Ironically it's when he goes on his "business trips" that Robbie and I can have some proper time together. I'm just a possession—but possessions must be guarded.

'He's slapped me about often enough in the past for daring to arouse his ridiculous suspicions. Can you believe I once got beaten up because I dared to chat to the postman? If he found out about Robbie and me, the consequences would be unthinkable—that's a euphemism for he'd beat me to a pulp, Mr Anderson. Our Inverness is a very small community, Superintendent. My husband's a powerful man with his spies everywhere. I can assure you there's probably someone in your police station reporting to him—it's the way he operates. So you see, to protect me, Robbie couldn't let me be his alibi. He was with me all that night, left sometime shortly before 10.00 in the morning.'

Carol put her face in her hands. 'God, it all seems so sordid. He has to sneak in and out through a hole in the hedge in the back garden. We've got very nosey neighbours. Bloody Neighbourhood Watch—just an excuse for being bloody nosey.

'The news will get out—it has to soon, but at a time of our choosing. You see we have to be ready. We, my four-year-old daughter Sally and I can't be in that house when the shit does hit the fan. We need a wee bit more time.

'I can see what you're thinking, Mr Anderson. How on earth did she get involved with Evans in the first place? Why doesn't this silly woman just leave the man and run off with her lover and live happily ever after? Unfortunately life's not that easy. He'd go for custody of Sally, just to spite me. You know what clever lawyers can do. At best they'd make life hell.

'It really embarrasses me to think of how I married him. My mother was dying of cancer. I'd just finished university. No job; my boyfriend—husband-to-be I suppose, had recently died in a climbing accident. I was in a mess. A devastated, pathetic, sad, lost soul. A successful good looking man comes along—at least he was good looking then, not the fat pig he is now. I craved the security, I suppose.

'Anyway, we're preparing our case, Mr Anderson. We're gathering the facts; piling up the shit to dump on him. We're almost there. We've got photographic evidence of his adultery—we hired a private detective; and we've got doctors' reports on my bruising after he'd knocked me about.

'Mental cruelty's more difficult, but we've got lots on that too.' Carol pulled a credit card from her bag and held it up. 'I've got no money, Superintendent. Credit limit one hundred pounds: just about enough for the shopping. Mobile phone: local calls only. He checks my calls on this and the home phone every time the statements come in. He demands to know who I've been calling.' She smiled and pulled another mobile phone from her bag. 'Robbie bought me this one on his account. I'll give you the number.' She pulled a pen and pad from her kit-bag, wrote down the number and handed the paper to Jock.

'Robbie's planning the whole thing like a military operation. What we don't need right now is for our adultery to be made public—for my health reasons, but also because we can't hand him that weapon against us.' Carol looked at her watch. 'I'll have to get back now, Mr Anderson—my time's up.'

It's not often that Jock found himself stuck for words, so he told her simply what she needed to hear: he believed her and that there would be no further talk of charging Robbie. Carol grabbed his hand, kissed him on the cheek and was gone.

Jock sat in numbed silence for fully five minutes. Once again he was back to square one.

Back in his office, Jock gave an account of his meeting with Carol Evans to Bob McLean.

Bob shrugged. 'Robbie was the most likely candidate sir, but I don't think either of us was convinced. And as for that lot at Dunmorey? Not much mileage there either.'

Jock looked at him and smiled. 'Glad we agree on that. No, I can't figure Dunkie or his family somehow. If it was one of them, we've bugger all evidence so they've got off with it.

'No, Bob. I think the answer has to lie down south. So unfortunately it's off to London—flight's booked for tomorrow afternoon.'

Bob McLean had been reading through the information on Richard Ogilvie he'd got from his London contacts. He tapped the file. 'I don't think our friends down there will be able to give you any more, sir. Ogilvie's been in their sights for a while.' He shrugged and laid the file on Jock's desk.

'There's folk down there who know more than they're letting on, Bob. Bankers are notoriously tight lipped about their activities.' Jock picked up the file. 'Bugger all in here from his bank. I've got to rattle that cage a bit.

'I've spoken to the new CEO of Ogilvies. He's a right plumby, snotty bastard: one Rupert Edmonds. With no great enthusiasm, he's granted me access to the hallowed precincts and permission to interview the staff. I'm meeting him at 9.00 day after tomorrow. Then I'll work my way down—to the tea lady if necessary. Bit of pleasure mixed in, though. An old pal of mine, Alex Telford, is with the Serious Crimes Squad. We'll be having a few drams tomorrow night. I'll be staying with him and his wife. There's an awful lot of stuff never gets put on paper, Bob.' Jock slid the file back to DI McLean. 'I'm hoping Alex's got some juicy gossip for me.'

Late that night, Jock lay in bed as Meg packed his bag.

'I'm only planning an overnight, Meg—maybe two nights.'

'You've got to look smart, Jock,' she said folding and packing another shirt. 'You're going to wear your best suit when you go to that bank: your nice tweed one. You're not going in dressed like some country bumpkin.

They'll be expectin' to see heather growin' out of your ears as it is—and your deerstalker's staying here. With that pipe o' yours and the hat they'd think you're doing a Sherlock Holmes.'

Meg sat on the bed beside him and took his hand. 'Could we go to London some time—you and me? I've never been nearer than Heathrow. I'd just like to see the place some day. Buckingham Palace, the Houses of Parliament: they look so grand on the TV.'

Jock put his arm round her and kissed her cheek. 'Of course we can love, of course we can.'

London: he hated the bloody place.

Chapter 23

Alex Telford and Jock hadn't met for over twenty years. They'd been cadets together at Police College, probationers in Inverness, stars in the Inverness Rugby Club, best drinking buddies for years—until Alex met an English girl who married him and took him off to London. Jock had been Alex's best man and he liked Alex's wife, Mary. They'd managed to keep vaguely in touch through Christmas cards and the occasional professional contact.

As they sat in Alex's lounge with a glass of malt, the years fell away and they spent the first hour of the evening laughing and reminiscing. Over a meal, Jock told Alex and Mary about the events on Dunmorey. Mary, it turned out, was well up in the banking business, an investment manager with one of the big banks and her ears pricked up at the mention of Richard Ogilvie. She'd had no professional dealings with the man, but there was plenty of talk in the city about him—loads of rumours.

Mary smiled at Jock. 'This place runs on rumours. Someone picks up a rumour that a company or a bank is in trouble and that's enough—shares go through the floor.' She told him about the CEO of a London company who started a rumour about serious troubles brewing in his business. When the shares hit rock bottom he'd arranged to have the shares bought up. The scare was all bollocks and he made himself millions. Highly illegal of course, but there are few morals or ethics in this business. Everyone knew what this guy had done. He'd given the nod to enough of his influential pals who'd shared in the feast. Insider trading—they all do it, and they think that the only crime is getting caught.'

'So what have you been hearing about Ogilvie, then?'

Mary sipped her wine. 'Recently? Well, there was talk of some deal in the States that he and his bank had been involved in that went pear-shaped. Not big by London banking standards, but quite a few millions involved, apparently.'

Mary smiled. 'When there's something in the offing, those at the top, naturally enough, want to keep things to themselves. But when these big boys are sitting in their clubs with a few whiskies down them, they can't help boasting about the latest killing they're going to make and how clever they are. Then when it all goes quiet and the millions don't start pouring in and it seems that maybe they weren't so clever after all, people start to wonder—and to speculate.'

'Spread rumours you mean?'

Mary shrugged. 'I've no idea what happened over there, but something went down with a bang, and no-one from Ogilvies is talking about it.'

'Anyone there I could target specifically?'

Mary got up and found her mobile, made a call, and Jock listened as she chatted to a colleague. She wrote something on her table napkin and handed it to Jock.

'These are the names and numbers of the two top boys who were with Ogilvie in America. The first is David Rubens: his shit-hot lawyer; and the other's Arthur Cavendish: his accountant and financial guru. I know Arthur quite well, actually. He's a very nice guy, a real gentleman; and quite a wit and raconteur. You'll remember him, Alex, at the Cranford's dinner party? He had us all in stitches.'

'Aye,' said Alex with a laugh. 'A hell of a man—that was a good night.'

Jock could have kissed her. The business in the States was probably a big red herring, but now he was going to the bank tomorrow morning armed with something—he had insider information, and that, judiciously dropped, would really scare them. Country bumpkin indeed.

Neither Alex nor Mary could offer anything more finite about Ogilvie beyond what Jock knew already. He'd sailed very close to the wind; the police wanted to nail him, the financial regulators wanted something on him, but he'd been too smart for either.

Jock hated opulence. A bit of affluence was fine: it was usually the product of hard work and he could respect that. He knew that Ogilvies was a small, discreet merchant bank and he had expected the premises to reflect that—maybe a modest old building in the City of London. The modern steel and glass structure surprised him; the opulent vulgarity of the decor horrified him.

Rupert Edmonds, the CEO of Ogilvies, immaculate in a pin-stripe suit, crisp white shirt and club tie more than matched his surroundings. After his wet, limp handshake, Jock felt like washing his hands. Edmonds was clearly very proud of his building. He informed Jock that on the death of the old Duke, Richard Ogilvie had transferred the business from the old premises in The City.

'Must hae moved right quick,' said Jock as he eyed a piece of "artwork" on a wall. 'The auld Duke's hardly cold in his grave.'

Edmonds gave Jock a cold smile. 'Mr Ogilvie had been planning the move for some time. His father favoured the old premises. Richard Ogilvie was progressive. He and I felt that this new structure better illustrated our dynamic new approach to the business.'

Jock was shown into Edmonds' plush office. Edmonds continued to be formally polite, coffee was ordered and Jock was subjected to an embarrassing eulogy on the late Richard Ogilvie.

'Och aye, A'm sure he wis a richt fine man. His tragic death must hae sorely hurt ye all in this fine wee bank.'

'Indeed Superintendent; a tragic accident indeed, but how may I assist you?'

'Och, it's probably nothin', Mr Edwards.'

'Edmonds. My name is Edmonds.'

'Oh Aye, Edmonds is it—A've a terrible memory fir names. Routine stuff ye understand, just a few wee loose ends tae be tied up. Ma Chief Constable just hates loose ends, so here A am, sent a' the way doon tae London tae ask a load o' silly questions an' tae tak gid folks like yersel' awa' frae their work.'

Jock hoped he wasn't laying on the brogue and dumb Scottish Policeman act a bit too thickly. From the hard eyes of Edmonds and his contemptuous smirk, he reckoned he probably had it about right.

Edmonds made a show of consulting his watch. 'You said on the phone, Superintendent, that you wished to interview my staff.'

Jock nodded. 'Aye, that's richt, Mr Edmonds, but A'll no' be needin' tae see them a' the noo: just the twa that wis involved in that wee spot o' bother in America. Mr Cavendish an' Mr Rubens will dae me fine fir noo. A'll be startin' wi' Mr Cavendish if that's a' richt by yersel'?'

Edmonds struggled to retain his composure—a slap on the face could scarcely have produced a more dramatic reaction. He rose stiffly, muttered that he'd see what he could arrange, excused himself and left the office. Jock could hear a raised voice through the office door—Edmonds was on the phone. Jock smiled to himself and sipped his coffee. This is what he called rattling a cage.

Arthur Cavendish seemed to be everything Mary Telford had described. When shown into his office and introduced, Jock felt that the smile was genuine and that the welcome was sincere; and when he learned that Jock was from Inverness he beamed at him. 'My mother's from Dingwall. She moved back there a few years ago after my father died. I love it up there—I'm going up soon to visit her.'

He sat back in his chair and lifted his hands. 'Well, Superintendent, what can I do for you?'

Jock decided to be candid, dropping the dumb Scottish Policeman act—he would be straight with Cavendish.

'Firstly, Mr Cavendish, just so you'll appreciate the serious nature of my visit, I . . .' Jock stopped.

Cavendish was laughing. 'I'm sorry, Superintendent, I'm sorry. You were taking the piss with that pompous fart Edmonds—you're not the McPlod Edmonds warned me expect.'

Jock couldn't help but smile. 'As I was saying, the serious nature of my visit . . .' He assumed a grave expression. 'What I'm about to tell you must remain confidential.'

Cavendish nodded. 'Of course Mr Anderson.'

'Your late boss was not killed in a shooting accident: he was murdered—an assassination well planned and executed.'

Cavendish's jaw dropped.

'Our initial investigations were directed locally, but we've eliminated all suspects. From what I've learned of Richard Ogilvie, I can well imagine he wasn't short of enemies. I need your help, Mr Cavendish.'

Arthur Cavendish sat forward and ran his hand over his mouth. He glanced at Jock, opened a drawer and took out a file which he laid on his desk.

'Richard Ogilvie was a very, very unpleasant person, Superintendent. He has been described as evil—I don't object to that description. A brilliant man: a brilliant, evil genius. He was extremely ruthless in business; an unnecessary ruthlessness which, I'm afraid, reflected his sadistic nature. I'm sure he had many enemies—I know he had many enemies. You're asking me if I can think of someone who hated him enough to kill him—or to have him killed?

'Ogilvie lived in two worlds, Superintendent. This world,' Cavendish waved his arm round the room. 'The respectable world of business and banking in which he was very, very successful. And another, darker world. Arms dealing, for sure, he was into—huge money there. No regime was too sick for him to supply. He was legally involved in the arms business, and that's how I learned about the illegal side.'

'Drugs?'

Cavendish shrugged. 'Probably, anything that made money. I wasn't ever part of his other world, but one hears things, deduces things. He was swimming with very nasty sharks. In that world you don't get killed because you're hated; all the players hate each other. No. You get killed for breaking their rules.'

Cavendish toyed with a pen on his desk. 'I only got close to his other world once. We were in America recently: in Florida. I got too close and it's been on my conscience since. While Ogilvie was around . . .' Cavendish shrugged. 'Call it loyalty, fear for my own skin; call it what you like, but I did nothing. Now he's gone, I can . . .' He pushed the file on his desk towards Jock. 'It's all in there, Superintendent. You'll see that there are two signatories. That's a joint statement by myself and David Rubens, Ogilvie's lawyer. I think you are scheduled to interview him next. What I suggest is that you read this now. I have an important meeting I must attend, but it shouldn't take more than an hour or so. Please make yourself comfortable; I'll order you some coffee.'

Jock had just finished reading the file for a second time, the cup of coffee untouched on the table, when Cavendish returned. With him was a small, thin, bespectacled man he introduced as David Rubens.

Cavendish took his seat behind his desk. 'Well, Superintendent. I would imagine that you'll have a few questions.'

Jock let out a breath and tapped the file. 'Gripping stuff, gentlemen. So you think this Capello character, this Don Luigi, had these four men killed?'

'We do. Scheiffer, we think, was tortured and killed.'

'Bloody hell. The authorities in The States have to be notified.'

Cavendish nodded. 'But not those anywhere near Paradise Glades. I'm sure they're all in Capello's pocket.'

'Your appearance this morning is timely, Superintendent,' said Rubens. 'Only yesterday I approached a colleague in Fort Lauderdale for advice on how we should proceed.'

Jock picked up the file he'd been given by Cavendish. 'This report goes into great detail about these four men, and will be of great interest to the American police. But Ogilvie seriously ruffled someone's feathers over the blown deal—and relieved whoever it was of five million. I'd think that person might just be pissed off enough to have Ogilvie killed; don't you agree?'

Both men nodded.

'You make no mention in the report of who that person might be. Still a bit afraid for your own skin, Mr Cavendish?'

Cavendish looked at Rubens who gave him a nod.

Cavendish turned back to Jock. 'We think his name is Steiner: Klaus Steiner.'

Jock enjoyed Chinese food, and Alex and Mary had chosen a real Chinese restaurant. Theirs was the only table of non-Chinese customers.

As the starters were arriving, Jock was telling Alex and Mary about his meeting with Arthur Cavendish, and of the significance of Mary's inside information: how it had led via Cavendish to both a name, and a likely motive for Ogilvie's assassination. Mary flushed with pleasure and toasted Jock with her glass of wine. Jock smiled, squeezed her hand and chewed appreciatively on his spring roll as he listened to Alex.

'Assassins—hit-men, are a special breed, Jock. Professional killers who make an awful lot of money and are determined to live free to enjoy it. Not many have ever been caught—alive anyway—so we don't really know much about them. Generally, they are assumed to be mainly ex-soldiers who're already well versed in the arts of planning and killing. It's all in the planning. Any fool can get hold of a rifle and try to shoot someone, but it's the smart ones who plan the job efficiently that get away with it again and again.'

Jock laid down his chop-sticks. 'So you want someone bumped off. How do you find yourself an assassin?'

Alex sipped some green tea. 'In that "darker world" Cavendish talked about, there are those who know how to make contact, and there are those who know those who know. A few phone calls—not too difficult. But there are definitely firewalls. I wouldn't mind betting that there are no top hit men whose actual identity is known by anyone: that's their only security. Nor is there a hit man who knows the identity of his employer—that's his security.'

'So even if we managed to get the man . . .'

'Or woman, they're at it too.'

'It wouldn't lead us to Steiner?'

Alex shrugged. 'Probably not. A contract's put out: if accepted, some of the money would be deposited, then it's up to the hit man to decide how and when to do the job. Unless, that is, the contract stipulates otherwise. An employer may stipulate a time and place. Hit men don't like that—much more dangerous. The employer may demand a gorier end if someone's really pissed him off. Bit of torture; maybe a few body parts removed first.'

Mary shifted uncomfortably in her chair.

'Gun, knife; drowning in the bath—poison even. Generally, as long as the contract's fulfilled the employer's happy and your man gets the rest of his money. There are apparently specialists around who are experts in whatever sort of end the employer may have in mind.'

Jock poked at a piece of pork with his chopstick. 'You seem well up on this Alex. Much of it going on in this country? All sounds a bit Hollywood.'

'You're lucky to be a policeman in Inverness, Jock, I can tell you. London's a cesspit. You wouldn't believe what goes on here. The killers here are maybe not so sophisticated, often just some moron with a gun who needs a bit of spare cash. In Serious Crimes section I see it all. To some of those thugs, paying to have someone removed is no more special than . . . than . . . a nice Chinese meal. But I think you're dealing with a very sophisticated imported assassin.'

Mary laid down her chopsticks. 'Can we please change the subject now? You're putting me off my food. Jock, forget about the job for one evening. Tell me about Meg. When are we going to meet her? You told us she'd like to visit London—you're welcome to stay with us.'

'No, Mary. Can you see me traipsing about London? Sight—seeing, fighting my way through that seething mass of humanity? And she'd want to go shopping. I couldn't face it, Mary.'

Mary shook her head. 'Jock Anderson. You're a miserable, macho old Scots fart. I know—I'm married to one. Your wife wants to see London, I want to meet her; so she's *going* to see London. Surely you must have some anniversary coming up. Her birthday maybe? When's your wedding anniversary?'

'Oh shit,' groaned Jock. 'Our wedding anniversary's next week: I'd forgotten all about it.'

'Point proven, I think. OK, her birthday then, when's that?' Jock had to think, then consulted his diary.

Mary was shaking her head in disbelief. 'I don't believe it. Alex, he's worse than you.'

'It's in June, in the middle of the summer, Mary—it's a bit of a way off.'

'How old will she be?' Mary wasn't letting up. She stared in disbelief at Jock's blank expression. 'Come on, how old—what age will she be?'

Jock sheepishly picked up his diary again. 'Eh . . . she'll be fifty.'

'And you don't think that's a wee bit special? You and your wife are coming to London for her birthday. I'll take some time off—you too, Alex, we're going to do this properly.'

Mary picked up her mobile. 'I'm going to call her right now, what's your number? You're not getting out of this, Jock. You can have a word with her yourself. You were planning to call her tonight anyway, were you not?'

Jock—totally bemused—nodded dumbly. He'd thought his Meg was a formidable woman—he almost felt sorry for Alex.

Chapter 24

On the Monday following his return to Inverness, Jock immediately called for a meeting of the team in the incident room. There was an air of expectancy when he and DI McLean entered. Jock knew that an injection of enthusiasm was required. When a case drags on and the trail gets steadily colder, lack of results invariably takes its toll. He gave a brief account of his visit to London and then reviewed what information they already had in the light of what he'd learned.

'We are going to assume that the driver of the green car was our hit man: he was in the area at least twice in the days before the killing. My guess is he was there more often than that. I think he spent days watching—setting it up; recording Ogilvie's movements in preparation.'

'But sir,' asked DS Clark. 'Is all this not a wee bit elaborate—a bit far-fetched even? Why follow the man all the way up here to kill him when surely he could just as easily have put a bullet in him in London?'

Jock shrugged. 'Maybe, but look at it this way. There are a lot more eyes and big mouths in London—and a bigger fan for the shit to hit. He couldn't have counted on Steiner and his stag—that could only be a very weird coincidence. Discounting that, he knew that he could count on ample time to get clear. He would probably have anticipated some sort of active response from us: airport clampdown or roadblocks, but he'd guess we'd be a wee bit flat-footed, and would take time to get organized. And he'd have known of course that we'd have no idea who we'd be looking for. He would've been well out of the area, half way to Edinburgh, Glasgow—or Aberdeen before we even got half-way up Dunmorey glen. No, I don't think it was such a daft plan. Could be, of course, that his contract stipulated that the hit must be made up here.

'Whatever, we're going to work on the assumption that he's our man. He was in the area for at least three days, probably more. He must have stayed somewhere. It's a long-shot, but we've got the description of the car and a description, of sorts, of the man himself from Hamish Robertson. We'll start with the hotels; then work down to guest houses. Our man will want to have been as inconspicuous as possible so I'd guess he'd want the anonymity of a big hotel.

'Car hire. Check with the local companies and at the airport. DI McLean will give you your instructions. I'll be taking a couple of you down to Dunmorey to ask around and have another look there.'

Back in his office, Jock was faced with a glum looking DI McLean. 'If our hit man's really the professional you think he is, we've got a right job on. I can't help thinking that it's unlikely we'll come up with something from a hotel. You think he'll have come up by plane?'

Jock shook his head. 'Unlikely. Too many surveillance cameras. He wouldn't have left by plane from Inverness either—too risky.'

'A trip to Dunmorey will probably be a waste of time too, sir,' said DI McLean. 'We covered every inch of that ground in the forest.'

'You're feeling right negative this morning, Bob. At least I'll get a nice cup of tea and one of Morag's homemade scones.'

Jock's mobile rang as they were leaving his office: it was Hamish Robertson, the vet.

'I've seen it sir—I've seen it.'

'You've seen what, lad?'

'The green car with the sticker on the back window: it's parked on Castle Street. I'm standing beside it now.'

'Stay where you are, lad, but be a bit less conspicuous. We're on our way. If there's a traffic warden round or if you can grab a policeman: but there's never one of them round when you want one. I want that car delayed, held somehow until we get there. If the driver gets back before you can arrange a delay, I want a description. Follow the car if you can; make sure you've got the registration number, but don't get involved with the driver: he could be dangerous.'

By the time Jock and DI McLean arrived, there was a squad car parked discreetly out of sight in the Castle car park and two policemen were with Hamish Robertson.

Hamish indicated the car. 'He's only got ten minutes left on his ticket, sir; so unless he wants a parking fine he'll be back any time.'

Jock had barely got his men in position when an elderly couple came struggling up the hill loaded with shopping. They stopped by the car, unlocked it and dumped their bags on the back seat.

Hamish was shaking his head. 'That's definitely not him sir: and he doesn't look in the least bit dangerous.'

The couple were American tourists: a Mr and Mrs Orcott, in Scotland tracing ancestry. Jock was given an account of their search so far. Their name, he was informed, was a phonetic perversion of Urquhart, and they'd traced their ancestry to a William Urquhart from Drumnadrochit, a victim of the Clearances who went to America in 1796. They were just off to visit their old clan family seat: Castle Urquhart on Loch Ness side. They were a really nice couple and Jock was happy to repay them for the good-natured answers to his questions by showing suitable polite interest in their quest.

Hamish may not have found the correct car, but he was in no doubt about the sticker: it showed the name of a car hire company in Edinburgh. Jock took the details from the couple's rental documents.

Back in his car, Jock grinned at DI McLean. 'We've got something, Bob—at last we've got something. The Orcotts said the hire folk took photocopies of their driving licences. With a bit of luck we'll be getting a photo of our man.'

It appeared, initially, to be better than they could have hoped for. The hire company was a small affair: only twenty cars, so it took no great search to identify the likely suspect.

A green Toyota hatchback had been hired for a week by a Michael W. Jarvis, from Saturday 18th to Saturday 25th August: the day of the killing. It had been returned at 2 o'clock on the afternoon of the 25th. It was a family car-hire business, but neither husband nor wife had any recollection of Jarvis. Their records showed that the open-ended booking had been made by phone on Friday 17th. His British driving licence had been scanned, not photocopied, so they were able to provide an excellent photograph. The licence was genuine, but its owner had died in a car crash two months previously. Payment had been with a credit card which was debiting to a Mrs Agnes Thorpe, a pensioner from Oxford. The company owners insisted that they always checked the photograph on the licence, but Jock wasn't convinced. DVLA had been approached for more details and a photograph. The airline companies had no record of a Michael Jarvis. If he'd come to Edinburgh by plane it was under another alias.

Jock sat at his desk toying with the photo from the driving licence. Enlarged, it had lost surprisingly little quality. It showed a man who appeared to be in his thirties, closely cropped hair, heavily moustached. He was wearing a pair of heavy framed glasses. Jock chewed his pipe impatiently. The lab in Glasgow was working on the photo, removing the glasses and moustache and replacing cropped pate with longer black hair. He'd also been promised a computer-generated profile. Jock had given up marvelling at what could be achieved by computers and was happy to accept the results: he just wished they'd hurry up and send them. He'd convinced himself, rightly or wrongly, that the driver of the green car was their man. With a decent photograph to show Hamish Robertson, then maybe he could be closer to confirming that.

A smiling Bob McLean came into the office; he was carrying two folders. He opened the first folder and slid it across the desk: inside were the results of the computer generation.

'This is great Bob! This could be the man Hamish described—he's even got a nice long nose in this profile. The Glasgow boys have done a good job on this.'

Bob McLean gave Jock a wry smile, opened and slid the second file across. Before Jock, was a colour photo of Michael Winston Jarvis and a copy of his licence application form provided by the DVLA.

Jock laughed. 'Bloody hell; he's a big black man.' Jock scratched his head. 'Well, at least we know the photo on the licence isn't the big black man; so the licence has been doctored. But the photo on this licence will have to at least resemble our man.'

An hour later, Jock was addressing his team. It had taken only half an hour to get a copy of the computer-modified photo to Hamish Robertson. Hamish said he couldn't, unfortunately, confirm with any certainty that it was their man. Jock had to be content that at least he couldn't positively eliminate him either.

'What we have may prove to be bugger-all, but it's all we've got. I think our man would be daft to be running on a driving licence with a photo that didn't at least bear a passing resemblance to the man himself. A simple routine check, or a traffic incident could rumble him and he's too much of a pro to risk that. But it's very likely that he'll have moved to another alias to register in some hotel. You're looking for someone registered for about a week. The car was hired on the 18th, so unless our man did a wee bit of sightseeing in Edinburgh for a few days I reckon he'll have booked in on the evening of the 18th, probably staying put for the week, and signing out on the 25th. Don't be looking for a week's advance booking—he wouldn't have known for sure how long it would take to do the job. You've all got the photo, you've got a name and you've got dates—so see what you come up with.

'I'm taking DC Ross and DC Annie Miller to Dunmorey.' Jock waved the photos of the suspect at the pair. 'I want everyone at Dunmorey re-interviewed and this photo stuck under noses. Take the thumb screws with you; I want memories jogged.'

It was a cold blustery day on Dunmorey. While his officers interviewed everyone currently available on the estate, Jock and Dunkie took a drive up to the area of woodland they'd identified as the source of the shot. Nick was along for the trip and he and Gyp were excitedly exploring the ground. There was very little wind in the pine forest, and the air almost felt warm. The trees had been brashed, branches removed to head height, so the movement of the men was unrestricted.

Jock looked round him. 'I think he was here every day, Dunkie. Probably every morning, and maybe every evening in the week before the shooting. Watching and waiting; planning for the shot, just picking his time. He must surely have left *some* trace behind.'

Dunkie kicked at the carpet of pine needles and sat where the shooter had supposedly taken his position, resting his stick as a rifle on the stump of branch identified by DC Ross. 'It's nae bad, Jock, right comfy an' steady. A could drop Lordie very nicely frae here. If this is how he did it he'd hae tae be a gid bit taller than me though; A'm sittin' a wee bittie too low.' Wee Dunkie was only about five foot eight. When Jock took Dunkie's stick and repeated the exercise he felt he was positioned perfectly. Jock was just over six foot; they had a bit more to add to the description of the shooter.

'I think Bob McLean's right though, Dunkie; we'll find bugger all in another search. As he walked out of the woods and leaned on the deer fence, a gust of wind almost took off his deerstalker. An ominous grey cloud shrouded the head of the glen. There were no eagles about.

Dunkie pointed up the glen. 'That lot'll be hittin' us soon, Jock.' Jock nodded and walked a few yards further down the hill, not knowing what he was looking for but feeling sure he wouldn't be finding it. He was already about fifty yards below the site of the shooting and was about to head back through the trees to the car when his eye was caught by the flicker of something white on the wire of the fence another ten yards below him. The first drops of rain were hitting him as he unhooked a white tissue from the wire, examined it and showed his find to Dunkie.

Dunkie looked at it in distaste. 'Somebuddy's gaed their arse a gid wipe wi' that, Jock, if A'm no' mistaken.'

'Aye Dunkie, and if we could find the mother lode it could maybe be right helpful. Let's have a wee competition.'

Jock called in Nick and Gyp and gave each of them a sniff of the tissue, narrowly avoiding Nick's attempt to eat it.

'OK you pair; time to earn your keep.' He waved the two dogs off: 'Seekit.'

Both Nick and Gyp were trained gun dogs and they knew what was expected of them. The two men watched as their dogs quartered the ground under the trees, tails going frantically in their excitement. The search lasted only a few minutes until Nick barked and began digging in the needles. Jock called him off, bent and gave him a big hug of congratulations then knelt where the dog had disturbed the surface needles. Digging carefully with a stick, about a foot down, at the base of the carpet of needles he found it. There were several more pieces of tissue beneath which was a load of dried up, but identifiable, faeces.

'Keep the dogs off this, Dunkie. I'm going to the car for a collection kit.'

When he returned, Dunkie watched in disgust as Jock spooned a good sample of the faeces into a tub.

'Funny how sweet corn just passes straight through: ye'd wonder why we bother eatin' it,' muttered Dunkie.

Jock chuckled at Dunkie's observation. 'DNA, Dunkie. From this smelly pile of shit we can get the shooter's DNA. If we can just find him, we can nail him.'

'Aye Jock, but dae ye no' think maybe it'll turn oot tae be the Jolly Green Giant?'

Back at Dunkie's house, Jamie and DC Miller were in the large kitchen drinking tea and enjoying Morag's scones. There was a homely warm fug generated from the old log-fired Aga. A full storm driven by a cold north wind was battering the windows as Jock and Dunkie joined the others at the table for a welcome cup of tea.

Jamie and DC Miller had come up with nothing new, but they'd only found a few of the interviewees, the rest were scheduled for the following day. Jock gave them an account of his findings.

Jamie, who'd been involved in the original search, looked sheepish. 'We must have missed it, sir.'

Jock shook his head. 'No, it was outside your designated search area. I was just lucky. If I'm right, our man got caught short. Maybe our good Highland cooking didn't agree with him. It had been right watery stuff. Maybe he wasn't as professional as we think or he'd have done an SAS in a plastic bag. He thought he'd gone a safe enough distance. Maybe he'd liked to have gone further but couldn't hang on any longer.' Jock smiled round the table. 'It happens.'

'Too bloody true,' laughed Dunkie. 'A remember one time after we'd had an Indian when we were in Edinburgh. Bloody gid curry it wis. It really hit me when we were drivin' home. Ye mind that Morag?'

'Aye, no easy tae forget. A had tae hold a travelling rug up tae hide ye frae all the cars—bit embarrassin' on the side o' the A9.'

Dunkie grinned. 'But A didnae care—A had tae get rid o' it.'

Jock was laughing. 'So there you are. If our man had a Dunkie experience he maybe had little choice. He did have time to scrape a decent hole but it looks as if a bit of Kleenex escaped; maybe a gust of wind took it off.'

He looked at Jamie. 'I'm assuming that none of your lot had a dump when you were making your search?'

'Not me anyway,' said Jamie smiling. 'No, sir, it wasn't us.'

'Well, while we can't totally discount the possibility that some estate worker, or even a rambler or birdwatcher got caught short—I think it was our man who left his mark.'

Chapter 25

The following Friday evening Jock was sitting with Meg in front of the fire. He'd filled her in on the day's events, and she was telling him about an outbreak of measles at the school when his mobile rang: it was John MacDougal, the stalker from the Steiner estate. Jock frowned and looked at his watch: it was almost 9.30.

MacDougal sounded agitated. 'There's somethin' no' right here Superintendent, somethin' no' right at all. Ye've got tae get up here quick. There's somethin' no' right.' A bemused Jock managed to calm MacDougal down and to extract a surprisingly articulate account.

MacDougal told him that they'd not been on the hill that day. No stalking had been planned and the weather had ensured that. He and two ghillies had been set on some maintenance work, and they'd been told by Steiner that they'd to be off down the glen, clear of the Lodge by 2.00, and not to report back until Monday morning: an arrangement which suited the men just fine. As the weather closed in and maintenance work was rained-off, MacDougal and his two men had a few drams watching the down-pour. MacDougal had sent his men off early intending to follow after doing some work on his Land Rover. Instead he'd had a few more drams and had fallen asleep on one of the beds in the old ghillies' room. He'd woken in darkness.

There was no power in the old ghillies' room, and, desperate to relieve himself, he'd groped his way to the door and had been about to go into the yard when he'd seen a figure silhouetted by lights from the Lodge: it was a man in combat fatigues with a gun, a rifle—an AK47 by the look of it, standing about twenty yards away. He'd heard the crackle of a radio. The man had unclipped a small set from his belt, muttered something unintelligible then moved off.

The lights in the Lodge were blazing and there was the sound of loud music. MacDougal was well accustomed to Steiner and his extravagances: there had been many wild gatherings before as Steiner partied with his rich friends. MacDougal knew that he was trapped, at least until the morning. He'd be in trouble with his boss if he tried to drive out tonight. There *was* no way out. The Lodge was surrounded by a three-metre fence topped by razor wire. The exit, a huge wrought iron gate, would be locked and presumably guarded. He had quietly relieved himself and was heading back to his bed and a half bottle of whisky when he'd heard a girl screaming. He'd peeked out again—the guard had gone, presumably continuing his patrol. He had pulled on his own camouflage jacket, stuck on his deerstalker and slipped out into the dark. The ground between the old stable block and the Lodge was lawn planted with shrubs. Moving cautiously from bush to bush, he had made his way to where he thought the scream had come from—the huge glass conservatory addition to the east end of the Lodge. He knew that the loud music would cover any noise he may make, but as he'd crouched beneath a bush considering his next move, another armed man had appeared from round the corner of the illuminated conservatory. The man had looked round and disappeared, heading back towards the front of the building. MacDougal had stiffened as there was another stifled scream. He covered the short distance to the Lodge unseen and had slipped through the door into the large kitchen. The room had been in darkness. Unsure of his next move, MacDougal had held himself against a wall when he'd heard a commotion in the corridor leading to kitchen. Suddenly a half naked young girl had burst through the door. MacDougal guessed from her naked immature breasts, that she was no more than a child: no more than twelve or thirteen years old. From the light of the corridor he could see her awful, terrified expression: her desperation. She had seen MacDougal frozen to the wall and made to move towards him, crying in some foreign language, when she was grabbed roughly from behind by a naked fat man who slapped her on the face and hauled her screaming back into the corridor, slamming the door behind him.

Jock had listened to John MacDougal's story in shocked silence, his mind racing. He told MacDougal to stay in the ghillies' room but to keep his mobile to hand.

In minutes, Jock had contacted DI McLean and organized a team including four officers from the armed response unit, and had them all meet at the station. Gathered round a map, they quickly formulated a plan of action. They had to get in there and catch Steiner and his pals in the act. Jock wanted photographic evidence. To do this they'd have to disable the guards before they could signal a warning to the Lodge. From MacDougal he knew there were at least two guards but he suspected that there would be more. Jock was tempted to recruit MacDougal for a reconnaissance, but to risk endangering a member of the public was unthinkable. MacDougal did, however, provide useful information on the Lodge's defences.

Jock and DI McLean remembered from their visit to the estate that the approach road was hidden from the Lodge until about the last fifty metres, so vehicles without headlights could make it undetected—and hopefully the music from the Lodge would cover engine noises.

It was an overcast night, and the cloud cover largely obscured any light from a weak half moon. The guard on the gate to Steiner's Lodge was cold and bored. It wasn't yet midnight, and he still had a long night ahead of him. He settled his rifle strap on his shoulder and lit another cigarette.

From the road below the gate he heard stumbling footsteps and someone singing; there was laughter and a second voice joined in the song. The clouds had cleared sufficiently for him to make out two figures in tweed jackets and plus-fours with deerstalkers on their heads slowly making their way up the road towards him and the closed gate. Both seemed to be drunk, and the larger figure had his arm round a smaller companion. The pair stopped and seemed to share a drink from a bottle before continuing unsteadily towards him. They were singing quietly together, the guard thought it sounded like *The Wild Rover*.

The guard smiled to himself and stubbed out his cigarette as he stepped out of the shadows and prepared to confront the two drunks. He'd been told to radio in if he saw anything unusual: since when were two drunks in Scotland unusual? He could deal with this. There was a locked gate between him and the visitors—they'd not be crashing the party. The guard watched as the two men stopped at the closed gates.

The larger of the two cursed and shook the bars. 'The fuckin' thing's locked, Bob. Wi' a wee leg up dae ye think ye'd get ower?'

The smaller man staggered backwards and looked up at the gate. 'No fuckin' way Jock; A'll end up wi' one o' they spikes up ma arse. A think we need a wee drink.' He was struggling to pull a half bottle of whisky from his jacket pocket when the guard showed himself on the other side of the gate and shone a torch in the faces of the two men.

'Pit that fuckin' thing away man; ye're fuckin' blindin' me. Let us in, will ye!' shouted the larger man.

'Fuck off the pair o' ye—ye're no' comin' in here. This is private property.'

'Ye hear that Bob—fuckin' private property, is it? Look you, we fuckin' work here—we just want tae get in fir a wee kip. Bob's missus has kicked him oot, says he's drunk—can ye believe that. A man canny hae a wee dram or twa wi' his pal on a Friday night—him that pits food on the table. A'll never understand wimmen. Nae fuckin' gratitude, nae fuckin' gratitude. Is that no' right Bob?'

Jock grabbed the bars again and rattled the gate. In the darkness the guard unslung his rifle and was raising the butt to hit Jock's knuckles when he grunted and staggered forward, his face crashing against the bars. Jock looked into glazed eyes as the man slid down the gate and rolled groaning on the ground

From the darkness behind him, with what looked like a shotgun in his hands, appeared the grinning figure of John MacDougal. 'Onythin' left in that bottle o' yours, DI McLean?—this is right thirsty work.'

Jock looked through the gate at the figure on the ground. 'You idiot, MacDougal, if you've killed him there'll be hell to pay. I told you to stay in the ghillies' room.'

'We can talk aboot that later, Mr Anderson,' muttered MacDougal as he tied the guard's hands. 'He's no' deid, just had a wee dunt on the heid. A'll just stick some o' this on that big mooth o' his.'

Jock heard the sound of stripping parcel tape.

'Ye'll be wantin' tae come in. Just gie me a minute.' MacDougal dragged the moaning guard clear of the gates and was lost in the darkness.

Jock turned to Bob McLean who grinned at him. 'He's ex-SAS sir. This is kid's stuff to him—he's loving it.'

There was a click, a whirring of an electric motor and the gates slowly opened. Jock hurried through and bent over the groaning figure of the guard. Deciding that MacDougal was right, that the man would have nothing worse than a sore head, Jock and DI McLean were whispering at the roadside when MacDougal returned.

'Nae need tae whisper lads. A've taken care o' the lot o' them—A've no' had sae much fun since the Congo.' He frowned at Jock. 'There werenae ony weak stomachs ower there, sir.' He prodded the recumbent guard with his boot. 'He's lucky A didnae cut his throat—through habit like. The bastard—he'd hae crushed yer fingers, Mr Anderson. Ye were still blinded wi' that torch; ye didnae see what he wis gaen tae dae, did ye?'

Jock shook his head. 'Thanks John, thanks.'

As Jock was pulling a radio from his pocket, two black-clad policemen appeared from the darkness behind MacDougal. One stuck a pistol to his head.

'Drop it—I'll only say it once.'

MacDougal smiled and dropped his shotgun. 'Ye silly buggers—ye're five minutes ower late.'

Jock called up the vehicles and the rest of the team gathered round near the gate. 'I want photographs: lots of photographic evidence. We'll have some of the best crooked lawyers in Europe descending on us screaming blue murder after this lot. They'll try to make it look like these bastards were having a nice wee tea party for some poor underprivileged girls. John here has taken care of the bullyboys, and he's had a good peek in through the windows of the big conservatory. There's a full blown orgy going on—at least five men doing God knows what to a bunch of young girls.'

Jock looked round the assembled policemen and women. 'Follow John—Sergeant John MacDougal, late SAS and 3rd Para—I think he knows what he's doing. Take your time, do this right. These bastards are enjoying themselves, set cosy for the night—let's not disturb them till we're ready. John says it'll be easy to take photographs through some open windows in the big conservatory. When you've got the pictures we'll meet at the back door of the Lodge and go in.'

He turned to Dr Paterson. 'Your team ready?'

The doctor nodded. 'How many girls are there?'

Jock looked at John MacDougal.

'A've counted eight, but there could be mair.'

Jock shook his head in disgust. 'Aye, they're planning a nice long week-end. There's maybe a few spare—in reserve for when some wear out.'

Only half an hour later the team was gathered by the back door of the Lodge. A grim faced DC Ross took Jock's arm. 'We've got to get in there now, sir.' He waved a digital video camera. 'It's all on this. Those girls are—'

'I know lad, I've seen what's going on.' Jock indicated his own camera and looked round at the other officers. Four grim faces, four cameras were lifted. 'You're happy you've got everything you can?

'OK, Go! Get the bastards!'

Jock had them all assembled in the Lodge kitchen. Five shivering, middle-aged, naked, overweight men made an unedifying picture. Three, too drugged or drunk to fully comprehend what was happening, were standing in numbed disbelief, but Steiner and an obscenely fat man were protesting loudly in mixed English and German.

Jock surveyed the group in disgust. 'Their pathetic little dicks could use a good swabbing, don't you think Doc?'

Dr. Paterson looked at him. 'How can this sort of thing happen, Jock? They're animals—fucking animals.'

Jock turned to Bob McLean. 'Read them their rights, Bob. And to be sure—just so that there can be no claims of any misunderstanding—DC Ross, will you please deliver the same in German. And I want all of this recorded on video.'

There were ten young girls. A team of four female PCs, a doctor, three nurses and two interpreters were trying to calm them in the still illuminated conservatory. The music and strobe lights were off, but the horror of the place was starkly revealed: the frame from which two naked girls had been untied—the bubbling Jacuzzi, a glass-topped table with lines of cocaine still drawn out; couches with ties for bondage.

The interpreters who'd been rushed in from town were doing their best but the girls were clearly terrified. They could communicate with only one girl: she was Latvian with broken Russian. Through her, they managed however, with the help of the empathetic female PCs and nurses, to convince the girls to trust them and subject themselves to the indignity of swabbing and a brief preliminary medical examination.

Two middle-aged women had been found asleep together in a bedroom in a far wing of the Lodge. German, butch and obnoxious, they were clearly not there to be sexually exploited. Jock refused to accept their claim to be caterers. He thought they'd look just fine in black Gestapo uniforms and suspected that, while they may indeed have catering responsibilities, they were in charge of the girls and ordered that they be taken in—but he allowed them the dignity of dressing.

It was after 3.00 in the morning before the ambulances with the girls, and police cars loaded with blanket-clad prisoners left the estate. Almost the last to leave were the three guards, one with his head bandaged. They were dumped, still bound, in the back of a Land Rover.

Jock, Bob McLean and John MacDougal were gathered in the big kitchen of the Lodge. John MacDougal took off his deer-stalker and ran his hands through his hair. 'What a fucking night—there must be some whisky aroond here some place.'

Jock smiled as John began searching the cupboards.

'Schnapps, schnapps an' more fucking schnapps! Nae wonder they Krauts are so fucked up drinkin' that stuff.'

'I think I saw a bottle in the orgy room,' said Jock. 'But don't touch anything else—that's a crime scene.'

MacDougal returned a few minutes later triumphantly waving a bottle of Black Label.

Jock grinned. 'I didn't see you do that.'

'Doing what?' DI McLean grinned as he lifting a glass for filling.

Jock turned as Jamie Ross entered the kitchen. 'That's the last of them off, sir. We had to cuff the two dykes: wrist and ankles. One of them took a swing at PC Harris. She'll have a shiner in the morning. The bitch obviously has had martial arts training—it took four of us to restrain her. She just about got me in the balls.' Jamie flinched as he rubbed his thigh.

'Well, you'd better get back to town for some treatment for that. And tell Jo I'm right sorry to have dragged you out, you being off duty, too. She'd best be getting used to it, her taking up with a policeman.'

Jamie flushed in embarrassment.

'Off you go lad, and well done. You had the video camera, didn't you?'

Jamie nodded. 'Aye, sir.'

'I've had a quick look. You got some great stuff. Get off home now—I'll be needing you in the office first thing.'

'He's a good lad,' said Bob McLean when Jamie left. 'He'll go places.'

'Aye Bob, he'd better. He'll no' stay a humble DC for long if Jo has anything to do with it.'

'How come he's here tonight? He was off duty.'

Jock accepted a refill of Black Label and smiled at Bob. 'Meg phoned up Jo a few minutes before the call from John came in. Jamie answered it so I knew where he was. I thought maybe he'd enjoy a wee trip out—good experience for him. Anyway, it'll teach him to keep his head down when he's off duty. I'll have another wee dram from that bottle of yours I didn't see, John, and then we're off. Busy day tomorrow. Bob, you're driving.'

Jock turned to John MacDougal. 'The shit's going to hit the fan tomorrow, John. The press and maybe TV will be on to this. They feed on this sort of stuff and they'll be wetting themselves for an inside story. Please keep your mouth shut if they get to you.'

Chapter 26

There was already mayhem in the station car park when Jock arrived just before 7.30. The press had got word that something big had gone down and were clamouring for details. Some folk likened the press to vultures. Jock thought they were more like flies—they somehow could smell shit from miles off. At least with vultures you could chase them off for a bit; but like flies, the press were straight back in your face. There was, however, a mutual respect between Jock and the local reporters. He appreciated that they had a job to do and he'd always try to give them some copy. This morning he had to deal with a load of hard men from the national press who smelt blood. Unfortunately for them there was little that he could give them beyond a statement that some men were in custody following a raid on a local property, but stressed, in answer to the inevitable question, that there were no terrorist implications, but yes, sex and drugs were involved and yes, the armed response team had been employed.

The reporters' appetites unsated, Jock retreated to his office with Bob McLean. Bob took a sip of his coffee. 'None of the five will say a word without their lawyers present. They're coming from all over, the first one's flying in from Germany—on a private plane of course. He's due in a couple of hours, and there's more to follow. Bit of local colour, though—Steiner's using Owen Evans. I think we can expect him any minute. Word is Steiner's Edinburgh lawyers won't touch this one.'

Jock smiled. 'Aye, nothing's too smelly for that slime ball. We'll have a bit of fun with him. We do this right and they can all go and screw themselves. Everything by the book, Bob, or they'll be shafting us.' Jock rubbed his hands. 'More coffee, I think, then we'll get all our lovely little ducks in a row.'

'I demand to see my client immediately.'

Jock stoked his pipe, smiled at Bob McLean and eyed the overweight little lawyer seated in his office.

'What's the hurry, Mr Evans? He'll hardly have finished his breakfast.' Jock slid a sheet of paper across his desk. 'Your authorization. You may visit your client at your convenience. Have you already met Mr Steiner, by the way?'

'No, but I fail to see the relevance of that question.'

'Well, just trying to be helpful. So as you'll recognize him, I'll show you some nice photos of the man.' Jock opened a file on his desk. 'I think you'll find these to be a good likeness.' He closed the file and slid it over his desk.

Evans, after a moment's hesitation, rose, picked up the folder and opened it. Jock was enjoying this and made no attempt to conceal his disgust.

'Stuck for words are we, Mr Evans? That's not like you. Well endowed for such a small man, don't you think? It's really great stuff that Viagra; or so they tell me. Must be a bit uncomfortable for that wee girl though. I assume you can see which orifice he's employing. There's a nice big blow up on the next sheet if you're in any doubt. That wee girl is eleven years old, Mr Evans—eleven years old. If you'll excuse me, Mr Evans, I'm very busy this morning. I'm sure you'll understand.' Jock got up and left the office leaving the lawyer looking through the file in stunned silence.

An hour later Jock was sitting with Hamish Gordon, the Procurator Fiscal. He'd had a verbal account from Jock and was flipping through his report. The files of photos were open beside him on his desk.

'Bloody hell, Jock, you've brought me a lovely can of worms beautifully wrapped up. Tell me Jock, is it wrong to be getting so much pleasure from this? I can't wait to get stuck into these bastards.'

Jock smiled and shook his head. 'They're scum, Hamish. Very rich powerful scum who think they can buy everyone and get off with anything. You'll see at the end of the report a wee resume of each one. Our friends in Germany and Switzerland are delighted. They've been trying to nail these slugs with something—anything would do. Even the Swiss couldn't be more helpful. Hatred of paedophiles transcends all boundaries, it seems. They had a big screen set up with downloaded child porn in their orgy room. Seems that's given our colleagues the excuse they needed to raid offices and homes. What else will they uncover on their computers, one wonders? Aye, a good haul it seems.

'The first load of lawyers has arrived so we can start asking our guests a few questions. They'll no doubt be screaming for bail.'

The Procurator Fiscal laughed. 'Bail! No bloody way. These worms are staying in my can—we can both enjoy watching them wriggle.'

By late afternoon the preliminary interrogations had been completed. Faced with the irrefutable evidence, the lawyers were floundering. Even Owen Evans, an expert on Scottish law and a master of loopholes could find no way through. Jock and the Procurator Fiscal had done their jobs well.

Back home that evening Jock was listening to Meg.

'She wasn't very amused about it. I think she had something more romantic in mind for his night off.' Meg kissed Jock on the cheek as he ate his dinner. 'But she'll forgive you. Jamie was full of it. He was very happy, so she's happy.'

Jock smiled at her. 'They wouldn't be if that dyke had been on target.' Meg punched him playfully on the arm as Jock continued. 'Seriously though. He got off lightly—he'll have learned, I hope, a very valuable lesson: to be more careful with female prisoners next time. Remember that young probationer who lost an eye when he was too casual with a drunk girl?—a wee slip of a thing with fingernails like claws.'

Meg ruffled Jock's hair. 'Anyway, she'll be switching phones off next time he's off duty. Eat your dinner. The news is on in twenty minutes and I want to see you on the TV.'

The incident had attracted intense national interest. Meg had missed the live Sky News coverage when Jock had faced the cameras late that afternoon, but with Sky's propensity to suck the juice out of every story, they were pretty sure they'd have an expanded version for their 7 o'clock news. Meg switched on the TV and took her seat on the arm of Jock's big armchair. It must have been a slack news day—Strathgellie was headline news.

'Oh no,' groaned Jock. 'It's getting the full Sky treatment.'

Meg hushed him as she turned up the volume.

'Late last night the Inverness Police made a daring raid on the Highland shooting Lodge of the Strathgellie Estate near Inverness.' Aerial pictures of Strathgellie Lodge came on screen. The helicopter circled and the camera zoomed onto the German flag flapping in a stiff breeze. The boundary fence was hidden for much of its length, but was, in many places clearly visible.

'Behind a three-metre, razor-wire-topped fence, and protected by armed men, it is alleged that a group of five middle-aged German businessmen were engaged in an orgy with ten girls; the youngest of whom was ten years old, the eldest thirteen.

'Under cover of darkness the police moved in, cleverly disabled the guards armed with AK47 assault rifles and apprehended the five men. It is believed that quantities of drugs were seized. Our Scotland correspondent is at the Strathgellie estate.'

A cold looking reporter appeared on screen.

'There is no doubt that yesterday night, in the Lodge behind me on the other side of these impressive gates, five men were engaged in an unspeakable episode with a group of ten young girls. We understand that all of the girls are of East European origin and that they are currently in the care of the local authorities. It seems that they are of several nationalities and the local police are appealing for any local Latvian or Romanian speakers to assist them as interpreters.

'I spoke earlier with the man heading up the investigation: Detective Superintendent Jock Anderson of the Highland Constabulary in Inverness.'

The scene shifted to the police HQ in Inverness, the camera focused for a moment on the board advertising the fact at the station entrance, then panned back and zoomed in on a group of three figures on the police station steps. Jock was flanked by DI McLean and DS Clark.

'Superintendent, what can you tell us about the events of yesterday evening?'

Jock frowned at the camera for a few moments. 'This is an ongoing investigation which is still at a very early stage, so unfortunately I am unable to tell you very much beyond my statement of this morning. I can confirm that five men are in custody in connection with an incident yesterday night. The men are under arrest and have been charged with people trafficking, indecent assault and rape of minors, and the possession of Class A drugs. They will also be facing fire-arms charges.'

'These minors, can you confirm that they were all young girls?'

Jock nodded. 'They are between the ages of ten and thirteen years.'

A BBC reporter asked if armed officers had been involved in the raid and whether it had been necessary to use firearms. Jock told them that yes, they'd had information that the premises were being guarded by armed men. They had been subdued, no weapons had been fired but armed officers had been involved.

'We have information, Superintendent, that the Strathgellie estate is owned by a German businessman, a Mr Klaus Steiner. Can you confirm that he is one of the five men under arrest and that all of the men involved are Germans?'

'Four of the men are German, one is Swiss. Mr Steiner is one of the men in custody.'

The BBC reporter had another question. 'Some weeks ago, Mr Steiner was involved in a hunting accident when the Duke of Dunmorey, the owner of the neighbouring estate, was shot. Is there any connection with that incident?'

'None. It seems simply that Herr Steiner is having a run of very bad luck.'

Jock evaded several other questions and excused himself, assuring the reporters that he would be making a fuller statement as soon as was possible.

A Sky reporter was back on screen. 'I have here with me Jimmy Campbell, a ghillie on the Strathgellie estate.'

An unkempt, unshaven middle-aged man in tweeds and deerstalker appeared on the screen. Behind him was the public bar of the Moray Inn.

Jock groaned. 'Shit, they've tracked him down to the pub the bugger'll be half pissed.'

'Mr. Campbell, you are employed on the Strathgellie Estate. What can you tell us about your boss, the owner, Mr Steiner?'

'Him? He's a right wee shite o' a man—we a' call him the Führer: a right little bastard he is.'

'Have you worked for Mr Steiner for some time?'

'Aye, A have that. Far too bloody long. A wis there when he bought the place aboot five years ago an' A stayed on.'

'Was Mr Steiner in the habit of entertaining guests on the estate?'

'Aye, he wis; every couple o' months or so. We were ey kicked off the place first though—he didnae want any riff-raff like us aboot the place. Just like yesterday, but we kent fine when he wis havin' one o' his wee private ceilidhs. Big cars up an' doon the glen; helicopters sometimes, an' lots o' loud music.'

'You had no indication that anything untoward was taking place?'

'Untoward? Ye mean did A ken that him and his Kraut pals were fuckin' a load o' children? No, A didnae, but A can tell ye A'm no' a bit surprised—he's a right nasty little shite o' a man.'

'Mr Campbell has painted a rather unattractive picture of his employer,' came back the reporter. The photograph of a round-faced man in wire-rimmed glasses, a Tyrolean hat on his head and sporting a small Hitler moustache came on screen. 'Herr Klaus Adolph Steiner.

'We understand that the Head Stalker on the estate, Mr John MacDougal, played an active part in last night's rescue operation.'

John MacDougal, in shirtsleeves standing at what seemed to be the open front door of his house, came on screen. He was smiling at the camera.

Jock groaned. 'Forego your fifteen minutes of fame John. Keep your bloody mouth shut.'

The reporter thrust a microphone in front of John MacDougal. 'Mr MacDougal, you are the Head Stalker on the Strathgellie estate.'

'I am.'

'What can you tell us about your employer, Mr Steiner?'

'He is an unpleasant wee German mannie.'

'Is that all?'

'Is that no' enough?'

'We understand that you were actively involved in the events of last night. Would you care to tell the viewers what happened?'

'No A widnae, an' ma dinner's on the table. Sorry viewers, but nane o' this is ony o' your business, so will ye please excuse me?' MacDougal turned, went into his house and closed the door behind him.

Jock clapped his hands. 'Good on you, John. Handled like a pro.'

Sky moved onto a story about another bit of political sleaze and Jock switched off. 'You'll get the STV news later, Meg. Maybe they'll have come up with something more for you.'

Chapter 27

Jock and Meg had a Sunday morning routine: a longish lie—in, a bit of Radio Scotland for the news, breakfast in bed made by Jock, and then, still in bed, the Sunday papers dropped off by a neighbour who was happy to make the trip to the shop in town for his own. His reward and thanks—a big bottle of malt whisky for Christmas and a few fresh eggs when the chickens were in lay, which seemed to be rarely. Meg kept telling Jock they'd passed it and they needed to replace them with a young flock but Jock hadn't got round to it. Anyway, he liked the old girls pecking round the yard. They'd produced an egg for each of them for their breakfasts, so sentence again deferred.

The papers all featured a story about the events at Strathgellie. *The Times* and *The Telegraph* carried a reasonably accurate account. *The Times* had a more flattering picture of Jock, *The Telegraph* a more elaborate spread. It was the neighbour's idea of a joke to provide the *The News of the World,* where, of course, it made the front page.

'Look at this,' said Jock waving the *The News of the World.* 'How do they come up with this stuff? If you believe this lot, they know more about Steiner than we do—maybe they do. Folk will talk to a journalist before a policeman, especially if they're slipped a few quid. Lots of lurid sex stuff as you'd expect. They've got Steiner heading up a white sex-slave trade in young girls—maybe he was, and they're tying in the Nazi Steiner with the dead

Duke. They've got him as the killer and want a full enquiry. That would be bloody interesting, would it not? Could embarrass a few folks in London if they were forced to take a good look.' He tossed the paper on the floor. 'Just as well for them no one with any influence reads that rag. They're on the right lines though, Meg. Our wee German mannie didn't pull the trigger himself, but how the hell do I nail the little bastard? I should have the DNA results from the shit sample tomorrow. Not much chance we'll get a match from the DNA bank. Maybe we should pop down to the church for a quick prayer to McGoddie?'

Meg dumped her paper on the floor. 'Will you just switch off for a bit: for at least half an hour—more if you're up to it. Come here and give me my well-earned Sunday cuddle.'

Interest in the case had died somewhat by Monday morning. The press charabanc had moved on. Even Sky could squeeze no more juice out of the story. The guilty were locked up and no lurid photos would be forthcoming; no more scandal on the horizon. The great unwashed had lost interest in a bunch of foreign perverts. Jock was mildly disappointed when there were only reporters from *The Scotsman* and the local *Press and Journal* to greet him on his arrival at the station. It was a cold wet morning. Jock took pity on the pair of them and he had them in for a chat over coffee in the canteen. They got their coffee and biscuits but not much more as Jock had nothing new he could give them. As they were finishing, Owen Evans arrived so Jock unloaded them onto him. The lawyer was delighted to have an audience for his accusations of police heavy handedness, general mishandling of the raid, and supposed infringements of the human rights of the prisoners. He would maybe provide the reporters with a few paragraphs for their papers, but Jock suspected that as there would be no public sympathy for the accused, their editors would be unimpressed.

Jock called Dr Paterson from his office. The doctor had two reports for him. The DNA analysis of the faeces from the woods had produced some excellent results but so far no match from any database. Doc Paterson had a good laugh about the Jolly Green Giant hypothesis.

The second report was more interesting—the DNA extracted from the cigarette end found at the scene of Hughie MacRae's death matched that of Richard Ogilvie. Jock slowly replaced the receiver. It was circumstantial, would never stand up in court, but there was absolutely no doubt in Jock's mind that Ogilvie had removed the one obstacle to his golf course plans by killing Hugh MacRae. He called Jamie Ross to his office to give him the news of the results.

On hearing the news Jamie swore under his breath but smiled. 'It's nice to be vindicated sir. I was planning to come and see you this morning with an update on my investigation into Hughie's killing.'

Jamie took out his notebook. 'I spoke to Dunkie at Dunmorey. He had no bother remembering the night—Hughie had been a good family friend. Ogilvie had gone off about 8 o'clock that evening in a foul temper. Apparently he'd had a business dinner arranged with his lawyer and accountant at the Moray Inn. He was late; the Range Rover had a puncture and the spare was flat so he took off in the old estate Land Rover. I've spoken to Owen Evans and Mr MacPhee and they've confirmed that they had a meal with Ogilvie at The Moray that night. They both agreed they all left about 10 o'clock, as the ceilidh was starting, when Ogilvie had got irritated by what he called "that awful, noisy, peasant music". MacPhee didn't like that—he likes his music. Actually, sir, I got the impression Mr MacPhee didn't like Ogilvie very much at all.

'Evans and MacPhee had ordered a taxi, but the Duke was determined to drive home even though he'd had a lot to drink. MacPhee said he'd had far too much. They were waiting for their taxi when Ogilvie drove off in his Land Rover.'

'And Hughie, did they see him?'

'I'm coming to that sir. Would you believe that Councillor MacPhee's a closet biker? Loves bikes—says he's got an old Harley at home in the garage.'

Jock laughed. 'Can't quite imagine the wee man on a bike, and certainly not a big Harley.'

Jamie smiled and nodded. 'Anyway, he'd noticed the blue Honda Varadero: that's Hughie's bike, when they'd arrived. It was parked right outside the front door. MacPhee couldn't identify Hughie, but the bike was driven out of the car park right in front of Ogilvie in his Land Rover; he'd actually peeped at Hughie who was apparently a bit slow in getting onto the main road.'

Jock lit his pipe and sat back in his chair. 'Evans. Did he see the bike?'

'No sir, he had very little to say—he was his usual surly self. What I'd like to do now, sir, is to get forensics to have a look at the old estate Land Rover. It's a very long shot sir, a really long shot. The chance of them finding anything now is a bit remote. But can you please authorize that, sir?'

Jock nodded. 'Aye lad, no harm in their having a look. I doubt if that old thing's ever had a wash so they might just find something. Well done lad, very well done—a nice bit of police work. Aye lad, the remaining obstacle to Ogilvie's grand design was removed. I doubt if we'll ever prove he killed Hughie but let's press on anyway.'

'You said the remaining obstacle, sir, but I think maybe there was one more.'

Jock paused in the filling of his pipe and looked at Jamie.

Jamie laid down his notebook. 'I was with Robbie Ogilvie yesterday. You'll remember that he's quite a good friend of mine. He's a grand piper; and he's great on the uilleann—the Irish pipes. We had a bit of a session, him and our ceilidh band yesterday evening. Him and myself and, eh, Jo went for a meal at the Moray afterwards. Jo asked him about the estate and what his plans were. He said that he was still thinking about it. He's really worried about the responsibility of it all. He loves that place but has no training in farm or estate management; says he's just a soldier. He really misses Colonel Sanderson: he was almost a second father. To lose his mother, his father and then Dougie, only a few months apart has hit him really badly. Without the support of Dunkie and his family he would have cracked up. Dunkie, he said, really *was* his second father.

'Colonel Sanderson knew the estate inside out. The old Duke and the Colonel were both really into the nature aspects of the place and the reserve was their big thing. Robbie was talking about the Colonel's responsibilities there, how he and his father had set it all up. The Duke was a very sick man and Robbie said his dad had made provision for the Colonel to be able to carry on with the development of the reserve after he died. I think, sir, that his father may have put something in his will about the reserve—something that involved Colonel Sanderson. Robbie had to dash off. He was on duty from Sunday night so I didn't get the chance to go into it any further.'

Jock leaned forward. 'The reserve. It's right in the middle of the proposed golf course.'

'Aye sir, just like Hughie's farm.'

Fort George is only a short drive from Inverness, and less than an hour later Jock was sitting in the office of the Duty Officer, who ordered coffee and sent off a soldier in search of Captain Ogilvie. Robert Ogilvie breezed in minutes later and they moved off to his office.

Robbie shook Jock's hand warmly and offered him a seat. 'I don't believe I thanked you properly for the way you handled . . .'

Jock lifted his hand. 'I was only too relieved to exclude you from the investigation, Captain. Carol's a fine girl, a lot of her father in her. I knew her dad very well; he was a good pal of mine. He was one of the best—and one hell of a rugby player.'

'You really knew him well, Mr Anderson? Carol will be delighted. He died so young. I don't think she's met any old friends of his. She never knew him. She has a memory of the day he died—somehow the trauma and tragedy of the day left a scar on her five-year-old brain. Her mother couldn't talk about it—ever. She never remarried, and Carol can't remember any other man in her mum's life. It was only after her mum died that Carol found all the old photographs of her dad. Do you think we could get together sometime and . . . ?' Robbie sighed. 'I'm afraid it'll have to be after we've sorted out her current, eh . . . domestic situation.'

Jock nodded. 'Good luck with that, lad. I'll look forward to getting together with yourself and the lass soon—very soon I hope, for the sake of the pair of you. I've got a load of old photos myself she'll be interested in.'

'But Superintendent, I don't think you came all the way out here for a coffee and a chat about all that. So what can I do for you?'

Jock told him about his conversation with Jamie Ross. 'The will: your father's will. Was there perhaps any mention of Colonel Sanderson?'

Robbie got up and crossed to a filing cabinet, returning with a photocopied document which he waved at Jock. 'A copy of my father's will. Most of it is the usual unintelligible legalese. It's all as expected: passing all, or mostly all to the eldest son and heir. I think what you'll be interested in are the last couple of pages.' Robbie passed the will to Jock. The penultimate page was handwritten, on the Duke's headed paper.

'An interesting codicil, Superintendent. And it's all totally legal. I know Richard tried very hard to contest it, but even the smart lawyers he hired in London could do nothing—though not for want of trying.'

The Duke's almost copperplate script was easy to read. There was only one written page, with three signatures at the bottom: the Duke's and two witnesses.

'The witnesses?'

'My father's secretary and his nurse. You'll see that the main will is dated the 4th of April of this year.'

Jock looked for the date on the codicil. '3rd of May.'

'Yes, Mr Anderson, the 3rd of May: the day before my father died.'

Jock re-read the page. 'According to this, your father bequeathed in trust to Colonel Sanderson—for his lifetime—the old croft house on the estate and an area of land he has defined as "The New Nature Reserve". He's very clearly defined this—all the map references are there. And he's provided two million pounds for its upkeep and development.'

The last page was a copy of a map, also with signatures, showing part of the estate with the new reserve clearly marked out.

'A good bit bigger than the existing reserve, is it not?'

Robbie nodded. 'Much bigger. All of the home farm and all the woodlands and the lochan—right up to the Lodge. Just about everything except the moors and the mountains.'

Jock whistled.

'Aye Mr Anderson. And Colonel Sanderson was charged to recruit a board of trustees for the future long-term management of The Reserve. Or, if he chose, to sign over the trusteeship—in perpetuity—to a national agency: Scottish Natural Heritage, RSPB, Woodlands Trust; whichever—it was up to him.'

'In fact he had carte blanche.'

'Indeed, Mr Anderson. It's a powerful bit of paper. I'm sure Richard couldn't believe his luck when the Colonel was killed before he could set anything up.'

Jock stroked his chin. 'Aye, he was lucky right enough. Right lucky.'

Back in his office Jock faced DI McLean. 'It's all back in the melting pot, Bob. It's back to the drawing board. Get the spanner out of the works, get the wheels greased, all stops pulled out—and while you're at it, get that poor black man out of the wood pile.' Jock searched for another metaphor but decided, from the smile on his face that Bob had got the message.

Jock sat back in his chair and chewed on his unlit pipe.

'I saw Richard Ogilvie at lunchtime at the golf club on the day of the Colonel's murder. He was with Owen Evans. I seem to remember he was supposed to be going to London on the afternoon flight. We never did check it out. Why would we, I suppose? Well, we'll need to check that now. And get onto Dunmorey. Ask Dunkie what he knows about Richard Ogilvie's movements on the day of Dougie's death.'

Jock had the Ogilvie file open on his desk—he puffed in exasperation. 'I must be getting past it, Bob. The computer and mobile phone belonging to Ogilvie were found in Dunmorey Lodge. They both were locked as I remember. They were sent off to the computer boys, were they not?'

'Yes sir, DC Miller dealt with it. She sent them off to Glasgow. We should have had them back by now. Slipped my mind too, sir.'

Jock rubbed his hands through his hair. 'Aye Bob, we've had a lot on, right enough. Chase it up, will you.' Bob McLean was half way out the door when Jock called to him. 'Another one for you, Bob: noses to the grindstone. Pass that one on, will you.'

DI McLean was back in Jock's office thirty minutes later. 'I've been on to the computer lads in Glasgow. Very sorry, but they've been snowed under; some big case most of them are on. Big backlog of work. Annie Miller didn't put a "priority one" on the job. I suppose back then there was no rush really. No red flag, so back of the queue. Anyway, I spoke to a pal of mine down there. Rob Nicholson—he's a real computer wizzo. I think he's got the message that we want results asap—says he'll do it tonight at home if he can.'

'If he can?'

'Aye. The phone should be no problem, but if the Duke was clever he'll have made sure that nobody would ever be able to access his computer. Rob said that some programs will automatically clear the hard drive if there's any attempt at tampering.'

'Bit like bomb disposal, eh?'

'Aye sir, something like that. He has had a look at the machine though, and he thinks it might be OK.'

'And I've had a quick word with Dunkie Munro at Dunmorey. Normally, when Ogilvie comes up, he's collected at the airport in the Range Rover. He uses it when he's here, then gets dropped back. Seems that the Range Rover was out of action: was in the garage in Inverness, so he had to hire a car. Dunkie says he was right pissed off about that—blamed him, of course. According to Dunkie, Ogilvie left Dunmorey on the Sunday morning; sometime after 11.00 he thinks. He was supposed to go to London on the Sunday afternoon flight, but reappeared at Dunmorey on the Monday morning "spitting nails", Dunkie said. He went back to Inverness for the Monday afternoon flight.'

'So, Bob, our man was on the loose in Inverness on the Sunday. I think we'll be having a wee chat with our friend Mr Owen Evans.'

DI McLean grinned at Jock. 'Aye sir, and I think we've got some serious developments in another direction. Jamie Ross—he struck gold at the Kings Hotel this morning.'

Jock gave him a blank look.

'Our assassin, sir—the hotel search. Jamie's struck lucky. He's downstairs—will I call him up?'

Jamie was smiling as he took a seat in Jock's office. 'The Kings Hotel, sir. They had a Mr Michael Jarvis for a week: the dates you anticipated.'

'So he's used the same name and credit card.'

'Aye sir. The manager was right helpful, knew all about our man. Seems that the old lady down south has twigged to the fact that she's been paying for a holiday she's not had. The credit card company have been onto the hotel.'

'And the photo: any joy with that?'

'I'm coming to that sir. I've spoken to all the staff, the ones on duty this morning and I've shown all of them the photos. It was weeks ago when our man was here, and this is a very popular and busy hotel. A couple of employees, one of them a receptionist, said they vaguely remembered someone who looked maybe a bit like our friend in the photo.'

'So no one really remembers bugger all,' groaned Jock.

'Not quite, sir. There are a lot of Polish girls working in the hotel. A couple of them were a wee bit more positive. They said that he looked like some-one who'd been a guest about that time. None had ever been addressed in Polish before by a guest so they remembered the man. They told me that a friend of theirs, another Polish girl, got quite friendly with the man. The girl they were talking about comes on duty at 6.00 this evening. I'll go back then and talk to her.'

'Good lad, take DC Miller with you. Give me a call when you're done—you've got my mobile number.'

Jock was just finishing his dinner that evening when he got the call from Jamie. 'I've spoken to the girl sir. She won't admit to recognizing the man, and she denies ever meeting any Polish man in the hotel. Her friends weren't lying, sir—I'm sure that she is. She was very flustered, her body language was screaming at me. The manager told me that they have a very strict policy: any hanky panky with a guest and you're out. That could be it. Maybe she's afraid for her job. She's definitely hiding something.

'I've got an idea sir. Jo's got a nice wee Polish girl working in the boutique. I thought I might get her and Jo round to visit her for a wee woman's chat. What do you think, sir?'

'Good idea lad. But not in the hotel. Get Jo's Polish lassie to phone her up tonight—you can brief Jo. Try and get her out for a coffee or something tomorrow.'

'Right sir, I'm just going to interview the evening shift, show the photo round.'

'You're off duty tonight, aren't you lad? Be sure to tell Jo it's not my fault you're working late. DC Morrison's on duty tonight, is he not? This is routine stuff—you should have passed this onto him. I'm no' wantin' Jo jumpin' all over me.'

Chapter 28

'It's like getting blood out of a stone,' puffed Bob McLean. 'All the information is on their bloody computers—where's the big deal in checking the passenger manifest? Anyway, I got what I wanted—finally. Richard Ogilvie was booked on the afternoon flight to Luton on the Sunday but didn't show. He booked again on the 7.00am Monday flight but it was cancelled at the last minute because of problems with the plane. He rebooked for the Monday afternoon and he was on that flight. Avis confirms the car was returned on Monday afternoon.'

Jock and Bob McLean looked at each other. Jock flipped through his directory, picked up the phone and tapped in a number. An irate Owen Evans answered.

'Something bothering you, Mr Evans? You sound upset. Perhaps I can cheer you up. Would you mind coming round to see me? When? Now, of course—or at least in the next hour. Yes, Mr Evans, it is important—very important. Concerning your client? Yes indeed, concerning a client of yours.'

Jock was grinning as he replaced the receiver. 'He might be a wee bit disappointed when he learns which client I was referring to. Cup of coffee while we sharpen our claws, Bob?'

An hour later a very disgruntled Evans was seated in Jock's office. 'I'm a very busy man, Superintendent—very busy, so can we get straight to the point? No, I don't want coffee. And would you mind not smoking?'

Jock blew another puff of pipe smoke. 'DI McLean, would you please give us some fresh air.' Bob McLean got up and opened the window beside Evans.

'Courtesy to a guest.' said the DI. 'I do hope that there's not too much of a draught for you.'

Jock sat back in his chair and relit his pipe. 'Richard Ogilvie. He was a client of yours?'

'If you mean the Duke of Dunmorey? Yes, he was. But I came here on behalf of Mr Steiner. You have some information for me? Have you come to your senses and withdrawn your objection to bail?'

Jock smiled at him. 'No, Mr Evans, you came here at my request. You chose to believe I was referring to Mr Steiner. Bail? If I have anything to do with it, it will be at least twenty years before your Mr Steiner breathes free Scottish air again. No, my interest is in Mr Richard Ogilvie, another client of yours.

'On the morning of Sunday 27th of June you were in the company of Ogilvie at the Inverness Golf Club.'

Evans nodded. 'I'll have to trust you on the date but I think I know the day you are referring to. I seem to remember you had the honour of meeting the Duke.'

Jock smiled. 'Indeed, a rare pleasure. Would you please give me an account of your day—with reference to Ogilvie, I mean.'

Evans visibly forced himself to stay calm. 'I had arranged to meet the Duke at the golf club at midday. I'd had a quick round in the morning. He had some business he wished to discuss before heading back to London. We had lunch and a bottle of very palatable South African red, if I remember correctly. And some brandies, I do believe. A very pleasant and constructive lunch. The Duke was a very entertaining personality: a fine man. We continued our discussions in the bar.'

'Over more brandies, perhaps?'

Evans scowled. 'The Duke had originally planned to take the afternoon flight to London, but as we had not completed our business discussions he decided to delay his departure until the Monday morning. I offered him the hospitality of my home.'

'When did you leave the golf club?'

'About 2 o'clock, or shortly after I think: not much later.'

'You drove home?'

'No, Superintendent. I suspected that we were both some—what over the limit so we took a taxi. We were home I believe by about 2.15. It's my habit to take a short nap after Sunday lunch, and the Duke was of a like mind. We recommenced our meeting about 3.30 and then spent a pleasant social evening together.'

'So you maintain that you were with Mr Ogilvie, the Duke, from midday Sunday until he left for his flight on Monday morning. Did he leave your house at all during the afternoon or evening?'

'No Superintendent, he did not.'

'The Duke was due to take the first flight the next morning. That would be at 7.00am?'

'Yes, I saw him off from home sometime before 6.00.'

'And how did he get to the airport?'

Evans sighed in exasperation. 'He drove, Superintendent—what did you expect? It's a bloody long walk.'

Jock stared at him and watched as the penny finally dropped. For a moment Evans seemed flustered. 'My wife . . . my wife took a taxi to the golf club and collected his car on Sunday evening.'

'That was very kind of her. And what time would that have been, Mr Evans?'

Evans flapped his hands, clearly very nervous—the man was not used to being on the receiving end. 'I don't know. You're asking me about events which occurred weeks ago. Sometime during the evening. The Duke gave her the keys—we were talking in the lounge. I don't know exactly when she went.'

Jock gave him a cold smile. 'I've no doubt that your wife will confirm your account.'

Evans flushed. 'You keep my wife out of this—I'll have you for harassment! What's all this about anyway? Chasing a dead man for a parking ticket or something—that's about the level of you lot. No wonder the public hasn't got any confidence in the police.'

Jock folded his arms as he listened to the tirade. DI Mclean was smiling to himself.

'Are you sure you wouldn't like a coffee, Mr Evans? Will you please excuse me for a few minutes? Perhaps DI McLean has some questions for you.' Jock got up and left the office.

'Nice mobile, Mr Evans,' observed the DI. 'Top of the line job by the look of it.'

Evans had taken his mobile from his pocket and was toying nervously with it. 'I'm a busy man, Mr McLean. I've got several calls I should make.' Bob McLean noticed that Evans's hands were shaking as he prepared and sent a long text message then returned his mobile to his pocket.

'Where's Anderson? Gone to the toilet, has he? He got constipation? Or something nicer—more serious? Piles or prostate problems, hopefully.'

Bob McLean was not a violent man, but he felt an almost overwhelming urge to punch the whining little lawyer in his smug little face. He smiled instead. 'I'm sure he's thoroughly washing his hands before he shakes your hand when you depart—then I imagine he'll want to wash them very thoroughly again.'

Evans turned visibly purple in the face as he left his chair and headed for the door, only to be met by Jock as he returned.

'Leaving us, Mr Evans? I'd be very grateful if you could spare us another few minutes of your time. I require a written and signed statement from you. Just a few lines, nothing fancy. Just what you told us, but missing out the abusive bits if you don't mind. DI McLean's been taking notes—he'll give you a wee hand if it seems you've forgotten anything.'

Evans knew he was beaten and left quietly with Bob McLean. Jock looked at his watch. Almost lunchtime—he could kill a beer.

A smiling DI McLean was back in minutes waving a paper. 'He did *not* want to sign this sir. I hope you're going to confirm the reason why.'

Jock clapped his hands and laughed. 'We've got the little bastard by his shrivelled little balls! I got her—Carol, his wife. She confirmed his story, except the most important bit. After a wee nap, the Duke left by taxi at about 3.30 to collect his car from the golf club. Evans offered to have Carol go, but the Duke would have none of it, said he'd got something else to attend to in town. He didn't get back until about 5.00.' Jock rubbed his hands in glee. 'While we were talking a text came through to her on her other phone.'

'Aye sir, I watched him write and send it.'

'She's sent me a copy, listen to this.' Jock pulled up the message. '"With Anderson. Asking about Duke's movements when he stayed with us. Duke told me to say he never left house on Sunday. If asked, confirm my story. Say you collected Duke's car from golf club Sunday 6 pm."'

Bob laughed and clapped his hands. 'Aye sir, we've got him.'

Both men were in high spirits when they got back from lunch. There was a message for Bob from Rob Nicholson, the computer wizzo, and Bob hurried off to return his call.

Jock was having a quiet smoke and a coffee when DI McLean burst into his office. He sat down and took a deep breath. 'Things are speeding up, sir. Rob's opened Ogilvie's phone for us. It'll be up here tomorrow morning.' Bob took another deep breath.

'Come on Bob, the computer, how did he get on with Ogilvie's computer?'

'No bother, sir; took him ten minutes. It's coming up too. Thing is, sir, it's not Ogilvie's computer. It's registered to Douglas Sanderson—it's Dougie's computer!'

'Shit, Bob. Bloody hell. The missing computer.' For a moment he was stunned by the implications. 'Ogilvie. It *was* him that thumped Dougie. He must have taken the computer in case there was something incriminating on it. Bloody hell.'

Jock rubbed his face. 'There are two innocent lads in Porterfield facing a trial for murder, Bob.' Jock rose from his chair. 'I'm going to see the Procurator Fiscal now. We'll never have anything more than circumstantial evidence against Ogilvie, but my God, now it's stacking up. Let's see what Hamish thinks.'

The Procurator was in his office when Jock arrived.

'You again, Jock! Not brought me more work, have you? I'm still working my way through the last lot. Thanks for the dykes by the way: they're piling up enough assault charges to keep them in for years.' He patted a thick file beside him—'Statements from all the young girls. That pair are real sadists—sadomasochists. Makes your hair curl to read this stuff. The trouble is, beasts like these thrive quite happily in a woman's prison. I'm not really sure what to do with them yet. Anyway, you've dumped the lot on me—my problem.' He smiled at Jock. 'I've had my bitch—your turn.'

It took over an hour for Jock to lay out the details of the Ogilvie story. The Procurator said nothing throughout; he just sat and listened in mounting horror.

'There are still a lot of loose ends, Hamish. We've still not had a look at Ogilvie's phone records, and who knows what's on Dougie's computer. But I've got much more on Ogilvie than I ever had on the two lads. Poor bastards were just in the wrong place at the wrong time.'

The Procurator looked at Jock. 'Bit less work for me, I suppose. They've still got the burglary charges to face, though.'

Jock shrugged. 'They're not bad lads. I'm sure they've learned their lesson. One of them was due to get married. Lovely girl: a nurse in Edinburgh. I had a visit from her, and she phones me up quite regularly. I think she has some magical faith that I'd eventually be coming up with the evidence to clear her man of murder. She'll keep him on the straight and narrow—not that I think that he'll be tempted to stray. They're a couple of very nice bright lads. It was all a big game to them. We were bloody lucky to catch them.' Jock laughed. 'It's wrong to admire crooks, but I got close to it with that pair. They'd cooked up a brilliant wee crime.'

The Procurator smiled. 'You're a big softie, Jock—how did you ever become a policeman?' He picked up the phone and tapped in a number. 'Andy, it's Hamish. The lads you've got there: the burglars up for the Sanderson killing. Aye, that's them. Can you get them round to me first thing in the morning. You can tell them they're to be released on their own cognisance tomorrow morning. We'll be rescheduling their appearance for the burglary charges. We're dropping the murder charge. Aye, you can tell them all that. For sure, I'm still up for golf on Saturday.'

Hamish laid down the phone and turned to Jock. 'He's golf mad, that man.'

'Andy Carmichael? Aye he is. Bloody good too. There's talk of him taking the club captaincy next year. You knew that Dougie'd been in line for the job?'

Jock was exhausted when he got home and he flopped straight into his chair by the fire. Nick laid his head in Jock's lap and Jock played with his ears as Meg poured him his whisky.

'Jamie and Jo were trying to get hold of you. Jo said something about a Polish girl.'

Jock sighed and looked at his mobile. 'It's dead, love; can you put in on to charge for me?' Meg took his mobile and handed him the walk-about handset.

Jock dialled Jo's number and Jamie answered. 'Been trying to get you sir.'

'Aye lad, I'm sorry, my phone was dead—what have you got?'

'You'd best have it first hand, sir. I'll pass you over to Jo.'

Jo told him that they'd had a meeting that afternoon—she and her Polish assistant—with the girl from the hotel. She said it had taken a bit of coaxing but they'd got it out of her.

'There's no doubt about it Dad: she'd got involved with the man you're looking for. She'd recognized him straight away from the photograph. She'd sneak up to his room when she finished work at night. She said he wasn't Polish—he was Russian, brought up in Poland. Seems he was quite a stud. She learned nothing about your man though; wasn't interested, she said. Claims she didn't even ask him what he was doing in Inverness. I don't think somehow that their relationship was cerebral. But she did see a passport: a Russian passport. It was in the name of Ivor Beliatski. She remembered the name: same as a friend of hers in Poland, she said.

'She's quite a character, Dad, and a very pretty little thing. We had a good laugh with her once she relaxed. Her and my Olga really hit it off very well—they'll become good pals, I think. Maybe as a waitress she just took room service a wee bit too far. She's terrified about losing her job, Dad. I had to put a bit of a squeeze on her. I told her you'd have her deported if she wouldn't talk to us, but that you'd not report her to the hotel manager if she helped you. Please keep it quiet Dad, she's a nice kid. There's one more thing; we thought you'd be pleased. Jamie's right happy about it anyway—we've got a photo! Seems your man was right camera-shy but she sneaked a picture of him on her mobile. She says she has to have a photo of all her . . . eh, boyfriends . . . and each has a performance rating. Your man got a nine out of ten. The highest local lad's only got a five—bit sad that, eh Dad?'

Jock sighed. 'Aye, these young lads today just can't cut it. Now if she'd been round thirty years ago . . . .'

Jo laughed. 'Aye, dream on Dad.' Jock heard a prompting from Jamie. 'Oh aye, and we've got a very good physical description, with a few, eh . . . quite personal distinguishing features.'

'Thanks very much, that's fantastic, love, you've done a great job. And don't worry; I've got what I need. I don't think I'll need to bother her again. If I do, you'll be in on it. You're a natural at police work. You getting a taste for it?'

Jo laughed again. 'Piss off, Dad. And we're switching the phones off now— just in case you're tempted to rope Jamie into any escapade tonight.'

Jock smiled as he laid down the phone. Nick nuzzled Jock's arm with his nose and Jock rubbed his head. 'Aye Nick, I think on balance it's been a pretty good day.'

Jock lay back in his chair and put his feet up. 'Any more in that bottle, Meg?' Meg topped up his glass and sat on the chair—arm beside him.

'Getting right domesticated, that pair. Has he moved in with her? He seems to be ey there.'

Meg kissed him on the top of his head. 'He's a fine man, Jock. They make a lovely couple. I've managed lunch a few times with them but I want to get to know him better—to spend more time with him. You being his boss makes it a bit difficult.'

Jock looked at her and shrugged. 'Aye, Meg, but I like the lad. He's got the makings. What I like is he's no grovelling arse-licker. None of your "yes sir, no sir, I'm so humble" stuff. Lots of confidence—maybe a wee bit cocky. Not surprising, I suppose, considering he's doing so well. He's not scared to come forward with ideas. We get on fine. Never even had to bollock him, which is unusual for a young bobby. It'll be fine. He reminds me a bit of myself when I was his age—but I had a real miserable bastard as a DS. If you'd been his daughter . . .'

'What do you think about Sunday lunch, Jock? Will I ask them round? What do you think?'

Jock squeezed her hand. 'Aye, that would be nice—and I promise I'll be on my best behaviour.'

Chapter 29

Jamie Ross had volunteered to have a go at Dougie's computer which had arrived back from Glasgow along with Ogilvie's mobile. Jock stood behind him and watched as he systematically searched through Dougie's files. There was a lot of stuff and Jock told him to ignore anything older than six months for the moment. He had no real idea what he was looking for but he had confidence that Jamie would have a nose for anything important. DC Miller was doing a similar job on Ogilvie's mobile phone. From his mobile provider she'd got a printout of all calls received and made over the last year—there was a lot of paper.

'You've got Colonel Sanderson's telephone numbers: landline and mobile. Anything to him from Ogilvie round May time: first or second week?'

DC Miller found the relevant page and ran her finger down the list, put a tick against a number and turned to Jock. 'Here sir, 8th of May made at 10.10 am to Sanderson's mobile. I've not come across any other calls to either to his mobile or land-line.'

'You've got Ogilvie's father's numbers; any calls to his father or from his father to him? Have a look in May, first week.'

Another tick. 'One here on the 3rd of May to his father's mobile. Made at 11.15am. Looks like a reply to a very short text message from his father asking him to call him—timed at 10.14am.'

'I've come across a few other calls to his father's mobile number. No pattern—don't look like regular dutiful son calls.'

Jock glanced through the listings. 'Seems there are quite a few calls to local numbers. Should be easy enough to identify the recipients.'

Annie Miller nodded. 'There are no regular calls to most of these though—except for a couple: quite a few to them.' She showed Jock the numbers but he didn't recognize them. 'I still need to check them all out. These land-line numbers will be easily traceable, but mobiles are more difficult to identify. Calls to pay-as-you-go numbers will be impossible if there are any of them.'

'This one?' asked Jock. He showed her the mobile number for Owen Evans and she consulted the list. 'Lots sir, over the last six months; at least two or three a week. Quite long calls too.' She checked another list. 'And lots from that number received by Ogilvie. Anything more specific for me, sir?'

Jock shook his head. 'Thanks lass, but please see if you can identify these local landlines for me—especially the ones he's made lots of calls to.'

Jock was about to leave the room when Jamie called him over. 'This could be an interesting e-mail, sir.' He handed Jock a printout. It read: "I need to talk to you urgently. Not happy with information I've picked up about Ogilvie's activities at Dunmorey. Please call me asap. Alex." The e-mail was from an alex_polinski dated 30th April.

'Are there any more from that address?'

Jamie nodded. 'Quite few old ones sir, but they're all about birds. You'll know Alex Polinski. I think his father was a Polish commando who stayed on after the war. As Scottish as you and me but he was brought up speaking Polish. Alex does all the Polish interpretation and translations for us. He's a paralegal in Owen Evans' office and was a birding pal of Dougie Sanderson's I think. You're a birder, so you know Alex is a well-known ornithologist.'

Jock was reviewing the file on the Dougie Sanderson case when Bob McLean joined him in his office. Jock was chewing thoughtfully on his empty pipe and looked up at Bob who was smiling at him.

'OK Bob; so you've worked it out. You've got your ducks in a row too, eh? You can go first.'

Bob opened the case file in his lap. 'I think it's all pretty clear what happened sir. Ogilvie knew his father was dying—it was only a matter of months. Behind the old man's back—behind everyone's back—he'd drawn up his grand plans for the new Dunmorey. There remained, however, the small problem with Hughie MacRae. Hughie would never sell. Ogilvie had to have that land so he had to kill MacRae, confident that he could extract the farm from his widow—and using our pal Evans, he'd acquired additional farms: all the extra land he'd need. Evans was clearly privy to the Dunmorey Golf Course project.

Jock nodded. 'The e-mail from Alex Polinski.'

'Aye, that's right sir. I phoned Alex at Evans's office and he's confirmed our suspicions. Alex got wind of what was going on and gave the nod to Dougie who passed on the news to the old Duke.

'We've checked Dougie's phone records. As you know, we only have his landline—I think Ogilvie must have dumped his mobile phone. Dougie had a long conversation with the old Duke on the 1st of May—I'm assuming that was after he'd had the meeting with Alex. The horrified Duke then contacted his lawyer. I've spoken to the lawyer: a right grumpy, tight-lipped old bugger, but he confirmed his conversation with the old Duke, and his advice about the preparation of a codicil. He even arranged for a visit from a top psychiatrist to confirm that the Duke was of sound mind. The Duke prepared the codicil which would scupper Ogilvie, and summoned his son for a meeting to have it out with him and drop the bombshell.'

'So Ogilvie was with his father the evening before he died?'

'Aye, sir. I got that from the old Duke's regular nurse. She seems to be quite a character: a local woman, name of Heather McEwan from Fort Augustus. She'd been with the Duke for quite some time. The Duke told her he was having a meeting with his son that evening and had sent her off. As a live-in nurse—there to provide twenty-four hour care—she said she hadn't wanted to leave him but he'd insisted he'd be OK.

'She'd been very worried about the planned meeting: she'd known that it was to be a show-down and a lot of dirty laundry would be coming out.

'The nurse knew, of course, that the Duke was a very, very sick man. Ordinarily, she'd said, he was more than a match for his son—that he was one of the few people Richard couldn't intimidate. But that day she'd sensed that the Duke was uneasy about the forthcoming encounter: he'd admitted to some nervousness. Heather and the old Duke had grown very close—he'd confided in her, apparently.'

Jock sat back in his chair. 'So he confided in his nurse then? Had she been told all about Richard and his pals raping Cathy?'

'She had sir. That news had badly shaken the Duke, and he'd felt guilty that he'd never found a way to punish his son. He'd considered disinheriting Richard but had been talked out of that by the bank's directors—Richard was much too valuable to the bank. The Duke had very reluctantly reconciled himself to the fact that Richard was his heir and would be the next Duke of Dunmorey. The nurse knew that some bank shares had been allocated to Robbie. With those, and the inheritance of his mother's entire estate, the old Duke felt that Robbie was well taken care of.

'So, much against her wishes—and her instinct, Heather McEwan had taken herself off to the cinema. She got back about 8.00 as instructed, when she'd found Richard Ogilvie standing by his father's bed holding a copy of the codicil prepared by his father. The Duke was in a bad way apparently—gasping for breath. The whole thing clearly had proved too much for the old man. It's quite likely it had been a very fiery meeting and the old guy had had another heart attack.'

Jock swore under his breath. 'He effectively murdered him Bob.'

'He did, sir. Ogilvie told the nurse his father had suddenly taken a funny turn and that he was just about to call an ambulance—the nurse didn't believe him but told him to do it immediately. Anyway, she gave the old man oxygen and some medication. He was rushed to hospital, but died the following morning. The nurse is in no doubt that Richard had deliberately delayed calling for help; he was clearly very angry that she'd returned when she had. Richard had wanted his father to himself for a bit longer—she presumed he'd wanted to get hold of the original copy of the codicil and destroy it. The original was in the office safe and only the Duke had immediate access.'

Bob checked his notes. 'Then a few days later: 8th of May, Ogilvie calls Dougie—remember his cleaning lady reported a pretty fiery conversation Dougie had with someone round that time? Maybe Ogilvie was having a go at sweet-talking Dougie. He knew that Dougie was going to be a real problem for him.

'He'd already got Hughie MacRae out of the way: he'd fitted that wee chore in with one of his business trips up here. Dougie either had to be talked round or eliminated. On that Sunday you saw him at the golf club—with a few drinks in him—he decides to pay Dougie a visit after he collected his car. With all the wine and a load of brandy still sloshing about from his heavy lunch he probably felt like having another go at convincing Dougie. Dougie of course was immovable and Ogilvie's notorious temper kicked in—he thumped Dougie who fell backwards down the steps and smashed his head.'

Bob sat back. 'That's my reading of it, sir. I doubt very much that he intended to kill Dougie that afternoon. Much too dangerous—sloppy, even. He must have been right relieved when the young burglars took the rap for that.'

Jock slowly nodded his head. 'That's my reading too, Bob; and the bugger is, we can't prove a bloody thing—not a bloody thing. But another wee bit of circumstantial evidence for you.

'The Chief Constable and I were right surprised, and a bit puzzled about being beneficiaries as well as executors of Dougie's will. We were good friends right enough, but not *that* close. I've asked Dougie's lawyer when he drafted the will. Want to make a guess?'

Bob McLean smiled as he flipped through his file. 'Well sir, I'd be guessing shortly after the presumed fiery conversation overheard by Dougie's cleaning lady. The week after the 8th May?'

'Right, Bob. He phoned his lawyer on the 9th for an appointment; the will was drawn up the next day. Dougie knew his life was possibly in danger. He knew Ogilvie only too well: what the man was capable of.' Jock sat back in his chair with a sigh. 'That day at the golf club: the day Dougie died—when I had the pleasure of meeting the Duke. I saw Dougie's face when he saw Ogilvie. There was a glimpse of something in his expression I couldn't identify at the time. I know now what it was—it was fear.'

Jock slowly filled his pipe. 'Aye, it's a real pity that Dougie didn't confide in us at the time. I suppose he thought that having made two top policemen his executors at least Ogilvie wouldn't get off with it eh?' Jock gave a humourless laugh and looked towards the ceiling. 'Well Dougie, if you're up there watching us poor idiots, I hope you're happy with the way things have worked out.'

Jock gave a wry smile. 'Aye Bob; unfortunately it's all circumstantial. But I spoke to the Procurator Fiscal earlier. He's confident we've got a good case, and he's sure that we'd have got a conviction. He says it's pretty irrefutable stuff, and enough to convince any jury.' Jock tapped a file on his desk. 'I've prepared a statement: the facts as we interpret them. For sure we'll be up for another hounding by the press when I finally let the news out. I've also spoken to Robbie Ogilvie and he agrees with me the truth's more important than the good name of the Dukedom of Dunmorey—the truth will out. Aye Bob, Ogilvie was a thoroughly bad bastard. Maybe our wee German mannie did the world a right big favour having him removed, eh? Let's us now just apply our efforts to tying in the little shit with the dead Duke.'

Chapter 30

'No, I don't need any help with the vegetables—I don't need you to be cutting yourself again. Everything's under control Jock. They'll be here in about an hour, so why don't you get out of my hair and take Nick for a walk? You're like a cat on hot bricks.' Jock grunted something unintelligible and did what he was told.

It was a clear, crisp morning with a brisk north wind, but well wrapped up, with his old deerstalker on his head, Jock didn't notice the cold. He took a deep breath and looked around. There was already some early snow on Ben Wyvis and the view over the firth and the Black Isle was spectacular. He had regular routes, loops which gave him the option of a long, medium or short walk. Nick chose the long option and Jock was happy to follow on. About half way round was Balmannie, an old croft house on the edge of his land. Set higher on the hill than the farmhouse, it had a similar, but even more spectacular out-look. Surrounded by half an acre or so of cropped turf and set cosily in a grove of mature oaks, it was Jock's favourite spot. He loved the old house, and he'd always stop there for a wee rest, a smoke and some contemplation. As a young man he'd often come to the remote old place to practice on his pipes or his fiddle. He smiled as he remembered the girlfriends he'd brought to the place. One day—when he'd got the spare money—he was determined to rescue the old house. It was a fine old building and he felt it held too many memories to be allowed to disintegrate. Supposedly his great-grandfather had been born and had died in the wee place, so he felt he owed it something. There was already some damage to the roof where an old oak had come down in a storm and taken off a load of slates. That, he knew, was beginning of the end if he didn't do something about it soon.

He did his usual tour of inspection, disturbing some wood pigeons that had taken up residence in the loft. The old house was still habitable and, except where the tiles had come off, it was watertight. He checked his watch: loads of time, no hurry to get back. Jock loved making fires, and within minutes he had a good blaze going in the big old fireplace. He brushed some bird droppings from the old leather armchair he kept by the fire, pulled a hip flask from one jacket pocket, his pipe and tobacco from another and sat down with a contented sigh. Nick, well used to the routine, lay happily in front of the fire. Jock had a lot to think about, but for the moment he was content to look forward to Sunday lunch with his daughter and the young man who may become his son-in-law. He lay back, put his feet up and toasted the world with a healthy swig from his hip flask.

A wet tongue licking his face woke Jock with a start. He looked at his watch and swore to himself, but gave Nick a cuddle of thanks—he'd been asleep for almost an hour. It was a twenty minute walk back home—Jo and Jamie would be there by now—he was late. Jock knew that Meg would be getting worried about him, imagining all sorts of dreadful scenarios to explain his absence. He stuck his old deer-stalker on his head, quickly locked up the house and hurried off down the track home.

He wasn't sure whether to be relieved or disappointed when his lateness appeared to have gone unnoticed. He heard the sounds of laughter as he opened the back door into the kitchen. Meg and Jo were clearly oblivious to his late return, and Jo got up and gave him a hug.

Meg sat him down at the big kitchen table and put a glass of red wine in his hand. 'Try some of this, love: Jo brought it, it's lovely.' Meg clearly had already sampled a couple of glasses herself.

Gordie ran in from the lounge and threw himself into Jock's arms; Jock picked him up and hugged him as he took a seat at the table and looked around. 'Isn't there someone missing?'

'No Dad.' Jo laughed and indicated with her head. Jamie was standing in the kitchen doorway with a can of beer in his hand. Jock winked at him and pushed the glass of wine away.

'You got a beer for me, Jamie?'

The girls had finished Jo's wine and were well through another bottle before the haunch of roast venison was even served. Conversation flowed freely and to the relief of all, the boss-junior employee relationship between Jock and Jamie disintegrated—and when Jock learned that Jamie was a very keen bridge player, his place in the family was secured.

After lunch the men retired to the lounge where a big log fire was blazing and Jock performed his only authoritarian act of the day by setting up the card table—he wanted to play bridge, so surely everyone else did. He was shuffling the cards when Jamie asked if they were allowed to talk shop.

Jock laid down the cards and took a sip of his brandy. 'Aye lad, it's a bugger this job, isn't it? You're either up to your neck in it or thinking about it.' He lifted his glass. 'This is meant to help you relax, but it just gets my brain going—but sometimes in right funny directions. So what have you been thinking about?'

Jamie refilled his own and Jock's glass. 'Well eh . . . I just happened to call by the station on the way here.'

Jock looked at him and smiled. 'Oh aye, since when was the middle of Inverness on the way from Culloden to here?'

Jamie shrugged. 'Maybe I needed to buy some wine . . . or something?'

Jock laughed. 'Aye, whatever. So what's on your mind?'

Jamie took a seat at the table and laid down his glass.

'There's an e-mail come in from the Spanish police. They've got him— our presumed assassin, Ivor Whatzisname. They picked him up on a motor cruiser in the Med this morning. At least they're assuming it's him: it's someone on a Russian passport with his name anyway. Their Special Branch boys are onto it—they said they'll let us have more details asap. I e-mailed big thank-you from you. I thought it was best to acknowledge it—didn't want them to think the Scottish police took the day off on Sundays.'

Jock beamed at him. 'Bloody marvellous! News like that's almost enough to put me off my bridge. Thanks lad, that's fantastic news. Here are the ladies; you'll be playing with Jo—me and Meg have an understanding. Do you play five card major? High or low no-trump?'

With wee Gordie tucked up in bed, the four of them played until almost midnight. In the end, the result was about as close to a draw as possible. They were equal in rubbers but Jock and Meg won the match by ten points. Jock was magnanimous in victory, joking that if he'd been on the whisky instead of brandy they'd have won more comfortably.

When Jo and Jamie left, Jock took Meg in his arms. 'That was the nicest Sunday I can remember in a long time—a very long time. Jamie's a bloody good card player. We must get him and Jo round again soon—how about next Sunday?

'On the subject of cards. If you continue to play yours right, all that brandy's lowered my resistance—I could be putty in your hands tonight.'

Meg kissed him, took his hand and led him upstairs. In the bedroom, as she slowly unzipped him she whispered, 'John Anderson ma Joe—you'd better *not* be putty in my hands tonight.'

Chapter 31

On Monday morning, straight after Morning Service, Jock was on the phone to Spain. Nothing more had come through, and besides, he preferred talk to impersonal e-mails.

Captain Carlos Gonzales of Special Branch couldn't have been more helpful—or professional. His English was less than perfect, but the fact that his son was apparently married to an Edinburgh girl really helped things along. It appeared that the suspect had been very unlucky. There had been reports of a cargo vessel offshore in the Med transferring drugs to pleasure cruisers. The customs and drug squads had been on high alert and were searching all boats entering port—without exception.

The suspect was on an eighty-foot luxury cruiser which had docked in the Alicante Marina. Normally customs clearance would have been cursory—for millionaires' boats particularly. Ivor Beliatski was travelling with a glamorous Swiss blonde named Ingrid Kessler. The motor yacht, with a four-man crew, was owned and registered to her husband, Hans Kessler.

Jock had circulated Beliatski's name to all the international police agencies, and a quick computer check had flagged the passport. Beliatski was now in police custody in Alicante.

Beliatski was not a happy man. Gonzales admitted that Spanish holding jails were not perhaps the most salubrious of places. The man had no idea why he was being held, and Gonzales had yet to enlighten him. Ivor was being deliberately obnoxious, presumably confident that the police could have nothing on him. He was refusing to co-operate, maintaining that he was Herr Kessler's Head of Security and would be suing for wrongful detention. Gonzales had clearly not taken to Ivor.

He said that Ivor must have been very concerned about Mrs Kessler's personal security. She had been under close observation. Very close—they'd been caught in bed together.

Jock explained his interest in Ivor and asked that he be sent a photograph and a DNA analysis of the prisoner. Gonzales was particularly amused as to how Jock came by the suspect's DNA. He told Jock he'd send a full report, he had some good photographs which he would forward immediately and he'd have a DNA test run that morning. Hopefully, paperwork completed, he could see no reason why Ivor shouldn't be back in Scotland very soon. Both he and Jock agreed that closer police co-operation and ease of extradition were one of the few obvious benefits of EU membership. Jock sat back and filled his pipe, a broad grin on his face. A perfect Sunday followed by a perfect Monday morning. He called Bob McLean to his office and gave him an account of his talk with Gonzales.

'Hans Kessler—not our Hans Kessler?'

'Has to be, Bob—one of Steiner's fat Kraut pervert friends who's nicely tucked up in Porterfield prison. Seems our friend Ivor was doing a fine job consoling the grieving wife. We've got him, Bob. Kessler must have lent our Ivor to Steiner for the job. He probably saved his pal a bit of money—if so, the tight bastard's going to regret that bit of economy. I doubt if we'll have to lean on the fat slug Kessler too hard to get the truth out of him. Somehow I think he'll find the promise of a few years remission for his wee bit of co-operation quite attractive. But we'll wait until we've got Beliatski's DNA confirmation before we go and dump on him.'

There was a knock on the door and Jamie Ross came in waving some photographs. 'These and a report have just come through from Spain, sir.

Will I go and see that wee lassie at the hotel—see if she can identify him? He looks like the guy in the photos she gave us.'

Jock looked at the photos and nodded. 'Aye, and Hamish Robertson the vet, see what he says. They've taken a nice profile for us, he may clock him too. Not important really, but it would be another wee bit of ribbon for our wrapping up, eh Bob? And Jamie, if the girl's in any doubt, e-mail Gonzales and ask him to photograph our man's bare arse. You told me she said there was a big scar on his right buttock—and anyway, she might like a copy for her album.'

Jock added his copies of the photos to the file. 'Bob, can you get onto the Procurator Fiscal. Make sure he's got what he needs to initiate extradition proceedings. Hopefully you'll be off to Spain very soon to see our man. I think I'll go and have a coffee with the Chief Constable—cheer him up this fine Monday morning.'

Jock Anderson was not a man noted for great patience. His confidence in Carlos' efficiency was eroding when Wednesday came and still the DNA results were not forthcoming. By Friday afternoon his little bit of remaining patience was finally exhausted and he made another call to Gonzales who was most apologetic. The test had been run, and he'd given instructions for the results to be sent on Wednesday morning—he'd go and "kick some ass". Like many foreigners, Carlos loved to use English colloquialisms—pity this was an American one Jock particularly disliked. Whatever he did to someone's ass, the results arrived minutes after the call, with a personal apology to Jock from Gonzales—confidence was restored.

Jock was no expert, but Dr Paterson had initiated him to the mysteries of DNA analysis. As far as he could see, the DNA tracing from the faeces sample in his left hand matched perfectly with the results from Spain in his right. He had the Spanish results sent to Dr Paterson for confirmation. Jock looked at his watch, got up, pulled on his jacket and called DI McLean. 'It's knocking off time, Bob. We're going for a drink. I think we've got something to celebrate.' The phone rang just as he opened his office door. He groaned as he returned to answer it.

'Bloody hell, Jock, I'll be having to take on another assistant if you keep this up.' It was the Procurator Fiscal. 'I've got all the stuff Bob McLean sent over about this Ivor chappie. I suppose you'll be wanting your man extradited pretty sharpish eh? It's not as easy as you might think, but at least it's not like the old days when Spain collected all our dross and wouldn't hand it back. It's likely to take a week or ten days, working days that is—you'll have everything you need this end from me as quickly as I can manage. Hopefully, if your friends in Spain get *their* fingers out . . . ? But you're going to have to send someone over there now to formally charge him and get things set up with the Spanish police. I'll have all the papers you need prepared by Tuesday morning hopefully.' Jock thanked him and suggested he join them for a beer.

'Fuck off Jock; fine for you plods and your comfy nine-to-fives. I'll be here for hours yet, thanks to you. Can I expect many more bodies, by the way? Porterfield's getting a bit full with your lot as it is.'

Jock laughed. 'No, hopefully that'll be my lot on this case.'

The Procurator grunted. 'Away and have your beer. And by the way, Jock—bloody good work, bloody good. You should be tapping the Chief Constable for a bonus.'

'Aye, that'll be right. You still OK for golf on Sunday?'

It was "happy hour" and the pub was already quite busy when Jock and Bob McLean arrived. Jamie was at the bar with a few of his young colleagues. The Old Mill, the nearest nice bar to the station was popular with the police. Jock and Bob found an empty table and Bob got the beer. The pint barely touched the sides. Jock would love another: he'd love a few more, but he knew he wasn't above the law and wasn't about to set a bad example—or risk a breath-test. He was reluctantly getting up to leave when Jamie came over and told him that Jo was coming to pick him up later. He offered to buy Jock and Bob a beer and suggested that Jo could give them all a lift home. Jock sat back down and grinned at him. Bob nodded—he was up for a few too. It had been a very long week and they did have something to celebrate. Jock rubbed his hands and phoned Meg to tell her he'd be a bit late home.

It was after 7.00 before Jo arrived. She had a quick half of lager then shepherded them all out. Bob, who lived in the opposite direction, insisted on taking a taxi. On the way home they discussed plans for the following evening, when The Dunmorey Ceilidh Band was booked at the Moray for their first professional gig. Jock was as excited about it as Jo and Jamie. He'd yet to hear them play, and it had been ages since he and Meg had had a good leg-up. They were still chatting about it when they reached Jock's house. Nick and Gordie ran out to meet them and Meg stood grinning in the doorway as she watched Jock and Jamie help each other out of the car and up the steps. Jo smiled, shrugged her shoulders, picked up Gordie and followed on.

'Men, they're all the same, isn't that right, Mum?'

Meg gave her a hug. 'Aye love, you're right—but would you really want it any other way?'

Inside, Jock had already poured the whiskies.

Later that evening as they were getting ready for bed, Meg laughed and cuffed Jock playfully on the head. 'For God's sake man, of course you've got to wear your kilt. It's a ceilidh—they'll all be in kilts.' Jock gave her a smiling scowl and tapped his gut. 'I want to wear my kilt: but will the thing still fit me? It must be three years since I've had it on. It probably won't go round—and my knees are right white . . . and it's bedtime.'

Meg puffed in exasperation. 'Two years ago; Brian and Flora MacIntosh's wedding. You're still the same size, you silly bugger. Try it on—I'll shift a buckle if necessary.' She took the kilt from the wardrobe and held it out to him. 'Try it on—right now.'

At 7.00 on the following evening, Jock was admiring himself in the big bedroom mirror. Much to his surprise and pleasure his kilt still fitted perfectly, and, in his casual tweed kilt jacket and waistcoat, he looked the perfect Highland gentleman. Meg, who looked stunning in a white blouse and long tartan skirt, stepped in front of him and put her arms round his neck. 'Jock—you look magnificent.'

Jock took Meg's face in his hands and kissed her. 'And you're more beautiful than ever. Aye, all that's missing is my pipes.' He eyed the pipe case in the foot of the wardrobe and bent to pick it up.

'Oh no you don't, not now. In your kilt with a couple of drams in you, you've got the urge again—but not tonight.' Meg pulled him towards the door. 'Come on, we're going to be late. I suppose I'm driving tonight—again.'

The Moray was packed when they arrived. The management had gone to town on the publicity, and everyone and their brother were there to hear the new ceilidh band. Meg and Jock went straight through to The Barn to find Jo and Jamie. Jo ran and gave Meg a hug, then stood back and admired her handsome father. She dabbed a tear from her eye and hugged him again. 'You look bloody marvellous, Dad. And you, Mum—drop dead gorgeous. You make a daughter right proud of the pair of you.' Lachie called her from the stage and she dashed off. Jamie was fine-tuning his banjo and gave them a big grin and a wave.

The line-up was impressive: Jo was on the fiddle, Jamie on tenor banjo, guitar, and bouzouki. Calum Munro was on the small pipes and whistle, and Colin Buchannan, up from Edinburgh for the weekend, had the five-string banjo. Ali, who'd come up with Colin, was on bodhran and vocals. Sitting stage left was Robbie Ogilvie with his Irish pipes, and beside him was Lachie Donaldson on the melodian. Completing the band was a lad Jock didn't recognize on bass guitar.

Meg had rarely seen Jock more excited—he wasn't a man to demonstrate much emotion generally. 'Takes me back, Meg. I just want to get up there with my fiddle and join them.'

Meg looped her arm in his. 'With a wee bittie practice I've no doubt you could show the youngsters a thing or two.'

Jock held up his left hand, wiggled his fingers and smiled at her. 'Aye love, you don't get a silver medal at the Fiddlers Rally for just turning up. Maybe I'll dig out the old fiddle and blow the dust off.'

For Jock, the first set was a complete whirl, physically and emotionally. He and Meg didn't miss a single dance, to music more breath-taking than the dancing. They played all the old favourites, but with unique arrangements which transformed the old tunes and raised them to a new level.

They all gathered in the bar at the end of the first set, Jock bought a round for the band and looked in admiration at each of the musicians, shaking his head. 'Un-bloody-believable. You lot are fantastic. Real Battlefield Band stuff.'

Jamie nodded. 'Aye, They're quite a strong influence right enough. We've pinched a few of their arrangements, but mostly they're our own. We're working on a lot of our own stuff too: we'll be doing a couple in the next set.'

Meg was chatting to Robbie Ogilvie; Jock congratulated Jamie again and moved to join them. Meg had not met Robbie before and was clearly impressed. Jock congratulated him on the music and, as a fellow piper, on his performance. Jock had never tried the Irish pipes, which are played seated. They have their own distinctive sound and have a versatility not found in the Scottish bagpipes. Jock was intrigued and Robbie promised they'd have a session together so Jock could try them out.

'Aye, Mr Anderson,' said Robbie, 'life's certainly taken a turn for the best.' Jock looked at him knowingly.

'No sir, I'm afraid that's not resolved yet.' His smiling face saddened for a moment. 'God, how I wish that she could be here tonight.' He looked at Jo and Jamie wrapped together at the bar and smiled. 'That should be us: Carol and me.'

Jock took Robbie to one side. 'If you can manage to hang on for a few more days, I think you'll notice a sudden change in attitude of our friend Mr Evans.' He gave Robbie a big smile and a knowing wink. 'Maybe as soon as Monday, in fact. I'll be calling yourself and Carol. Make sure you're both free early Monday morning.'

A bemused Robbie was called away for the start of the second set. Jock downed his dram, took Meg's hand, and followed on back into The Barn.

Jamie tapped a mike and called for a bit of shush. 'A couple of announcements to make.

'Firstly, it seems that the landlord is quite impressed by our music.' Jamie looked round the packed hall. 'And with the turnout—so he's booked us again for a month today.' The place went wild at that.

'I'm sorry to be taking up so much valuable dancing time, but just one more announcement. I suppose you could say it's about another musical engagement.' Jamie pulled Jo to his side and took her hand. Jamie cleared his throat. 'I've never done this before, and intend never to do it again. I want to announce the official engagement of myself, Jamie Ross, to this beautiful young lady and magical fiddler: Jo Anderson.' Jamie pulled a ring from his waistcoat pocket and theatrically slipped it on Jo's finger. He and Jo were oblivious to the uproar of cheering as he took Jo in his arms and kissed her. A wildly happy looking Jo then held up her left hand—what looked to be a very large diamond sparkled in the spotlight.

Jamie once again called for silence. Jock and Meg were in the middle of the dance floor, tears were running down Meg's cheek and Jock had a silly grin on his face.

Jamie addressed Jock. 'With your permission of course, sir.'

Jock whooped, grabbed Meg and gave her a birl. He called up to Jamie. 'Aye lad—seems quite a good idea—go for it!' Jock and Meg found themselves surrounded by friends and well-wishers eager to congratulate them, Jamie and Jo came down to join them and there were tearful hugs all round. Jo and Jamie returned to the stage and finally Jock managed to draw Meg away. He looked into her happy smiling face. 'You knew, didn't you? You weren't in the least surprised.'

Meg nodded, wiped a happy tear from her eye and blew her nose. She stood on her tiptoes to kiss him. 'Aye love, but I was sworn to silence.'

Jock hugged her tight and whispered in her ear. 'It's marvellous, so bloody marvellous.'

The mike was tapped again: it was Jo. She looked at her mum and dad and laughed. 'If you pair have finished having it off on the dance floor maybe we can get on with the ceilidh. To kick off the next set, we're going to do one of our own compositions. As my Dad seems to be quite happy.' She waved her left hand. 'We're going to make him even happier, I hope. This tune is dedicated to a wonderful man, that miserable old fart: my Dad. The tune's called *Jock Anderson's Rant*, or if you prefer, *A Ranting Jock Anderson*.' Jo struck up on her fiddle. After a few bars the band joined in, not en mass, each one crept in in its turn to finally produce a hair-tingling crescendo. For a few moments, Jock, with a large lump in his throat, stood transfixed as the incredible music washed over him. Meg handed him a tissue to wipe away the tears he'd tried, but failed, to suppress. Then he whooped again, grabbed Meg's hand and pulled her into the wild dance—they'd written a tune just for him and he was going to make the most of it.

Chapter 32

The routine Monday morning chores out of the way, Jock sat in his office with Bob McLean and DS Alan Clark. Bob and Alan were booked to fly to Alicante the following day.

The three men reviewed every detail together—there could be no slip-ups. There were plenty of perfectly good police cases blown through bad paperwork or sloppy procedure. The international dimension was a further complication, but they'd have to rely on the Procurator Fiscal to keep them right there. It was almost 11.30 by the time they'd finished.

Jock dismissed DS Clark and called for more coffee. He looked at his watch. 'He should be here any minute.'

They were expecting Owen Evans. Jock and Bob McLean were due to interview Hans Kessler early that afternoon and Kessler had nominated Evans as his lawyer, and on that professional pretext Evans had been called to the station. Dead on time, at 11.45 Evans blustered his way into Jock's office. He was already demanding details and the reason for the latest interrogation of his client before the door was closed behind him.

Jock held up his hands. 'All in good time, Mr Evans, all in good time. Will you please take a seat? But if you'll please excuse me for a few moments, I've something to attend to.' Jock was pulling his mobile from his pocket as he left the office. Evans gave his usual grumble about being a very busy man and sat down. After only a few minutes, Jock returned to his office and resumed his seat. 'DI McLean, will you please give Mr Evans a copy of his previous statement made to us.

'This statement, Mr Evans, refers, as you will recall, to the relative movements of yourself and Richard Ogilvie on the 27th of June, the day I had the pleasure of meeting the Duke at the golf club.' Bob McLean drew a folder from a file on his lap and handed it to Evans. Jock smiled at the lawyer. 'Mr Evans, would you please read through your statement.'

Evans scowled, grabbed the folder and quickly read through the contents and handed it back to DI McLean.

'You are happy with the statement Mr Evans? You have no desire to make any amendments?'

Evans, in his infuriatingly pompous whine, replied that there was no need to change a word.

Jock took the folder from Bob McLean and opened it on his desk. 'If I may summarize? You have stated that Richard Ogilvie was a guest in your house from shortly after 2 o'clock on the afternoon of Sunday the 27th of June. You maintain that he did not leave the house at any point during the afternoon or evening, and that you saw him off to the airport early on the morning of the 28th.'

Evans got up from his seat and crossed the office, leant both hands on the desk and leaned threateningly towards Jock. 'Look, Superintendent. I've got no time for this. I demand the information relevant to my client.' He spat out the words contemptuously, and continued glaring at Jock.

Jock looked at him coldly. 'Mr Evans, you can demand all you want. I have told you, all in good time. Will you please resume your seat. DI McLean, will you please hand Mr Evans the statements taken from Mr Roger Mansfield, Mrs Norma Brown and Mrs Mary Grayson. These, Mr Evans, are your neighbours, left and right and over the road at number 24. I think it's very heartening in these days where urban crime is so rampant that your Neighbourhood Watch operates so efficiently.'

Evans took the three folders from Bob McLean, read through each, then contemptuously dropped them on the floor.

'These stupid old codgers. You insult me, Superintendent, if you take their word over mine!'

Jock shrugged. 'I accept that one witness statement could perhaps be disputed—but not three, I'm afraid. You clearly do not know your neighbours, Mr Evans. Mr Mansfield is a retired Chief Constable from Aberdeen, Mrs Brown is a local psychotherapist, and Mrs Grayson is a Chief Librarian. Not one of them is over sixty-five years old, and all have perfect vision—through spectacles, I accept. Intelligent, fine upstanding members of the community I'd say. Old codgers? Most certainly not.'

Jock flipped through the files Bob McLean had retrieved from the floor. 'They all seem to contradict your statement, Mr Evans. Not all witnessed the return of Ogilvie later that Sunday evening, but all confirm the fact that he did leave at about 3.30 pm, seen off by yourself. Mrs Grayson at number 24 saw him return about 5 o'clock to be welcomed by yourself at the door. Mrs Brown also saw his return, but being to the left and somewhat behind your house, missed the greeting. Mr Mansfield, no longer working in his garden at round 5.00, only saw you seeing Ogilvie off. Pretty convincing stuff, I'd say.'

A red-faced Evans dismissed the statements as a load of rubbish. 'And besides, my wife will confirm my statement.'

Jock gave him one of his cold smiles.

Realization dawned on Evans. 'The bitch: the fucking bitch, is she saying . . . ?'

Evans got up and made for the door to find his way blocked by DI McLean who hissed at him. 'Mr Evans . . . we can, if you choose, arrest you for obstructing the course of justice and conspiracy to murder, or you can sit down, shut the fuck up and listen to DS Anderson.'

Jock glared at the lawyer. 'You're in trouble, Mr Evans—more than you realize.'

'What's all this about murder?' blustered Evans.

'As I said, Mr Evans, more trouble than you realize. A false signed statement made to us is enough to ruin you as a lawyer and you know it. What I'm going to say now is between the three of us. You are now going to go home to your wife. She's got a very reasonable request to make of you: an offer I suggest you don't refuse. Should you agree to co-operate with your wife, I can promise you that this "rubbish" as you call it: this statement—these very incriminating files, they will indeed become shredded rubbish—they will disappear. On the other hand, if . . .'

'I've got the message, Anderson: you don't have to spell it out.' Evans moved towards the door and made to leave.

'Mr Evans, don't forget, please. 2.30 at Porterfield for the interview with your client Mr Kessler.'

Jock and Bob were having a quiet pie and a pint in the pub when his mobile rang: it was an ebullient Carol Evans.

'How did you do it, Mr Anderson? How did you do it? The bastard came storming into the house ready to kill me, I'm sure. I wish you could have seen his face when he saw Robbie, him all dressed up in his uniform. He just crumpled, deflated like a balloon—just sat there with his head in his hands. He didn't say a word, just nodded when I told him I wanted a divorce with no dispute over custody of my daughter. We'd got ourselves organized right after you called us. I don't know how Robbie got here so quickly. I told the bastard I was leaving immediately; everything was already packed. All my stuff and what little I wanted from the house were in the cars outside. I told him I wanted nothing from him—nothing. That he could keep his bloody house and all the bourgeois crap he'd collected and made me live with for years. God, did I enjoy myself, Mr Anderson! I didn't know it was possible to hate anyone so much. It's over Mr Anderson—it's all over. Here, have a word with Robbie.'

'I think she's described it pretty well, Superintendent. We can never thank you enough. I somehow suspect we'll never know how you did it: how you put the squeeze on that bastard's balls, but it sure as hell worked. I hope you've not made any trouble for yourself. This seems a wee bit beyond the realm of normal police work.'

Jock laughed. 'Don't worry, lad; strange as it may seem I did him a big favour. I just expected a little something in return.'

'I hope so, Mr Anderson. The die is cast for us anyway. Whatever the bastard might try, we're ready for him. Three weeks on Saturday—Dunmorey Lodge. We'll be having a big celebration, everyone will be there. And Mr Anderson—rosin up your bow; bring your fiddle along.'

Jock disconnected and grinned at his DI. 'Worked a treat, Bob; they shafted the little worm and they're finally free. But we'd best get going.' Jock rubbed his hands. 'I'm looking forward to this afternoon's interview. I hope Evans can keep his mind on the job—we didn't upset him too much this morning, did we?'

Bob McLean laughed. 'One thing though, sir—isn't Evans also representing Steiner? Bit of conflict of interest if we're asking Kessler to crap all over his old mate?'

'No Bob. Steiner's dumped him: not too politely either, I gather. He's found another slime ball in Edinburgh. In his current mood, Evans will be ready to shaft anyone—hopefully Steiner will suit him fine.'

The Governor of Porterfield met Jock and Bob when they arrived. He told them that Evans was already closeted with his client, and Jock asked him to call Evans to his office.

Evans was his normal objectionable self, but listened in silence to Jock as he outlined the developments on the Ogilvie case and the role of his client Herr Kessler. To Jock's surprise, Evans seemed to be unaware that the case was ongoing, that Ogilvie had, in fact, been murdered. Jock had no illusions that information security at the station was watertight and had somehow expected that a leak in Evans's direction would have been inevitable.

Evans was no fool, insisting that the offer of some leniency for his client—in recognition of his co-operation—be made official, and demanded a written statement from the Procurator Fiscal. Jock smiled and drew a sheet from his file and passed it to Evans. Evans scanned the paper and gave the nearest thing to a smile Jock had ever observed.

'Three years remission. Very nice; four would be nicer?' He looked at Jock who shook his head.

Evans sneered. 'You must really want to nail Mr Steiner and this Ivor character.' Evans knew that Kessler would be facing at least eight years, possibly more. Three years off plus what he'd earn for good conduct, he could possibly be out in two years. What Evans wasn't aware of, was that the police in Germany were building another solid case against Kessler. On release from a sentence in Scotland he'd be immediately extradited to Germany.

'I'd like now to talk with my client. I can promise you nothing—unless of course you were prepared to offer bail; when, I believe, I could obtain immediate acceptance of your offer.'

Jock glanced at Bob and nodded. They'd expected this: Evans always drove a hard bargain. Jock passed Evans a second sheet of paper. Somehow a grin from Evans looked more like a grimace.

Forty-five minutes later, the policemen were facing Evans and Kessler in the interview room. Evans granted permission to officially record the interview and Bob McLean started the machine with the formal introduction.

Kessler's English was excellent, he had a full understanding of his situation and was willing to co-operate. He explained that he had been approached by Steiner for his advice. Steiner had made no mention of whom he wished terminated, but was looking to put out a contract. Kessler owed Steiner some favours and volunteered his man Ivor who used to be, he stressed *used* to be, in that line of business—assuring the policemen that he, Kessler, had never used him in that capacity. Ivor was, as he claimed, his Head of Security. Somehow Jock believed him. A disgruntled Ivor wouldn't be slow to dump on his old boss if he thought that would gain him any mileage.

Evans handed Jock several handwritten pages. 'My client's written and signed statement, Superintendent. I thought I'd save us all some time. You will note that Mr Kessler has provided you with impressive documentation of events, including dates of his communications with Herr Steiner. My client has an amazing memory. You will also note that he simply put Steiner in contact with Ivor. He has no knowledge of their subsequent relationship, or their financial arrangements.'

Jock read through the statement, grunted in satisfaction, passed it to Bob McLean and stood up abruptly. 'Thank you, Mr Evans, Herr Kessler. You realize, Herr Kessler, that you will be expected to testify in court?'

Kessler nodded sullenly.

'I would recommend that you appoint a new Head of Security as soon as possible. Your erstwhile friend Mr Steiner is likely to take steps to eh . . . discourage your attendance.'

On their way back to the station Bob lamented the decision to grant bail. Jock agreed but told him that it was likely they'd all, with the exception of Steiner, be granted bail. Neither he nor the Procurator was happy about it, but Hamish was under a lot of pressure. The prisoners were very highly connected and a diplomatic incident was looming.

Jock shrugged. 'As long as Kessler takes good care of his hide it should be OK. Somehow I doubt if the man will be venturing far from his big chateau for a while. Even once Steiner's convicted, Kessler'll be a marked man. I think our Mr Steiner's likely to be a wee bit vindictive, don't you?'

Chapter 33

His large frame crammed into a none-too-large seat in economy on the flight to Alicante, Sergeant Alan Clark was distinctly uncomfortable. His knees were jammed into the back of the seat in front which produced complaints from the fat lady sitting there.

Bob McLean took a swig of his beer and reclined comfortably. 'Seems there are some advantages to being a skinny short arse. We'll be in business class coming back. But hopefully you'll be chained to an assassin, so I suppose you'll still be moaning.'

The extradition process had proved to be extremely quick. Assuming the papers in Bob's briefcase were all in order, Ivor would be returning with them to Inverness. Bob admitted to some nervousness. He had never been involved in such an exercise before. Ivor was a hundred and eighty pounds of muscle: a hired killer no doubt schooled in the martial arts. What if he started playing up? Sergeant Clark was some kind of security, but his two hundred pounds was certainly not all muscle. Bob tried reading a magazine but dropped off to be woken by a none-too-gentle poke in the ribs by Clark as the plane began its descent to Alicante.

It was red-carpet treatment on arrival—they were called forward to exit first, and on the tarmac was a police car with a smart young policeman waiting to drive them to headquarters. As the policeman's English didn't extend, it seemed, beyond "Good morning, sir"—and it now being late afternoon, Bob gave up any attempt at conversation and sat back to enjoy the trip. He rolled down his window to feel the warm Mediterranean breeze in his face. Having left a cold wet Inverness, the warm sun was a real treat.

Captain Gonzales was effusive in his welcome, insisting they join him for a coffee. Unlike Inverness where a guest would be treated to a cup of mediocre stuff from the canteen, the Captain ushered them out to a street café round the corner from the police station. 'Coffee in police station it bad—prisoners too they not like drink,' he explained as he ordered three large espressos. 'Also we must drink the brandy. We celebrate you come to my Alicante, yes?' It wasn't really a question, and three large brandies arrived with the coffee. The thought crossed Bob's mind that the Captain and Jock would get on just fine.

Bob took the extradition papers from his briefcase and tried to interest Gonzales in the contents of the file—this apparently was not the Spanish way.

'Inspector—the business do inside. Here enjoy coffee and sunshine. You must stay some days; you Scottish people you so white. Tomorrow I not work; you come with me on boat. My son he married to Scottish girl—she from Edinburgh. My son and she come—and my wife she come. I know quiet place we make the nice picnic. I love English word the picnic. In the Spain we have no word for the picnic so we make your word. Yes, we make the nice picnic.'

The Captain smiled as Bob made to protest. 'The papers, we wait papers they come Madrid. I like tomorrow they come. If no papers . . .' The Captain shrugged and raised his hands. 'Tomorrow we make the picnic. Now I think you make visit the *Señor* Ivor.'

The police station was an old building: if not quite dilapidated, it certainly required some serious renovation. The interview room smelt of vomit and disinfectant, the vomit smell winning out. Ivor was led in, manacled hand and foot. He had a large bruise on his left cheek and a plaster above his right eye.

Bob looked questioningly at Gonzales. 'He make big the trouble; he not like food, he make fight big with my men.'

Gonzales ordered the prisoner to sit and dismissed his two guards.

'*Señor* Ivor, the gentlemen they the police officers: they come from England they visit you.'

Ivor looked grimly at Bob. 'I hope the fuck at least you'll tell me what the fuck all this is about. I can't get any sense out of these monkeys.'

Gonzales rose threateningly from his chair and Bob waved him back.

'Indeed,' said Bob. 'Mr Ivor Beliatski. You are charged that on the morning of the 25th of August of this year you murdered Mr Richard Ogilvie, the Duke of Dunmorey. You are not obliged to say anything, but what you do say may be taken down and used in evidence against you.'

The colour drained from the prisoner's face. He forced a dismissive laugh. 'I've not murdered anyone. I've never even been to Scotland. I've been in Spain for the last six months.' Ivor spoke in perfect, cultured, accentless English, and Bob was reminded of Ivor's Russian history. Was this one of the groomed products of the old KGB? He suspected that was the case as he looked coldly at the prisoner.

'Did anyone mention Scotland? I don't believe they did, Mr Beliatski. I have here the necessary extradition papers. On completion of the formalities here in Spain, you will accompany us back to Inverness, which, as you are aware, is indeed in Scotland. My hope is that you will only have to tolerate Spanish prison food for another twenty-four hours or so.'

'Extradition! You can't just extradite me. I demand to see a lawyer—I'll fight it.'

Gonzales got up, stood behind Ivor, bent and spoke in his ear. '*Señor*, we have for you outside a lawyer. Now you speak him. Then he make for you appeal. The appeal he make to Judge Alberto Mendez. He what you say, make the dismiss. If we make fast all this we make finish today. You be happy with the gentlemen, *Señor*. You no like we make hospitality. Extradition maybe it take too much months. I tell *Señor*—us monkeys we make a long time for you very not nice.' Gonzales resumed his seat and crossed his arms.

Ivor looked up. 'You bastards—you've stitched me up.'

Bob McLean shook his head and told him all was being done totally legally, that he was just lucky—his case had been fast tracked.'

The men moved to Captain Gonzales' office where an old ceiling fan turned lazily, and an early evening sun illuminated the tidy room. The office, with a smart, new-looking computer, and a general air of efficiency was totally out of keeping with the rest of the building—Gonzales clearly took pride in his own little patch.

'Well gentlemen, you happy I think? I too be the happy that man he gone. He very dangerous—one my men he in hospital. Him he kick; very expert is Señor Ivor—four ribs he break.' Gonzales flipped through the extradition papers presented by Bob McLean. 'All I think good. Now we go for the drink and we eat the tapas.'

Bob McLean and Alan Clark were treated to a heavy dose of Spanish hospitality and their innate reserve evaporated after the first few drinks. They had no idea what they were drinking, but it tasted good and had its effect. From the tapas bar they went to a restaurant for a huge *catapallana*—and more drinks. They ended up in a nightclub, and for the first time in their lives, both men experienced live pole and lap-dancing. At the end of the evening, photographs of both of them with naked girls on their laps were taken and presented—but by that time both men were too drunk to care. Both, however, declined Gonzalez's offer of companions for the night, even though one girl seemed to have taken a particular shine to Alan and he was obviously sorely tempted.

It was after 1.00 in the morning before Gonzales dropped them off at their hotel. 'Eight o'clock, gentlemen. I come you at the 8 o'clock—we go make the nice picnic.'

Bob McLean somehow made it down for breakfast—he'd not had such a bad head since student days. Alan Clark was none the worse for the night and was tucking into a full English breakfast when Bob joined him at the table. The smell of the food nauseated him but he forced down some orange juice and toast.

'A great night, eh Bob? These Spaniards sure know how to enjoy themselves. Imagine if our pal Carlos came to Inverness. What could we offer him? A picnic in the rain, a few pints in the pub and an Indian or a Chinese? Would be a bit embarrassing, eh? Aye Bob, this is the life.' Alan pulled a photo from his pocket. 'Mimi. She's bloody gorgeous, isn't she? I think she really fancied me, Bob. You won't believe what she was whispering in my ear—what she was going to do to me.'

Bob took off his glasses and rubbed his eyes. 'Aye Alan, this is the life right enough. I'll leave you here if you like. What message do you want me to give to your wife?'

Alan Clark grinned at him and tore up the photo. 'I don't think Marie would appreciate my wee souvenir.'

They were just finishing their coffee; Bob was starting to feel a little better, having scrounged some asprin from a waiter, when Carlos arrived in infectious good spirits. He had a plastic bag for each of them.

'You not I think bring the clothes for picnic? I think this they fit you. You put on now. My family on boat, they wait.'

The beach clothes fitted reasonably well: garish T-shirts and long striped baggy shorts—outfits that neither man would normally have been seen dead in, but they had to go with the flow. Carlos had even found them each a pair of flip-flops and sunglasses. Bob had never worn a baseball cap before but Carlos assured him he'd need it to keep the sun off.

The family was already drinking wine when they arrived at the marina. The boat was a fifty-foot cabin cruiser: what Bob would call a gin palace. Carlos was obviously reading Bob's thoughts.

'My father boat, Bob. My father he businessman, a very—you say, successful businessman. I not have interest in the business and he not forgive me for not be with him in the business and that I policeman. From my money from policeman maybe I buy like that one.' Carlos indicated a little inflatable moored to the stern. He shrugged. 'It is good my father is wonderful and very generous man. Come, I introduce you to family.'

Carlos' wife Maria was a buxom dark haired beauty, well over forty, with the figure of a woman half her age and a bubbly, vivacious personality. Roberto, his son, was something out of a fashion magazine, as was his beautiful blonde Scottish wife Maggie. To Bob's surprise they were both doctors at the local hospital. Both had engineered the day off and were clearly determined to enjoy themselves as it was their first day off together for a month. Carlos made sure his guests had their wine, stuck on his captain's hat and started the engines.

Bob sat back and sipped his wine. His headache had gone and he felt well up for the day. He suddenly burst out laughing and raised his glass to Alan. 'This *is* the life, Alan—if only Jock could see us now.'

The boat motored about ten miles or so up the coast from Alicante to what Carlos called his 'private beach'. Carlos moored about fifty yards off-shore, Bob and Alan were loaded into the inflatable with Carlos and Roberto, Maggie and Maria swam the short distance to the sandy beach. Hidden from the beach by some rocks, Carlos had built his own barbeque, and with yet another glass of wine in his hand, he had been determined to get the fire going immediately to boil water for coffee.

It turned out to be a magical day. Carlos grilled fresh fish, from freezer boxes Maria produced more food that could ever be consumed, and count was lost of the number of bottles of wine consumed. Roberto was a Glasgow Celtic fan and spent the whole day talking football with Alan Clark. Carlos and Bob, both fanatical policemen, talked shop all day while the women talked woman things, drank wine and sunbathed.

The sun had almost set before the boat was moored back at the marina. Despite the application of copious amounts of sun cream, both Alan and Bob were showing the effects of sunburn. When Carlos dropped two very tired, slightly drunk but very happy men back at their hotel, Bob lamented to Carlos that if he ever came to Scotland they could never reciprocate this type of hospitality.

Carlos laughed. 'You crazy? I come Scotland next year, in summer. Maggie, her sister Jennie—she get married in Fort William. They make me promise a "real Highland wedding". You make for me the kilt? I need meet your famous Jock. Bob and Alan—you and me make up your Ben Nevis and drink the whisky.' Carlos was being serious and both men were drunk enough to show enthusiasm for the climb.

A police car brought the two policemen to headquarters the following morning. A beaming Carlos pulled them into his office. 'Later we have the coffee—here good news.' He sat down and waved some papers. 'All ready. *Señor* Ivor he go Scotland.' Carlos consulted some notes on his desk. 'You go 11.30 BA Gatwick, and after quick flight Inverness.'

He looked seriously at the two men. 'Our *Señor* Ivor he dangerous man. He animal: he killer. I think he kill many men before Duke. You very careful my friends.' Carlos smiled. 'I make it he be very sleepy. The doctor give him needle. He have handcuff to you, Alan. Also you make handcuff to other hand to seat. You not let him from handcuffs—he wet trousers, you not let him go toilet.' Carlos opened the drawer of his desk, pulled out a small revolver and handed it to Bob McLean. 'This you take—you not I hope need you shoot. Ivor, he make me nervous. He very clever. You know he before a big KGB man?'

Bob nodded. He hadn't known but was pleased that his hunch had been correct.

A squad of armed men accompanied the policemen and their prisoner to the plane. They ensured that Ivor was securely cuffed to Alan Clark on his right and to his seat-arm on his left. Bob McLean still felt very nervous. He'd read all about the KGB and their operatives, and had asked that Ivor's feet be shackled also—Carlos was very happy to oblige. Carlos wished them both a good journey and warned them again to take no chances. Bob fingered the revolver in his pocket. He'd never fired a revolver. The instructions he'd been given by Carlos were very cursory—basically point it and fire. He seriously hoped that he wouldn't have to.

The flight to Gatwick was uneventful. Ivor, heavily sedated, slept throughout the journey. Alan Clark, obliged to eat with one hand, complained as predicted. They were met by armed police and escorted to the Inverness flight where Ivor was once again secured. He was, however, beginning to recover from the sedation and half-way to Inverness he began to struggle and protest very noisily. Other passengers, many having seen that Ivor was obviously a prisoner, were becoming nervous as he struggled against the handcuffs; and Alan Clark's wrist was becoming painfully chafed. The Captain was considering emergency landing in Edinburgh when Bob McLean discreetly drew the revolver from his pocket, leaned over Sergeant Clark and pressed the gun painfully into Ivor's ribs—the gun worked as well as any sedative.

Chapter 34

Bob McLean picked painfully at his peeling nose as he made his report to Jock. He, of course, got no sympathy from his boss.

'And what did the wife have to say about all your shenanigans then?' asked Jock with a laugh.

'I missed out the bit about the nightclub—and don't you be telling anyone, sir.' Bob dabbed some more cream on his nose. 'Carlos, Captain Gonzales, will be over here next summer. I'm telling you sir, even you would have trouble keeping up with him and the drink. I really do think he's serious about dragging Alan and me up Ben Nevis. We, you and Meg—all of us are invited to the wedding. It's going to be a right big do—Glenfinnan House Hotel. Me and Alan are going anyway.'

Jock smiled at him. 'I'll pass on your wee climb up Ben Nevis, but you really think I'd let you lads have all the fun; that me and Meg would miss out on a leg-up? You know the dates?'

Bob nodded.

'Best to book us all in now. If it's full-up there's another place up the road, try that one. Maybe they've not booked a band yet—I'm sure The Dunmorey Ceilidh Band would be well up for it.'

Jock lay back in his chair. 'Glenfinnan, eh? It's beautiful there: really really lovely. Me and Meg spent some of our honeymoon at the Glenfinnan House so it'll be a wee trip down memory lane for us. Pity the bridal suite will probably be booked, eh? Summer wedding on the west coast? With a bit of luck it might not be raining on the day. Have you warned Carlos about the midges? I suppose the wedding will be in the wee Catholic church on the hill?'

'Oh no; that's what I thought too. But there's to be no religious stuff. Maggie said her sister's a staunch atheist. It'll be a short civil wedding at the hotel. Carlos isn't too happy about that—they're right religious folk, the Spanish.'

'Aye,' said Jock smiling, 'but hopefully they'll have the consolation of a good ceilidh. And what's all this about a gun? Thank God no one saw it—there would have been hell to pay if you'd fired the damn thing. Don't know who's the daftest one: you or your man Carlos. Where is it?'

Bob sheepishly took the small revolver from his pocket and passed it over the desk to Jock who picked it up and flipped it open. 'It's empty: no bullets. Did you take them out?'

Bob shook his head. 'I wouldn't know how.'

'Maybe your man Carlos wasn't so daft after all,' sighed Jock. 'I'll have this sent back to him.' Jock slipped the revolver into a drawer, tucked a large file under his arm and stood up.

'Let's go and have a wee chat with Mr Ivor. He'll be needing a lawyer, I suppose.'

Bob McLean smiled at him.

'Don't tell me—bloody Owen Bloody Evans again! Call him up. Tell him to get his arse round here now. We'll go down and see our Ivor anyway. I want to size him up—and he just might be feeling talkative.'

Ivor, with a uniformed constable on guard, was drinking tea when Bob and Jock entered the interview room. Jock dismissed the constable and introduced himself. The pair sat down facing the prisoner. 'This is not a formal interview, Mr Beliatski. Your lawyer is not present but we expect him shortly. He's a very busy man, or so he keeps telling me. I trust the food is to your taste—the tea, it's OK?'

Ivor looked coldly at Jock but said nothing.

Jock patted the fat folder in front of him. 'This is your file. You'd be surprised what we know about you—very surprised.'

In truth, Ivor's was a fairly modest file—the padding was for psychological effect.

'You'll no doubt be wondering how you ended up here. You, the international assassin, master of his trade; brought down by a bunch of Highland plods. You, the clever KGB man that fooled the best of them: Interpol, CIA, FBI, MI5.' Jock tapped the file again and Ivor shifted uncomfortably on his chair. 'Well, I'm not about to tell you how we got you, I'm afraid—we policemen like to keep our little secrets. What I will tell you, though, is that we know that you shot the Duke of Dunmorey. We know, and can prove that you were there—we know how you did it.' Jock paused and smiled coldly at the prisoner. 'And we know who ordered the hit, *and* we know who paid you. In fact there's not much we don't know.'

Jock made a show of flipping through the file. He drew out a photograph. 'A wee sampler for you.' He slipped the photo over the desk between them. 'Not a bad photo eh? These wee phone cameras are amazing, are they not? Taken by your little girlfriend in the Kings Hotel. She gave you a nine by the way.' Jock smiled at Ivor's puzzled expression as he shrugged and tossed the photo back to Jock.

There was a disturbance outside the door: it was Owen Evans, his whine was unmistakable. The familiar figure burst through the door loudly protesting.

'This is my client—you have no right to interview him unless I am present.' He turned to Ivor. 'I hope you've said nothing.'

Jock smiled at the lawyer. 'He hasn't even said good morning—which I thought was very rude. This is not a formal interview, Mr Evans, just a friendly wee chat and your client has been informed of the fact. We are in fact finished, so we'll leave you now. I'm sure you have an awful lot to talk about.' Jock handed Evans a manila folder. 'These are the details of the charges against your client.'

'That's one hard bastard,' muttered Jock as they made their way back up to his office. 'I'm glad we'll not be having to push him for a confession. In fact, I don't think we really need to talk to him at all. He's going to tell us bugger all anyway. We do need him to finger Steiner, though. I want that one wrapped up—I want Steiner formally charged. Evans will no doubt be up in a bit when he's finished with our Ivor. I think we'll maybe manage to make a wee deal. Can you arrange to have Ivor shifted to Porterfield. But tell the Governor that this is no ordinary prisoner. I want solitary with maximum security. And be sure to tell the Governor that he's getting a wild man who's right handy with his feet.'

Jo and Jamie had brunch at Meg and Jock's on Sunday morning. It was a crisp, clear morning and Jock suggested a brisk walk to help their digestion. With Nick leading the way and with wee Gordie on Jamie's shoulders, they took the long loop which took them to Balmannie: the old house.

'I've not been here for years,' said Jo with a sigh. 'I love this old house.' Jamie was also very smitten with the place and was concerned about the missing slates. Jo pulled Jock to one side and whispered in his ear. 'I used to bring my boyfriends here.'

Jock laughed. 'You little minx. It saw a quite few of my girlfriends too. And your Mum: she has fond memories of the place.' He nudged a blushing Meg. 'The big old bed's gone, though. I liked that bed: it was a nice old piece of furniture.'

'I've got it in the flat Dad. Didn't you tell him I took it, Mum? Got a new mattress though, the old one was a bit eh . . .'

'Aye it was. I bet that old mattress could have told a few stories.

'Mum and me have been thinking. It's a shame having the poor old house sitting here doing nothing. Would you like to have it Jo—a wedding present from us?'

Jo whooped, threw her arms round Jock, hugged him and her mother and ran off to find Jamie who was checking the place out. The pair came back, grins all over their faces. Jock dug in his pocket and pulled out the big key for the old wooden front door, and with a theatrical gesture presented it to the excited couple.

Jock called to them as they ran to the house. 'Needs a bit of work mind; it's not too . . . eh, salubrious right now. Aye, a right lot of work.'

Jamie unlocked the door, they all went in and Jo and Jamie scurried round excitedly, already planning the renovation.

On the walk home, Jo hung on Jock's arm. 'I'm so excited, Dad—we're both so excited. It'll work out just great. Alison, Jamie's sister, is graduating in the summer as doctor. She'll be coming to work at Raigmore and will be needing somewhere to stay, so she can have Jamie's place near Dunmorey.'

'It's going to cost a bit to do up, love.'

'We'll manage just fine, Dad. I've still got some money Auntie May left me—and of course I'll be selling the flat. And from Jamie's mum and dad—there was money that went to Ali and Jamie when they got killed. It'll be lovely Dad, I can just picture it—I can't wait to get started.'

Always the practical one, Jamie said he'd have someone look at the roof on Monday for starters. 'Andy Johnston our bass player—he's a builder: I'll get him on it.'

Chapter 35

At his desk the following morning Jock wasn't in the best of humour. He'd started a toothache the previous evening and he was stroking his jaw as he read the statement made by Ivor. Bob McLean had already read it and was sitting back with a coffee.

'Aye sir, whatever we may say about Evans, he doesn't hang about. It's all here in Ivor's statement, chapter and verse. It's amazing what the promise of a wee bit of remission can do. A hundred thousand dollars: I wonder if that's the current rate for knocking someone off? At least he'll have no bother paying Evans. I see that he even had a face-to-face meeting with Steiner—nice that. He can formally identify him to the court.'

'Aye Bob. Right sloppy of Ivor—of both of them. It's great how over-confidence nets us so many villains.' He slid the statement over to Bob McLean. 'I've got a dental appointment at 11.00, Bob. Can you get over to Porterfield and formally charge Steiner. I'd been looking forward to doing that myself.' Jock flinched and drew air into his mouth. 'Another bloody root canal job, I think. Lawyers and dentists: necessary bloody evils.'

Bob smiled at him. 'Aye, sir, and there's them that say the same thing about the police.' Jock grunted, sent him off, and tried to concentrate on some paperwork but the pain was too intrusive. He reached into the bottom drawer of his desk and took out his emergency whisky and a glass, poured a healthy dram, popped a couple of asprin and washed them down with the whisky. He looked at his watch. Another hour. He thought maybe another dram would help—he took one anyway.

Jock was in better spirits by the time he got home that evening. His face was a bit swollen but the pain had mostly gone. Meg gave him a consoling hug and poured him a whisky.

'Right gentle, that new dentist. Nice young chap he is. Davie MacGregor, a local lad. That old Archie Wilson was a right butcher by comparison. Did you know he'd retired? Good riddance; he was a grumpy old sod too. I hardly felt a thing with this youngster. The bugger's lined me up for a couple of fillings though.'

Meg grinned at him and decided a change of subject was in order. 'Lots of activity at Balmannie this morning. Jo was up with her builder and an architect.'

Jock looked at her. 'An architect? Why does she need an architect?'

Meg refilled his glass. 'Regulations, love. They're going to have to go through all the planning permission nonsense. They want to extend the house into the old steading on the end so they'll need formal plans.'

'Load of bloody nonsense.' He smiled and gave Meg a hug. 'Nothing to do with us, eh? We'll just let them get on with it.' Jock sat back in his chair. Planning permission? He felt a little penny drop in the back of his brain.

Jock was back on all cylinders the following morning. He was on the phone when Bob McLean came into his office. He finished the call and turned to Bob. 'What do you know about our Councillor MacPhee?'

Bob thought for a moment. 'Other than the fact that he's a right pain in the arse, not much. He's an accountant; just himself, works out of a wee office at his house. Bit of an expert on tax. Word is, if you don't want to pay tax, go and see wee MacPhee.'

'So he specializes in tax avoidance then?'

'Aye, that and tax evasion. I remember I once heard someone in a pub boasting what a great job MacPhee was doing for him: it was Connor O'Reilly—you know him, the second-hand car merchant and scrap metal dealer.'

'Know him!' laughed Jock. 'I'd love to nail that smart little bastard. I'm sure he's processing most of the cars stolen round here. Anyway, about MacPhee. Does all right, do you think?'

Bob shrugged. 'It seems so. He swans round like a big shot; dapper little sod in smart suits. Drives a top of the line Merc, as does his wife. His wife's a big spender. My wife knows her—she's on her golf team. Apparently she's always dressed up to the nines—all the right golf gear; a flashy kind of woman. Not much of a golfer though, apparently.'

Jock smiled at the picture of a bunch of gossiping golf wives.

'You remember Jimmy Grey; died a couple of years back?'

Bob shook his head.

'Anyway, he was my accountant. Self-employed, he was. A bloody good accountant and right busy. I mind him telling me how difficult it was to make much when you're on your own—there's not enough hours in the day. He could only cope with a limited number of clients. He did OK mind, charged enough I can tell you, but no big Mercs for him and the wife. Jamie Ross interviewed MacPhee after the burglary—he was in his house; give him a shout, will you Bob.'

A few minutes later Jamie was seated in Jock's office.

'A wee test of your powers of observation, Jamie. You interviewed Councillor MacPhee after his burglary. His house—nice is it?'

Jamie looked a bit puzzled by the question. 'It's a nice house sir. Stone built. Not huge, only four bedrooms, but it's immaculately kept. Doctored lawns, not a weed in the big flowerbeds. Not that they do any work in the garden themselves. They've got an old guy who does three days a week. I had to interview him about the burglary.'

'And inside?'

'Nice, if you like that sort of thing, I suppose; but not my style: vulgar and ostentatious. I was minded about the old saying that money can't buy taste. Light coloured, almost white carpets. You feel you should take your shoes off to walk on them. And the settees: they were white. How anyone can live with that I can't understand. Aye sir, the place was like something out of a Vogue magazine. Bloody horrible, I thought.'

Jock sat back in his chair. 'If I remember right, when wee MacPhee was shouting down the phone at me about his bit of bother, he said he'd just got back from a wee holiday. Did he tell you where he'd been?'

Jamie smiled. 'No sir, but that wife of his did. Caribbean: a ten-day cruise. Among all her blubbing she had to tell me about it. First class all the way, apparently. "Nothing but the best for me and Archie," said she.'

'So you got the impression that they were quite well-heeled then?'

Jamie nodded. 'If he could afford fifteen hundred pounds for a wee Persian rug just before a jaunt to the Caribbean he can't be short of a few.'

Jock thanked Jamie, sent him off and raised his eyebrows at Bob McLean. 'I've just been on the phone to Duncan MacRobbie, the Provost. You ever had any dealings with the planning committee?'

Bob shook his head.

Jock carefully filled his pipe. 'I'd remembered hearing somewhere that wee MacPhee—Councillor MacPhee—was supposed to be on the planning committee. Well, he's not just on the committee; Duncan told me he's now the chairman. Pretty influential position you'd think, eh? And you'll never guess who else is on the planning committee.'

Bob frowned and shook his head.

Jock grinned at him. 'Councillor Owen Evans.'

'I'm sorry sir, you've lost me.'

Jock liked folk to get there on their own and ploughed patiently on. 'I asked the Provost, hypothetically like, how the council would view an application to build a great big golf course with all the trimmings in the area. He didn't exactly say no bloody way, but just about. On principle, he said, anything that would benefit the area could be looked on favourably, but nowadays apparently there are so many other considerations: mostly environmental. He said for an area of bog doing nothing, needed by no-one and in a locality which interfered with no-one, you could probably get your permission. Unless, of course, the bog was a place of special scientific interest, which meant it only needed to have a rare flower or rare newt or something. A place especially rich in wildlife, the habitat of rare birds or other beasts, then forget it. Even a wintering area for wildfowl was sacred. Special interest groups tend to appear out of the woodwork, it seems. I asked if there had been any such applications—he said there had been none.

'The planning office is apparently very important Bob. If the planning committee approve and back a proposal; which means the proposal is, they feel, overwhelmingly in the public interest, then you're most of the way there. If the local authority goes for it you can pretty well forget the special interest groups and most other considerations.'

Jock smiled at Bob who was still looking puzzled.

'You remember, Bob, all that carry-on about that horrible big new supermarket on the edge of town? Seemed that nobody wanted the damn thing. An eyesore on a greenfield site—they had to knock down all those lovely old croft houses to build it. I remember even I signed a petition against it, and I'm not big on petitions—bloody waste of time. That got the OK, went through no bother. I always reckoned a lot of money changed hands on that one. Aye Bob, the special interest groups can make a lot of background noise but can usually be ignored—if the planning committee approve, that is.' Jock looked at Bob, who had finally caught up.

'What you're saying, sir, is that under normal circumstances there's no way Ogilvie would have got approval for a golf course on Dunmorey.'

Jock nodded while lighting his pipe.

'So you think Ogilvie had Evans and MacPhee in his pocket?'

Jock blew out a cloud of smoke. 'Aye Bob; that would be my guess. With Evans and MacPhee pushing together; a bit of heavy persuasion, plus a bit of money maybe to lubricate any sticky wheels? I'm getting a bad smell, Bob. That bit of influence would be worth a good bit of money to Ogilvie, I'd say. True democracy in action, eh? Trouble is, that's the way this whole bloody country's run—there's always some sort of payback somewhere along the line for some bugger. I hate corruption, Bob. If that pair were in cahoots with Ogilvie, the chances are they're more than susceptible to other persuasion. I wonder if they had a hand in the approval for that bloody supermarket?

'You remember all those calls to a local landline made by Ogilvie? They were traced. Most were to MacPhee, his home and office numbers. They were as thick as bloody thieves.'

Bob McLean shook his head. 'It'll be a bastard to nail them, sir. They're two clever little sods. I bet there'll be no money trail to follow. Bit of pocket money put down as legal fees and accountancy fees? The rest stuck in some numbered accounts somewhere? MacPhee would have no bother setting that up. Aye sir, it smells, right enough. Any ideas?'

Jock sat back and puffed quietly on his pipe for a few moments. 'You're right—I don't think we can nail them. But we can have a good go at trying to scare them. I want them off that planning committee and off the council. A wee bit of hard evidence would be nice, but circumstantial evidence—if there's enough of it—is good enough for us, eh Bob? Let's just have a bit of a think about it. And another thing. There's no way Jo and Jamie will get planning approval for their wee project. That pair of bastards are sure to find a way to block it just to get at me—and I'm not having that. Aye, let's us just have a wee think. Maybe our brains will work a bit better with a beer. Come on, it's almost lunchtime.'

Bob looked at his watch. 'But sir, it's only 11.30.'

'Aye, that's what I said—it's almost lunchtime.'

Bob shook his head and followed on.

An idea came to Jock half-way through his first pint. 'It may be just a wee bit elaborate, and will cost a wee bit. I best go and have a chat with the Chief Constable. Just you stay and finish off your pint.' Jock downed the last of his, and left a bemused Bob McLean chewing on his half-eaten pie.

The Chief Constable was on the point of leaving for his lunch when Jock rolled up. The golf club did a good lunch so they headed off there. Jock hadn't touched his pie in the pub so he was now ready to eat—and to have another beer.

Jock and the Chief Constable met regularly, socially and professionally, and Jock always ensured that his friend was abreast of every investigation— chief constables hate nasty surprises—especially ones that leave egg on their faces. There was a strong mutual respect between the two men, so when Jock explained the suspicions he harboured about Evans and MacPhee, and his idea about outing them, the Chief Constable was obliged to take him seriously. He had some serious reservations about Jock's scheme but supported him and would authorize the necessary funds.

'It might work Jock, but you'll never get them into court—and it could rebound.'

'Aye, Willie. I'll risk that; but if I can get them out of public life and their sticky wee fingers out of that cookie jar I'll be happy enough.'

The Chief Constable didn't seem quite so happy but raised his wine glass to Jock. 'Here's to—what will we call it? How about . . . eh—"Operation Rat Catcher"?'

'Aye Willie, that'll do nicely; "Operation Rat Catcher" it is then.' Jock didn't go much on silly names but sometimes it was good to humour the boss.

When Jock outlined his plan to his DI, Bob burst out laughing. 'If nothing else, it will be fun. They're greedy little bastards: they won't be able to resist it. Might take a few days to set up, though.'

In an Inverness hotel room, Councillors MacPhee and Evans were in conference with a suave Argentinian businessman, *Señor* Manuel de la Cruz.

La Cruz smiled at the two men seated opposite him. 'It too very kind that you to meet with me. You I think be busy men, and I thank to you *Señor* Macafee for to meet me at airport. I sorry I not tell of why I come on telephone. Must make careful to say on telephone, you understand? Forgive me I not make the nice talk gentlemen, I am to be direct. We make the nice talk at the dinner, yes?'

The Argentinian cleared his throat. 'I ask that you gentlemen to trust you say to no-one, yes?' He looked at Evans and MacPhee and both men nodded. 'I before a business—I think to say English—associate of *Señor* Ogilvie; an *amigo*, a friend Señor Ogilvie. He dead it make me so sad. I lose friend, I lose good business. *Señor* Ogilvie he want me business partner in what he make on *estancia*—on estate. So sad. I like very much idea. I make too many talks with my good friend. We talk, he tell me many problems. He tell to me you help him yes? I like very much idea, I think I like do same. I do before many business with the *Señor* Steiner. You know the *Señor* Steiner yes?'

Evans smiled and nodded.

'Poor *Señor* Steiner, he now have the big problems. *Señor* Steiner he now he sell estate. I think I like buy; I do same like *Señor* Ogilvie. I make very special place for the special people.'

The Argentinian produced a roll of plans and opened them on the table. 'These, you say very quick, they what you say . . .' He searched for the word.

'Provisional?' suggested Evans.

'Yes yes, provisional. Much provisional.' The map was upside down to Evans and MacPhee and they had only a brief look at it before their host pushed it aside. 'We look good later. *Señor* Ogilvie tell to me to make building, to make the land to use different make problem and that you help him, yes? I like you help me.' Evans and MacPhee exchanged glances and smiled.

Room service arrived with coffee and the Argentinian poured for his guests.

Evans sipped his coffee, replaced his cup and looked at the Argentinian, smiling. 'I think we can help you, Mr de la Cruz.'

'Please—I Manuel.'

'Manuel. Did Mr Ogilvie tell you how—in what way we helped him? How we were going to help him?'

The Argentinian nodded. 'He tell you make the permission that he make the golf course.'

'I am a lawyer, Manuel. I helped Mr Ogilvie to buy land. I gave him a lot of advice.'

'Good, good, you to help me. But I not to buy if I not do what I want— you help to me?'

Evans glanced at MacPhee and shifted in his chair. 'Mr MacPhee and myself serve on the planning committee of the local council. You understand planning committee?'

The Argentinian nodded.

'For a consideration we would ensure that the plans for his project would be approved.'

'Mr Ogilvie give to you money to make good?'

'Yes, Manuel, he give us money to make good.'

The Argentinian clapped his hands and smiled broadly. 'I give many money make good me also. You men very clever; I like work with you. You do for me? You make like same before—you make me no problem? I buy not can build big problem for me.'

Evans smiled at him. 'We do this many times before. I promise you no problem. Perhaps I must pay a little to other people . . . ?'

'Pay little, pay big OK. I pay you good; you pay people, I like no problem. I so happy I like kiss you. Yes, I do to buy the *estancia* of *Señor* Steiner. Yes we do the good business. We go the bar make nice talk. I like too much the whisky. I not before drink the whisky in Scotland. Come I buy you drink.'

As they left the lift they were met by Jock and Bob McLean. Jock shook hands with the "Argentinian".

'Great job, Carlos, you should have been an actor.'

Carlos beamed at him. 'The pleasure, *Señor* Jock, the big pleasure.'

Jock turned to the crestfallen Evans and MacPhee. 'I'd like to have a few words with you pair. Would you mind accompanying us to the station?'

'You bastard!' blurted Evans. 'You'll never get away with this Anderson! This is entrapment. I'll have you, Anderson. I'll make you regret this.'

A small crowd had gathered, drawn by the smell of something interesting. Evans and MacPhee looked round nervously, dreading to see, or be seen by anyone they knew.

Jamie Ross and DC Miller came out of a neighbouring lift behind Evans and MacPhee, and Jamie nodded at Jock.

Jock took Evans's arm. 'Shall we go gentlemen?'

Back at the station, Jock forced the pair to watch the video of their meeting with Carlos. He ejected the CD and faced the two men. 'DC Ross and DC Miller witnessed and further recorded the meeting from the bedroom—a bit of extra insurance. I think you'll agree we've got you cold, gentlemen.

'But you're right, Mr Evans, entrapment it is; but my God you greedy bastards made it easy for us, spilling the whole bloody can of beans without making a single check.' Jock turned to Carlos. 'Mind you, Carlos here was damned convincing, could have fooled anyone. But he shouldn't have been allowed to fool you, Evans—you're a lawyer, for God's sake. Anyway, thanks for being so greedy and gullible.'

Evans glared calmly at Jock, but beside him MacPhee slumped in his chair, clearly close to tears.

'I note, Anderson,' said Evans with a sneer, 'that this conversation is not being recorded. You're a maverick, Anderson. You must know you can't get away with this. You know damned well that a good lawyer will rubbish that recording. You'll be the one in the dock over this.'

Evans sat back and smiled smugly as he crossed his arms. 'We, respectable councillors, suspicious of his motives, were *of course,* merely setting up "*Señor* de la Cruz" only to expose him. Our records as councillors are, I think, quite impressive—impressive to the public if not to you. To give you just one example of many: we are responsible for bringing Holbrook Engineering to the town—a cutting edge computer software company; over one hundred and fifty jobs.'

'One wonders, Mr Evans, what kickbacks you got on that one? And do we have you to thank for that monstrosity of a supermarket?'

Evans reddened, but maintained his cool and continued. 'Mr MacPhee, in his role on the Police Relations Committee, has done sterling work improving the policing of this area. Perhaps I should say *attempting* to make improvements in the face of your persistent resistance to his efforts.'

Jock glared at him. He couldn't let that pass without comment. 'Perhaps if Councillor MacPhee devoted more effort to increasing the police budget and less time harassing us, he would have found his efforts more gratifying.'

Jock steepled his fingers and looked at the two men. 'I have no intention of charging you two. I'm going to make it so easy for the pair of you—so simple you'll probably want to hug me.'

Jock fingered the CD recording of the meeting and glared at Evans and MacPhee. 'You will resign immediately as councillors. God knows what you got up to on that planning committee; how much silver has crossed your grubby little palms. You disgust me. You're elected as councillors to serve the interests of this community. You greedy little slugs were only ever interested in serving yourselves. It's over. The gravy train's hit the buffers. You can go now and prepare your resignations, but before you leave, I'd like the names of the others on the committee who were benefitting from your little schemes.'

Jock waved the CD at the men. 'You misbehave and this gets shown to the Provost. I don't think you'll like that now, will you? You'd both be ruined, you know that. I don't mean to ruin you—I simply want you out of public life.' At that point the Chief Constable came in and smiled at Jock. Evans was now outgunned and he knew it.

A red-faced Evans stood and faced up to Jock. 'This is fucking blackmail, Anderson—fucking blackmail.'

'You call it what you like,' said Jock calmly. 'I would call it rough justice. The names of your associates please; then get out of here the pair of you. Get out of my sight.'

'There are no others, Anderson. I was pushing . . .'

'Aye, Evans, don't tell me—pushing for more money. Get out.'

An hour later, a group of very self-satisfied, very happy policemen were gathered round a table in Carlos' hotel. The Chief Constable joined them for a quick drink, thanked Carlos, congratulated his men and then discreetly left—but not before giving the OK to an expense account for the evening.

Jock walked with him to the door. They smiled at each other and shook hands. Both men knew they'd sailed very close to the wind on this one, and that the Chief Constable's timely arrival in the interview room had probably tipped the balance.

'Bloody expensive wee operation, though, Jock. But you're right, it was worth it. You're lucky you don't have to worry too much about budgets; you're ey spendin' money. You realize what it cost to get the two forensic lads up from Glasgow to look at that Land Rover from Dunmorey? No, and I don't suppose you care,' said the Chief Constable with a laugh.

Jock grinned at him. 'Aye Willie, but that was worth it too—whatever it cost. I got the report back this morning. They found a wee fleck of blue paint in a scatch on the wing of the Land Rover—a perfect match with the paint from Hughie MacRae's bike. If that bastard Ogilvie was still alive we'd have enough to prosecute. Let's just hope the bastard's rotting in hell. Mind you, he'll probably be quite happy there—he'll be amongst his own kind of folk eh?'

Jock returned to the table and interrupted the excited noisy conversation. He lifted his newly filled glass of whisky. 'A toast, gentlemen. To international police co-operation and to "Operation Rat Catcher".' Jock took a small sip from his whisky as Carlos drained his own. Jock smiled, leaned over and refilled Carlos's glass. Bob had implied that Carlos could drink him under the table—Jock was pacing himself with care.

Chapter 36

A **smiling** Bob McLean waved a copy of the popular local daily, the *Aberdeen Press and Journal* as Jock entered the station the next morning. He handed over the paper and Jock read the headlines.

"'Shock resignation of eminent Inverness councillors".' Jock smiled. 'Aye, that'll do just fine. They'll be trying to dig for some dirt. What excuses did they give for resigning? The usual, eh? For reasons of ill health? To spend more time with the family? Or just the good old standby: personal reasons?'

Bob took back the paper and scanned the article. 'No reasons offered. Seems that Evans and MacPhee are refusing to comment.'

'They'll be having to come up with something, Bob. Tongues will be wagging.

'How's Carlos this morning?'

Bob laughed. 'No idea, sir. Last I saw him, Alan was half carrying him to his room. He was in a right state. Did you see him? He was drinking whisky like he'd drink wine. I think he enjoyed himself though.'

Jock flipped through some mail on his desk. 'You could give him a ring later. He'll probably have a right head on him—and it's the big do at Dunmorey tonight; he'll want to be fit for that. Are you and the wife coming?'

Bob looked at him in surprise. 'Too bloody right we are—it'll be a great night. Sheena wants me to wear my kilt; are you wearing yours?'

'Of course, it's a ceilidh isn't it? The band's playing and it's going to be a real leg-up. And it'll be a wee treat for Carlos. He's already a bit disappointed that folk in Scotland don't wear kilts all the time. Can you find DC Ross for me Bob. I've got a wee job for him.'

Jamie arrived a few minutes later and Jock grinned at him. 'All set for tonight?'

'Aye sir, you bringing your fiddle?'

'Not the fiddle. My pipes maybe. Been trying a few tunes, but I'm a bit rusty. All this music stuff's right infectious. I took my pipes for a wee walk up to your Balmannie for a bit of a blow. Aye, I might just bring them along. But I've got a job for you.'

Jock handed Jamie a large file. 'The Ogilvie case. It's wrapped up as well as it'll ever be. Can you go through the file and prepare a nice tidy account; make it nice easy reading, cut out the extraneous stuff. I want to send a report nicely wrapped up in red ribbon to those snots they sent up from London—a wee souvenir for them. You think you can do that?'

'Of course sir. Might take me a few days—we've got a lot on at the moment.'

Jock waved him away. 'When you've got time lad, but quick as you can—but by the end of next week.'

Jock had just finished dealing with his mail when there was a call from reception: he had a visitor. A Mr Arthur Cavendish would like to see him. It took a moment for the name to register before he asked that he be sent up. The last time he'd met Cavendish was in Ogilvies, the bank in London. Jock had liked the man very much and he'd be happy to see him again.

Cavendish greeted Jock warmly and accepted the offer of coffee. 'I'm visiting my old mother in Dingwall. I'm here for a week and I thought while I was up here, I'd pay you a visit.'

Jock recalled Cavendish's Scottish connection and asked how his mum was.

'In hospital actually. That's why I'm in Inverness. They tell me it's nothing serious; had a funny turn—her heart I think. Got herself a bit too excited about my visit, I expect. I don't see nearly enough of her, and she's getting on a bit.'

'It's good to see you again, Mr Anderson.' Cavendish looked a bit uncomfortable. 'That awful business about Ogilvie in America. I still feel bad about that. I thought you might like to know what happened. You'll remember Rubens and I had prepared a report for the American police?'

Jock nodded.

'Well, it really hit the fan over there. Rubens passed our report to someone near the top in the Department of Justice. Turns out that the Capello character—the owner of Paradise Glades—is, as we expected, a big Mafia boss. None of the men involved in the scam were ever seen again. We'll carry the guilt of that forever, Mr Anderson. We should have had the courage to report our concerns earlier: much earlier. Those poor men could have still been alive.

'Anyway, I don't know all the details, but Capello's in custody. They're still building the case against him but seem very confident they'll nail him for the murder of the missing men. A lot of others: most of the senior officers in the local police are going down, too. Unfortunately, Rubens and I will have to go over there and testify sometime.' Cavendish smiled wryly. 'I suppose it's the least we can do.

'Your visit to London was very odd, Mr Anderson. You left us all feeling somewhat perplexed. We had believed that Richard Ogilvie was the victim of an unfortunate shooting accident. Your visit was very unsettling. So has the case been resolved?'

Jock looked at Cavendish and fiddled with his pipe. 'Mr Cavendish, what I'm about to tell you is in confidence. The facts are soon to be made public; I'll be issuing a statement very soon, but for the moment I must ask you to be discreet.'

Arthur Cavendish vowed to keep his own council and sat in shocked silence as Jock told him the story—as a dessert, Jock added the tale of Steiner's orgy.

'My God,' said Cavendish. 'I knew something about the Steiner affair; it was, I remember, on the news and in all of the papers. But all this about Ogilvie. It's like something out of a cheap crime thriller. One doesn't expect such things to happen in real life—and especially not in the Highlands of Scotland. Please Mr Anderson, can I tell all this to Rubens? He has to know.'

Jock arched his eyebrows, smiled and nodded. 'Aye, OK but only your pal Rubens, mind.' Jock asked how things were at the bank.

Cavendish shrugged. 'Settling down finally. Ogilvie was a bastard: but a very, very clever bastard. He made the bank a lot of money—and he was a very strong leader. That's not easy to replace. The CEO you met: Rupert Edmonds—he's gone, thank goodness. We've a new CEO. He's a good man. He was head of one of the big banks so we're back on track. Officially Robert Ogilvie is the Chairman and is the major shareholder of the bank now. He'll have to attend the odd board meeting but he has no interest and is determined not to get involved in the running of the bank. A wise decision on his part I think—the bank doesn't need a square peg in a round hole.'

'You know Robert Ogilvie well?'

Cavendish laughed. 'Robbie? Yes, very well. We're great friends. His mother was a good friend, a very good friend of mine. The Honourable Richard hated that, of course. Yes, we had a few wild times down at the farm in Devon. I've known Robbie since he was a kid.'

'In that case, you better come along as a surprise guest tonight. Robbie's having a big party at Dunmorey Lodge—and I think he'll have an awful lot to tell you about.'

'But Mr Anderson . . .'

'For goodness sake man, my name's Jock.'

'OK, Jock, and I'm Arthur. I'd love to come but I'm not exactly dressed for a party.'

Jock looked at him. 'Aye, ye're right. We've got to do this properly.' Jock smiled mischievously. 'Come with me, man, we'll soon get you sorted out. But we'll have to hurry—it's an early kick-off.'

Dunmorey Lodge was already filling up when Jock and his party arrived, and Jock was pleased that everyone was in Highland gear. Robbie, looking magnificent in full regalia, strode over to greet them. Over Jock's shoulder he spotted a familiar grinning face. Jock stepped aside to reveal the kilt-clad figure of Arthur Cavendish. Robbie gave a joyful laugh and the two men hugged each other. 'How the hell did you get here? I don't believe it!' Robbie looked at Jock who grinned and shrugged innocently. Robbie put his arms round the shoulders of the two men. 'Come on, the bar's over here—I think we all deserve a drink.'

Jock accepted a large malt and left the two men laughing together.

Meg had been whisked off somewhere by Morag, and Jock wandered into the huge dining room which had been cleared for dancing. Jo and Jamie were knocking out a reel on fiddle and banjo on a stage at the top end of the room and Jock gave them a wave. He saw wee Dunkie and tried to make his way over to him, but the place was full of people, many of whom he knew, and he seemed to be stopped at every step by happy folk who wanted to shake his hand. It was a heady atmosphere.

It had been some weeks since Jock had seen Dunkie and he'd prepared himself for the worst—he had seen the decline of other cancer sufferers. To Jock's surprise, however, Dunkie looked in the best of health, and his ruddy complexion owed nothing to the whisky he was drinking.

Dunkie read his thoughts. 'Yon bloody doctor didnae ken bugger all, Jock. Morag took me tae a specialist. One lung's pretty well buggered right enough—but it's no' cancer. They think it's from some bug that A picked up on ma foreign travels years ago. A mind A had a right bad pneumonia when A wis oot in the Congo. A wee bit got left as a souvenir maybe. Some lads got the clap—A got this. It's a sort o' big dry abscess or somethin'. A'm still on medication, an' maybe A'll be needin' a bit o' surgery, but A'm fit fir a few mair ceildhs Jock: a lot more.' Dunkie put a hand on Jock's shoulder. 'Man, yer glass is empty—we canny hae that.'

Robbie, with his arm round Carol, was still at the bar with Arthur Cavendish. Carol broke away, threw her arms round Jock and there were tears in her eyes as she kissed his cheek. Jock hugged her and checked the flow of thanks. Jo and Jamie had handed the music over to Lachie on the accordion, and joined them. Jo hung on her dad's arm while Jamie got the drinks, and Jock introduced her to Arthur Cavendish and explained their connection. Jo thought it was a hoot and introduced him and Jock to her friend Annie Wallace; a tall, very attractive athletic looking blonde who'd just arrived. Annie told Jock she was a friend of Jo and Carol's from the gym.

Jo gave Jock a nudge and indicated with her head. Annie was leading Cavendish towards the big hall. 'I think Annie's taken a shine to your friend, Dad. Is he married?'

'Divorced,' said Robbie who'd overheard.

'And I'm sure he'll be up for some real Highland hospitality,' said Jock with a big grin. Jo punched him on the arm and took her drink from Jamie.

There was a commotion at the door and everyone turned. Carlos, in full Highland gear with Alan Clark and Bob McLean in tow had made his entrance.

Carlos spotted Jock, hurried over and put his arm round his shoulder. '*Señor* Jock, I love you. I must to meet your friends—where is the whisky?'

The best of ceilidhs take a wee while to get going, which means time for folk to get a bit oiled-up. When he sensed the time was right, Robbie gave the nod to the musicians and called the first dance: a *Strip the Willow*.

There was barely enough space for all the sets and there were a few collisions. And even more on the next dance, an *Eightsome Reel*. Carlos had a bit of trouble with the moves but just about got the hang of both dances by the end—there were plenty of willing helpers.

A bit winded, Jock and Meg were taking a breather in the lounge, when they were joined by Robbie who flopped on the settee beside Meg. 'Carol's been hijacked by your pal Carlos. Where did you find him? Life and soul, isn't he?'

Jock grinned and told him it was a long story.

'So what are your plans then?'

Robbie lay back smiling. 'I've resigned my commission. A wee bit sad, I suppose. I loved the army, but I love the alternative even more—and life's pretty awful for an army wife. We'll live here. There's more than enough for me to do. I love this place, and with all the new land Richard bought, the home farm's more than three times the size—there will be lots to do. It's a challenge. I'm off to Aberdeen next week to do a course on estate management. My guys here are great, they'll help me, but I hate knowing bugger all.'

Meg, who sat in the middle, elbowed both of the men. 'Come on, I'm for another dance. And you, Robbie, you better come and rescue your woman.'

Sometime in the middle of the evening—no one was counting the time—the band took a break and everyone tucked into the huge buffet Robbie had laid on. Carlos, poncing round in his kilt, was blown away by the whole experience. He'd learned about whisky the previous evening and was intoxicated by the atmosphere, not the drink. He found Jock by the bar and threw his arm over his shoulder. '*Señor* Jock, how I thank you? You take me from hell of Alicante, this you show me. *Señor* Jock—your Scotland—this is the life.'

Jock led him to the buffet where they loaded up their plates and joined Meg at a table. Jo, a plate of food in her hand, came and sat on Carlos' lap, kissed him on the cheek and put an arm round his neck. 'You look wonderful in your kilt, Carlos. We'll have to get some nice photos for you to take home.'

Carlos gave her a hug. 'Yes, my wife not believing this—Carlos in skirt! A photo please with new friends in the skirts.'

Jo and her dad, arm in arm, took a walk outside for a breath of fresh air. It was a beautiful, calm, clear but cold night. The almost full moon was reflected in the lochan and illuminated the mountains round. Jo and Jock wandered over the lawn towards the lochan. A young couple were sitting, hand in hand, on a log by the shore and Jo introduced them to her father. Their names meant nothing to Jock, but they clearly knew about him.

'Gus MacRae,' explained Jo as they headed back to the Lodge. 'Hughie MacRae's cousin: Hughie that got killed by the Monnie Bridge. Lizzie, the girl with Gus had been Hughie's wife. Gus and Lizzie are an item, been together for a wee while now.

'Robbie's been really good to Lizzie. He offered to give her back the farm she'd sold to Richard. But she didn't want to go back there. It had been Hughie's place—too many memories. Gus and Lizzie have got a nice house in the village now. Robbie's given her half a million pounds. He was right embarrassed about it. Money can never compensate, but he felt he had to recompense somehow for what his brother had done. Lizzie didn't want to take it but we talked her into it. She's getting over Hughie's death, but it'll take time. Gus used to work with Hughie, and he's taken on Hughie's garage. It seems to be going well. Aye, they'll be fine.'

They were almost back at the Lodge when Jock stopped and hugged Jo. 'I've written two tunes: the first is *Dunmorey Lament*, the second's *Dunmorey Celebration*. I composed them last week at your Balmannie—it's a right inspiring wee place.' Jock hugged Jo again, went over to his car and took out his pipe case.

At the first skirl of the pipes, folk began to spill from the Lodge. Jamie draped his jacket over Jo's shoulders and put his arm round her as a haunting lament filled the glen. Jo buried her face and sobbed in Jamie's chest. 'He wrote it for Hughie and Dougie. God Jamie, it's beautiful.' Almost a hundred people stood and listened in awe. When the music died there was a wonderful unearthly silence.

'That,' called Jock, 'was the past. The past is in the past. Now—the future.' Within moments the mood was transformed and the lawn filled with dancers as Jock played his *Dunmorey Celebration*: a wild reel. Jo ran inside and grabbed her fiddle. She didn't know the tune but jamming along was easy. Jamie found the bodhran and the three of them played and played until the dancers were exhausted.

As Jock was packing his pipes in their case, wee Dunkie handed him a dram. 'Ye wis ey one o' the best Jock. Ye wis a wee bittie rusty tonight but that wisnae bad, nae bad at all.' From Pipe Major Dunkie Munro that was praise indeed. Jock put his arm round his old friend, drained his glass and the two headed back to join the ceilidh.

Back in the big hall folk had gathered again for the dancing. Robbie Ogilvie found himself a beer crate to stand on and addressed his guests.

'I think you've all enjoyed yourselves so far this evening.' Robbie lifted his hands and silenced the cheer.

'I have an announcement to make. While at the moment it's not technically possible, I want to announce that Carol and I intend to get married.' Someone had found another beer crate and Carol stood up beside Robbie. Robbie calmed the cheering crowd again.

'That Carol and I can be together; that we can have this ceilidh tonight, or even begin to contemplate getting married, is thanks to one man, our piper this evening: Chief Superintendent Jock Anderson.'

Jock found himself pushed forward amid wild clapping and cheering. Robbie stepped down from his beer crate to try and get Jock to say a few words. A reluctant Jock, whisky in hand, stepped up and looked round the sea of silent expectant faces.

'The course of true love wasn't running too smoothly for this pair. I have to admit that I applied a wee bittie oil that maybe made it a wee bit easier for them—but they'd have got there just fine without me. Piping's right thirsty work so I'm going to have another wee sip o' this and I'll ask you all to do the same and we'll drink a wee toast to the happy couple. Then for God's sake, Jo, will you play that fiddle o' yours and get me out of this.'

The toast drunk, Jo struck up on her fiddle, the rest of the band caught on and the ceilidh took off again.

Jock stepped down from the beer crate, Robbie shook his hand, and Meg led Jock away. 'A bit much for you, love?'

'Aye, Meg, it is. I suppose you'll be up for more dancing?'

Meg took his hand and led him onto the dance floor. 'Too right I am.' She pulled him into a set with Carol and Robbie for a *Dashing White Sergeant*.

By 1.00 in the morning a few folk were looking the worse for wear. There were already a couple of bodies asleep on lounge settees—one of them being Carlos. Meg rearranged his kilt and made him a bit more decent, found a blanket and laid it over him.

The dance floor was thinning out as Jock took Meg in his arms for a slow waltz. Arthur Cavendish was tightly wrapped up with Annie Wallace. He caught Jock's eye and gave him a wink.

Jock whispered in Meg's ear. 'I've brought a sleeping bag for him, but I don't think he'll be needing it.'

Meg looked across at the couple. 'He's a fine looking man Jock—and he looks great in the kilt.'

'Aye, an' Annie's no' bad looking herself—a fine couple.'

Meg hugged Jock tightly. 'That nice big four-poster we've got tonight: it looks real comfy. Morag told me it's likely Queen Victoria was conceived in that bed.'

Jock kissed the top of her head. 'That's great, love, let's go—I just hope they've changed the sheets since.'

Chapter 37

It was a warm Saturday afternoon in early summer. The car park was full to overflowing, and Jock had to park along with many others in a neighbouring field. A good crowd of people were gathered in front of an old farmhouse. A large sign over the door, erected only the day before, advertised its purpose: *The Sanderson Wildlife Centre*. It had taken many months of work to create something appropriate: something Dougie would have approved and been proud of.

As executors of Dougie's estate, Jock and Willie Ferguson the Chief Constable, were charged with the job of utilizing the significant amount of money left by Dougie. Under the terms of Dougie's will, his only stipulations were that the legacy be used to produce something of lasting value to wildlife in particular and the community in general. There had been agreement that some sort of centre be created: something that would celebrate Dougie's life and work. There had to be an educational aspect and it had to be sited in an area with a diverse wildlife population. Any facility created should also have the capacity to generate the funds required for its upkeep—which meant basically it had to attract paying visitors. It had to be located somewhere near Dougie's hometown of Inverness—it was a pretty tall order.

Armed with a list of properties for sale round Inverness, Jock and Meg spent many pleasant but sometimes frustrating weekends searching for somewhere suitable. They'd all but given up when one cold wet Sunday afternoon in December, at the end of a fruitless day's exploring, Meg suggested they call in and see old Angus McKenzie. Angus, a local farmer, had been Jock's father's best friend, and Meg and Jock had not seen Angus since his wife's funeral some two years before.

They were immediately struck by the dilapidated state of the farm. The garden of the old house, once the pride and joy of both Angus and his wife Jean, was an overgrown jungle of weeds and brambles. When they knocked the rusted old clapper on the weather-beaten door, a half-hearted bark sounded from deep in the house. As there was no other response to their knocking, Jock tried the door handle: the door was unlocked. Jock pushed it open and called out for Angus. From somewhere at the back of the house they heard a call for them to come on in. They found Angus in an armchair in the big back kitchen, and beside him on the floor was a very old collie which struggled to its feet and growled at Jock and Meg as they entered. Angus patted the dog and it settled back on the floor. A black and white TV flickered in a corner, the only heating in the room was from a single bar electric radiator and the room was very cold.

'Jock, ye old bugger, an' you too Meg; come on in. Sorry the place is a bit o' a mess, ma legs are no' very good an' A've a wee bit o' bother gettin' aboot.'

Meg and Jock were horrified. The state of the kitchen was indescribable, and the smell of rotting food, old dog and old man was overpowering.

Angus grinned at his visitors. 'A could fair use a cup o' tea.'

How Angus had survived alone for so long was amazing. From the pile of empty tins it looked as if he had been living on sardines and beans.

Meg looked sternly at the old man. 'For God's sake, Angus, why did you not call us? You can't live like this, man. Is there no-one looks in on you?'

Angus told her that old Mrs McLeod from along the road who, it seemed, was about as decrepit as Angus, would phone him up to see if he was OK and ask what he needed. The local shop then delivered the groceries to his door for him.

'Och A've been doin' just fine, lassie. Only the last few weeks wi' the cold ma' legs have been gettin' a bittie worse—but A can manage fine, dinnae you be worryin' aboot me.' As if determined to prove his mobility he took his walking sticks and began struggling painfully to get out of his chair. Meg gently pushed him back down, filled the kettle and searched for some clean cups.

By 8.00 that evening, Angus was in Raigmore Hospital in Inverness. Meg and Jock assured him it would just be for a few days, only until they got his legs feeling a bit better. Angus of course made the predictable protests but in his heart he knew it was the best thing. He was more concerned about Ben, his old dog. Ben went home with Meg and Jock, sharing the back with a very curious Nick.

When Meg visited Angus the next morning he was in great form, entertaining the others in his ward with his stories, mercilessly teasing the young nurses and in his quieter moments, revelling in the large colour TV.

The doctor said he was in remarkably good health. What Angus needed, however, was a bilateral hip replacement. He was only seventy-two and the doctor was sure they could get him mobile again. Angus was concerned about Ben, and Meg told him not to worry, that he was getting his share of TLC at the vet's. He was having his teeth done: they were in a terrible state and were preventing him from eating properly. He'd also be getting a good flea wash, shampoo and grooming, and Meg promised she'd bring him in to visit the following morning. The hospital didn't allow pets on the wards, but Meg had talked the management into a compromise: Angus would be trollied to the reception area.

On an evening visit a couple of days later, Jock was explaining how he and Meg had come to visit him the previous Sunday. Angus had been intrigued by the Dougie Sanderson story.

He had looked at Jock and grinned. 'Well man, ye can hae ma' place if it's ony gid tae ye—it's daein' bugger all an' A'll no' be fermin' it again A'm thinkin'. They're talkin' aboot pittin' me intae one o' they sheltered hoosin' places. A dinnae want that Jock. Maybe you and me could cam tae some kind o' arrangement eh?'

Angus's old farm proved to be perfect for their requirements. Set on the shore, there were about eighty acres of good arable land. All had been rented out to neighbouring farmers for grazing or hay production, and it had been many years since any crops had been sown. The land was exceptionally fertile and Angus had never liked to use chemical fertilizers—he reckoned dung had been good enough for his father and was good enough for him. The farm had always been run, as far as possible, using traditional methods. Angus was well aware of the damage to the environment that the removal of old hedges caused, so all hedges and shelter belts had been retained.

There was a broad strip of mature native woodland close to the shore, and it had also been unmanaged for years. In one walk, Jock had seen several roe deer and three badger setts; he had been especially delighted to find red squirrel.

The jewel for the birders was, however, the foreshore and salt marsh into which a small river drained. Jock had reckoned there to be at least thirty acres of marshland, and even in summer it was full of birds.

Angus had been reluctant to sell his farm. He'd agreed to lease the property, for a nominal fee, to The Sanderson Trust. On his death, the trust would assume full ownership. Angus had no family to inherit, his only son having died in a tragic tractor accident on the farm many years before. In turn, the trust would renovate one of the old worker's cottages for Angus to live in. He was determined that he'd die on his own land as his father and grandfather had done before him.

For the trust, it was an eminently suitable arrangement. They'd need to spend nothing to acquire land and there was more than enough in the bank to fund the project. With the land available, they could expand the scope of the project.

Close to Dougie's heart had been another interest, one which Jock shared: the survival of rare breeds. Jock reckoned he could fit in quite a few on eighty acres. The Centre, sadly, had to generate an income, and unusual animals were attractive to visitors—and it was visitors who brought in much needed money.

Everyone had wanted to be involved. Robbie, flush with new knowledge gained from his estate management course, together with Donald Cameron, his farm manager, had drawn up a management plan for the farm. With advice from the RSPB and Scottish National Heritage, plans for the marsh and woodlands had been produced, and nature trails had been created through the old woodlands and fields. A concealed walkway terminating in a large comfortable hide had been built, and this provided a panoramic view of the marsh and foreshore.

Old Angus, the hip operations a great success and walking now with the aid of only one stick, was actively involved at every stage. His knowledge of the farm and its wildlife was invaluable—and besides, he was a great character to have around.

Jock and Meg walked arm in arm towards the large group of people by the house. Most of Jock's colleagues were there. DI McLean and DS Clark with their wives, DC Miller and her boyfriend and many others from the station were in the gathering.

Jock was met by the Lord Provost of Inverness. Sensitive to the need to keep the local authority on board, Jock had suggested that the Provost be invited to officially open the Centre. The Provost was happy to oblige—he loved having his photo in the paper and there were plenty of journalists present who were happy to oblige him. The Chief Constable, himself never shy of good publicity, put his arm round Jock's shoulders and called the assembly to the side of the house where a large marquee had been set up on the lawn. Inside, a small stage had been erected and chairs lined up. At the back, a large buffet had been provided and there were many early drinkers being served at the small bar. Already at the bar, wee Dunkie saw Jock and lifted his glass of whisky in greeting.

When all were seated, the Chief Constable and the Lord Provost mounted the stage—Jock had been offered to join them and the chance to say something, but had declined. The Chief Constable, a consummate politician, was a great talker and gave an interesting and, at times, very humorous account of the creation of The Sanderson Wildlife Centre. Jock smiled to himself as his friend somewhat exaggerated his own role and contribution to the effort. He also—much to Jock's serious embarrassment—exaggerated Jock's own contribution. Listing and thanking all those who'd played their part, he finally handed over to the Lord Provost who made a brief speech and formally declared The Sanderson Wildlife Centre officially open.

Jamie Ross, who'd been heavily involved in the project, had been given the job of tour guide for the morning and led guests off to view The Centre. The large old house had been cleverly modified to meet requirements. One room on the ground floor was dedicated to Dougie. On one wall was a record of his life with many photographs, and central was his framed Victoria Cross with the original citation. On the other walls were arranged many of Dougie's lifetime collection of bird pictures. Dozens of others were displayed round the Centre. Many originals were hundreds of years old, many were unusual, many exotic, most were very valuable; but all were extremely beautiful. There were many Peter Scott originals. Peter Scott had been Dougie's personal friend and all the paintings bore a written dedication to him. One small room had been designated a library, for which Dougie's many books would be the nucleus. Most of the ground floor had been modified to accommodate a small cafeteria and a large gift shop. The plan was that the Centre be manned by volunteers of which currently there was no shortage.

Upstairs was the educational area where there were many computers and worktops—the first visits by school groups were planned for the coming term. The many old cattle-sheds and barns had all been cleaned out and renovated, some had yet to be allocated a purpose. There were several old farm cottages. These had also been renovated to provide accommodation and work space for research students. Two PhD students from the University of Edinburgh were already in residence.

The Chief Constable, who was well into hunting shooting and fishing, had been left Dougie's fine collection of rifles, shotguns and fishing gear. The picture collection and Dougie's extensive library of books on natural history had been willed to Jock. Jock had, however, nowhere to display so many pictures, and his own bookshelves were already full. He wasn't about to sell any items so the collections had been donated to the Centre.

The insured value of Dougie's collection—pictures and books—was close a million pounds. The Victoria Cross alone would be worth many thousands to a collector. Jamie had contacted Duncan Lewis at Ex-Cell and he'd happily agreed to install an alarm system free of charge.

Angus's old farm, unspoiled by modern agricultural practices, was something of a time capsule. One PhD student, a botanist, would be assessing plant species distribution, comparing those on Angus's property with those on surrounding farms. It was a rare opportunity to attempt to quantify the impact of modern farming practices on the environment. The second student, an animal ecologist, would be involved in a similar study into the distribution of animals. The post grads would act as joint wardens of the reserve.

Meg and Jock leaned on a fence admiring the small herd of Highland cattle loaned by Robbie. Dunmorey Laddie, a son of the prize-winning Arthur, stood beside three grazing cows with their young calves. Only three years old, Arthur was already a magnificent animal with an impressive spread of horn. Attractive, though not rare, the Highland cattle would soon be joined by others of interest like Dexters, Belted Galloways, Blue Greys and Luing. Jock had a serious interest in truly rare breeds and intended to acquire as many of these as the place would support. Sadly most, if not all, of the old British breeds were in danger: many having already been lost, supplanted by more productive imported breeds and hybrids.

He wanted not only rare breeds of cattle. Rare breeds of sheep, pigs and chickens were also on his list. He had already sourced Soay and North Ronaldsay sheep, but he wanted some Boreray, the old sheep of Saint Kilda. There was a depressingly long list of endangered native domestic animals, and he wouldn't have room for them all.

Jock turned as someone addressed him: it was John MacDonald and beside him was Ian Forbes, the two former burglars. Each had a pretty girl on his arm.

John cleared his throat. 'We never did thank you properly for what you did for us, Mr Anderson.'

Jock smiled at them as he introduced Meg. 'Och, I don't know about that. I got a very nice letter from you, and that bottle of malt—that nice Glen Morangie went down a treat.'

MacDonald shifted awkwardly. 'Aye, I know sir, but you know what I mean.' He introduced his wife, Flora—whom Jock had already met when she'd visited him at the station—and Forbes' girlfriend, Judith Armitage.

Jock shook their hands and addressed the two lads. 'I trust you've both learned your lesson.'

'Too right they have,' said Flora. 'The silly buggers. If only I'd known what they were up to. I was visiting my sister in Australia while they were at it. How did they think they were going to explain where all the money came from? He should have known I'd have nothing to do with stolen money. His folks are devastated, Mr Anderson. John was brought up right. His father's a respected man: he's an engineer with Edinburgh City Council, and his mum's a lawyer. You can imagine how they feel. Aye Superintendent, they've learned all right.'

Jock looked at John MacDonald. He had his head down and was kicking at the gravel with his toe—this wasn't the first time he'd had this from his wife.

Jock knew that the two lads were out of prison on their own cognisance—
it had been his recommendation to the Procurator Fiscal. Their case was
coming up at the end of the following month. Flora told Jock that Ian Forbes
and his girlfriend were due to open an antique shop in Inverness. Judith
Armitage, she said, had been a workmate of Forbes in Edinburgh. She was a
specialist in fine art and Judith told Jock she'd work the shop on her own until
Ian had served his jail sentence. Jock learned that MacDonald had the offer of
a job with Ex-Cell, the company he'd misrepresented during his crime spree.
He was already involved with them in further Research and Development,
working with his old flat mate Frank MacTavish. Flora proudly told Jock that
Duncan Lewis, Ex-Cell's boss, had said that he'd identified a real talent and
wanted John to start up and manage their Highland Division. Jock already
knew from Jamie that Ex-Cell's business had improved dramatically as a
result of the burglaries—there was a huge demand for their state-of-the-art
anti-burglar systems and the company was expanding.

Jock thought it likely the lads would escape a prison sentence. All the
stolen goods had been recovered, the lads themselves had been fully co-
operative and he felt that, as both had stable relationships and good future
employment prospects, the court would be impressed—and hopefully
lenient. Jock himself intended to put in a good word for them. To Jock, a
few months community service would seem more appropriate than a jail
sentence. He wondered if a bit of hard labour at The Sanderson Wildlife
Centre could be considered as community service—he made a mental note
to check that out.

Flora was a nurse. She had been working in Edinburgh but had got a
job in Raigmore Hospital to be near her man in Porterfield Prison. She'd
met old Angus McKenzie in Raigmore Hospital and he'd told her about the
Sanderson project. She'd nursed him through his hip operations and they
were now great friends.

Jock noticed that both of the lads had binoculars round their necks. 'Birders, are you?'

Both lads nodded and gave him wide grins. 'Too right sir; we're away down to the hide now.' Jock gave them a tip as to where they might see a woodpecker and some long-tailed tits. They thanked Jock again and hurried off.

Meg watched them as they trouped off. 'Nice pair of lads.'

'Aye, Meg, a bloody lucky pair of lads.'

Jock and Meg were sitting on a long wooden bench, donated to the Centre by Dougie's old regiment, when they were joined by the Chief Constable who was a wee bit the worse for wear.

'I see DI McLean and DS Clark are here.'

Jock reminded him that both men had been very actively involved in the establishment of the centre.

'Even better then.' He pulled some papers from his jacket pocket and handed them to Jock. 'Came through this morning. Finally—official notification of McLean's promotion to DCI and Alan Clark's to DI.'

Jock waved the papers. 'It's about bloody time, too. It's ridiculous. Bob McLean's been doing a DCI's job since Alex Lauder retired. Why does it take so bloody long for the obvious to be approved? Bloody ridiculous. Same with Alan. Mind you, neither of them complained about their extra workload.'

The Chief Constable smiled at Jock. 'Money, Jock—money and budgets: it's all about money. We've got to pay them more if they're promoted. Anyway, I was going to tell them on Monday, but it would be nice to add to an already happy occasion—what do you think?'

'I think, man, that you've had a few drams and you're feeling right happy. Me too. Last I saw them, they were at the bar. I don't think it's maybe the most professional way to do this, but bugger it, come on—let's go and give them the good news.'

When Jock rejoined Meg on the bench, he had a silly grin on his face. 'I remember when I was promoted to DCI—real formal it was, but my Chief Constable was a stuffy old fart. Bob and Alan didn't seem to be bothered by the informality.'

Meg laughed. 'Aye, I saw them both do a wee jig when you told them. They wouldn't have done that in the Chief Constable's office—but mind you, they wouldn't have been half drunk in the Chief Constable's office.'

Jock and Meg headed back towards the marquee where Jo, Carol and wee Dunkie's daughter Cathy, were sitting chatting and sipping orange juice at a table in the sunshine. Jo and Jamie had got married in February: registry office followed by a big do at Dunmorey. Carol's divorce, uncontested and fast-tracked, had come through in March, and she and Robbie had got married shortly after—a big wedding followed by an even bigger do at Dunmorey.

As Meg and Jock joined them, Jo and Carol were laughing and kissing Cathy. Jo got up and hugged her mother. 'It's wonderful Mum. Cathy just got the results—the latest IVF's worked—she's eight weeks pregnant!'

Everyone turned at the sound of the pipes: it was Robbie. He had pestered Jock for the musical scores for *Dunmorey Lament* and *Dunmorey Celebration*. Dressed in his full Highland gear, he was doing this properly and Jock had a lump in his throat as Robbie gave a perfect rendition of the lament. He'd had to agree with wee Dunkie that his own performance had been maybe just a wee bittie rusty. For the *Dunmorey Celebration* Robbie marched round the house followed by a string of dancers—led by the Lord Provost.

Meg squeezed Jock's hand. 'Aye, Jock, you've done Dougie proud.' Jock put his arm round her as he looked at the large crowd of people enjoying themselves in the farmyard, and at Angus's old house now beautifully renovated, the garden returned to its former glory.

Jock smiled as he read the large sign over the farmhouse door. 'Aye—*The Sanderson Wildlife Centre*: a nice name. I think you're right Meg; it's no' a bad job right enough. I'm sure Dougie would be fair chuffed. Worth a wee dram to celebrate, don't you think?' He took Meg's hand and they headed into the marquee.

Jock had kept only one of the paintings left to him by Dougie. Set above the big fireplace in his lounge, with its own little light above it, was a large oil painting of two magnificent golden eagles circling over a Highland glen—with a wee bit of imagination, it could be Dunmorey.

The Dunmorey Trilogy:

Mischief in the Glen.

The Long Road's End.

Almost Lost.

Lightning Source UK Ltd.
Milton Keynes UK
UKOW050630310812

198307UK00004B/33/P